GW01048758

## THE M(AN?)
## BEHIND THE PLAN

Jack looked at Michael. He didn't have to ask how Michael was doing. No matter how bad the state of the world economy, there were lots of people around with big money, and Michael Kir was invariably their contact when it came to buying diamonds and other precious gems. His jewels were worn by Elizabeth Taylor, Sophia Loren, Jihan Sadat, Queen Nour of Jordan, Princess Grace, Esmelda Marcos, and the former Empress Farah. Kir was a sharp businessman and a consummate ladies man. With his grace and charm, he could manipulate and take advantage of people, but he was able to do it in such a way that they ended up believing that he was doing them a favor.

Today on the tennis court, though, there was something different, something unsettling about Michael. Jack could feel it. His friend had the killer instinct. He'd always had it, but today, with every shot, Michael went straight for the jugular. He showed no mercy.

We will send you a free catalog on request. Any titles not in your local bookstore can be purchased by mail. Send the price of the book plus 50¢ shipping charge to Tower Books, P.O. Box 511, Murray Hill Station, New York, N.Y. 10156-0511.

Titles currently in print are available for industrial and sales promotion at reduced rates. Address inquiries to Tower Publications, Inc., Two Park Avenue, New York, N.Y. 10016, Attention: Premium Sales Department.

# PROJECT NOROUZ

**Rebecca Swift**

TOWER·BOOKS   NEW YORK CITY

**A TOWER BOOK**

Published by

Tower Publications, Inc.
Two Park Avenue
New York, N.Y. 10016

# CHAPTER ONE

Michael Kir balanced precariously.

The Texas air was hot and still. The anxious dancing of Kir's feet on the red clay of the tennis court created a small dust storm around his heels, coloring his white tennis shoes and socks sienna red. His long, powerful body was hunched over slightly, and the muscles of his thighs strained as he moved quickly on the balls of his feet. Yet, above the recoiled tension—the movement of his body—Michael Kir's eyes were trained on the ball with a look of calm, steely concentration. The tendons of his left arm tautened as he instinctively gripped the racquet tighter. He moved quickly to the net. In a split second Kir's racquet made contact with the ball, and with great finesse Kir chipped the ball over the net. The ball, loaded with backspin, dropped over the net into Jack Tucker's court and died, leaving Jack frozen in his tracks.

"Game and first set to you," Jack said, smiling graciously. That bastard has had me running around the court like a goddamn idiot, Jack said to himself. Jack Adams Tucker, Houston Tennis Club Champion, pressed the terry-towel sweatband on his wrist to his freckled forehead, damming the rivulets of streaming sweat. He motioned with his upstretched racquet. "Come on, Mike, old pal, let's take a break."

The two men walked toward the portable cooler sitting in a shaded corner of the court.

"Mike," Jack said, opening the spigot of the water cooler, "you really caught me sleeping, old buddy. Hell, I figured that a guy like you, with chronic jet-lag, would be a pushover. Not so," sighed Jack, as he handed a paper cup full of luke-warm water to Kir. Jack filled another for himself and gulped it down. He refilled his cup and put it to his parched mouth again, this time forcing himself to drink slowly. The sting of his humiliating defeat in the first set of the match was beginning to ebb away.

Jack Tucker and Michael Kir had been friends for years. They had roomed together for four years at Stanford, class of '65, and had played together on the varsity tennis team. After graduation, each went his separate way. Jack went back to Texas, where he built a successful career for himself in the booming oil business centered around Houston, while Michael entered his family's prestigious international gem business.

Shortly after Kir's graduation from Stanford, his father died. Kir assumed control of the family business, and so began his nomadic life. He traveled incessantly; the entire world was his domain. He searched the Far East for its vivid hued stones; India for star sapphires; Bangkok's gem market for rubies and emeralds; South Africa for diamonds; South America for the most perfect emeralds. Kir sold his dazzling gems to the world's rich and privileged in Paris, Monte Carlo, London, Tokyo, New York, and Beverly Hills.

But it was the Middle East where Michael Kir found his best marketplace: in the hustle and bustle of Lebanon, torn by civil war; in the ornate white palaces of Saudi Arabia, Kuwait, Bahrain, and the United Arab Emirates; in the boom town of Tehran before the Islamic Revolution in 1979. Kir sold to high-flying entrepreneurs, princes, and sheikhs. The Middle-East was a violent, tumultuous, and extravagant society that often confused and intimidated the rest of the world, but could not be ignored. The world had grown to understand that, most painfully. Under the Middle East's shifting sands and turquoise blue waters lay the lifeblood of the industrialized world, three-quarters of the world's proven oil reserves, hundreds of billions of barrels of black gold.

Michael Kir was no stranger to the Middle-East; Iran was his country of origin. He was born into one of the best families in Iran: an old, wealthy family that had been involved in gem dealing for seven generations. His ancestors had sold to the wildly extravagant Qajar kings, absolute rulers of Iran (or, as it was then called, Persia) during the eighteenth and nineteenth centuries. In the early part of the twentieth century, when Reza Shah the Great overthrew the decadent Qajar rulers and founded his own short-lived Pahlavi dynasty, Michael's family had continued to provide the most fabulous stones to Iran's new royalty. Diamonds and the famous rose-colored rubies that Michael Kir's grandfather had sold to Reza Shah graced the ill-fated Peacock Throne.

Michael Kir's family was a curious blend of East and West. For generations the men in his family had traveled, studied, and lived in Europe. Michael Kir was a product of both cultures and felt equally at ease in both, but like his father before him, he made no one place his home. Kir had a co-op in New York, an apartment along the Croissette in Cannes, and a condominium in St. Moritz, but he lived his life in hotels: the nature of his business demanded it.

Jack Tucker and Michael Kir usually managed

to see each other once or twice a year, renewing their old friendship, and long rivalry on the tennis courts. They traveled on the same circuit, so to speak, the Houston-London-Riyadh Shuttle. During the past few years, however, the circuit had become shorter. In the days when they were places of consequence, Beirut and Tehran had been star links in that circle of influence. The whole circle, indeed the whole Western world, had become weaker and more unstable with the loss of Iran in 1979, four years earlier.

Before 1979, Tehran had been one of the favorite meeting places for Michael and Jack. There, in the hot, dry, rarified air of the Imperial Club at the foot of the Alborz Mountains in northern Tehran, the two had played tennis frequently. It was in Tehran that Jack had hustled his multimillion dollar oil deals, and rubbed elbows with some of the richest, most influential people in Iran, and, therefore, the world. That was during the early and mid 1970s, the time of the Great Boom, when Iran was forging its way into the twentieth century, full speed ahead. Iran was the superpower of the Middle East; oil-rich, powerful, and ruled by Mohammad Reza Shah Pahlavi Aryamehr, King of Kings, Light of the Aryans. But only four short years ago the Islamic Revolution had rocked Iran, and the entire world had never been the same since.

Jack and Kir sat on the wooden bench in the blazing midday sun. Both men were breathing heavily, and their shirts were soaked with perspiration.

"You're out for blood today, Mr. Kir."

Kir flashed Jack a friendly smile and shrugged his shoulders. He pulled off his sweat-soaked cotton T-shirt and took a fresh Fila tennis shirt out of his bag. Pulling the T-shirt over his head, Kir asked, "How's the oil services business these days, Jack?"

"Couldn't be better, Mike. International Oil Services is in great shape. Thanks to that big pipeline sabotage in Iran last year and the way those goddamn OPEC radicals, like sharks smelling blood, put the squeeze on us, the Europeans are sinking more wells in the North Sea almost daily. It looks like a goddamn pin cushion out there."

Jack looked at Michael. He didn't have to ask how Michael was doing. No matter how bad the state of the world economy, there were lots of people around with big money, and Michael Kir was invariably their contact when it came to buying diamonds and other precious gems. His jewels were worn by Elizabeth Taylor, Sophia Loren, Jihan Sadat, Queen Nour of Jordan, Princess Grace, Esmelda Marcos, and the former Empress Farah. Kir was a sharp businessman and a consummate ladies man. With his grace and charm, he could manipulate and take advantage of people, but he was able to do it in such a way that they ended up believing that he was doing them a favor.

Today on the tennis court, though, there was something different, something unsettling about Michael. Jack could feel it. His friend had the killer instinct. He'd always had it, but today, with every shot, Michael went straight for the jugular. He showed no mercy. It was unnerving to Jack, and he tried to push it out of his mind. The next set is mine, Jack thought to himself as he stood up. Picking up his racquet, Jack said, "Come on, Mike, let's play another set."

The two men walked back to the court. The sun was directly overhead, hot and searing, working in tandem with the suffocating humidity to make things as unpleasant as possible out there on

Court 12.

Court 12 was the only one of the fourteen courts at the new Houston Tennis Club that was occupied. It was too hot an afternoon for all but the most dedicated of tennis fanatics to be playing. Even the diehards were sitting out the afternoon sun. At two-thirty, as Jack and Michael were beginning their second set, the courts were still empty. No one else had ventured out.

Usually, Jack Tucker liked to play on Court 12. Although it was fairly far from the clubhouse and in a corner of the court area, it was one of the three competition courts at the club. Concrete bleachers on either side of the court provided seating for several hundred spectators. At times they'd been filled to near capacity, all eyes directed toward Court 12, where Jack Tucker played in one club tournament or another. Yes, Court 12 at the Houston Tennis Club had been the scene of many victories for Jack Tucker, and today he was damn glad that there was no one watching this fiasco. Kir had been toying with him like a cat with a trapped mouse.

Michael Kir bounced the yellow Slazenger ball on the ground a few times as he prepared to serve.

"I'll get that son of a bitch this time," Jack assured himself. Jack Tucker took his tennis very seriously and friend or no friend, he was not going to let Michael Kir make an ass out of him on the court this afternoon.

The swollen beads of perspiration gathering at Kir's left inner elbow and banded wrist trickled in reverse direction as he raised his arm to serve. The force with which Kir hit the ball belied the apparent effortlessness of his graceful move.

"Fault," Jack called out. "A bit long," he said, indicating with his index finger and thumb that the ball was a few inches out of the service court.

Jack continued to mutter to himself, "I knew he'd fall apart in the second set; the heat's getting to him." Jack automatically relaxed, waiting to receive the second, usually softer, serve.

Kir tossed the ball up in the air. In one smooth, powerful motion, the racquet connected with the ball, forcing the ball across the net with a velocity that left Jack stunned.

"Ace," Jack yelled. Then he muttered to himself, "You S.O.B."

It had started again.

While her husband continued his struggle on Court 12, Jeri Tucker freshened up in the ladies' lounge of the Houston Tennis Club clubhouse. Straight from a shopping trip at the Galleria, where her Neiman Marcus credit card had seen considerable action that Saturday afternoon, she and her friend Cheryl had arrived at the Club late, expecting to see her husband and that good-looking friend of his relaxing in the air-conditioned, potted-palm coolness of the clubhouse, like all sane persons on such a hot day. But no, Jack and Mike were out there, hitting the ball as if their lives depended on it. Jeri was a little miffed that she had to get changed out of her brand new silk dress, but she was dying to show off that doll, Michael Kir, to Cheryl, and since it was considered bad form to parade around the tennis courts in street clothes, she was obliged to change into her tennis clothes. Jeri stepped out of her dress. She deliberated on undoing her bra. It was only a couple of tucks that Dr. Watson had done when she'd had that little breast lift in the spring, but she didn't want to go around spoiling Dr. Watson's beautiful work by bouncing too freely around the court. Besides, Jack would have a fit if she paraded around the Club braless. Jeri left her bra on.

"You don't really want to play, do you, Cheryl?" asked Jeri, looking over at her friend squirming to get out of her tight Italian designer jeans.

"In this heat, Jeri?" Cheryl said. "You've got to be kidding!"

Jeri sat down on the sky-blue Naugahyde sofa, waiting for Cheryl to get dressed.

Cheryl pulled on her tennis socks and looked at Jeri. "Don't you think we should have gone in the locker room to change? I think it's against club rules to change in the clubhouse bathroom, Jeri."

"Screw the club rules," Jeri said nonchalantly. Sometimes Cheryl really annoyed her. She could be so suburban. If Jeri didn't know better, she'd swear that Cheryl only went to PTA meetings and screwed her husband once a week. Well, come to think of it, Cheryl does screw her husband once a week, but he's lucky she can fit him in at all, considering the way she gets around, Jeri thought to herself.

"What if someone comes in?" Cheryl continued, a worried look on her face.

"Don't worry, no one is going to come in. Don't worry so much," Jeri reprimanded her friend. God, sometimes she's so childish, thought Jeri, but men didn't seem to mind in the least. It must be that "I'm-so-helpless" Marilyn Monroe syndrome that gets them every time. She glanced down at Cheryl, who had seated herself at one of the several stools by the low formica countertop. A look of serious concentration was on Cheryl's face as she reapplied another coat of black mascara to her eyelashes, upper and lower, thick brooms that framed Cheryl's baby-blue eyes. A brush of glimmery blue eyeshadow across her lids, a coat of coral lipstick that exactly matched her long manicured fingernails, a light dusting of translucent powder over her nose and chin, and her

12

face was retouched.

Cheryl examined the roots of her blond hair carefully as she brushed it.

"I'll be due for a touchup in a week or so, don't you think, Jeri?"

"Don't be silly. Your hair looks fine." Jeri didn't go for the labored look. Unlike Cheryl, with her vintage Farrah Fawcett hair, Jeri's hair was cut in an easy-to-manage, natural-looking style, free and easy, except that it was neither of those. It was an expensive, painstaking process to keep up the free and easy look. *Au naturel* was as serious a business as *au plastique*.

Both women were in their mid-thirties, and very well kept. They considered the preservation of their bodies and faces as a profession, a profession at which they were most successful. The results spoke for themselves: trim, tight bodies that never failed to attract admiring glances and forward proposals, which were often accepted. Without fail, Jeri and Cheryl gave their bodies brutal workouts at the gym every day. They then rewarded themselves with saunas, massages, pedicures, manicures, facials, and the occasional nip and tuck performed by a top Houston plastic surgeon. Jeri and Cheryl made use of every service, product, and technique that their husbands' money could buy to maintain their ages at a steady thirty-three. The two women were buffed to a sheen. And what massages, whirlpools, clay masks, and facials couldn't do for their skin tone was done by the musclemen gym instructors, the tight-assed tennis pros, and the bisexual hairdressers. The well-buffed look was synonymous with the well-fucked look, a true status symbol.

"Move your tail, honey," urged Jeri. She lit a cigarette and took a long, languorous drag. "You know, Cheryl, that tennis instructor of mine has been teaching me my backhand all wrong. At least, that's Jack's impression. When Jack and I played mixed doubles last Sunday with the Nortons, Jack was furious, absolutely furious." Hands on her hips, brows furrowed, Jeri mimicked her husband. "'Christ, Jeri, at fifty bucks a lesson you should at least be learning to do it right!'"

"Well, Jeri darling," replied Cheryl, "the fifty dollars I spend for my pro Skip, learning to do it right, is definitely worth it. One of these days I might even try learning to play tennis," deadpanned Cheryl.

"Let's go," said Jeri impatiently.

"Jeri, don't rush me," Cheryl squealed. "I almost forgot my tennis panties!" Cheryl reached into her Gucci tennis bag and pulled out a pair of frilly lime green panties. She quickly pulled them on, smoothing down her short skirt of the same color.

"Cheryl, did I see writing on the back of those things?"

"Sure did, honey." Cheryl turned around, lifting up her tennis skirt, exposing two apple cheeks across which were written, "Number One Rodeo Sport."

"Present from Tex, the Rodeo Champion," Cheryl said with a wide grin.

"You are so subtle," Jeri said, smiling.

"I'll leave being subtle to someone else, thank you," said Cheryl, digging around in her bag.

"Come on, Cheryl! Let's get a nice cool drink and go down to Court 12 and watch Jack play some old friend of his."

"Jeri, you dirty old lady! That's a switch, you going down to watch your husband move his ass around the court!"

"Honey," Jeri paused, "you should see *what* he is playing."

The heat hit the two women with unexpected force as they walked down the gravel path to the spectator stands. Jeri took a sip of her frosty gin and tonic as they walked toward Court 12. She was enjoying the way that she had dangled the proverbial carrot in front of Cheryl's horny little nose. Jeri was taking her time to reply to Cheryl's stream of questions about Jack's tennis partner. "No, Cheryl, I don't think you've met him before. You'd probably remember this one! He's from New York, mainly, but he travels all around." Then throwing in another morsel, Jeri continued, "Maybe you'll recognize him, he was in *Town and Country* last month." Jeri stopped for a theatrical pause. "A big photograph of him and some princess at a party in Paris." Then she added dramatically, "In color!"

"Really, Jeri?" asked Cheryl. She was very impressed. To Cheryl, "making it" was getting your picture in *Town and Country* magazine, but most people she knew who had "made it" had only managed a small black and white photo at the back of the magazine, taken at some charity ball in Houston or Dallas.

Two men, one dark-haired, the other fair, came into focus as the women approached Court 12. The women's attention was quickly riveted on the dark-haired figure. Both women unconsciously quickened their step, like predatory animals who'd caught the scent of fresh meat.

Jeri and Cheryl waited outside the gate to the court until the point was over. Through the wire fence they stared at Michael Kir in the far court, as he waited to receive Jack's serve. Kir was slightly hunched over, eagerly anticipating the ball. With the back of his hand he pushed a few

15

strands of damp, curly hair off his brow. His eyelashes were long and thick, forming a natural sunshade for his eyes as he squinted into the sun. His cheekbones were high, and his jawline square and well defined. The muscles in his left arm rippled as he gripped his racquet tighter. His legs were long and well-muscled, leading up to a trim, perfectly proportioned torso. The white tennis shorts and unbuttoned-at-the-throat Fila T-shirt contrasted with his tanned skin which was covered with just the right amount of masculine, dark hair.

Kir moved swiftly on the court. His smooth, graceful moves were imbued with confidence and virility. The thin, white cotton T-shirt clung to the curve of his spine and broad shoulders, creating a T-shaped strip of sweat. His buttocks were rounded, beautifully shaped, and, the two women could tell from the way he was moving around the court, rock-hard. But their attention was focused elsewhere. The fabric of his Fila shorts was pulled tightly across the crotch area, creating an enticing relief to a relatively flat surface.

"What a doll!" whispered Cheryl breathlessly as she gingerly opened the gate into the court.

"Hurry up," Jeri ordered, as they tiptoed beside the waist-high railing that separated the actual court area from the bleachers. Jack, who was in the court nearest to them, bounced the ball methodically as he prepared to serve, waiting impatiently for the women and their rattling ice cubes to get out of the way. Jack, his face flushed, glared at Jeri. She grabbed Cheryl by the arm, stopping her abruptly at courtside.

Cheryl didn't mind in the slightest. From this close proximity she could better observe the stranger; his strong large hands, the deep green of his eyes. She took in everything, not too interested in his tennis prowess, but fantasizing about his obvious sexual prowess. In her mind's eye Cheryl watched Michael Kir's unclothed body move around the court. Her pulse quickened.

Michael Kir came racing toward the net to get Jack's drop shot. He skidded to a stop against the net, having missed the ball, and then turned to the two women nearby. He smiled politely at them, in acknowledgment.

He was gorgeous! He had a beautiful smile, brilliant white teeth, and a sexy, sensuous mouth. Cheryl was in love, or, at the least, in lust.

"Point's over," whispered Jeri, nudging Cheryl. "Let's sit down." They climbed the concrete steps to the bleachers to get a bird's-eye view, and be high enough up so that they could talk without disturbing the players.

"My God, Jeri, I see what you mean!" Behind the dark Oscar de la Renta sunglasses, Cheryl's mascara-fringed eyes strained to look at Michael Kir, to drink in the entire figure. His exotic good looks and the way he wore his tennis clothes—very tight, very neat, no baggy shorts and loose green and yellow striped T-shirt flopping over a paunch—told Cheryl that Michael Kir definitely was not American.

"Where is he from?" asked Cheryl.

"Umm . . . I'm not really sure. He might be Iranian. I think one of his parents is Iranian, or something like that, but he doesn't act like one," Jeri said, remembering the bearded, fanatical students that she had grown to despise during the U.S. Embassy crisis. "At any rate, he's from somewhere near there," Jeri said, pointing with her arm, as if to signify the direction of Michael Kir's homeland.

Jeri and Cheryl sat in silence, seemingly engrossed in the match being played below. But, unlike most tennis audiences whose heads turn from side to side following the ball's movement, the girls' eyes were riveted on one figure, Michael Kir.

"Is he married?" Cheryl asked.

"No, I don't think so."

"Does he have a girlfriend?"

"Doesn't he look like he has a girlfriend?" Jeri looked at Cheryl. "Girlfriends is more like it!"

"I mean a girlfriend, a steady girlfriend?"

"I don't really know," Jeri replied evasively, as if gossip was hardly a subject of interest to her. "He travels all the time, that might make it kind of tough." Then, beginning to speculate, Jeri continued, "Probably a girl in every port. One time we ran into him in New York at the Pierre and he was with the most gorgeous girl I'd ever seen. So sophisticated and tall." Jeri's last comment alluded to Cheryl's diminutive five-foot-two stature.

"What about an Iranian girlfriend? Do you think he has an Iranian girlfriend, a serious one, I mean?"

Jeri let out a howl of laughter. "Are you kidding? Those Persian bitches couldn't fuck their way out of a paper bag."

But I'm sure I can, and then some, Cheryl thought. And she'd love to show Michael Kir her considerable boudoir abilities, perfected by tireless bouts of practice. She continued to watch Kir's every movement. And he could show me a thing or two, I'd bet, she thought to herself.

On the court below, Jack and Michael continued the game. Jack, a fiercely competitive man, was not about to give in, and he continued to hustle for every ball. Michael Kir controlled the game with an almost mechanical precision, setting the pace and sending Jack running from one side of the court to the other. With a vengeful, hard, forehand shot, Jack sent the ball flying high over the chain-

18

link fence separating the courts. Like a burnt-out meteor, it dribbled to a stop in a corner of the adjoining court.

"Sorry about that, Mike," Jack said. "I was a tad off on that shot. Too bad there are no ballboys here like at the Imperial Club, eh pal?" At the Imperial Club in pre-Revolutionary Iran, no self-respecting Persian, or foreigner for that matter, would think of going out on to the courts without at least one ballboy.

Kir felt an unexpected pang of nostalgia for a life that would never be again. Playing tennis at the Houston Tennis Club, deluxe and exclusive as it was, was a far cry from tennis at pre-Revolutionary Tehran's Club Shahinshahi—Club of the King of Kings—or, as it was otherwise called, the Imperial Club. It was the most important and elite country club in all Iran. The Shah himself had given the land, and members of the royal family, as well as the cream of Iranian society and the most important members of the foreign community, played tennis, golf, or swam there. The Imperial Club was the place where the rich Iranian women went to show off their latest Paris fashions while playing endless hours of pinochle in the club's Old England lounge, and where the enormously wealthy Iranian businessmen ate lunch in the upstairs dining room, the luxuriously appointed Dariush Room. At 1:00 P.M. on any day during the 1970s, the net worth of the patrons in that small dining room made the Dariush Room the greatest concentration of wealth in the world. The children of the members of the Imperial Club, in their California surfing trunks and French bikinis, talked about grade points and cocaine as they lay on chaise lounges around the blue-striped swimming-pool deck. Overhead was the noise of helicopters as generals and court ministers arrived in their Bell 206's for a game of tennis.

After the Revolution, the name of the club had changed. The Imperial Club was renamed the Revolution Club, but the elitist system that had prevailed before still continued. The name of the club and the names of the people who counted had changed, but the story was the same. The select few of the reigning Revolutionary Council had assumed the rights of the powerful pro-Shah individuals they had executed. Although the transfer of power had not been smooth, the transfer of privilege was done neatly and quickly.

"Got it," Jack yelled from the neighboring court. He waved at Michael, then up at the two women.

Michael turned and looked up high into the gray cement stands. He saw what looked like two colorful bonbons, one pink, the other lime green, in an empty candy box. He watched Jeri in her pink scoop-neck T-shirt and the shortest of shorts now standing up and waving back. The other woman was dressed in a bright-green tennis outfit and was carefully planting her oversize sunglasses in her blond hair. Yes indeed, they did look like delicious sweets, a cherry tart and a Key-lime pie, good enough to eat, which, Kir correctly assumed, was the idea they were trying to project.

Jack was back on Court 12. He batted the errant ball to Kir. "Play ball," he yelled, anxious to get the game going again. He felt he was about to break Kir's serve and he wanted to keep the momentum going. Jack knew that the psychological advantage of winning this game away from the server could turn the game around. Jack desperately needed that edge. He had no intention of losing. His eyes were trained on the ball, unwilling to concede a single blink.

Cheryl's and Jeri's eyes were trained on Michael

Kir. The two women had systematically been working their way down his body, from head to toe.

"Honey, did you see those hands?" Cheryl exclaimed. Jeri nodded knowingly. Both women, after years of laboratory-type testing, considered it a scientific fact that the size of a man's hands was directly proportional to the size of his penis.

"Lordie, they are huge, absolutely huge!" Cheryl continued excitedly. "And beautiful!" Cheryl Smith took the science a step further. She felt that the shape, the look, of a man's hands was a dead giveaway; a sneak preview of what she would be getting, if she wanted it. Short and stubby, pink and pudgy, was enough to tell Cheryl she was wasting her time. But that was not the case with the dark, magnetically attractive man she was watching on the court.

"Gorgeous, absolutely gorgeous!" Cheryl raved, oblivious to the action on the court.

Jack had fought unsuccessfully to break Kir's serve and now floundered, near the brink of defeat. The score in the second set was five games to three, in Michael Kir's favor. Kir was now serving for set point and the match.

Damn bastard, five fucking games in a row. I shouldn't have let down my guard after winning the first three games, Jack steamed inwardly. "Jack Adams Tucker, you aren't going to lose this game! Time for a comeback," he told himself, trying to muster the surge of adrenalin needed to turn the game around.

Jack wiped his sweaty right palm on the terry-cloth pocket lining of his shorts. He stood three feet behind the baseline, hunched over, nervously shifting his weight from one foot to the other, anticipating Kir's deadly service. Jack's eyes never left the ball that Kir methodically bounced as he prepared to serve.

Kir tossed the ball in the air with one hand, while with the other, his left hand, he simultaneously pulled the racquet behind his shoulder. As the ball reached the zenith of its arc, Kir's upstretched racquet connected with the ball.

Jack gripped his racquet tighter, following the ball's trajectory toward his backhand side. Jack slammed his powerful two-handed backhand, low and fast, straight into the net.

"Shit," Jack muttered. "Set," he yelled to Michael.

"Good show," he said, walking toward Kir. The women on the bench clapped politely as they stood up.

"You've turned into a monster on the courts," Jack said in a joking voice, but he really meant it. Jack didn't know what it was, but he sensed that his old friend seemed driven by something more than just winning the tennis game. Jack tried to shrug the feeling off as he hung his sweaty arm around his friend's damp neck. "I don't know if I can take you anymore, Mike."

"You put up a good fight, Jack."

Jack shook his head from side to side, embarrassed by his poor showing. "I'll get you next time, Mike. I'll be ready for you. We should play more often."

Michael nodded in agreement, but he knew that it would be quite a while before he and Jack could get together for another game.

"Mike, let's get out of this goddamn heat!" Jack said, motioning toward the stands for Jeri and Cheryl to come down to the court.

"Come on, girls," he yelled impatiently. Jeri and Cheryl clambered down the concrete steps to Court 12.

"You boys must be simply roasting! We got hot up there just watching you play," Cheryl said, smiling sweetly.

Jeri absentmindedly gave her husband a peck on his wet, flushed cheek, then turned and greeted Michael Kir.

"Jeri, how nice to see you again," said Michael as he kissed her lightly on the cheek. "It's been such a long time."

"Mike, I'd like you to meet Cheryl Smith," Jack said, "a good friend of ours."

Michael Kir smiled at Cheryl and shook her hand.

Cheryl, her eyelashes batting like butterfly wings, looked up at Kir. "Charmed, absolutely charmed to meet you," she said.

"My pleasure," Kir replied, sporting his most winning smile.

"Come on, folks," Jack said. "Let's go get a drink."

"Good idea," Kir said, looking at the others. The four of them started toward the clubhouse.

"Mike," Jack said, putting his hand on Kir's shoulder, "next time we'll have to play at the Houston Country Club."

"It's a deal," Kir said, smiling at his friend. Next time we'll play at the Imperial Club in Tehran, Kir thought. He'd stake his life on it. In fact, he already had.

# CHAPTER TWO

For at least the third time that day, Mark Rowan reviewed his U.S. State Department briefing materials on Iran. He flipped the pages until he found what he was looking for.

NOROUZ (pronounced "New Rooz"): the Iranian New Year. Norouz (literally, New Day) usually falls on March 21 or March 22, with variances due to the fact that Iran follows a solar calendar. It coincides with the sun's vernal equinox, the exact moment of which is regarded as the beginning of the New Year . . . . Norouz is a pre-Islamic holiday, the only one still celebrated in Iran. It is uniquely Iranian, and has been celebrated continuously since the days of the Achaemenid Empire, or at least 700 B.C. Reliefs at the ruins of Persepolis (dating from approximately 600 B.C.) on the walls of the *apadana* (audience hall), depict the people of Iran paying tribute to the ruler of Iran as part of the Norouz ceremonies. Iranian poets through the ages celebrated Norouz in verse . . . . Norouz is traditionally a very festive holiday, involving feasting, exchange of gifts, dressing in new clothes, preparation of traditional foods, much socializing, etc. . . . Throughout Iranian history, the public was admitted to a royal audience with the reigning Shah . . . . Under Shah Mohammad Reza Pahlavi, great public Norouz ceremonies and festivities were held . . .

Since the Islamic Revolution in 1979, the celebration of Norouz has changed drastically. The

Ayatollah Khomeini changed Norouz (which was an Iranian, but non-Islamic, holiday) into a deeply religious Islamic holy day. Norouz became a day of prayer and meditation. Festivities and joyful celebrations are no longer permitted, and have been replaced by publicly broadcast prayers led by the leaders of the Islamic Republic. Despite the fact that even private celebration of this most ancient of Iranian traditions has been discouraged, Norouz remains the best loved of all holidays by the Iranian people, and is the most eagerly awaited yearly event . . . .

Mark Rowan closed the white notebook and got up from his desk. He walked over to the window of his north Connecticut Avenue apartment. It was a typical late summer day in Washington, D.C. The gray skies were breaking open into the humid air, unleashing a rainstorm of almost tropical intensity. Mark watched as the tennis players on the courts below scattered, running for cover against the torrential downpour.

Mark shut the window and walked back across the room, carefully stepping over his half-packed suitcase on the carpeted floor. He went over to the bookcase, pulled out his Farsi grammar book, and tossed it into the open suitcase. He then paced around the living room of his three-room apartment, glancing occasionally at the white notebook on the desk. The notebook was his reason for staying indoors all day; it would probably keep him captive for the rest of the Labor Day weekend.

Mark Rowan was a lean, lanky man, whose thick head of sandy-blond hair and clear, light-blue eyes made him look younger than his thirty-six years. His boyish All-American good looks belied his intellectual capacity and professional accomplishments. Fluent in Arabic, Turkish, and Farsi, Mark Rowan was a top-notch Mid-East intelligence specialist with the U.S. State Department.

Mark walked into his tiny kitchen to see what there was to eat. There wasn't much. It was late in the afternoon, and Mark could not decide whether to go to Armando's for a quick pizza, or wait until after his phone call and then to go the Café De Artistas in Georgetown. The sound of the rain made him decide on the latter. He went to the refrigerator to get a drink and a snack to hold him over until after nine o'clock. Juggling a can of Coke and a tin of Planter's peanuts, he went over to his desk and picked up his heavy white plastic notebook. Only one word—Iran—was written on the notebook's cover. Mark carried the notebook over to the couch. He sat down on the couch and put his feet up on the wooden coffee table.

He lifted the cumbersome book onto his lap. The notebook was the casebook on Iran issued by the State Department. New books were compiled yearly; the one Mark balanced on his lap was the latest one, dated August 1983. The book contained basic background information on Iran: tabbed markers divided the general background material into sections on geography, history, culture, and society (past and present), health and social welfare, ethnic groups, religion, and economy. The Iran casebook also contained extensive classified information and personality profiles on key Iranians, the result of information collected by various intelligence-gathering agencies.

Information on Iran was hard to come by. Westerners were not generally admitted into Iran, and the few foreigners still allowed to enter the country were closely watched. Aerial reconnaissance was difficult because, with the exception of a few commercial flights, foreign aircraft were not allowed into Iranian airspace. Much of the latest information contained in the U.S. State Department Iran casebook had been compiled from unauthorized aerial photography and information obtained by the CIA, Interpol, Mossad (the Israeli intelligence agency), and other Western intelligence-gathering agencies. Mark had studied the book carefully, and was familiar with all of the information it contained. But he still read and re-read it, trying to absorb everything.

Mark flipped through the dividers. A wry smile crossed his face as he passed over the religion section. Only since the 1979 Islamic Revolution in Iran had the U.S. State Department placed any emphasis on religion; in 1979 the State Department completely rewrote the briefing books on every Middle Eastern Islamic country. Islam, once the exotic and far-off religion that the West had perceived as fairly innocuous, had become the catapult that made Khomeini a household word, added the words "Sunni" and "Shi'ite" to the vocabularies of most Americans, and turned the "arc of crisis"—that Moslem-dominated section of the globe stretching from Ethiopia to Pakistan—into the chronic hot spot in the world.

Mark came to the pages he wanted to review: a synopsis of the major events and upheavals in Iran since the 1979 Islamic Revolution. But before starting in on these pages, Mark quickly reviewed the background information on twentieth century Iran, through 1979.

Iran had been an agrarian, semifeudal society up until the time of Reza Shah the Great, only about sixty years in the past. Reza Shah, an illiterate army officer who became Shah of Iran by means of a coup d'etat and founded the short-lived, ill-fated Pahlavi dynasty, had pulled Iran up into the twentieth century by its bootstraps. The Pahlavis—first Reza Shah and then his urbane, Swiss-educated, Westernized son, Mohammad

Reza Pahlavi—instituted ambitious industrialization, modernization, and Westernization programs that inevitably restructured Iranian society.

The Pahlavis stripped away the status and power of the old landed ruling class as oil exports became a larger and more important part of the Iranian economy. The Shah enraged the mullahs, the Moslem clergy, by expropriating much of their vast land holdings, and by severely curtailing their powers. In matters of daily social and economic life, in which the mullahs had reigned supreme for centuries, Shah Mohammad Reza Pahlavi made civil authority supreme. The Shah felt he had effectively castrated the clergy, but it was the clergy, secretly fermenting and agitating, who orchestrated the Islamic Revolution that ousted the Shah.

The bazaar merchants, or the *bazaaris*, were another group that had been disenfranchised by the Shah. The nine-mile-long, serpentine, covered labyrinth of shops that made up the Tehran bazaar had been the commercial heart of Iranian society. But with the massive industrialization and ambitious commercial exploits of the Shah's regime, the *bazaaris* were supplanted by the Harard Business School graduates who dealt with businessmen from Tokyo, Frankfurt, London, New York, and Houston from ultramodern offices and banks on Takht-e-Jamshid Street in downtown Tehran.

By the late 1970s, when opposition to the Shah's autocratic rule caught fire in Iran, pitifully few Iranians had reaped the benefits of industrialization and modernization. A corrupt elite, a narrow segment of society, ruled Iran, and became fabulously wealthy in the process. The daily lot of the masses, an estimated eighty-five percent of

28

Iranian society, was not greatly improved, and what advances that were made in the name of progress were offset by the social upheavals created by the economic boom. The benefits of modernization for most Iranians were double-digit inflation, and a view northward, up the smog-free slopes of the Alborz Mountains, of the palatial homes of businessmen, generals, and government ministers, not to mention the high-living Pahlavi family. SAVAK, the Shah's hated secret police, ruthlessly crushed opposition to the Shah's rule, but by 1978 the situation had gotten out of hand. The concentration of wealth was top-heavy, the corruption too glaring, and SAVAK too repressive to stem the tide of anti-Shah sentiment. In mid-1978, the Shah belatedly realized the gravity of the situation and attempted to make amends. But it was too late, and Iran fell.

Mark turned the page. There was a subchapter of information on 1979 Iran, compiled by the CIA. At the time of the Revolution, Iran had some very sophisticated aircraft: two hundred and fifty F-4 Phantoms, approximately two hundred F-5's, and seventy-five F-14A's. The U.S., fearful that the new Revolutionary Government of Iran would use these aircraft, or that they might fall into Soviet hands, attempted to track these aircraft down, and keep tabs on them. However, U.S. Intelligence was unable to locate over forty percent of the aircraft. All reports said that they had simply disappeared.

Mark gave a quick glance to the intelligence profile on Ayatollah Khomeini, and passed over the reports on ex-Prime Minister Mehdi Bazargan, Ibrahim Yazdi, Ayatollah Shariat-Maderi, ex-Presidents Bani-Sadr and Rajai, all of whom had become, by death, execution, or political disfavor, persons of no consequence. There was a thick file, complete with photographs, on the U.S. Embassy hostage crisis.

Mark pulled out profiles on the key figures in the present Iranian government. The thickest dossier was on the Ayatollah Hassan-Ali Khalaghani, the head of the current government, the Third Islamic Republic of Iran, and the third Ayatollah to rule post-Revolutionary Iran.

Mark knew that the profile on Khalaghani was merely a composite of educated guesses and a few facts, compiled by the foremost U.S. authorities on Iran. Like Khomeini, the first Ayatollah to rule the Islamic Republic of Iran, Khalaghani was an enigma to the West. Mark read over the parts of the profile that he had underlined.

*Khalaghani, Hassan-Ali:* Born 1907 in Arak, a town in central Iran . . . rose from an obscure position during the rule of Khomeini to become the most outspoken proponent of exporting the Iranian revolution to other Islamic nations . . . . Served as head of Religious Affairs in the Revolutionary Council, 1981-82 . . . a staunch enforcer of strict Islamic justice . . . upon assuming control of the government after the death of Ahmed, son of Khomeini, there was a resurgence of public floggings and executions . . . . Over the past two years, Khalaghani has become increasingly fanatical and irrational . . . believed to suffer from brucellosis, commonly known as undulent fever, which causes recurring high fevers and can eventually lead to madness . . . Khalaghani is considered highly unstable . . . dangerous . . . pathologically xenophobic . . .

Mark made a few notes in the margins, and moved on in the casebook.

Iran under Khalaghani was burdened by problems that had been left unresolved from the early days of the Revolution when Khomeini had managed to disenfranchise most segments of Iranian society. There had been a brain drain: U.S.-educated Iranian professionals and technocrats who feared the Khomeini regime fled Iran. A U.S. Immigration report of 1979, represented in the casebook, showed that seventy-five percent of U.S.-educated Iranians had petitioned either to stay in the United States, or to return to the U.S. from Iran. The Iranian immigration situation had been similar in France and England, with Iranians who had received university degrees in those countries returning to them.

The once well-paid laborers who had made up the bulk of the work force no longer had government projects to work on, highways to build, apartment buildings to construct. The middle class, the technocrats, and the merchants fought a losing battle to carry on business as usual, when, in reality, there was no business.

Mark turned to the appendices at the back of the casebook. He found the appendix he wanted: Status Reports on Major Iranian Industries. He scanned the first report in the section, a report on the Peykan car factory:

. . . the combination of two factors—fleeing management (both foreigners and Iranian nationals), and a lack of foreign-produced parts—caused the rapid demise of the Peykan car factory, once one of the largest factories in Iran, and an important part of the growing auto industry in Iran . . . . Depleted stock inventories, heavy debts, dissatisfied workers, and, above all, fear of the new Islamic government, caused virtually all upper and middle level management to leave Iran. All those who had been in management before the fall of the Shah who did not resign their positions were dismissed. In their place, revolutionary committees ran each plant . . . people who had neither the expertise nor practical

31

experience to run the factory . . . . by early 1981, the Peykan car factory had stopped receiving knock-down kits from Hilland, U.K. . . . The factory closed shortly thereafter . . .

Mark flipped through the appendices on major Iranian industries. The reports were all the same. The auto industry was a classic example of what had happened to industry in Iran after the Revolution. The few remaining industries in Iran that still functioned did so only on a subsistence level, with productivity falling every year.

Under the Shah's reign, Iran's oil industry was developed, making Iran one of the world's major oil exporters and one of the world's richest nations. During the 1970s, oil revenues brought in more than twenty billion dollars a year. The world's largest oil refinery was at Abadan, in the southwest corner of Iran. After the 1979 Revolution, oil production dropped drastically. In late 1980, during the war of attrition between Iran and Iraq, the Iraqis destroyed a major part of the Abadan refinery complex. The Iranians partially rebuilt the refinery, enough to resume production on a limited scale, but reconstruction was halted by late 1981. Iran was paralyzed by governmental crises. But the flow of Iranian oil, although only a fraction of what it had been under the Shah, continued through Abadan. The Western world counted on it, and paid for it, enough to keep the merry-go-round governments of Iran functioning.

In April 1982, antigovernment terrorists dealt yet another devastating blow to the Islamic Republic of Iran. And, as in the bombings of Tehran government buildings, no group claimed responsibility for the act. A crippling sabotage of the Iranian oil-pipeline system occurred. A massive set of explosions, carefully planned to destroy the whole pipeline, wracked the pipeline network, and cut off the supply of oil to the tanker-loading facility at Kharg Island, and to the Abadan refinery. The oil-pipeline sabotage left Iran without a cash flow.

The radical element of OPEC—dominant within the cartel—now seized the moment. Realizing that the delicate balance of world supply and demand had been upset, the cartel engaged in unprecedented opportunism. They reduced oil production drastically, thus elevating prices to a record high, strangling the world's economy.

While economic and political aftershocks of these catastrophic events were being felt around the world, another incident occurred that further heightened instability in the Persian Gulf region. Sovereignty over the tiny but strategic island of Abu Musa, near the Straits of Hormuz, was wrested from Iran by the United Arab Emirates only three months after the April 1982 pipeline sabotage.

By then, the problems left unresolved by the Revolution, the pipeline sabotage, and internal anarchy forced the government of the Islamic Republic of Iran to turn its focus inward. Compounding the growing problems in Iran was a natural disaster. The winter of 1982 was the most severe on record. Food supplies and oil reserves were nearly totally depleted.

Poor bastards, thought Mark, as he closed his eyes, and leaned back in his chair. Without the twenty-billion dollars a year in oil revenues, there was no money to import food. Agricultural self-sufficiency had been one of the aims of the Shah's own White Revolution, but somehow, in the excitement of becoming the Mid-East Superpower, the Shah forgot about that. Back then, oil-revenue rich Iran could easily afford to export carpets, pistachios, and dried fruit, and import nearly everything else—more than eighty percent of all its food. The agricultural program had been a failure, a flagrant example of Iranian mismanagement and corruption. Enormous tracts of arable land that the Shah took from the clergy and other feudal landowners, divided up, then gave to small farmers, somehow ended up back in the hands of one individual, a developer. The land was once again parceled off and sold for housing projects, factories, or just left empty, awaiting a better price on Iran's inflated real estate market. The fertile tea- and rice-growing area around the Caspian Sea was used for luxury seaside condominiums and houses for Tehran's wealthy. Yes, thought Mark, many mistakes had been made under the Shah. Still, they in no way compared to the blunders committed in Iran since the Revolution.

Mark rubbed his eyes, and returned to the casebook. He still had a lot to do before he talked to Kir. He returned to the information on the Third Islamic Republic of Iran.

By the winter of 1982, there was starvation, anarchy and chaos in Iran. Adding to and perpetuating Iran's problems was the fact that the populace was armed. All the weapons that had been taken from military bases, barracks, and police stations during the early days of the Revolution in 1979 were still held by the people.

Armed political splinter groups, primarily the Mohjahidin and the increasingly anticlerical Feydayeen, felt that they had been cut off from the Islamic government that they had helped to bring to power. The Mohjahidin and the Feydayeen continued their armed underground struggle against the government—and against each other—contributing to the general anarchy in the streets. By the time Khalaghani assumed power, a potentially potent new underground movement, the Zurkhaneh, had developed. Reports on the Zurkhaneh were sketchy, but they were said to be a liberal, prodemocratic, clandestine group, an illusive, but seemingly well-organized antigovernment force.

By 1982, Iran was rife with problems; it was a hotbed of seething discontent that seemed ready to boil over, and Khalaghani realized that, in order to effectively control the Iranians, he had to disarm them. An armed, hungry populace was dangerous.

Khalaghani seized upon a plan—guns for rice. In the harsh winter of 1982, when many Iranians were starving, and most others were very hungry, Khalaghani issued a call for national unity—and a call for all good Moslems to turn in their weapons. For each gun a loyal Iranian turned in, he would be given a five-kilo bag of rice.

The plan worked. People lined up outside of the government's hastily set up collection center, eagerly waiting to trade their weapons for food. In less than two months, the Iranian people were disarmed. Any possible opposition to Ayatollah Khalaghani and his Third Islamic Republic had effectively been neutralized. As conditions in Iran deteriorated, Khalaghani continued his theocratic, increasingly tyrannical rule.

"Those poor bastards," Mark said aloud, as he stood up. He went to the kitchen to get another Coke, then continued reading.

Mark read over the grim statistics on the state of the Iranian economy, as of mid-1983. Tables of statistics included figures on estimated productivity, numbers of persons employed in the few still-active sectors, unemployment, and other related information. Only essential industries such as textiles and food processing continued, but production in most of Iran's factories had dropped to between ten and twenty percent of capacity. By August 1983, unemployment in Iran was estimated to be upwards of sixty-five per cent.

Mark shook his head slowly from side to side. It's all such a damned shame, he thought to himself, sadly remembering what a booming, prosperous economy Iran had enjoyed only a few years before.

Mark turned to a section of maps on Iran: detailed topographical maps, colored Earth Resources Satellite photographs of agricultural activities and demographic studies of population shifts. The demographic maps plotted the movement of the people away from the cities and back into the countryside. Increased areas of land were being used for agriculture, but without significant increases in food production. Modern farming methods were, for all practical purposes, nonexistent, and insufficient water supply, especially in south and central Iran, was a constant problem.

A map of Baluchistan, the province in southeast Iran, caught Mark's eye. The terrain was rough and mountainous, inhabited by the bellicose Baluchi tribesmen, who were extremely hostile to the Islamic government. Mark trusted the map's accuracy—as it had been provided by Mossad, the Israeli intelligence organization.

Mark reviewed the rest of the maps. He paid special attention to the map of Qom, Iran's capital city since 1981. The map had been drawn from an aerial photograph of Qom, and was not as detailed as he would have liked, but it was the best he'd seen. He made a note on the steno pad to obtain a more up-to-date map of Qom.

Mark moved ahead a few pages in the casebook until he came to the section on aerial surveillance, satellite photo-reconnaissance, and intelligence reports on the status of pipeline repairs in Iran. Mark looked at some photos of southwestern Iran, where the border of Iraq meets the Iranian border, the province of Khuzistan. Mark brought his high-intensity light closer to him and pulled the photos out of the cellophane packet. The most recent photos were dated August 15, 1983. Mark studied the highly enlarged satellite photos of the work being done on the Iranian pipelines. The pipelines stretched south from the oil fields and north from the tanker-loading facility at Kharg Island. Mark reviewed the entire series of satellite photographs that dated from sixteen months ago, when the massive sabotage occurred, until just last month. Mark interpreted the progress of work on the pipeline network. Repair and rebuilding of the pipelines had been hampered by the constant harassment and subversive activities of the Sunni Arabs of Khuzistan.

Mark's brow furrowed as he read the health and social welfare section of the Iran casebook. Communicable diseases were on the upswing. Public immunization programs were nonexistent. The breakdown of public services which had occurred after the 1979 Revolution had especially affected the areas of health and sanitation. The expulsion of foreigners had not been limited to Westerners, and the thousands of Indian and Pakistani physicians—who had been the only doctors willing to practice in the Iranian countryside—had also been forced to flee Iran. Diseases that had been nearly extinct, or under tight control for years, reappeared. Bone tuberculosis was (according to Radio Baku, a Soviet station near the Irano-Soviet border) rampant all along the Caspian Sea area, in the north of Iran.

"Christ," Mark said aloud. "It must be hell getting any information from Iran if we're moni-

37

toring Radio Baku."

As he continued reading, the furrow on his forehead deepening. Cholera areas dotted Iran, especially in the areas of Baluchistan, in the southeast, and in Khuzistan and the Zagros mountains, in west-central Iran. A cholera outbreak amongst the Baluchi tribesmen in 1981 had killed an estimated four thousand people. Smallpox, which had been declared extinct by the World Health Organization in 1978, had broken out in some nomadic tribes, chiefly the Qashqai tribe. The Irano-Turkish border, which the Qashqai had previously freely crossed, was closed by Turkey. A 1981 WHO report stated that smallpox was still present in Iran, but was unable to provide any statistics. Mark sighed, and turned the page.

A table of figures was at the top of the page. Mark skipped over them. He knew most of the figures by heart: infant mortality was up more than fifty percent in the past five years, and the estimated number of children under the age of twelve suffering from malnutrition was seventy percent. Mark considered most of these statistics —all of them from outside Iran—too low. Mark knew from experience that, in such cases, reality was usually worse than the statistics belied. Mark speed-read over the rest of the health section, his eyes stopping only at the section on venereal disease. With the lack of antibiotics, medical care, and condoms, and the increase in prostitution and homosexuality (both the result of the Islamic clergy's ban on nearly any male-female activity), the rise in venereal disease could not be accurately estimated, but it was several times what it had been five years before.

The social welfare information was equally grim. Women were particularly repressed under the Islamic Republic. The Shah's landmark Family

Protection Act of 1967—which gave women the rights to abortion, contraception, support in case of divorce or desertion by the husband, and abolished forced marriages and raised the legal age for marriage to eighteen—was repealed by Khomeini almost immediately after he assumed power. In one fell swoop, all the hard-won rights, financial and legal, of Iranian women were destroyed. *Sighe*, legalized concubinage, was reinstated, despite the protests of hundreds of thousands of Iranian women. And because many educated Iranians had fled the country, there was an insufficient number of teachers for both girls' and boys' schools, so female children no longer went to school at all. Mark glanced at his watch, and turned to the last section of the casebook.

The personality profiles of important Iranians, both in Iran and in exile, were the most well-thumbed pages in the Iran casebook. Mark read and reread the profiles, trying to commit to memory as much information as possible about the past, present and would-be leaders of Iran. Mark turned quickly to the page he wanted.

*Bakhtiar, Shapour:* Prime Minister of Iran for three weeks, between January 16, 1979, and February 10, 1979, a period of Regency Council, between the departure of the Shah from Iran and the Islamic Revolution . . . . Escaped from Iran during the first days of the Islamic Revolution, to France . . . . Has been residing in France since 1979 . . . Death sentence *in absentia* pronounced by Islamic leader Khalkhali, at the same time the Shah and members of the royal family were sentenced to death, regardless of the fact that Bakhtiar was anti-Shah for twenty years preceding the Revolution . . . . Bakhtiar was educated (Ph.D., political science, Sorbonne) in France, and lived there for a number of years during his youth. Upon returning to Iran, he became a leader of the National Front, the moderate-liberal opposition (to the Shah's autocratic rule) group . . . . Before the Revolution, Bakhtiar had had wide-spread popular support . . .

Bakhtiar surfaced in Paris several months after the Revolution. From 1979 through 1981 he conducted a campaign against the Islamic government in Iran. He lectured, held press conferences, published pamphlets, etc., lambasting Iran from France, Italy, England, and West Germany . . . . Now lives in hiding in France and Switzerland . . . . Of late, there have been reports of anti-Islamic, underground Bakhtiar tapes being circulated in the border areas of Iran . . .

Mark underlined the last sentence, and closed the notebook. His mind was teeming with images of Iran: endless, flat expanses of desert; lush green forests; inferno-like orange flames rising above the oilfields; huge modern factories, the Shah's camouflage-painted helicopters flying to and from Niavarin Palace; gleaming turquoise-and-gold domed mosques; sloe-eyed veiled women; angry, machine-gun toting men; silhouettes of tribal children against the boundless, azure-blue sky. But that was the Iran he had known several years before, before the Revolution. He wondered what Iran looked like now.

Mark Rowan stretched out on the sofa and began studying the notes he'd just made. He wanted to be prepared when he spoke with Michael Kir that night.

# CHAPTER THREE

The sun beat down on the four figures walking up the gravel path toward the clubhouse.

"Go ahead, girls," Jack said as they walked past the entrance to the men's locker room. "We'd better shower first."

"Fine, dear," Jeri said. Both she and Cheryl eyed Michael Kir's ass as the two men walked into the locker room.

"Ooh, love that ass!" Cheryl said, once the men were out of earshot.

Jeri smiled in agreement as the two women hurried out of the heat, toward the clubhouse.

Jack dropped his bag on the tiled floor and walked over to the stack of thick white towels piled high on a rack near the showers.

"Here, Mike!"

Michael Kir caught the towel as it winged across the spotless red and white tiled locker room. "Thanks, Jack. God, I can't believe how hot it is out there today! It must be in the nineties, with the humidity about the same."

"Hot is right, but it didn't stop you from beating the shit out of me!"

Defeat had always been a hard pill for Jack Adams Tucker to swallow, perhaps because it hardly ever happened to him, either on the tennis courts or in business. And it was especially hard to accept defeat today, since Jack had been confident that he would beat Kir. Jack had been playing a top-notch game of tennis at least five or six times a week for the past three years, and he was the club champion.

Jack glanced over at Kir, who was walking toward the shower, only a towel hung around his neck. Christ, no wonder Kir beat me, he's still got the body of a twenty-nine year old, Jack thought. Michael looked the same as he had in college, lean and in top condition.

Jack peeled off his damp tennis clothes, dropping them in a pile as he pushed open the swinging doors of the shower stall next to Kir's. He turned on the shower, full force, and began lathering up his salty skin. What the hell, I can't complain, he thought. Jack's body was trim and hard from his many hours spent on the tennis court and jogging track. He soaped down his torso, feeling the edges around his waist, his "love handles" as Sandy, his secretary, called them. They were firm, but they were still there. Age can't help but begin to show. I am nearing the big four-oh," Jack thought. But Michael was thirty-nine, too. "Mike," Jack yelled over the noise of the shower, "you're in great shape. How do you do it?"

"Women," Kir replied, water running down his face as he rinsed the soap out of his thick head of hair, "they keep you young."

"They keep you poor," Jack replied. He poured his fifteen-dollar-a-bottle French shampoo for "fine and thinning hair," that Jeri had insisted he buy, onto his head and gently massaged the amber liquid along his receding hairline.

He visualized Kir in the shower stall next to him. And the goddamn son-of-a-bitch is hung, too, Jack thought. Jeri's constant harping on hair loss, sexual staying power, and the daily morning ritual of the "pinch test" was getting to him. One more "Special K Day" and he would tell her what she could do with the half a banana she sliced on top of his 237 calories. No wonder Mike has a full head of hair, Jack thought enviously. He doesn't have a wife to prematurely age him.

"Jack." Kir's voice rose above the sound of the water. "It's been such a long time since we've talked. Whatever happened about that money you were trying to collect from the Revolutionary Government, the first tone, Khomeini's, I mean? How did International Oil Services make out, finally?"

"Not too badly. We finally managed to collect over twenty per cent of all outstanding debts. Better than a lot of companies, actually. That's because we followed your suggestion. As you know, we went back into Iran right after the Revolution, and started collecting bits and pieces and then got the hell out before the embassy takeover. After that fiasco, things went right down the tube for Americans over there. You could kiss your money and equipment in Iran goodbye, not to mention your ass. Since then, I haven't been able to get any real information on the economic status of Iran. Nobody knows anything. The Iranians fucked us over, but I think they did an ever better job on themselves."

"You hit the nail on the head, Jack," Michael replied.

"What do you hear, Mike?"

"It's all through the grapevine, naturally, but it looks very bad."

"Mike, let's face it. You always had the best grapevine in Tehran and that place was a goddamn vineyard. What the fuck actually happened?"

"It's a mess, an absolute mess. All the projects,

good and bad alike, of the Shah's regime have gone to hell. Mills, factories, and refineries that were in production during the Shah's reign have fallen into ruin. Productivity in the few still-functioning industries is down to nothing. Just to give you an example, Jack, the National Steel Company was not able to get the coke needed to fire all its furnaces and as a result the furnaces began to cool down and crack. Ruined. Now the National Steel Company works at under ten per cent of its pre-Revolutionary capacity."

"Christ!" Jack said. "Is any business going on there? What is still running?"

"*Sharh-e-now*, New City," Michael said. "The mullahs can't hold down free enterprise."

"Yeah, you can't keep a good girl down," Jack replied. He had been to Tehran's New City once back in 1976. It was a separate city within a city, in the south of Tehran, populated entirely by prostitutes, male and female, of all shapes and sizes. They hung out of windows, leaned on doors, wearing their *chadors*, the head-to-toe body veils, as immodestly as possible. Dark, kohl-painted eyes. Black platform-boots. Mini-skirts and low-cut dresses beneath the *chadors*.

"After Khomeini had a number of prostitutes executed, New City went underground, but it's still flourishing," said Michael.

"God damn, sounds like the whores have the only business left! I can't help but smile thinking that those Iranians are screwing themselves." Jack paused for a second. "Sorry, Mike, I didn't mean it that way. They're your people, your country."

"They're not my people, Jack, those lunatics that run the country. And Iran is not my country anymore," Kir said coldly as he turned off the shower. Kir wrapped a white towel around his waist as he stepped out of the shower. Jack followed suit, and the two men walked into the massage room.

Michael Kir stretched out on the hard, terry towel-covered table, Jack on the massage table next to him. "This was a great idea, Jack," Kir said. He closed his eyes as the strong hands of the masseur, slippery with almond oil, kneaded the knots in the muscles of his back. Kir could feel the tensions leave his body.

Michael Kir was no longer in the clubhouse of the Houston Tennis Club, but thousands of miles away and years back in time, with people who no longer existed. Michael Kir was a boy again, in his grandfather's summer house near Khoy, in the heart of Azarbaijan, in the northwest corner of Iran. He and his grandfather were sitting on a sun-bleached carpet, on the wide balcony of his grandfather's large wooden summer house. The summer sun warmed Michael's body, while a light, fresh breeze perfumed the air with the scent of honeysuckle and widely-opened Persian roses. Michael was wearing Western clothes, as he always did, while his grandfather enjoyed wearing a loose-fitting cotton shirt and baggy pants, a traditional, timeless costume worn by generations of Persians.

Michael had loved his grandfather very much. He wished he could have become a kind and gentle man like his grandfather, but the times in which Michael lived precluded that. He had grown into a hard man, a solitary man; his grandfather would not have approved of the man he had become. In retrospect, Michael was glad that his grandfather had died seventeen years ago, during Michael's last year at Stanford, that his grandfather had not lived to see the Revolution and the ensuing chaos and misery. It would have broken his heart. He had had such high hopes and dreams for his country.

The Revolution would not have been so hard on Michael's father, who died a year after his grandfather, because Michael's father had never felt that he belonged there, in Iran. Michael's father had left Iran many years ago, and had married an American girl. He had made sure that his only son was born an American citizen. Kir's father, always conscious of his—and his half-Iranian son's—identity as an Iranian, and as a Jew, had told Michael, "I am doing this for your own good. We don't belong in Iran and one of these days they will drive us out." His father had been right, and after the Revolution the Persian Jews realized that Iran was no longer their country, too. The lucky ones left. Kir now understood his father's insecurity, and considered himself lucky to be an American citizen.

Michael's mother died when he was eight years old, and although his father kept the family home in New York, his peripatetic lifestyle required that Michael spend much of his youth in boarding schools in England and Europe. But Kir spent his summers in Iran with his grandfather, and those summers were the happiest times of his youth. They were the only times that he felt truly at home.

Jack's voice jarred him. "So Mike, is the latest Iranian government still blaming all its problems on Uncle Sam?"

"Sure, the government still loves to use the United States as a scapegoat, but that's getting a little old. The people are finally beginning to realize that things were a lot better for them when the Shah and the imperialist Americans were there."

"So why the hell don't they do something about it?" asked Jack.

"The Third Islamic Republic was very efficient at rounding up all the weapons in the country. Ayatollah Khalaghani literally took the guns out of the people's hands." Kir winced as the masseur started in on his shoulder muscles. "The hell with that country, Jack. I need a drink, after this conversation," Kir said, sitting up on the table.

"If you think you need a drink, how'd you think the President feels?" Jack asked, climbing off the table. "Iran won't be his problem much longer. It'll be Joseph Sullivan's."

"You think so?" Kir asked.

"Absolutely. Since the President won't run again, due to his declining health, Senator Sullivan will be a sure winner for President in '84. I mean, who the hell else would want the problems that the next administration will have to face? But Sullivan thinks he has all the answers, and it seems as if the American public is willing to grasp at straws at this point. Jesus, I need a drink, too," Jack said, "just thinking about Sullivan as President. I'm sure you're aware that the oil industry has been trying to dig up another skeleton in Sullivan's closet—just to have something on him, to keep him in line."

"I think his closet had been picked clean," Kir said, heading toward the shower. "I've got to rinse off, Jack. I'll be quick, the girls must have wondered what happened to us."

Jack wasn't listening to Kir. "Well, I guess the world won't be hearing anything from Iran anymore, will they?" Jack asked.

"No," Kir said, the sound of the water drowning out his lie.

# CHAPTER FOUR

Ali-Reza Raissi drove up to the front of Mehrabad Military Base. He left his orange 1975 Range Rover, running, in front of the main entrance, Gate 1, and hopped down from the driver's seat. A light cloud of dust rose from the dry ground as his feet hit the earth.

Ali-Reza was a tall, lean man of thirty-three. His full beard and moustache were pitch-black, as were his long, thick eyelashes and full head of hair. He had light-olive skin, a slightly aquiline nose, prominent cheekbones, and intense dark-brown eyes. He was a ferociously handsome young man.

The late afternoon sky was a cloudless pale blue, and the still air was dry and searingly hot, a typical early September day in Tehran. Ali-Reza unbuttoned the top button of his beige cotton shirt as he walked toward the gate. The gate was closed with a perfunctory, half-rusted padlock; there was not even a single guard left to control access to the base. Ali-Reza fished the key-ring out of the back pocket of his tight, worn jeans, selected the right key, and opened the gate.

He got back into his Range Rover and drove through the gate, past the empty guard-house, past a wall with metal doors, one of the side entrances to the cavernous, 12,000-square-meter warehouse, through the vacant parking lot, and pulled up in back of a large, rectangular building, the Base Administration Building. Ali-Reza got out of his car and walked along the side of the long building toward the front entrance. He walked up the few steps leading to the portico that graced the entrance to the Base Administration Building.

Standing on the portico, Ali-Reza pushed his aviator-style sunglasses to the top of his head, paused and blinked for a few seconds as his eyes grew accustomed to the new light, and looked all around at the bleak, deserted base. The lone guard standing just inside the heavy double glass doors of the Administration Building caught sight of Ali-Reza and nodded to him. Politely, Ali-Reza nodded back. A hot wind rippled the few scraggly blades of grass which still grew in what had been, less than five years ago, a well-tended garden in front of the Administration Building. Looking out at the silent, grayish-beige landscape before him, Ali-Reza found it hard to reconcile this harsh reality with his memory of Mehrabad Base as a humming, throbbing center of activity.

Mehrabad Military base, adjacent to Tehran's Mehrabad Airport, had been an Imperial Iranian Army aviation base; it had been the helicopter division of the old Imperial Iranian Army. Mehrabad Base's official name was IHSRC: Iran Helicopter Support and Renewal Company. In its heyday, which started in 1973 and lasted until late 1978, over 5,000 people worked at IHSRC. About 1,500 were Americans, all employees of Bell Helicopter International or one of the smaller, specialized service companies subcontracted to Bell Helicopter. Working together with the Americans were about 3,000 Iranians, under contract to the Imperial Government of Iran, whose work—for many of them, at least—counted for military service. Several hundred soldiers, drawn from all over Iran, had been permanently stationed at Mehrabad; maintaining tight security had been one of their main functions.

IHSRC had been an ambitious, high-priority project of the Imperial Government of Iran. Comprehensive training programs for technicians, pilots, and computer operators were conducted on the base. With its Administration Building, huge Computer Center, several warehouses, barracks, and its own buses, cars, and gas pumps, IHSRC was considered one of the finest military bases in Iran.

IHSRC was one of the Shah's pet projects. The Shah loved helicopters, plain and simple. And, with Iran's thousands of miles of borders, mountainous and desert areas, combined with the immense expanse of oil fields, no one could deny that helicopters were a most useful type of aircraft. The Imperial Iranian's Army's helicopter fleet, comprising over 1,200 helicopters of various models, sizes, and capabilities, was the largest helicopter fleet in the Middle East, and one of the largest in the world.

The Shah had wanted to have a completely self-sufficient helicopter fleet, and he had been close to reaching his goal. The master plan was that IHSRC would eventually be able to fly, maintain, repair, trouble-shoot, and train pilots for all of Iran's helicopters. In short, IHSRC would be capable of performing all functions necessary to keep a helicopter fleet of great magnitude airborne. But Americans on the base wondered about the Shah's own abiding faith in his mechanics. All of the Shah's personal helicopters were maintained by an American crew. No Iranian was allowed within a hundred yards of them. The Shah's helicopters were kept in a separate hangar

—for American eyes and hands only.

IHSRC had been supplied with the best American-made equipment that money could buy. The Computer Center, brimming with the newest and most sophisticated Honeywell Computer Equipment, contained the fully-automated Parts/Materials/Storage System, "pimss" for short. The "pimss" was the ultimate inventory system. Tens of thousands of types of hardware, software, and ammunition, at many locations throughout Iran—some classified, some not—could be pinpointed quickly and efficiently. The sophisticated Honeywell equipment that filled the gleaming glass and stainless steel interior of the Computer Center contained comprehensive information on over 100,000 line items used by Iran's aircraft. Within the thin metal walls of the Honeywell computers lay information about all materiel used by the Imperial Iranian Army Aviation and Air Force. All the records and information concerning Iran's thousands of military aircraft, and spare parts for them, were in the Computer Center at Mehrabad Base.

The gargantuan 12,000-square-meter warehouse at Mehrabad was the complete helicopter check-up, maintenance, and repair center for all the Imperial Iranian Government's helicopters. The interior of the warehouse had been divided with corrugated aluminum and plywood into various sections: electronic, hydraulic, mechanical, and paint shops. The Flight Line, where last minute checks on operationally ready aircraft were made just before takeoff, was the largest and most important part of the vast warehouse.

A small warehouse, behind the 12,000-square-meter one, contained a fully-equipped print shop that reproduced technical manuals, teaching materials, and statements of official policy of Bell

Helicopter International, for the Americans. During the final days of the print shop's operation in January 1979, the presses ran late into the night. They churned out security bulletins reassuring the Americans that the firebombing of eight Bell Helicopter employees' cars in north Tehran had nothing to do with the rumor that anti-American feelings in Iran were running high—pure coincidence. Reassurances from the U.S. Embassy were printed for BHI employees: the situation in Iran was not critical, merely fluid.

The situation had turned out to be critical, and the red brick barracks near Gate 1 and the remains of the Air Traffic Control Tower were reminders of that. In February 1979, during the final days of the Bakhtiar government, the barracks that housed the five hundred soldiers stationed at Mehrabad had provided a hideout shelter for the several dozen Americans trapped on the base during the Battle of Tehran. In the distance, far beyond the barracks, was the air traffic control tower, or what was left of it. During the Battle of Tehran, a base colonel had commandeered a Bell 206 helicopter in a desperate attempt to escape from Tehran, away from the frenzied mobs, thirsty for revenge against those who represented the Shah's authority, that thronged the streets. But the colonel, in his hurry, flew straight into the control tower, shaving the top part of it right off.

The surrender of the Imperial Iranian Armed Forces at Mehrabad to the Revolutionary Forces on February 11, 1979, signaled the end of IHSRC. Of the helicopters still on the base that day, about two-hundred fifty were operationally ready, ready to fly immediately upon fueling. The new commanders of the Revolutionary Forces ordered that many of these helicopters be flown to other areas of Iran, where they were needed. Soldier-pilots who had joined Khomeini's Revolution flew dozens of helicopters to Azarbaijan, to Baluchistan, and to Kurdistan. But many pilots at Mehrabad, still loyal to the Shah, brazenly stole choppers right off the base, and escaped in them to undisclosed destinations. From Doshen-Tappeh Air Force Base in Tehran, and the Imperial Flight Hangars, other loyal pilots did the same. All types of aircraft, including F-4's and F-5's, and even a few F-14's, vanished into thin air. During the days of total anarchy immediately following the Revolution, the same thing occurred at military bases all over Iran.

Its ranks broken, the Imperial Iranian Armed Forces disintegrated within days after the Revolution. As Khomeini's Revolutionary Courts were executing the Shah's generals and top-ranking officers, about half the soldiers simply walked out of their barracks and went home. The remains of the great Imperial Iranian Army were a pathetic sight; leaderless, disorganized, undisciplined, and demoralized troops.

At Mehrabad Base, practically anyone who wanted to could call himself a helicopter pilot; with the old military order gone, there was usually no one around to dispute such a claim. The result was numerous helicopter crashes and accidents. Some were relatively minor, a broken tailboom or a crumpled rotor blade. But most resulted in horribly mangled metal, or a mass of consuming flames, with a disfigured human body, or pieces of one, found scattered around the blackened wreckage.

Helicopters, along with the F-14 Tomcat fighter planes, had been the first items of the Islamic Republic of Iran's Armed Forces to fall into disuse. Two things essential to keeping the aircraft flying were missing: technical know-how and spare parts. Foreigners, meaning essentially Americans, had provided the know-how. Whether the Iranians admitted it or not, Americans were essential to keeping Iran's military aircraft flying. But the Americans had been evacuated, and they weren't coming back.

The Computer Center at Mehrabad stored all information concerning the whereabouts, status, and quantity of all parts and equipment relating to helicopters and all other aircraft in Iran. For spare parts and other information, the Revolutionary Committee of Mehrabad Base turned, naturally, to the Computer Center. The problems for the Islamic Republic's military aircraft began and ended here, very quickly. The upper-echelon Iranian IHSRC computer personnel had been arrested, shot, gone into hiding, or disappeared. Most of the personnel left at the Computer Center were lower- and middle-ranking IHSRC employees, who, taking full advantage of the almost total lack of "people at the top" in the center, now billed themselves as "experts" and "directors." But these computer personnel were not, as it turned out, as technically competent as they had believed, or bragged. In addition, further compounding the problem, members of the newly formed Revolutionary Committee of Mehrabad Base, most of whom had never before seen a computer, let alone used one, now joined the computer crew. Within hours, the computers were all jammed or short-circuited, and were completely nonfunctional. Millions of dollars worth of Honeywell computer equipment was a tangled, broken, disarray of metal, punch cards, paper, and tape. The destruction of Iran's military aircraft system had been effectively realized by this one act.

The entire organizational structure at Mehrabad—and of the entire country—had collapsed. The gaping holes in the organization meant gaping holes in knowledge and know-how. With the state of anarchy that prevailed in Iran after the Revolution, it was impossible to restructure the organization of Mehrabad Base, the Armed Forces, or any other facet of society.

At Mehrabad Base, as with most other Government of Iran property, the Revolutionary zeal for "liberating" anything that had been part of the old order turned into looting. In the first euphoric days following the Revolution, with the Imperial Iranian Army no longer Imperial and all-but-officially disbanded, Mehrabad, like other military bases in Tehran, overnight became *terra libra*.

Small groups of lower and middle class apartment dwellers from the nearby Taj and Shahyad residential areas walked into the "liberated" Mehrabad Base, at first stealthily in the black of night, then more openly, and helped themselves to whatever appealed to them. A vinyl-covered swivel chair from a secretary's desk, and a sack or two of rice from the cafeteria storeroom would always come in handy. A box of pencils or brightly colored felt-tip pens was considered a prize find. The more sophisticated scavengers availed themselves of rolls of American-made toilet paper, boxes of film from the photographic lab, and the electric teakettles from some of the Americans' offices.

The most ambitious liberators set about to furnish as much of their homes as possible courtesy of Mehrabad Base. They removed large wooden desks from the directors' offices (the standard four-drawer metal desks wouldn't do for such a discriminating crowd of thieves), wooden and metal coat racks, desk lamps, and even some loose (and pried loose) helicopter seats. There was even a rumor that, in a neighborhood close to the base, an outdoor wedding party was held under a tent made of sewn-together parachutes.

The "liberating" of government property finally came to a halt when the government of the new Islamic Republic was able to organize itself sufficiently so as to restore a marginal amount of order and stability, and close many of Iran's military bases. Mehrabad was ordered closed. It was of no use to anyone; the Computer Center had been destroyed, the base looted, and the helicopters left in the warehouse waited vainly for maintenance.

The vestiges of Iran's helicopter fleet, left at Mehrabad during the Revolution, remained crippled and grounded. Parts could not be traced, the U.S. refused to send another rotor blade or toggle switch to Iran, or to train any more Iranian pilots or technicians in the States. The IHSRC 12,000-meter warehouse became a helicopter graveyard. But there was no order even in this graveyard. Small 206 helicopters, once used for observation flights, competed for floor space with narrow, camouflage-painted Cobra helicopters, which had been used by the Imperial Army for "crowd control" during the street demonstrations against the Shah. Two white choppers, both badly damaged, sported the emblem of the Red Lion and Sun, the Iranian Red Cross, on their doors. Half-repaired electric cables dangled out of the bellies of the helicopters; the cement floor was stained with hydraulic fluid and oil that had leaked out of these sophisticated and expensive aircraft, rendering them useless.

The days of latest-model helicopters, high-flying potent aircraft, billion-dollar arms purchases, and plans—approaching reality—of being the fifth military power in the world were part of another era, the Shah's era. The bleak wasteland that was now Mehrabad Base was a sad monument to past dreams.

Ali-Reza's dark eyes scanned the desolate base, making sure that he was the only one on the base, except for the lone guard. Ali-Reza looked in all directions, but there were no people, no cars or other vehicles around. Ali-Reza turned and walked into the Administration Building.

The guard greeted Ali-Reza first.

"Hello, sir. How are you?" the guard said, bowing slightly toward Ali-Reza.

"I'm well, thank you. And you?"

Ali-Reza, as a formality and sign of respect for the guard's position rather than out of necessity, pulled his Civil Aviation identification card from his shirt pocket. The guard waved his hand to indicate that Ali-Reza should put his card back in his pocket. Ali-Reza nodded in acknowledgement and appreciation.

"Do you have any cigarettes, sir?" the guard said to Ali-Reza.

Ali-Reza smiled. This was the game the guard always played with him, asking for cigarettes. Ali-Reza knew that he was under no obligation to "tip" the guard. Ali-Reza's status as second in command of Islamic Iranian Civil Aviation automatically gave him free access to all military bases, both active and inactive, in Iran. But Ali-Reza knew it was better to stay on the good side of the guard, to placate him with a few cigarettes, sometimes even a whole pack. Besides, Ali-Reza felt genuinely sorry for the man. He had probably been, like most Iranian men, a dedicated cigarette smoker: Winston and Marlboro had been the two brands smoked almost exclusively in Iran. In one of the many acts of senseless violence against the Pahlavi Regime, just prior to the Revolution, the state-owned cigarette- and tobacco-packaging plants had been burnt to the ground by Khomeini followers. And after the Revolution, cigarettes imported from abroad were scarce and expensive. A black market in cigarettes (like so many other goods) flourished, at five dollars a package.

But as the value of the rial decreased and the cash money situation grew tighter, the black market cigarettes filtering up from the Persian Gulf soon became a luxury affordable by only a privileged few. The only "Marlboro men" in Iran were the mullahs and the Revolutionary Guards, and an ingenious few such as Ali-Reza. With his job as second in command of Iranian Civil Aviation, Ali-Reza knew the pilots and cabin crew who flew the six weekly Iran Air international flights. They frequently brought him a few cartons of English, French, and American cigarettes.

Ali-Reza took a full pack of Winstons from his pocket and gave it to the guard.

"Thank you very much," the guard said, holding his right hand to his heart and bowing slightly from the waist. The guard was very pleased. Winston was his favorite brand of cigarettes. Before Khomeini, he had smoked only Winstons. Before Khomeini, he had done a lot of things. The guard was a simple man and a religious man, but he still missed the adventure movies that he had gone to see in the old cinemas, in downtown Tehran—at the Empire, the Diamond, the Metropolitan. He missed music as well. Tehran before the Revolution had been a city full of stereo and record shops, but when Khomeini outlawed music the shops were forced to close. The cassettes for the tinny cassette deck in the guard's car had worn out long ago. It had become too expensive for him to buy blank cassettes and then use some friend's or relative's records to tape the banned songs of his favorite singers, Googoosh and Heydayat. He did not understand the harm in listening to a little music. It only made him laugh and dance. But he wouldn't think about that now. He fingered the cellophane on his precious package of cigarettes.

Ali-Reza looked at the lined face of the guard and felt deep compassion for him. A sense of resolution surged inside of Ali-Reza, strengthening him for the difficult and dangerous months ahead.

Ali-Reza had changed greatly over the past few years. He came from a moderately well-to-do land-owning family, the type of family known in Iran as a "good" family. His family sent him abroad to study, to Italy, where he took a degree in design at the University of Florence. During his years in Florence, he learned what Italians teach best, radical-chic living and politics—form with no sub-stance. In his expensive Gerard of Florence clothes, Ali-Reza breezed on to the business school at the University of Chicago in 1975. With a hefty allowance from his parents, Ali-Reza had ample money to buy a fire-engine-red Alfa Romeo and to act the part of a foreign Romeo. He impressed all the American girls with his dark good looks, charming personality, and custom of never going "Dutch."

When Ali-Reza returned to Iran in 1977, he acutely felt the Shah's regime to be repressive and unjust. The political philosophy he had acquired abroad and the exhilarating sensation of liberty that he had experienced in the U.S. and Europe combined to make him feel frustrated and dis-satisfied in Iran.

"A cigarette, sir?" the guard said, politely holding out the just-opened package of cigarettes to Ali-Reza.

*"Mersi,"* Ali-Reza said, taking one. The guard lit

it for him. *"Mersi,"* Ali-Reza said, taking a puff as he walked toward the staircase.

"I won't be long. I'm checking some things," Ali-Reza said over his shoulder to the guard.

The guard nodded as Ali-Reza climbed the travertine stairs of the Administration Building. Ali-Reza slowly walked down the second-story corridor. The doors to most of the offices were open. Ali-Reza couldn't help but remember what a bustling, lively place this had been four or five years ago, when he'd come to Mehrabad on business.

About halfway down the hallway, Ali-Reza paused. He walked into the Publications Department, and sat down at a desk. Except for the gaping holes left by the missing furniture, and the disorder of scattered papers and left-open drawers, it was almost as if he had come into a place where time had stopped, as if he had stepped into a suspended animation zone. The only telltale signs of change were the large squares on the walls, lighter color than the rest of the walls, where pictures of the Shah, Empress, and the Crown Prince had hung. A large photograph of Khomeini now hung on a tilt above the door to the office. How naive I was in those days, believing that Khomeini would be a change for the better.

Ali-Reza had been one of the millions who had cheered Khomeini along the carnation-strewn roadway leading from Mehrabad Airport to Behesht-Zahra cemetery that fateful February 1, 1979, when Khomeini returned to Iran in triumph. But the Revolution that Ali-Reza had participated in with naive enthusiasm soon disillusioned him.

Ali-Reza wanted a more democratic, liberal Iran, with the fruits of progress touching a broader spectrum of the Iranian population. He favored a republican form of government for Iran and the expansion of the role of the prime minister. Ali-Reza supported Prime Minister Shapour Bakhtiar, who headed the Regency Council that tried to govern Iran from the day the Shah left, January 16, 1979, until Khomeini and his supporters overthrew Bakhtiar on February 11, 1979. Ali-Reza realized that Bakhtiar was a competent and forceful man, probably the only man who could save Iran. But because Bekhtiar had been appointed by the Shah, he had the taint of the Pahlavis on him and was denounced by Khomeini. With the Revolution, Khomeini seized control of Iran, and the rest was history.

Ali-Reza had soon realized that Iran under the Shah was nothing compared to Iran under the rule of the fanatic Khomeini. Within a few months after the Revolution, after giving the new government all the chances he possibly could, making rationalizations to himself and hoping against hope that the deplorable situation in Iran was only temporary, Ali-Reza came to the ugly realization that the new government was much worse than the previous one. In fact, it was hell. Ali-Reza felt that nearly all sense of freedom had been squelched out of him. While most of his friends, who had also quickly become disenchanted with the repressive and dictatorial rule of the clergy, packed up and went back to Europe and the States, Ali-Reza chose to stay behind. After much soul-searching he decided to stay and plan and, eventually, when the time was right, fight for a free Iran: no more King of Kings and no more Imam to end all Imams.

Ali-Reza still believed that there was a better way than the corrupt, top-heavy rule of the Shah, and he also knew that it could never happen as long as the fanatical clergy held power. Ali-Reza's once fashionable student liberalism had turned into the deadly serious, pragmatic politics of the underground movement, the Zurkhaneh.

The fight had not been exactly what Ali-Reza had first envisioned. He had begun his struggle with romantic notions of "going underground," taking a small band of compatriots and hiding out in the hills, training as guerrillas and then undermining the religious rule of the country. He soon realized that that was an implausible idea; Iran was a country of guerrillas. Ali-Reza knew that he would have to beat the system, chaotic as it may have been. To form the nucleus of a self-styled group of freedom fighters, Ali-Reza recruited young, professional, liberal-minded Iranians, largely educated in Western Europe or the U.S. Many of these had held positions of responsibility during the Shah's Regime, but were far enough down the ladder to have escaped Khomeini's wrath. They were men and women who had been financial managers of government-run industries, assistants to the government ministers, lower management in government agencies, private industry, and banking. They were mostly people who had lost their positions of power in their organizations because of their connections with the Old Regime, but who had been kept on because they were the only ones who knew how to run the organization. It was a case of being banished from the executive offices on the top floor, then being given an office with the junior accountants on a lower floor.

These were the people who, as the situation in Iran grew more intolerable, as personal freedoms were restricted even more, as the secular government lost power completely to the clergy, as the economy disintegrated, joined together to form a clandestine underground liberation movement.

They called themselves the Zurkhaneh, or the House of Strength. The historical origin of the name "Zurkhaneh" served to identify the purpose of Ali-Reza's group. The Zurkhaneh started in the eighth century, when Persia was conquered by Moslem Arab invaders. Persian youths from all social classes gathered in secret to train and prepare for the day when they would drive out the invaders. Gradually, the Zurkhaneh developed into a traditional element of Persian culture. At the House of Strength, men performed special highly stylized rhythmic exercises, while in the background a chorus of elders chanted verses from the *Shah-nameh*, the beautiful eleventh century Persian epic poem, and musicians beat animal-skin drums. Many of the exercises performed by the members of the Zurkhaneh involved the use of shields and bows, testament to the military origins of the Zurkhaneh. This, coupled with the anti-Moslem origins of the Zurkhaneh (the eighth-century Arab invaders enforced Islam on the Persians), had caused Khomeini to declare the House of Strength *haram*, forbidden.

But there was one other factor that had caused the vengeful Khomeini to forbid the existence of the Zurkhaneh. The Zurkhaneh, as one of the oldest, purest Iranian traditions, had been a personal favorite of the Shah and Shahbanou. In the still heat of the summer of 1980, armed bands of Khomeini's followers, enflamed by his rhetoric, plundered and burned all of the buildings of the Zurkhaneh. Although this effectively ended the 1200-year-old institution of the House of Strength, the spirit of the Zurkhaneh lived on.

Ali-Reza's organization was a confederation of extremely well-disciplined men and a few women, who gathered in secret to prepare for the day when they would drive out the enemy; this time, the enemy was the repressive and dictatorial clergy. But outside of their meetings, Zurkhaneh members conducted themselves like loyal citizens of the Islamic Republic of Iran. They hardly looked like freedom fighters. They were mainly professional people, who still carried on as usual, who still went to work, if there was work. They were biding their time, waiting for the right moment.

The main Zurkhaneh group was in Tehran, with smaller groups in Isfahan, Abadan, Shiraz, Tabriz, the Caspian Sea area, the Persian Gulf area, and Qom. The Zurkhaneh members met with each other, planned their strategies with calculated, businesslike skills, waited, and tried to prepare themselves for the time when they would act, when the moment would be ripe for them to come forth and participate in the liberation and reconstruction of Iran. They kept their Revolutionary spirit alive.

As head of the Zurkhaneh, Ali-Reza, like the others, was forced to live his life on a tightrope. He was careful never to step out of line or bring attention to himself, because he had become a trusted member of the establishment who worked under the thumb of the mullahs. He had been able to keep his middle-management job with Civil Aviation after the Revolution. He ingratiated himself with the ruling clergy and through skillful maneuvering had been able to achieve his high-level post with Civil Aviation. The man above him, the head of Civil Aviation, was a mullah, and knew nothing about the organization he commanded. The actual running of Civil Aviation in Iran was left to Ali-Reza.

Ali-Reza was in charge of all airports in Iran. Some smaller airports such as Ramsar, which had serviced the casino and hotel on the Caspian, had been closed down. Others, such as Bandar Abbas in the south, Tabriz in the northwest, and Kermanshah in the west, now only had once-a-week flights, in and out. Abadan was no longer an international airport. Zahedan Airport had been seized by the Baluchis and could not be considered within Ali-Reza's jurisdiction, but he was involved in on-going negotiations to return the airport to Iranian Civil Aviation control. As general overseer of all Iran's airports, it was Ali-Reza's duty to keep all airports and equipment in working order, notwithstanding Civil Aviation's limited resources. With the serious post-Revolutionary internal disorder in the Air Force, the line between civil and military aviation had become more blurred. Ali-Reza had gradually assumed greater responsibility for military airports, including meteorological reporting, and all radar functions. Military and civilian technological resources were pooled. By 1983, they formed one cohesive unit under Ali-Reza's direct supervision.

But Ali-Reza's visit to Mehrabad Base this September day had nothing to do with his Civil Aviation responsibilities. He was here to hoard precious supplies of gasoline he would soon need. Gasoline was in very short supply. Ali-Reza had already started accumulating gasoline over a month ago; he knew it might take him months to get all he would need.

Ali-Reza looked at his watch—it was nearly six o'clock. There was no more time for reminiscing. His cousin was expecting him soon at his uncle's house, and the drive into Tehran would take at least half an hour. He stood up from the chair.

Ali-Reza walked down the hall, and ducked into the men's washroom, the door still adorned with the carefully lettered sign, "Mans Toylit." Spiderwebs draped across the cracked glass of the high lone window. Ali-Reza turned on the cold water tap, hoping to be able to cool his face and neck. A few spurts of rust-colored water shot out from the faucet, spattering the dusty white sink. Disgusted, Ali-Reza turned off the faucet, walked over to the row of grimy urinals, and unzippered his fly. As he urinated, a bit of eye-level English graffiti on the wall directly in front of him caught his attention. "For a good blow job see Kathy in Personnel Records Dept. Home telephone 23-31-16." A broad grin came automatically to Ali-Reza's face.

Freedom of expression, any kind, that's what I long for. Not to mention a good blow job, Ali-Reza thought as he zipped his fly and hurried out of the washroom.

Ali-Reza walked to the far end of the hallway and down the back stairs. He let himself out the back door of the building, and went to his Range Rover. He pulled back some blankets strewn on the back seat, uncovering six large plastic jerry cans. Ali-Reza quickly carried the containers into the Administration Building, leaving them just inside the door. He rearranged the blankets on the seat, then slipped back into the building.

Carrying two containers at a time, Ali-Reza quietly continued down the corridor to the Graphic Arts Department. He left the two cans behind the large door. He repeated the trip twice, until all six containers were in the Graphic Arts room.

Ali-Reza closed the door behind him, and pulled his key ring from his pocket. He walked to the far wall, where four large metal cabinets stood. He opened the double doors of the first cabinet. On the dusty shelves were a dozen twenty-liter, opaque-green plastic jerry cans, all filled to the brim with gasoline—an unimaginable sight in Iran, as strict gas rationing had been in effect for a year and a half, ever since the pipeline sabotage.

Ali-Reza put the six new containers into the cabinet and locked it. Now the cabinet was nearly full. On his next trip, he would start to fill another cabinet.

Ali-Reza had not dared store the gasoline in his home; it would have been too risky. As an upper-level government employee, his apartment was routinely searched, and he kept no incriminating materials there. But using Mehrabad Base as a hiding place worked perfectly.

Ali-Reza walked back down the corridor. He left through the back entrance, and climbed into his Range Rover. He put the Range Rover in gear, and drove out of Mehrabad Base through Gate 1.

# CHAPTER FIVE

Swiveling back and forth in her white leather chair, Cheryl slowly undid the top button of her tennis shirt, then the second, then finally the third button. Taking a small bottle of perfume out of her bag, she gently opened the bottle, then pressed the cold Lalique crystal stopper to her now exposed cleavage. The alcohol in the perfume evaporated quickly in the cool, processed air of the clubhouse.

Cheryl smiled at Jeri and positioned her chair so that she could have a better view of the whole room, the clubhouse of the Houston Tennis Club, Houston's newest and most exclusive racquet club. Here the city's elite—bankers, financiers, oilmen, politicians, successful con-men, carpet-baggers, and their pampered wives—would meet for a pre-game drink, or a couple of post-game rounds. Urban cowboys in Cutter Bill ostrich boots, six-thousand-dollar gold belt buckles, 5X beaver and mink Stetsons, and city cowgirls in Ralph Lauren outfits, would pass an hour or so watching their friends and their enemies on the courts and off, while they sipped iced bourbon.

Cheryl turned her gaze toward the door as Jack and Michael walked in. Jack was only a blur as Cheryl focused in on Michael Kir. Kir wore a pair of white jeans, not too tight and not too loose, just right, and a white Fila T-shirt.

"Jack Adams Tucker, where have you been?" Jeri asked.

Jack and Michael quickly took seats at Jack's usual table by the window. Preoccupied, Jack ignored Jeri's question and peered anxiously around the room while Michael apologized to the women for keeping them waiting. Jack craned his neck to see if anyone could have seen the massacre on Court 12 from this vantage point. God, he didn't want that! If Jeri and Cheryl could just keep their mouths shut about this humiliating defeat no one would be any more the wiser.

Jack straightened himself up in the chair. "Let's have a drink," he said, rubbing his hands together. "What'll it be, girls? Mike?"

"I'll have another gin and tonic," said Jeri, emphasizing the fact that she had been kept waiting by looking at her diamond and tiger's eye watch.

"So will I," added Cheryl, as the waiter approached their table.

"Could you turn the air conditioning down a bit, please, Peter?" Jeri Tucker addressed the white-jacketed waiter in a slow, honey-sweet voice, confident that her request would be fulfilled, even at the discomfort of the other guests in the clubhouse.

"Good for you, Jeri," Michael said. She looked at him strangely. Why is he commending me, she wondered. She only wanted the air conditioning turned down because it was blowing in her eyes and drying out her soft contact lenses.

Jack picked up the conversation, realizing that Michael was commending Jeri on her energy awareness. "During the first days of Carter's energy saving reforms," Jack explained to Kir, "the laws on temperature controls were strictly enforced around here, but now, with this President, it is more a matter of whether you can afford it. And with the steep membership dues at this club, it sure as hell had better be nice and cool when I come in here!"

"Air conditioning certainly has become a luxury item," said Jeri, who loved to flaunt frigid temperatures in her air-conditioned Cadillac. Jeri turned slightly in her chair to address her husband. "Honey, what about those drinks?"

"Right," Jack said, signaling for the waiter. "O.K., so we've got two gin and tonics, and, what'll it be, Mike? They pour a mean Jack Daniels here, I can tell you that."

"Vodka lime, please, Jack."

"You want vodka, tonic, with a squeeze of lime?" Jack asked Michael as the waiter wrote down the order.

"Actually I want vodka, with lime juice, Rose's lime juice, and soda."

Jack turned to the waiter. "Got that?" The waiter nodded.

"I've never heard of that," Cheryl said. She was put-out by Michael Kir's taste in drinks. How was she going to play up to this here-for-only-a-few-days gorgeous piece if she couldn't even peg him by what he drank? That was one of Cheryl's yardsticks, she measured a man by his drink as well as his hands. She knew what to do with martini drinkers, straight bourbon drinkers, even beer drinkers. But this? Yet, Cheryl knew she definitely wanted to have this "vodka lime" on her already extensive bar list.

With only a couple of not too obvious glances, Cheryl had appraised the physical attractiveness of Michael Kir—close up. He wasn't that tall, at least by Texas standards: just under six feet, fairly narrow build, but good shoulders, terrific shoulders. His well-muscled torso tapered downward, in a modified inverted triangle. His stomach was absolutely flat, his entire pelvis area had that trim, smooth look that looked so purely European to Cheryl's eyes. And his ass! Cheryl had to bite the inside of her lower lip, just thinking about his ass, imagining how those smooth, tight buttocks would feel under her palms and fingertips. Yes, he had the best ass Cheryl had ever seen, and she had seen more than a few.

Kir's skin was tanned, but it was not too dark. His emerald-green eyes were mesmerizing, and Cheryl was trying to refrain from staring. Thick dark hair covered his chest, revealed by the translucent cotton of his T-shirt. The dampness from his shower, just beginning to evaporate in the dry cold of the clubhouse, made the white, light cloth cling to his chest, the curls and tight spirals of dark, moisture-matted hair. His nipples, defenseless against the sudden shock of cold air, were erect, stretching the already taut cotton even further. Cheryl's nipples were hard just from the thought of biting his.

Her reverie was interrupted by the clatter of plastic coasters hitting the table.

"Let's have a toast," Jack said. "To Michael. To a successful trip."

They all raised their glasses and toasted.

"Where are you going, Michael?" Cheryl asked.

"Europe." Kir smiled and looked at Cheryl, who, with her pretty face, white-blond hair, and wide blue eyes, resembled a life-sized Barbie doll. "London, Paris, the usual places," he added.

"Shopping trip?" Cheryl asked, that being the first thing that came into her mind. "Just a vacation?"

"No, business, I'm afraid," he said smiling at her before turning his attention back to Jack.

Cheryl pressed a paper cocktail napkin daintily

to her mouth, being careful not to wipe off her lipstick. Damn, but he was such a good-looking man!
She sat up straighter in her chair, pushing her
shapely breasts out to full advantage. Michael Kir
glanced her way. Now that she had recaptured
Kir's attention, her composure and sense of attractiveness regained, she pursued her line of conversation.

"And what business are you in, Michael?"

"I'm a gem dealer."

"Michael Kir sells the biggest and best
diamonds in the world," Jack added.

"Oh, how absolutely fascinating!" Cheryl tit-
tered, as visions of diamonds and emeralds and
rubies exploded in her head like fireworks on the
fourth of July. Cheryl had a weakness for jewels,
but then again, she had a weakness for handsome
men. She felt she'd hit the jackpot with this one.

Michael Kir was feeling a bit uncomfortable.
Subtlety was not Cheryl's strong point. Kir was
tempted. No doubt that Cheryl's actions were not
false advertising, but at this moment he was too
engrossed in his own needs. What he most definitely needed was a woman with class. Well, he
would see; tomorrow he would be in London. Kir
involuntarily let out a low sigh. God, he hoped
Victoria Graham wouldn't be like this. Gripping
his glass firmly, Kir closed his eyes for an instant,
as he listened to Jack inquiring about the success
of the women's shopping expedition that morning.

"Michael, another vodka lime?" Jack asked. The
sound of Jack's voice brought Kir's attention back
to the table at the Houston Tennis Club. No one
seemed to have noticed his psychological absence.

"No rush, Jack."

"Vodka lime," Jeri remembered. "Isn't that
what they drink in Iran?" She had been wondering
where she'd had that drink before and now she

72

was elated that, having rummaged through her memory, she had found what she was searching for.

"What they *drank* in Iran, Jeri," Jack interjected. "Liquor was one of the first things to go after the Revolution," Jack explained to the girls, "along with the foreigners, that is."

"And the Royal Family," Kir added.

"Do you see any of them, Mike?" Jack added, conspiratorially lowering his voice. "Princess Shams, Princess Ashraf, any of Ashraf's sons, like good old Mr. Five Percent? What about any of the old generals? What the hell happened to all of them? The ones who got away, at least." Jack continued talking as if he had been an old intimate of those people, partly to impress the girls, and partly hoping to squeeze a little information out of Kir. Not that it really mattered anymore. Those people, the Pahlavis, the generals of the Imperial Iranian Armed Forces, were no longer people of consequence. But for that reason alone, perhaps Kir might be more willing to talk about his relationships with them. Jack had always suspected that Michael was much better connected than he claimed to be. "Do you ever see any of that old bunch, Mike?"

"Why should I see any of those people, Jack?" Michael asked innocently. "No one sees any of them nowadays, or even hears anything about them, for that matter. That's the way the governments that have given them refuge want it; out of sight, out of mind. Anyway, who do you think I am," Kir said smiling, "some VIP that I should get flown to a top-secret hideaway for dinner with the ex-royalty of Iran?"

"You're right, a nobody like you." Jack smiled, but he knew that Kir never talked about his connections, a rare character trait for an Iranian.

Nevertheless, Jack was certain that Michael had been very well-connected under the old regime.

Jack's own lucrative business career in Iran had been cut short, thanks to the Revolution, but he had managed, during his frequent trips to Iran in the 1970s, to form certain impressions and arrive at a degree of understanding of Iranian society. In those days Jack had been an Iranophile; a Persian groupie. He was one of a small minority of foreigners who came to Iran and really enjoyed it. He loved the weather, hot and dry, unlike the debilitating sauna-bath humidity of Houston. He enjoyed the novelty of skiing at 300-meter high Dizin, with its blue skies and corn-powder snow, then driving the hour and half back to Tehran to spend a January afternoon playing tennis. Jack enjoyed fresh Iranian caviar, frozen vodka, and the ritual of smoking opium, the latter being so exotic that it canceled out any conservative feeling that he had had about drugs in America. Jack was unlike most American businessmen who came to Iran, who hated the convoluted way of doing business, who hated the lousy service at the Hilton and Intercontinental, who hated the hair-raising traffic, and who usually couldn't get a date. Then, if they finally did get a date, they felt as if they were having a Dun and Bradstreet check run on them. If the D & B checked out favorably, then, and only then, did they end up spending the night in bed with a shaved pussy. But Jack loved it all!

Iranians were the archetypal inscrutable "Oriental"; that, Jack realized early in the game. One could never be too certain as to how well Iranians knew one another, or how much they liked each other. And then, with foreigners, they took it even a step further. Iranians had terrible inferiority complexes, they never wanted to show their failings, their Achilles' heels. No matter how polite, how gracious was an Iranian's hospitality to a Westerner, the Iranian was always on his guard, there were no chinks in the armor. The Shah himself was the classic prototype: ram-rod straight, elegant, charming, and aloof.

In Michael Kir, however, there was a dichotomy. Kir could be the typical unreadable Persian, but he possessed one trait that was atypical of Iranians: he made fun of his own failings, his faults. That was what Jack liked about Michael. Jack had seen Michael in action in Tehran many times; at glittering cocktail parties and sumptuous dinners, joking, laughing, charming even the most pompous former camel-driver-cum-billionaire in the grand old Persian tradition of *tarof*, roughly, ass-kissing, but of a most genteel and Byzantine fashion. *Tarof* is completely different from ass-kissing in the West, where it is only a way of doing things, getting things done more quickly, very pragmatic. In Iran *tarof* had been raised to an art form, and Kir not only used it to make a sale or make a woman, but he used it on everyone. With a *tarof* master like Kir, one was never able to ascertain the depth or quality of a relationship.

Jack Tucker was filled with admiration for his old college roommate. Kir led a charmed life—plenty of money, travel, and, no doubt, all the beautiful girls he wanted. Dinners with the right people, at the right places, but all the time, working hard, pursuing his business with a passion. Except this time. Michael didn't seem to want to discuss business at all. Usually he was interested in the contacts that Jack had for him, but not this trip. There was something strange, thought Jack, something about Michael seemed to have changed. Jack couldn't put his finger on it, it was barely perceptible, but the feeling was ominous.

The waiter set a bowl of corn chips in the center

of the table. Kir hesitated a moment to see if the women would reach for the bowl. When they didn't he proffered the chips to them.

"I swear, Michael, you are such a gentleman!" cooed Cheryl. But I could make you an animal in bed, she thought confidently.

"But I can only be a gentleman if there are ladies present to inspire me," Kir replied.

"Ooh, I swear," Cheryl said, giggling as she raised her eyebrows to Jeri, then, turning back to Kir, "you say the sweetest things."

You old "taroffer," Jack thought. Jack raised his squat glass of bourbon. "A toast to my old friend Michael. It's great to see you again, buddy. We've had some fine times together," he said, raising his glass toward Michael.

Jeri scrutinized her husband. Fine times together, she thought. When Jack traveled to all those far-off places, the Middle East, Indonesia, Venezuela, as he had for years, did he screw around, she wondered? She could just imagine those exotic hot-spots with gorgeous willing girls hanging like over-ripe fruit from the trees, just waiting to be plucked by traveling businessmen. But even if Jack did, she thought smugly, it was not as much screwing around as she did while he was away.

Jeri thought about the many times Jack had been in Tehran. Maybe in Tehran it had been one of those Iran Air stewardesses, one of those high-voiced Irish or English girls whose notoriety as easy, but expensive, lays had even reached Texas. Or perhaps it had been one of those Iranian girls, one of those conniving bitches with their long red nails and velvety brown eyes and God-knows-what Oriental sex tricks, eager to trade themselves for greenbacks, or better yet, Green Cards. No, probably whores, or cellulite-thighed secretaries. Jeri

76

rubbed the outside of her slim thighs, confident that there were no orange-peel-like dimples on her legs. With all those long trips Jack had made to Iran, he must have had some sort of steady lay there. That was the only explanation for Jack's peculiar fascination with Tehran. What else could it have been? Not Tehran, that's for sure.

Jeri remembered the one and only time she had been to Tehran. It was in September 1977. As the Iran Air 747SP circled Tehran's Mehrabad Airport, she looked down through the gray pollution haze at the little cubes of beige, like so many cardboard boxes overloading the gray-beige landscape. The monotony was relieved by vast networks of roads leading into the city and a large circle of green, on which stood a graceful white arch. Jeri looked dutifully in her guidebook that Jack had bought her.

> Shahyad Monument, standing 148 feet high, is the first major monument encountered by visitors entering Tehran from Mehrabad International Airport. More than just the gateway to the city, it symbolizes Iran's gateway into the twentieth century. Tehran offers the visitor . . .

Jeri shut the book. She was not the type that liked to go sightseeing. All she wanted to do was buy some turquoise and gold jewelry and a Persian carpet or two. And the first view of Tehran had not been too encouraging.

The ground level view of Tehran was not much of an improvement. After being greeted by surly customs officers, they were forced to take a rickety old orange jalopy, which passed for a taxi, because Jack's driver had not shown up at the airport.

Then, Jeri was treated to the most frightening

ride of her life, from the airport to the Hilton hotel in north Tehran. She had been warned that the Tehran traffic was the world's worst, but never in her wildest nightmares could she have imagined how bad it really was. The little orange taxi darted in and out of the paths of huge, bald-tired trucks barreling down the expressway. Jack pointed out the different half-completed housing complexes, Eckbatan and Farazad, which were more like satellite cities than mere housing projects. But Jeri was too busy watching the horror show unfolding in front of the windshield: Iranian Peykan cars making lefthand turns from the far lane, trucks stopped on the crests of fly-overs, picnickers who had simply parked their Mercedes sedans in the inside lefthand lane of the freeway and were calmly sitting on the grass on the center dividing strip of the freeway. Jeri stared at the women wrapped in flowered *chadors*, squatting beside portable barbecues, cooking lamb kebobs and tending the samovars, as the menfolk lay on the grass drinking tea, while the children literally played in the traffic.

Jeri was dumbfounded; she had never seen anything like it. She kept her eyes closed for the rest of the way, only involuntarily opening them as the taxi driver swerved to miss a family of four, all riding on one small motorcycle. With her knees weak and her nerves shot they finally arrived at the Royal Tehran Hilton. She didn't notice the beautiful snow-capped Alborz Mountains directly behind her, nor did she notice the line of gleaming blue Mercedes sedans with Imperial Court plates waiting for a group of European dignitaries who were walking past her. All Jeri wanted to do was to go up to her room and lie down, but it seemed to be one fight after another. Their reserved room at the hotel had mysteriously become "unreserved" and they were informed that the hotel was fully booked. Jack reassured Jeri that everything would be taken care of: all that was needed was a little palm greasing. Jack surreptitiously slipped a five-thousand rial note, about seventy dollars, to the desk clerk, but he returned it to Jack. The desk clerk explained that, this time, the hotel truly was fully booked. He explained that it was a very bad time in Tehran, the International Trade Fair and the Ayramehr International Tennis Tournament were both on. "Why, we even have tennis players sleeping in the sauna, Mr. Tucker!" said the desk clerk. Jeri couldn't believe it! She didn't want to risk another taxi ride to some other hotel.

Jack was getting desperate, because usually a simple little bribe did the trick. Jack dialed the Intercontinental and asked for Room 701. He kept his fingers crossed that Michael Kir would be in town. He was.

The next thing Jeri knew, Mr. and Mrs. Tucker were being escorted to their suite at the Royal Tehran Hilton. "In Iran, it's not *what* you want, but *who* you know," Jack had explained to the puzzled Jeri.

The Houston Tennis Club waiter interrupted Jeri's daydreaming. "Can I get you folks another round?"

"Another round," Jack said. He continued his conversation with Kir, while Cheryl pretended to hang on every word. Jeri couldn't believe it, Jack and Michael were still talking about the good old days in Iran. Who cared about their old business associates? The important ones were either dead or in self-imposed exile, and no one cared about the others. Iran, at least as her husband had known it, was dead and gone. Jeri wondered when Jack would slip in a question about his old Persian girlfriend. The love affair that Jack had had with

Tehran probably had nothing to do with Tehran. It had to be a girl; there was nothing else there.

Even the famous Tehran Bazaar had been a disappointment to Jeri. She had expected to wind her way down long dark corridors brimming over with exotic spices, frankincense, myrrh, silks, gold, and turquoise. Instead, she saw Day-Glo orange and green plastic buckets, mops, Lee jeans, and Panasonic radios and cassette decks. The exotic smells were naft cooking fuel and unwashed bodies. The fabled beauty, romance, and mystery of Persia was, as far as Jeri was concerned, only fable.

Yes, thought Jeri, Jack's enthusiasm for Iran had to be because of only one thing—a woman! And Jeri Tucker hated Persian women even more than she did most women. They were so haughty, with their dark-haired, dark-eyed, dark-skinned beauty. A bitter taste came to Jeri's mouth as she remembered the business dinners in Tehran with Jack's clients and their wives at the phoney French restaurant, Chez Maurice, where each time, compliments of the management, she was given a long-stemmed red rose before dinner and a case of Tehran tummy after, which sent her running to the bathroom all night long.

Those Persian women were all the same, so aloof and condescending, with their clammy deadfish handshakes and expressionless faces. They had made her feel so damn inferior, and there weren't many women who could make Jeri Tucker, and her beautiful body clothed in Halston and Calvin Klein, feel inferior. Unless it was those Persian women with their St. Laurent and Balmain dresses, which were no *pret-a-porter* from Neiman Marcus, but clothes that Yves and Pierre had personally draped on their thin shoulders. And those jewels! They were unbelievably huge, so huge that in any other place one would have sworn they were fakes. The diamonds Jeri displayed, ordinarily so proudly, looked absolutely minuscule in such exalted company. God, she had hated those evenings in Iran.

Jeri Tucker admired the 2.6 carat diamond solitaire on her own left hand. It might have been dwarfed in Tehran by massive brilliants on small dark hands, but it was certainly big enough here at the Houston Tennis Club. Jeri gave into temptation and nibbled at the corn chips as she listened to Jack talking earnestly to Michael.

"Mike, I can trust you to have the right information. Right after the Revolution, I tried to get one of our Iranian managers at our old Oil Services office in Abadan to track down some lost equipment." Jack looked at Michael. "I use the word lost very loosely—stolen is more like it. The guy gave me some run-around, telling me he couldn't find it, that ten million dollars worth of heavy equipment in Khuzistan Province had just disappeared. But after hearing about the state of anarchy with the Arabs in that area, I guess I can understand how things got misplaced. Hell, bigger things than my equipment got misplaced—F-4's, F-5's, Bell Cobra helicopters. Geez," said Jack, shaking his head. "What are they doing with that stuff? Building houses and planters for themselves out of the remains of the great Imperial Iranian Air Force?"

"Considering the effectiveness of the Iranian Air Force these days, Jack, those planes would be put to better use as planters," Kir said.

"I just can't help but think about that ten million bucks in equipment!" In spite of himself, Jack Turner was getting flustered recalling the loss. He tapped the tabletop with his fingers, the volume of his voice rising. "Thieves, what a bunch of goddamn thieves!"

"Honey," said Jeri, "no sense in crying over spilled milk. That was four to five years ago! There is no way you'll ever see that stuff again, Jack. Just be glad you made out as well as you did. A lot of people lost their shirts."

"Or their lives," Michael added.

"You're right, honey," Jack said, patting his wife's ringed fingers. "No sense dwelling on the past. Can't do a damn thing about it now. But, I'll tell you, Mike . . ."

"Lord, aren't those drinks ever going to get here?" interrupted Cheryl. She disliked not being the center of male attention, and if they were going to keep discussing business she wouldn't be able to get to first base with Michael Kir. She coyly wet her already moist lips with her tongue, a gesture that, when Cheryl Smith did it, bordered on the obscene.

Jack reached his arm out to signal the waiter, who was busy serving drinks to another table. The clubhouse was filling up. Everyone was stopping in for a before-dinner drink and a glance at who was at Houston's choicest watering hole. The waiter nodded to Jack, and hurried over to their table.

"The drinks are on the way, Mr. Tucker."

"Fine," Jack said, and turned to the girls. "Sorry to be rehashing old stuff, gals, but Mike and I had a lot of catching up to do, right?"

Michael could only nod in response, for he was already ensnared in a conversation with Cheryl. He smiled politely while Cheryl told him of how often she was alone because her husband traveled a lot, and what good friends Jack and Jeri were, and was he alone in Houston, and where was he staying? Her rapid-fire conversation was punctuated with calculated exposure of the pink tip of her tongue, frequent crossing and uncrossing of legs, and wistful sighs. Michael could only nod and smile.

"Excuse me," Jack said. "So what'll we do for dinner tonight, folks?" He immediately answered his own question. "Why don't we go down to San- chez's, the best Mexican food in Texas, if you don't have any preferences, Mike? You probably haven't had a nice two-alarm Mexican meal in a long time. And, old buddy, if you want good Mexican food, Texas is the place for it! Gals?"

"Fine with me," Jeri said.

"Sounds great," Cheryl said. "Just as long as you boys give me an hour or so to freshen up be- fore dinner." Cheryl was tickled pink that Jack had suggested dinner at Sanchez's. With its flattering candlelight and serenading guitarist, it would be just the place to have dinner with Michael Kir, even if Jack and Jeri had to be there, too. She would forsake ordering her favorite Mexi- can dish, *pollo con ajo*, chicken with garlic, pre- pared so divinely at Sanchez's, so that the sweet after-dinner treat she planned to present Michael Kir with later in the evening at her apartment would not be marred by garlicky breath. Cheryl was already deciding which dress she would wear that evening. There was the brand-new Ted Lapidus dress hanging in her closet, the price tag still on it. Or there was that mauve silk-jersey dress with the slit skirt. After only a moment's consideration, she decided on the mauve jersey; it had more decolletage than the Ted Lapidus. She didn't want to take any chances by being too subtle; her husband was expected back any day.

"I'm awfully sorry, Jack, but I won't be able to make it," Kir said.

"Come on, Mike. Are you sure?"

"Really, I can't. I'm expecting a couple of important phone calls tonight, so I'd better wait in the hotel. But please don't let me interfere with what sounds like a terrific evening."

"Aw, come on, Mike. We don't have to make a whole night of it, just a couple of drinks and some good food. Then we'll drop you off at your hotel. I can't stand to think of my old friend eating a chicken sandwich in his room while just a few minutes drive away I'll be dining on guacamole dip and enchiladas," said Jack.

"Really, Jack, I'd love to, but I can't make it. My agent in Bangkok will be calling tonight. Final negotiations for a large purchase of stones. Business before pleasure, unfortunately," he said apologetically, as he finished off his drink.

"What the hell, let him call you back. You aren't in Houston every night!"

"No, I'm very sorry, Jack, but I will not be able to accept your kind invitation tonight. I really must wait for those telephone calls."

There was a decisive tone in Kir's voice, something hard and determined, that closed the subject. Jack did not press the matter further.

Cheryl was crushed. Her plans for a nice dinner out and a great lay afterwards were ruined. Christ, what could be so important, she thought angrily.

"I guess I'll just have to eat your share of enchiladas," Jack said, eager to put everyone at ease.

"And he'll have to force himself to drink your share of the margueritas," Jeri added. As much as Jeri enjoyed looking at Michael Kir, that handsome face of his and that beautiful body, she didn't care that he would not be part of the social scene that evening. And, as much as Jeri would have liked to get into Michael Kir's pants, and feel his hard cock against her body, within her, she didn't stand a chance. Michael Kir was one of her husband's oldest friends. Moreover, she knew that he was also one of the few men in the world who wouldn't jump at the chance to fuck his friend's wife. Especially if that wife was as attractive and enticing as she was, Jeri complimented herself. She wouldn't be getting any from him, so no big deal. At least this way she wouldn't have to watch that tart of a friend Cheryl flirt all evening long.

The crowd at the clubhouse was thinning out. The Houston Tennis Club set was heading home this Saturday of Labor Day weekend. Back to the ranch, to a split-level home on a half-acre of land in a chic Houston suburb, or to a sumptuous new apartment in one of the slick new complexes in town. Home to bathe, change clothes, spruce up, before an evening out at a fine restaurant, or with friends at an intimate dinner party: but never too far from home. The gas ration coupons didn't go far. Most people would opt for dinner at home, preferring to save their gas for driving to the club the next morning.

"Since we can't have dinner together, Mike, let's have one last round," Jack suggested.

Jack was still disturbed by Michael's behavior. Michael seemed changed, more closed, and Jack felt an undercurrent of tense self-control in Michael that he had never noticed before. Well, people change, he thought. Three years has been a long time. A lot of things happen in three years, so who knows?

The compassionate side of Jack Tucker was emerging. Who could tell what problems Michael had had in business or what losses of friends and relatives during and after the Iranian Revolution? Jack had vivid recollections of the mysterious midnight trials conducted by the then mere mullah, Khalaghani, now the head of the government of Iran. Jack would never forget the photos of bound and blindfolded men facing the firing squad, and the chilling pictures of the bullet-riddled bodies of the dead Nasseri, former head of SAVAK, the Shah's dread secret police, and ex-Prime Minister Hoveyda, laid out in a morgue. And Jack was pretty sure that the fact that Michael Kir was Jewish hadn't made things any easier for him or his family. Perhaps he had lost somone near and dear to him; it would have been enough to harden any man.

A loud voice and a hard slap on the back broke Jack's train of thought.

"Howdy, Jack," boomed a big, tall man, one of his huge hands resting on Jack's shoulder. "Folks," he nodded a hello to the three others seated at the table. "What are you all doing settin' here so quiet? Better fill up them empty glasses and get things rollin'."

"I'm one step ahead of you, Ralph. The drinks are on their way," Jack said. "Can I get you something?"

Ralph held up an ice-cube filled glass of Scotch. "I'm doin' fine, ole buddy."

"Ralph, I'd like to introduce an old friend of mine, Michael Kir." Michael rose to meet Ralph's outstretched hand. "Michael, Ralph Robinson."

"Pleased to meetcha," Ralph grinned.

"A pleasure."

Ralph turned towards the girls. "So, how are the two prettiest gals in Texas doin'?"

"Just fine, Ralph," replied Jeri. "Why don't you sit here?" She motioned to a spot between Cheryl and herself.

"Couldn't have picked a better place myself," said Ralph, taking off his black Stetson and laying it carefully on the table.

"Join us in another round, the last one," Jack said.

"Can't, Jack. I'm waiting on Penelope. She should be changed in a minute."

"Aw, come on. Just a short one," insisted Jack.

"You talked me into it." Ralph turned to Michael. "New here in town, or just passin' through?"

"I'm just passing through. I stopped here to see Jack," replied Michael.

"Ralph works the whole Mid-East circuit, Mike. He's with Northern Industries. You two must know some of the same people," said Jack.

"What do you do?" Ralph asked Kir.

"I sell gems, diamonds."

"Well, that explains it. Who else can afford diamonds these days, only the A-rabs." Ralph looked at Michael quizzically. "You're not American, are you?" he asked, eyeing Kir.

"My mother was American, and I'm an American citizen, but my father was Persian," Kir said coldly.

"I thought it was something like that. You don't look American, but you don't sound like a *feranghi*, either." Ralph thought he'd throw in a foreign word, hoping to impress Cheryl, who he knew to be one hot number.

"Cheryl, honey," Ralph said, "*feranghi* in Iranian means foreigner."

Cheryl sucked on her straw, ignoring Ralph, as she continued to gaze at Michael Kir, getting hornier by the moment.

"Anyway," Ralph said, "glad to hear you're one of us."

Michael dismissed Ralph's comments. Kir was used to receiving unpleasant responses from Americans once they found out that he had Iranian blood in his veins. He had long ago given up trying to explain his position and he could easily sympathize with Americans who were mad as hell about what had happened in Iran.

"So Ralph, when were you last in the Middle East?" Kir asked.

"Hell, I guess about six weeks ago. I just fly in and fly out. I was in Jeddah and Cairo. July in Jeddah. God, was it awful, but let's face it, the Middle East is the best market for your business, and mine."

"The only place," Kir agreed.

"Yeah, but it used to be better a few years back, that's for sure. First Lebanaon blew up—didn't affect my business that much, but it sure put a cramp in my social life." Ralph smiled broadly. "I mean it *really* put a cramp in my social life!" Ralph emphasized. "Beirut's where I met Penelope. She was a flying-gal for MEA." He turned to Cheryl, as if acting as his own interpreter. "That's Middle East Airlines, honey."

Cheryl nodded, not that she gave a shit about what airlines "Pen" had flown for. She couldn't stand that snobby English bitch and she was tempted to screw Ralph just to spite Penelope. But, as selective as Cheryl was not, she couldn't bring herself to flirt with that hulk sitting next to her, especially when the beautiful Michael Kir was sitting across from her. She still wanted Kir. Perhaps there was a glimmer of hope.

"Yeah, as I was sayin', Mike, nowadays everybody has to hustle a bit harder for the bucks. It must have been rough on you after the Revolution." Ralph's abrasive manner seemed to be mellowing as he finished off his double Scotch. "Are you planning a trip to the Middle East?"

"Quite soon," Kir answered. "What exactly do you do for Northern, Ralph?"

"I'm in arms, SAMs—surface-to-air missiles—mostly. I spend most of my time hustlin' up business in Saudi, Egypt, and the United Arab Emirates, settin' things up and making sure that everything runs smooth, as smooth as this Scotch." Ralph held up his glass.

Jack took the hint. "Another drink, Ralph?"

"If you insist. As I was sayin'," Ralph continued, "You must do a lot of business with the same people I do. Do you know Prince Hamid bin Mohammed, grandson of the Saudi king? The guy lives in Riyadh, but spends a lot of time in London. That guy is a real sport! He hands jewelry out like some people hand out business cards."

"No, can't say that I do, but, Ralph, there are an awful lot of princes in Saudi Arabia, with an awful lot of money."

"Let's see, who else might you know? In the Emirates, Sheikh Zam-something, Sheikh Zamin?"

"I'm afraid not."

"Oh, I know one person you must know! The Sheikh of Dubai, Sheikh Rashid! Wonderful man, Rashid! Let me tell you, it is a pleasure to do business with him."

A red-haired, brown-eyed woman appeared at the table.

"Hi, Penelope," Jeri said, raising her head from an intense discussion—of new fall '83 nail polish colors—that she was having with Cheryl.

"Michael, I'd like you to meet my wife, Penelope. Pen, Michael Kir."

"How do you do?" she said with an affected upper-crust English accent, as thick as Devon cream on a scone.

Penelope immediately joined the women's discussion in progress, which had now moved from nail colors to eye shadows for autumn 1983.

"My wife's English," Ralph said proudly.

"Yes, I noticed," Michael said, who could hear Penelope's explanation of what shade of black

"Japanese Black" really was. So this is what happens to a stiff upper lip when it gets a Texas twang in it, Kir thought. Penelope sounded like a forty-five record on thirty-three.

"You must know him," Ralph continued.

"Who?" Kir asked.

"Rashid, Sheikh Rashid."

"Yes, as a matter of fact, I have met him a couple of times. A very nice man. And," Kir leaned forward, "Ralph, he bought a number of stones from me for part of a necklace he presented to the Queen of England when she made her tour of the United Arab Emirates, Bahrain, and Qatar in 1979."

"No kidding! Pen was really impressed with all the great gifts the Queen got from those sheikhs, especially that solid gold sculpture of one of those Persian Gulf boats, what are they called?"

*"Dhows."*

"Oh, right, a gold model of a *dhow*, pearls, bars of gold and some terrific necklace."

"That's the necklace I was talking about."

"Geez, don't let Pen hear me, but," Ralph lowered his voice, "what cheapskates those Brits are! In return for all those expensive gifts, the Queen gave those sheikhs pictures of that barge they call the Royal Yacht." Ralph took a sip of his drink. "Well, I'm off on a trip to Cairo, Riyadh, and the UAE next month," Ralph said. "Everybody's beefing up defense. They're worried."

"And hell, they should be, the Persian Gulf is a powder keg," Jack added.

"And things don't look too rosy here in the good old USA," Ralph said. He raised his glass. "Here's hopin' for a mild winter," he said, clinking his glass up against Cheryl's. Cheryl looked at him quizzically. She hadn't been listening to the conversation. "Ralph, it's always nice and mild here," she said.

"Not us, honey," Ralph said. "It's those damn Yankees.. Christ, those goddamn Easterners are like vampires, draining our oil. It was cold as a witch's tit up in the North last winter and them Yankees used up our stockpiles of fuel. If those damn Northerners have another bad winter this year we are all gonna be up shit-creek without a paddle. Excuse my French, ladies," Ralph added.

"You mean more gas rationing again, Ralph?" Cheryl asked, a worried look on her face.

"Maybe, honey, maybe. Hell, what am I doin' getting ulcers over this thing," said Ralph. "It's out of our hands." Ralph put his arm around Penelope. "Listen, Mike, Pen and I are having a barbecue Tuesday evening around sundown. Jeri and Jack are coming. You too, Cheryl? And your hubby?" asked Ralph.

Cheryl's eyes threw daggers at Ralph. Did that oaf have to remind everyone of the fact that she was married? "Ralph, I'd love to," she said, smiling sweetly, "but I'm afraid it'll just be little ole' me. Lance won't be home for absolutely ages." She gave Kir her most lascivious look.

"Sounds great, Ralph. I'd really love to, but I'm leaving tomorrow. Thank you," Kir said.

"Well, hell, just call 'em and tell 'em you'll be a little late. We've got some good-lookin' gals coming." Ralph winked.

"You know how business is, Ralph. I've got a tight schedule the next few weeks. But, next time. As a matter of fact, I've really got to be going. I'm expecting a call at my hotel," Michael said.

Jack looked at his watch. "Six o'clock already. We'd better be getting along, too. Gals," he said, standing up.

Ralph pulled a business card out of his wallet and gave it to Kir. "Anytime you're passing through Houston, just take a chance and give me a call. If I'm in town, we'll get together."

"Will do," Kir said, looking at Ralph's business card before putting it into his wallet. Kir made a mental note to ask Mark, when he called tonight, to run a check on Ralph Robinson. Ralph didn't know it, but Michael Kir was one of his customers.

# CHAPTER SIX

"This is the ABC World News Weekend Report," came the voice of the announcer as the words *Saturday, September 3, 1983,* were typed out across the television screen. Michael Kir stretched out on the couch of his Houston hotel suite. He was tired, and his body ached from the long, hot afternoon of playing tennis. The nattily-dressed anchorwoman, Barbara Peters, appeared on the screen.

"A scene not witnessed within the memory of most of the population of the United States greeted the American public this Labor Day weekend," Barbara Peters said. "The highways of America were virtually abandoned this long weekend as a result of the government's ban on the selling of gasoline for a five-day period that started Thursday and will be in effect until midnight Tuesday. It was a drastic and ominous portent of the winter ahead as the President sought to conserve every drop of fuel possible to tide America over during the inevitable oil shortages this winter. For the most part, Americans reacted well to the surprise ban. Most motorists decided to stay at home, or very close to home, saving their gas for essential driving to and from work and school. We have a report tonight from Tim Davidson, above the Washington Beltway, and one from Serena Jeffreys, in Pecatonoka, Illinois."

On the screen flashed a picture taken from a helicopter above the all-but-deserted Washington Beltway, one lone patrol car traveling down its eight lanes.

"Only essential vehicles were on the country's highways and interstates this weekend," said the voice competing with the whir of the rotor blades. "Motels, restaurants, and gas stations along the highways are all but deserted and throughout the country this holiday weekend, the story is the same. For some this ban on gasoline sales has meant no vacation; for others, no business. But there is some good news. This Labor Day weekend's highway death toll will be way, way, down. Tim Davidson for ABC News, above the Washington Beltway."

"Here, in the backyard of the Martin family's house in Pecatonika, Illinois," said Serena Jeffreys speaking into her microphone, as she stood beside a smoking barbecue, "this has been a different kind of Labor Day Weekend. Usually Mr. and Mrs. Martin and their four children get into their car and drive to Peoria for the annual stock car races, but not this year, with the President invoking a five-day ban on selling gas. We asked Mr. Martin how he felt about the situation." The reporter turned to the man at the barbecue. Mr. Martin took off his chef's hat and wiped his hands on his "Come 'n' git it" red and white apron.

"Well," said Mr. Martin, leaning forward to speak into the microphone, "it hasn't been so bad. This year we just invited the neighbors over, and any friends within walking distance. Frankly, I've gotta admit this beats spending my weekend driving, and it's a whole lot cheaper." Mr. Martin smiled. "Hamburger meat costs a lot less than gas."

"Thank you, Mr. Martin," Serena Jeffreys said,

turning to the camera. "As you can see, some Americans have turned this negative into a plus. As one person at this backyard barbecue noted, 'This is a time of crisis for America and we have just got to brace ourselves for worse to come.' This is Serena Jeffreys in Pecatonika, Illinois."

"Admirable sentiment," said Barbara Peters, "but not all America feels that way this weekend. Owners of motels, amusement parks, and resort towns were up in arms. They plan a march on Washington tomorrow. A few motel owners in the Washington area picketed the White House this morning, as well as the steps to Capital Hill as the members of Congress returned from their interrupted summer recess. An ABC poll conducted recently shows that most Americans, seventy-eight percent, have come to accept the fact of life that the gas situation is going to get a lot worse before it gets better. And now this . . ."

A commercial flashed on the screen, and Michael Kir got up from the couch and went over to the refrigerator to get a drink. With his back to the screen, he heard the three-hundred-thousand-dollar minute of advertising time (paid for by Exxon) promise the salvation in gasohol. "Our technicians are working day and night to develop a gasoline of the future," said the earnest voice narrating the commercial. "The breakthrough is at our doorstep, and all that we, the people at Exxon, ask of you is to abide by Exxon's ten energy-saving commandments, and we'll do the rest. For your free booklet, walk, don't drive, to your nearest station. Walk, don't drive—our first commandment . . ."

"Shit," Kir said, turning around, half expecting to see Billy Graham on the screen selling *The Ten Commandments According to Exxon.*

Kir sat down on the couch, put his feet up on the

table and reached for his just-delivered-by-room-service roast beef sandwich as Barbara Peters reappeared on the screen. "Phillip Britton in London has a report on a new development in the Persian Gulf."

A map of the Persian Gulf, with a small red light flashing at the mouth of the Persian Gulf, came on the inset screen behind the handsome announcer in the ABC News Room in London.

Michael sat bolt upright in his chair, dropping his sandwich back on to its plate.

"Another terrorist alert has been issued by the State Department for the Straits of Hormuz, that vital waterway which links the oil of Saudi Arabia and other Gulf states with the industrialized world." Kir leaned forward.

"This has been the second major terrorist alert in the past six months," continued Phillip Britton. "The previous terrorist attempt last May was stopped before the terrorists entered those narrow straits that lead into the Persian Gulf. Admiral Jamshid Mahmoud, head of Iran's Islamic Gulf Fleet, caught a group of splinter PLO terrorists with a rocket launcher on board a small Arab boat, a dhow. The terrorists' intention was to blow up the Shell supertanker passing through the Straits of Hormuz. Iran's Gulf fleet once had the world's largest fully-operational Hovercraft squadron. Although greatly reduced in size since the ouster of the Shah in 1979, the fleet, commanded by Admiral Mahmoud, is the only effective branch of the armed services left in Iran. However, the other Persian Gulf countries are not trusting Iran to thwart a terrorist attack again. Although the terrorist report may only be a false alarm, the recently strengthened Saudi Arabian navy is on full alert."

"Thank you, Phillip," said Barbara Peters, turning away from the monitor. "Today, in a Senate Special Session, Senator Joseph Sullivan spoke out on this latest terrorist warning. We have a report from the U.S. Senate building.

The camera switched to the tall, ruggedly handsome Senator Sullivan, his finger jabbing into the air as his voice boomed. "We, the United States of America, will not be held hostage to threats of terrorism. The Persian Gulf region must be made secure. It is our number one priority. The American people must have security."

"Oh, shit," said Michael, shaking his head. "Shut up!"

"We, the American people," Sullivan continued, brushing a forelock of wavy hair off his forehead, "must be able to go to bed at night and sleep easily, knowing that no bands of international hoodlums have their hands around our throats."

Michael reached over and began dialing the phone. He turned his head back to the television screen when he heard Barbara Peters say, "Correspondent Helen Mills in New York was able to speak to former Secretary of State Walter Singer for a few minutes and ask him a few questions." Kir dropped the phone back into the cradle.

"Dr. Singer," said Helen Mills, as she caught him walking up the stairs to his Eastside brownstone, "could you comment about the latest terrorist alert in the Persian Gulf?"

"Yes," replied the man with one of the most familiar faces on earth, as he stepped down one step to speak into the reporter's microphone. "The situation is hardly the crisis that some politicians have made it out to be, to aggrandize their own power. The Persian Gulf problem is not so simple. It goes back to the Revolution in Iran in 1979, when the U.S. made its big mistake by not supporting its loyal friend for thirty-seven years, the Shah of Iran. Any problems in the Gulf exist because Iran is no longer the policeman of the Gulf."

"Dr. Singer," interrupted Helen Mills, "what do you envision for the next little while?"

"There is no next little while," Walter Singer said. "This is just the way it is. We have not been able to even begin a dialogue with Iran's fanatical Ayatollah Khalaghani, so I see no change in sight. The American people have no choice but to accept the U.S. government's severe rationing, and total gasoline bans such as the one this weekend—as well as the accompanying economic consequences."

"Thank you, Dr. Singer. This is Helen Mills in New York for ABC News."

Michael Kir reached for the telephone and began dialing again. He waited impatiently for the telephone to be picked up on the other end.

"Walter, Michael here. I just saw you on the news. Christ, Walter, can you do something about shutting up that goddamn Sullivan? He sounds like he wants to send the Marines in there, take over the oil fields in the name of mom and apple pie. Walter, you know that attention in the Gulf is the last thing needed. The situation is dicey enough as it is. Yes, Walter, I know you can't stand his guts, but through your connections let him know that he has just got to stop grandstanding. It is downright irresponsible. Thanks, Walter, I'd appreciate it . . . uh-huh . . . Oh, Walter, it looks like you lost weight . . . . Five kilos, really? Not bad, it certainly does show . . . O.K. Thanks, Walter, goodnight." Kir hung up the telephone.

As the energy segment came on the nightly news, Kir turned up the volume on the TV with the remote-control unit. Energy was now a feature segment on most evening news programs, devoted solely to energy-related problems. Slotted between the special segments and the anchorman's closing remarks, it dealt with doomsday predictions of the winter of 1983 being worse than the winter of 1978, and gave pertinent and inflammatory information on energy: where to pick up gas coupons; hints to conserve energy; updates on gasohol; the coming ice age—anything to feed Americans' abject obsession with oil.

Michael looked at the screen. A chart showed the steep, almost vertical rise of heating fuel costs.

"Americans are now paying almost fifty percent of their expendable income on fuel, and the latest figures show that the cost of heating fuel will rise again next month," reported Myles Goldman, ABC's special Energy reporter.

"ABC has learned that gas rationing may come into effect early this winter, and with a reduction in coupons per family. A high-level government official emphasized that the rationing is intended to tide us over the winter months, and will be lifted in the spring. The Department of Energy would neither confirm nor deny . . ."

Kir picked up the remote-control unit. "Enough, enough," he muttered to himself, changing channels, stopping when he heard the editorial-styled voice of Doug Canal. "The new American Frankensteins, we created them and now they rule us; the seven sisters oil companies, the Arab cartel, they are our own creations. What can we do about it all, we ask ourselves. It is time to face up to the fact that . . . ." Michael Kir flicked off the switch in mid-sentence.

The telephone rang loudly. Michael reached over in the dark and fumbled for the phone on the bedside table.

"Oh, hi," Kir said, his voice thick with sleep. He listened for a few seconds. "Would you like me to come downstairs to the lobby? . . . No, sure, come on up." He put the phone back in the cradle and looked at his watch laying on the table. Almost midnight. He must have fallen asleep after Mark Rowan's call from Washington at eight o'clock. Kir picked up the telephone again. "Front desk, please. Hello, this is Mr. Kir, I have a guest on the way up to my room. . . . Yes, thank you." He pressed down the button on the phone. "Room service, please . . . a bottle of champagne. . . . Yes, Cordon Rouge is fine."

Michael Kir got out of bed. There was a light knocking on the door. "Coming," he said, grabbing his robe.

He opened the beige and gilt door. "Cheryl, how nice to see you. Come in."

"Hi, Michael," she said, as she sauntered into the room. "After Jack and Jeri dropped me off at my apartment and I went into my bedroom and saw that big ole lonely bed, I got to thinking that there you were, stuck in your hotel room all night waiting for that dumb phone call." Cheryl smiled at Kir seductively. "And I thought maybe you'd like some company."

"Cheryl, how considerate of you," Michael said, putting his arm lightly around her waist and leading her to the sofa. "I ordered champagne."

"Oooh, how nice," said Cheryl as she sat down on the sofa. She slowly slid her shawl off her shoulders, revealing a mauve silk-jersey dress, fashionably décolleté. Michael took the shawl from her and placed it over the back of the chair.

"A beautiful dress on a beautiful woman."

"Why, thank you."

"Please excuse my attire, Cheryl, but as you can see I was already in bed."

Cheryl glanced over at the rumpled bed and then at him. "Honey, you look fine, just fine," she said, looking into his eyes.

With the sound of the buzzer, Kir turned away from her gaze. "Excuse me, Cheryl, that must be room service." He pulled out a couple of bills from his gold money clip that lay on the dresser and answered the door. Exchanging the tip for an iced bucket of champagne and two tall, narrow champagne glasses, he shut the door, and sat down again next to Cheryl on the sofa.

As Kir opened the bottle, Cheryl looked around the high-ceilinged cream room, admiring the gilt moldings and crystal chandeliers. "My, this is a beautiful suite."

"Well, it's a bit much for me."

"Oooh, I just love French provincial!"

Cheryl studied Kir's profile as he poured the sparkling wine, his straight, well-shaped nose, the high planes of his cheekbones, the slight shading of his cheek, his strong chin, and the straight, tight jawline. His hair was thick and curly, but cut fairly short, side-parted and brushed away from his face. He had a few flecks of gray around his temples which Cheryl found sexy; she found everything about Michael Kir extremely sexy.

Cheryl took the glass of champagne that Kir handed to her and touched her glass to his. She was getting more excited by the moment and didn't know how long she could stand any more of these niceties. She imagined his naked body beneath that brown velour robe. She moved closer to him.

Kir put down his glass, and slowly moved to her. His warm, strong hands touched her cool cheeks. With both hands he gently pushed her hair away from her face. The touch of his fingers on the nape of her neck sent shivers down her spine. Gently he kissed her lips, and as she parted them ever so slowly he pushed his tongue into her warm champagne-flavored mouth.

Her body registered no surprise at this bold move. He kissed her harder. She was passive, but receptive. He was orchestrating the seduction and she let the maestro continue. With velvet-soft kisses he brushed his lips across her cheekbones, to her ear-lobe, warm and perfumed as a hothouse flower, down her neck to her collarbone.

He took her firmly by the waist and maneuvered her until she was sitting on her knees, straddling his thighs and facing him. Her sweet-smelling hair brushed against his face. Unbuttoning the buttons on the back of her dress, he continued to kiss her collarbone, along her now bare shoulder, as his hands moved down the length of her firm and graceful back. He undid the final button, and pulled her dress forward off both her shoulders and let it rest, his hands moving beneath the silky cloth, touching her warm, soft skin. As she faced him, half naked, he admired her body.

Cheryl stood up. Kir rose to meet her.

Her right hand slipped inside his robe, her fingers running through the hair of his chest and along his hard, flat stomach. Her left hand moved to undo the knot in his robe as her right felt his hard cock, sending a thrilling sensation to her core.

His hands were now against her skin, exploring every curve of her body, and he kissed her passionately as his hand traced a line down her stomach to the velvety wetness between her legs. His finger touched her clitoris, caressing, tantalizing, moving with increasing urgency. Her body writhed against his hard cock until she could stand it no more. The excited movement of his finger stopped. She was moaning for more. "Don't stop, don't stop," she begged breathlessly, as she teetered on the brink of orgasm. But he did stop. He was manipulating her totally, and his forceful control was exciting Cheryl even more.

He kept her in a state of suspended agitation as his tongue parted her half-opened lips, her mouth aching as much as her throbbing cunt. His finger teasingly touched her clitoris again. With increasing intensity, Kir manipulated Cheryl, building another orgasm on her already unfulfilled first. Her arms wrapped around his shoulders, her nails dug into his muscles as he refused to allow the release of her pent-up feelings. She was begging him, crushing her body against him, but his mastery of her body was total. She was at the verge, but he would not allow her to go farther, as his lips and teeth gently titillated her heaving breasts.

Kir pushed her down on the bed and entered her. Cheryl let out a moan of relief as he filled the aching, tortured space. He pushed hard inside her, moving with increasing intensity. The pent-up sexual tensions inside her, the continuous stimulation of her clitoris was driving Cheryl mad with passion. Cheryl's nails pressed against his buttocks, his back, desperately wanting him deeper inside her, faster, harder. The explosion of her wracking waves of orgasm overpowered his, as he came in her, bathing her burning sex.

Cheryl stared up at the ceiling, thinking about what she would tell Jeri. She had never been fucked so well, with such style. That's what she would tell Jeri! With such style. Cheryl rubbed her hand along Michael Kir's long muscled thigh. She felt his large, beautiful cock hardening in her hands. Cheryl smiled. With most men, Cheryl insisted that they do it until they get it right. With Michael Kir, she just wanted to do it all night.

"Cheryl." Cheryl pushed her hair from her face and looked at Kir. His emerald green eyes were sleepy.

"Cheryl, I have an early plane to catch, so I must get some sleep. Let me take you downstairs," he said getting out of bed. "Did you come by car or taxi?"

"Taxi," Cheryl said, admiring Kir's naked perfect body.

"Where are you going tomorrow, Michael?" she asked as she watched him dress. He put on a pair of beige gabardine pants and turned to her as he buttoned up his shift. "London, very early."

Cheryl slowly pushed aside the sheets and got out of bed. She walked over to Kir, picking up her dress off the chair. She pressed herself against him, running one hand across his chest as she felt for his ass with the other one.

"Cheryl!" he chastized her. "Come on, get dressed," he said, kissing her lightly on the mouth.

Cheryl quickly slipped on her dress. Michael retrieved her shoes from under the marble table and brought them over to her as she brushed her hair in front of the mirror. Kir grabbed his navy blue blazer and Cheryl's shawl as he ushered her out the door.

The air was still warm and humid at 2:00 a.m. as they waited outside the lobby of the hotel. The doorman hailed a cab.

"Michael, I do hope that you'll come to Houston again very soon. Please let me know in advance and I'll arrange things so that we can have a welcome-back party, just the two of us." A taxi pulled up. Kir bent down and kissed her gently. As she got into the car, Kir walked around to the driver's side and handed the driver the cab fare.

"Have a good trip to London, Michael," Cheryl said, smiling as the cab pulled out.

"I'll try," Kir said, waving goodbye, smiling.

Kir turned and walked back into the hotel, the thought of what was ahead weighing heavily on him.

# CHAPTER SEVEN

"Nice to see you, Mr. Kir. Dreadful weather, isn't it?" said the chalky-faced Sotheby's assistant, as he took Kir's dripping umbrella and raincoat.

"Are you close to Lot 105 yet, Sydney?" Kir asked, as he scanned the crowded Main Gallery.

"No, sir, we are only in the low 70's, Item 73 I believe, sir. If you'll excuse me a moment, I'll find a seat for you, sir." Michael raised his hand. "Don't worry, Sydney, I'll find my own seat."

Kir made his way into the main gallery. Almost every seat in the house was taken, and all eyes faced the Chairman's podium. As Kir moved along the side aisle next to the moss-green felt wall, he could feel the tense, charged atmosphere that energized the staid main gallery of Sotheby's, London—the most famous auction house in all the world. Behind its rather unimposing facade, Sotheby's was conducting an "Extraordinary Islamic Sale" on this gray and wet day, September 5, 1983. The room was filled with damp, nervous, bidders and observers, vying for jewel-like miniature paintings, intricate and delicate silk carpets from Isfahan, Qom, and Nain, and gracefully carved eighteenth-century nephrite jade bowls. But the most important artworks were the calligraphy—elaborate examples of Persian and Arabic handwriting, a unique and exotic form of art. The thin, fragile, parchment leaves, from Korans or books of poetry such as Omar Khayyam's *Rubiyaat* or Ferdowsi's *Shah-nameh*—the eleventh-century Persian epic—were painstakingly inscribed with styles of script that were more like the work of master weavers than of scribes. All this and more was being auctioned to the highest bidder.

Kir watched as a magnificent fourteenth-century *Shah-nameh*, the *Book of Kings*, was put on the block for auction. Like all Iranians, Kir knew the legendary story of the kings and heroes of ancient Persia—Rustam, Esfandiyar, and Zal. Kir noted that the bidding for the *Shah-nameh* was running high.

Kir could not see the girl in the crowd. It was a sea of black and tones of gray—men in their Saville Row suits, the monotone occasionally relieved by the bright white of an Arab in his flowing *dish-dasha*, or the startling pastel Fortrel leisure suit of a rich American tourist observing the elite of the art world at work.

Michael Kir caught a glimpse of honey-colored hair, but from where he stood, he couldn't be sure that she was the one. He inched his way along the side aisle. There she sat, in a water-spotted raincoat, her blond hair pulled back in a sober bun, peering intently over a pair of tinted tortoise-shell glasses. Her handbag and umbrella occupied the seat to her left.

"Excuse me, may I?" Kir said.

"Of course," she said, not bothering to look at him as she moved her possessions on to her lap. She seemed engrossed in the bidding on a rare black-and-white ceramic plate, its sole decoration being the elegant black Arabic script encircling the rim.

"Sold," said the chairman. Above the chairman's podium was a huge digital board, which computed the price paid in dollars, pounds sterling, French francs, Swiss francs, yen, Deustchmarks and Arab riyals. She noted down the astronomical sum achieved for this piece of pottery, oblivious to the clinical analysis that the man next to her was making of her person.

Kir leaned slightly toward her. "May I please look at your catalog for a moment, if you don't mind?" he asked in a hushed voice.

She put down her pen and looked up from her catalog, slowly taking off her glasses. Then she turned to Kir and smiled as she handed him the catalog.

Michael Kir almost dropped the catalog. He was completely taken aback. Michael Kir was not an easy man to impress, but Victoria Graham was more startlingly beautiful than any of the photographs that he had seen of her. Her eyes were the most amazing iridescent Mediterranean blue, framed with long feathery lashes, and her lips were gracefully curved and sensuous. The combined effect of those heart-stopping eyes and seductive smile pleased Kir immensely. He had made a perfect choice.

Regaining his composure, Kir smiled and nodded thanks. The catalog was bent open to the pages he was interested in, Lots 100 through 11, the Persian calligraphy. He knew that this was what she was interested in, too.

The chairman was about to begin the bidding on the first piece of calligraphy in the sale. An assistant brought out a glass-framed, yellowing sheaf of parchment, displaying it, front and back, to the audience. It was a leaf from the tenth-century Koran, covered with masterfully stylized Kufic script. The ink on this parchment was more than mere lettering, it was a masterpiece. The lyrical script, a fantasy of flowing curves, arrowlike serifs, and long, bold shafts, was a work of exotic, exquisite beauty.

The bidding went smoothly as the chairman's eagle eye watched those participating in the bidding for a signal: a nod, the raising of a pencil, a two-fingered tap on a catalog, the almost imperceptible arch of an eyebrow. The bidding stopped, and the chairman's soft-spoken voice asked, "Any further advances on twenty-two thousand pounds?" His intense eyes focused on those who had participated in the bidding. There was a pause, then he tapped his small ivory gavel on the podium.

The next item, a tattered-edged, almost translucent sheaf of parchment, pressed between two pieces of glass, was displayed to the audience. "Lot 101, ladies and gentlemen, in your catalog." A murmur of approval ran through the hall. The audience appreciated the value of this rare twelfth-century piece of calligraphy from northeastern Persia. Victoria Graham's focus of attention remained fixed straight ahead to the chairman's podium. She became noticeably more tense, but Kir knew that she would not be participating in the bidding. She was the seller.

"One of a kind," Kir whispered to Victoria Graham.

"Yes, indeed," she answered politely.

"It is one of a kind, my dear Miss Graham," continued Kir, "but, unfortunately, not on sale here today. The real piece is in the private collection of Mr. Yusef Tabeti in Asunción, Paraguay."

The blood drained from Victoria Graham's elegant face. She looked like an alabaster doll. Staring straight ahead, not denying anything, silent, she tried to quickly comprehend who this stranger was, and how he knew that these pieces of calligraphy being auctioned here today at Sotheby's were mere copies. Only she and one man knew the true story of the calligraphy, and in the eyes of the world, that man was dead. The calligraphy forgeries were a bargain that had been struck between Mr. Tabeti and herself, no one else.

Yusef Tabeti had been one of the wealthiest industrialists in Iran, old Imperial Iran, the Shah's Iran. Tabeti was the owner of plastics factories and food canning plants, sweat shops that had made him a very rich man. From the spoils of business, he had been able to acquire one of the world's most comprehensive private collections of Persian art, including an especially fine collection of calligraphy.

It was in 1976—the year that Victoria Graham had moved to London from her native San Francisco—that she had first met Tabeti at the Curzon's Club in London. Across the *chemin de fer* table, Tabeti had spied Victoria, the most beautiful woman he had ever seen. She was an object that he wanted to acquire, and acquire her he did. Like his beautiful objets d'art, Victoria Graham could be bought. Victoria pleased him with her companionship, affection, and sexual favors, and he showered Victoria with money, jewels, and furs, and established her in a Mayfair apartment and villa in Antibes.

When the first anti-Shah riots began in Iran in early 1978, however, Victoria Graham came to realize that the objects of Mr. Tabeti's greatest affection were his precious works of art. He implored Victoria to help him smuggle his calligraphy and Persian miniatures out of Iran. With these beloved possessions, he would take no chances. So Victoria took a job as a stewardess with Iran Air; her fluent French allowed her to be based in Paris, and she flew regularly from Paris to Tehran and back. Over a period of nine months, between February and November of 1978, she smuggled out of Iran virtually every piece in Tabeti's art collection. Tabeti paid her handsomely for rescuing his artworks from impending doom.

Tabeti himself, however, was not as lucky. He was still in Tehran when Bakhtiar's government fell in February of 1979. Tabeti knew that the Revolutionaries would arrest and kill him because of his close business connections with the Imperial Court, so he went into hiding. Three months later, he managed to escape from Iran: dressed as an old woman, wrapped in a black *chador*, riding a donkey, Tabeti crossed the Turkish border—the border guards having been well-paid to look the other way—to freedom.

But it was only freedom of a sort. All of Tabeti's factories, homes, and property in Iran were confiscated by the Revolutionary Government. Since his name was on the Revolutionary Tribunal's death squad hit-list, Yusef Tabeti decided that the best thing for him to do was to go into hiding in Paraguay, have reports of his death circulated, and never surface as long as the Revolutionary Government ruled in Iran. He would get by; he still had about sixty million dollars in a Swiss bank account, and, in Victoria's care, his beloved art collection.

Tabeti contacted Victoria from Paraguay, and she arranged for his artworks to be returned to him. But Victoria had known that there was more money to be made from the "late" Mr. Tabeti, and that was why she was at Sotheby's that September afternoon in 1982. With the money that Tabeti had paid her for secreting out his art, Victoria had taken the catalogued pieces of calligraphy and (with Tabeti's tacit understanding) had them copied. Mr. Tabeti was given the originals, and she had the copies. She did not have to worry, the originals would never surface. Dead men tell no tales—her secret was safe. Or so she had thought.

There was a pause in the bidding. Victoria looked up at the board. The last price on one of her pieces of calligraphy stood at thirty-seven thousand pounds, but she could hardly keep her mind on the bidding. How did this stranger sitting next to her know about the forgeries, and what did he want from her?

"Sold," said the chairman, as he tapped his gavel, signaling the close of the bidding. All of Victoria Graham's pieces of forged calligraphy had been sold at handsome prices, and she was now a very wealthy woman. At that moment, however, it was not a particularly comforting thought.

Michael Kir whispered to her. "Shall we go, Miss Graham?"

Knowing that she was in no position to argue, Victoria got up from her chair. Kir gently took her by the arm, and led her out of the main gallery, down the stairs, and into a waiting Silver Phantom Rolls Royce.

"Simpson's-in-the-Strand," Kir ordered the chauffeur. Kir turned to Victoria. "Permit me to introduce myself, Miss Graham. My name is Michael Kir."

The Rolls moved down New Bond Street. It was warm and dry inside, as Victoria looked out the rain-stained window at the stream of shiny black umbrellas, each jockeying for position on the narrow sidewalk. Having regained her composure, Victoria, in her most casual manner, asked, "I'm interested, how did you know, Mr. Kir?"

Taking her hand reassuringly, he said, "I'll explain over lunch."

The car pulled up in front of Simpson's-in-the-Strand, its sooty facade streaked with rain. The doorman held a large black umbrella for them as

Kir escorted his beautiful luncheon guest into the restaurant, an archetype of staid English elegance with its gleaming brass and deep rich mahogany.

"Let me freshen up," Victoria said to Kir as he took her coat and handed it to the cloakroom attendant.

Victoria looked into the mirror in the powder room. She pulled out the tortoise-shell combs that held her thick blond hair in a bun, so that it fell loose to her shoulders. She brushed her hair lightly and studied her face in the mirror. She was thirty years old, but looked twenty-three. She'd lived an adventurous life; she'd lived more in her thirty years than most people had in a lifetime. She applied a quick coat of rose-colored lipstick to her lips, then took a small atomizer from her purse and sprayed Madame Rochas perfume on her wrists and neck.

For an instant it occurred to her to bolt, to run away, to escape. Her life was on the line and she knew it. Still, thought Victoria, even at a critical moment like this, an incredibly handsome man with a fascinating story to tell was not to be deserted, under any circumstances.

Victoria straightened the collar of her ice-blue silk dress, opening the top button, then the next. Hanging from the fine gold chain around her neck was a small square object, white and blue enamel with gold. Arabic writing, "Allah and Ali," repeated endlessly, covered the surface of the miniature Koran. It had been given to her by Tabeti, on Norouz, many years ago.

Kir watched as Victoria entered the main dining room, and walked toward him with athletic grace. As she approached the table, he stood up and pulled out her chair. When they were both seated he lifted the leather-bound menu from the crisp linen tablecloth and handed the menu, opened, to her.

"What would you suggest, Mr. Kir?"

"Please, call me Michael," he replied with a warm smile. "Well, what do you like, Victoria?"

"The potted shrimps," she said, picking the first thing on the menu that caught her eye. At that moment, she was not too interested in food.

Michael Kir nodded slightly, and the obsequious waiter glided to their table. "Yes, sir, you wish to order? Thank you, sir."

"Potted shrimp for the lady and smoked salmon for me—sliced very thin."

"Thank you very much, sir. Thank you," repeated the waiter, backing away from the table, his head bobbing like a turtle's.

Victoria studied Michael Kir, while they made polite small talk, ate their appetizers and drank the chilled white wine.

Kir glanced at Victoria's barely-touched plate. "You aren't eating your shrimps." He leaned forward slightly, and said, almost confidentially, "I must admit they are a far cry from the Persian Gulf shrimp we used to eat."

"*We* used to eat?" she said. "Mr. Kir, you seem to be quite well informed about everything. You know about the calligraphy, and that *we* used to eat Gulf shrimp in Iran, yet I know that we have not met before. Tell me, Mr. Kir, what else do you know?"

Now pressed, Michael Kir began to answer her question, replacing amiable chit-chat with a cold, business-like account of the past seven years of her life. It was played back to her with uncanny accuracy as she sat in the dining room of Simpson's-in-the-Strand: the meeting of Mr. Tabeti at the Curzon's Club in 1976, the description of her Mayfair apartment, her numerous visits to Tehran, her January 1978 application for Iran Air, comprehensive lists of the art that she had smuggled out of Tehran for Mr. Tabeti during the subsequent months, her November 1978 resignation from Iran Air. The period from when she had had the calligraphy copied until the past six months was a little sketchy, but it was fairly obvious to Victoria that during these past six months or so Michael Kir had had her followed. Listening to Kir's voice, she automatically looked over her shoulder, half-expecting to see a man taking notes on her every move. There was no one there.

Victoria glanced down, feeling very uncomfortable, almost violated, trying to avert Michael Kir's chilling eyes. She looked at his briefcase resting on the floor next to his feet, the folds of the rich brown leather expanded to the maximum. No wonder it was so full. She imagined the complete documentation of her life inside that leather case, and knew that only the dread SAVAK could have gotten all this information on her.

Kir put down his glass, and took her hand in his. "I must apologize for this invasion of your privacy and the way that I acted at Sotheby's, but I have a favor to ask of you."

The tone of his voice was pleasant, but his cold hard stare sent a shiver down her spine. Favor! This is downright blackmail and you know it, she thought.

"Please, continue," she said, as she took another sip of wine, trying to slide it down smoothly, the knot in her throat being so tight she was afraid she would gag.

"Well, Victoria, there is not much to tell." Then Kir qualified his terse remark by saying, "There is not much that I can tell you. I need about seven months of your time. I need your help, and I will be honest with you, there is some danger, but it has been minimized." He put his other hand on top of hers and said, looking into her eyes. "You must

114

trust me. Later on I'll be able to clarify your position."

"Trust me," she said, repeating his words. "My dear Mr. Kir, that is not much to go on."

"I think we understand each other's position well enough, Miss Graham. There is obviously not much to discuss." His voice was icy. "Rest assured, your secret about the calligraphy will be safe with me. Now, enjoy your meal and we will talk more later. Would you like the roast beef? And for wine? A bordeaux, perhaps something lighter?"

Michael Kir called the wine steward over. She watched him as he discussed the wine list, the merits of a 1955 bordeaux versus a 1957 vintage. A strange man, she thought, one minute charming and warm and the next, frighteningly hard and intense. She could feel that beneath all his courtliness and charm he was driven. Victoria understood that he was not asking her to help him out. He was telling her.

Yet, now as they sat at their table, as he played the amiable host, smiling, pouring more wine, telling funny little stories, she relaxed and tried to enjoy herself.

Kir's sleek Silver Phantom, with its dark smoked-glass windows, was waiting outside the entrance to Simpson's. It was raining even harder now. Victoria glided into the Rolls and sunk back in the pearl-gray calf-skin leather upholstery. The bar and telephone were set in recessed ivory boxes along a panel of burled wood. The interior of the Rolls felt like a beautiful cocoon, perfect on such a dark, rainy summer's day as this.

"Is that a Nain—how beautiful!" she said, referring to the strip of carpeting beneath her feet. It was a beautiful silk and wool Persian carpet, in delicate shades of blues and pale creams, the luminous silk threads outlining the medallions and borders, creating a more definitive design and giving the appearance of slight relief.

"Yes, it is beautiful," Kir said. "The previous owner had it custom-made for himself. Unfortunately, or fortunately for me, after the Revolution he could no longer afford to travel in the style he was accustomed to. So, now it is mine. Would you care for a drink, perhaps a brandy, on such a miserable day?" he asked her. Victoria nodded. "Ah, September in London. Terrible, isn't it?" said Kir, undoing the latch to the liquor cabinet. It was filled with gleaming Baccarat crystal decanters and glasses. He took out two snifters, poured the rich amber liquid into them, and handed one to her.

Victoria sat back, warming the glass in her hands as the Rolls, caught in the London financial district's afternoon traffic, idled noiselessly.

"So tell me, Mr. Kir, what exactly can I do for you?"

Kir handed her a Louis Vuitton briefcase. "Please, open it."

As Victoria opened the latches she noticed her monogram "VLG" on the case. "Very good, Mr. Kir, you even got the middle initial right," she said.

"Inside, Victoria, you will find an appointment book, airline tickets, and money. Appointments have been made for you for the second week of September, at various places in Paris. Do try to keep all of them, as we will not have time to reschedule."

Victoria opened the appointment book and began leafing through it: Monday, 11:00 a.m., House of Dior, fitting; Thursday, all day, Carita: then, flipping back to Tuesday, 12:00 appointment with Mr. Hubert Givenchy; Wednesday, 9:00 a.m., appointment with Swiss Bank Corporation.

She looked up from the book as Kir began to speak. "Victoria, your assignment begins now and will terminate the end of March 1984. You are an ingenious girl, and I know you will have no problem thinking up a suitable excuse for your friends and family to explain your absence. Your parents live in San Francisco, isn't that right?"

"Right, again, Mr. Kir. With all the information you have, are you sure you never worked for SAVAK?"

"Positive. You are to leave London this weekend for Paris. Check your appointment book for flight number and time."

She looked in the book he had just given her. "Here it is; Air France, Flight 201, London to Paris, leaving Saturday night, 8:10 p.m."

"The ticket is in your attache case. You'll be met at the airport, and taken to the Ritz. My people will be with you constantly, to assist you in every possible way. Please refrain from questioning them about the, shall we say, arrangements that you and I have made. All your expenses will be taken care of and there is ten thousand dollars in an envelope in that briefcase for incidentals. Someone from the Swiss Bank Corporation will meet with you Wednesday morning at your suite at the Ritz to discuss payments. You will be paid one hundred thousand dollars; fifty thousand before and fifty thousand when your assignment is completed at the end of March. The banker can assist you with your money matters, and I would suggest that you contact him concerning your earnings today on the sale. He will be able to help you on that matter, too. Here is his card."

She took the card and put it in her handbag. She noticed the Rolls had turned into her *cul de sac*, a semicircle of white colonnaded townhouses.

"Now, Victoria, I must drop you off at your apartment. I am sure you have a lot to do, and I have a plane to catch."

The car pulled up in front of Victoria's white two-story townhouse. Michael Kir stepped out of the car and held the door open for her.

The rain had finally stopped, but Victoria hardly noticed. She gripped the still-wet, black wrought-iron railing as Kir escorted her up the stairs to her front door. Her mind was filled with questions, but she knew Kir would tell her nothing more.

At the top of the stairs, Victoria turned to Kir and extended her hand.

"I guess, Mr. Kir, we have a deal."

"Please, call me Michael."

Victoria smiled.

"We will meet again in Paris, Victoria," Michael Kir said, taking her hand.

"Of course," Victoria replied. She knew she had no choice.

Victoria pulled the diaphanous ivory nightgown over her naked body. She turned down the covers on her four-poster mahogany bed, and slipped between the cool embroidered sheets. Although it was only ten o'clock, Victoria was exhausted. All day she had pondered her luncheon meeting with Kir, but he remained an enigma. As Victoria lay in bed she reflected on the events and twists in her life that had led to this situation—whatever it was —with Mr. Kir. She had no regrets.

The mysterious Michael Kir intrigued her. And she had to agree with something he had said during lunch; they were cut from the same cloth. The idea of embarking on the unknown, the hint of danger, stirred Victoria's psychological libido.

The shrill ring of the telephone interrupted her

thoughts. Victoria reached over and picked up the receiver. She listened to the long distance beeps until a voice came on the line.

"Miss Graham? Miss Victoria Graham?"

The accented voice seemed familiar to Victoria. She was certain she'd heard it many times.

"Yes," Victoria said.

"Walter Singer here."

# CHAPTER EIGHT

*"Benvenuti a Roma, signore e signori."* Alitalia's white, red, and green DC-9 touched down at Leonardo da Vinci airport. Michael Kir felt good. It was great to be back in Rome, one of his favorite cities. A navy blue Fiat Mirafiore was waiting in front of the terminal to take him into the city center.

"Welcome, Mr. Kir, nice to see you again," the chauffeur said as he lifted Kir's suitcase into the *portabagagli*. A cushioned thud sounded as he closed the trunk.

"Thank you, Eduardo, nice to be back."

*"All' Hotel Hassler, vero?"*

*"Vero."* Kir sat back as the driver screeched out of the parking lot. Kir got a kick out of Italian drivers; the faster and more aggressively they drove, the more macho they were. Red lights, speed limits, and other such silly traffic rules were for old women and *cornuti*, cuckolds, to obey. They were certainly not for real men. Kir noticed that the speedometer needle hovered at about 110 kilometers as they headed toward Rome.

Even in the air-conditioned comfort of the Mirafiore, Kir could almost feel the hot September sun. It had turned the grass along the highway yellow and brittle, and made the road appear to shimmer. He watched the billboards, which extolled the virtues of Sicilian wines, TWA, and the Rome Cavalieri Hilton, flash by, as the open farmland quickly turned to cantilevered office buildings. The highway continued past the large stretches of low-cost apartment housing, the inevitable result of urban sprawl, and then funneled into a winding twolane road that led into the city.

The car continued its high-speed chase into the heart of Rome, tires squealing as it made a controlled drift around the magnificent pockmarked Colosseum, down the wide boulevard flanking the Forum, and into Piazza Venezia, Rome's largest square. The car rushed past the "Roman embarrassment," the gigantic wedding-cake-style monument to Vittorio Emmanuele that dominated Piazza Venezia. Kir's driver propelled the Fiat down Via del Corso, Rome's main street. Eduardo wove the car in and out of the crowds of tourists and darkly tanned Romans who jammed the Corso. Suddenly, Eduardo slammed on the brakes, coming within an inch of shaving-off the pink-and-white houndstooth polyester-clothed backside of a female tourist, ambling across the street on the green *Avanti* signal.

"Jesus Christ," moaned Kir. "You've almost hit five people already, Eduardo! Slow down."

"Cows," Eduardo said flatly, "all cows."

The car whizzed past the famous Spanish Steps and expertly took the steep hair-pin street tucked behind it, skirting the obelisk planted in the middle of the road between the Church of Trinita dei Monti and the top of the Spanish Steps. The Fiat came to a screeching halt in front of the Hassler.

*"Ecco,"* exclaimed Eduardo as he leaped out to open the trunk. The doorman opened the Fiat's back door and Kir got out. He stretched his legs and drank in the familiar view. God, he loved this

city! He had always held a special place in his heart for Rome, the Rome of *la dolce vita*, Soraya at *Piccolo Mondo*, the beautiful people on the Via Veneto, Ferraris and Lambourghinis triple-parked outside the Excelsior Hotel. Alas, those days were gone, and although the high life of Roman society had been forced to move indoors, and the rich and famous lived in fear of kidnapping and violence, there was no denying that Rome was a lovely city, crippled by fear and instability, but still brimming with life.

The doorman pushed the revolving door open for Kir as he walked into the lobby of the Hassler Hotel, the *crème de la crème* of Roman hotels, a dignified, traditional, home-away-from-home for the princes, dukes and duchesses, presidents, cardinals, kings, and commoners who had passed through its doors. The Hassler, with its dark wood, gleaming marble, and touches of gilt, was truly elegant. It was Michael Kir's favorite hotel in all the world.

"*Buon giorno, Signor Kir*. Nice to see you again," said the concierge as he stepped out to greet Michael Kir. "It has been a while since we last saw you. We have a lovely room with a view ready for you on the fourth floor; allow me to show you."

Together, Kir and the concierge crossed the lobby and followed the well-worn Persian runner to the *ascensore*. The concierge bowed slightly as Kir walked into his room. A valet was already unpacking his suitcase, hanging his suits in the rosewood *armadio*.

"This will be fine, thank you," Kir said.

The room was completely paneled in deep rich reddish-burgundy rosewood. A large bed with a wine-silk bedspread and canopy was situated against a slightly smoked mirror.

Kir opened the double doors to the balcony. He looked down on the cobblestone piazza below, at the couture houses of Valentino, Angelo, and Anna Manieri; the little Scalinata di Spagna *pensione*, and the top of the travertine balastrade of the Spanish Steps. He looked up, past the terracotta tiled roof tops, the green latticework, flower-filled terraces, past the red Crusader cross on the white background of the flag of the Knights of Malta fluttering in the hot breeze. Far in the distance was the dome of the Vatican, St. Peter's majestic against the fluffy cumulus clouds filling the blue sky. Kir may not have been a Christian, but St. Peter's was a sacred place to him. As a youth he had aspired to be an architect, and during his vacations from boarding school he had often come to Rome to sketch *San Pietro:* the facade of Maderno, the cupola of Michelangelo, and the colonnaded piazza of Bernini.

Kir had fallen in love with Rome: the fabulous buildings, the piazzas, the fountains, the clear, uniquely Roman light, as well as the beautiful women of Rome. It was a good apprenticeship for a young man. He learned proper appreciation of beautiful things—of all kinds.

He smiled at the memories that came flooding back as he stood on the balcony. Realizing the uncommon quiet that had descended on the streets, he looked at his watch. It was two o'clock, *l'ora di pranzo.* Everything had stopped as every Roman indulged in a three course meal, complete with great quantities of *vino* and a late afternoon siesta.

There was a knock on the door and a trolley draped with fine white linen was silently wheeled into the room. The waiter ceremoniously unveiled a club sandwich beneath the solid silver server. Then, with great panache, he poured San Pellegrino mineral water into the crystal glass. After receiving a generous tip, the waiter let himself out, shaking his head sadly at the American's idea of lunch.

Kir knew he would not really have time for anything more than a quick shower and a change of clothes before his seven o'clock appointment with his friend Gianni Bruni. The shops opened at 4:00 p.m., and Kir wanted to do some shopping while he was in Rome. For his type of body, European clothes fit better. During the past few months, although Kir had been in Europe numerous times, he had been so busy that he had not had a chance to buy the clothes he would be needing. He needed cool, lightweight clothing, since, on the island where he was going, it would be hot and humid. Michael knew he didn't have to go far to find what he wanted, just across the small piazza, to Angelo, the best men's store in Rome.

Kir looked at his watch. It was nearly 7:00 p.m., and he and Angelo had just finished their third frozen vodka in the back of the store.

"Have a good trip, Michael," Angelo said, raising a small, tubelike, frosted glass. "You will be the most chic man in the whole desert of *Arabia Saudita*, Saudi Arabia."

Kir smiled and raised his glass, *"Salute."*

Angelo saw him out to the door, and directed the clerk to take Kir's parcels over to his room at the Hassler. *"Arrivederci,* Michael. Try to come to Rome more often!"

Kir waved back to him as he hurried toward the Spanish Steps. A cool, fresh breeze was washing away the daytime heat as the distant sun eased itself down. Kir paused a moment to admire the clear, pale light of the Roman twilight, then walked quickly down the well-worn Spanish

Steps. At the foot of the steps, he crossed the Piazza di Spagna, and made his way down Via Condotti.

The Via Condotti, with Gucci, Ginori, Janetti, Bulgari, Ferragamo, and Bruni was the most exclusive shopping street in Rome. Elegantly dressed Romans, still bronzed from weeks at chic seaside resorts, crowded the Via Condotti as they shopped for *altissima moda*, high fashion from the trend-setting Italian designers.

Kir decided to stop for a quick *espresso* at the Antico Caffe Greco, once the haunt of famous expatriot literary geniuses like Byron and Keats. Keats, dying of tuberculosis in his tiny house at the corner of the Spanish Steps, had received his meals from this ancient cafe. But with the crowd around the bar this night, thought Kir, Keats probably would have died trying to get a coffee. Next to Canova's, in Piazza del Popolo, there was not a gayer place in all of Rome. Kir decided against the coffee and went across the street to his friend Gianni Bruni's store, one of the most fabulous jewelry stores in the world, if not the most fabulous. The Bruni name was synonymous with the finest jewelry money could buy.

Kir rang the buzzer at Bruni's. A man peeked out from behind the velvet-curtained glass door, and opened it when he saw Kir. A closed-circuit television camera was focused on him as he waited; then, a second door, this one of bulletproof glass, was unlocked from the inside.

Oblivious to the showcases which contained a king's ransom—glittering velvet-lined boxes full of twisted ropes of red coral, pearls and diamonds, flat heavy chains of diamond-encrusted gold, and delicate earrings and rings—Kir walked down the long, wide corridor. Tiered crystal chandeliers reflected in the black and green marble floor that led to the inner sanctum. Gianni was expecting him.

Kir had dragged Gianni back from the beach to discuss the setting of a very large diamond into a necklace that Gianni had designed for an Arabian princess. Pleasing an Arabian princess who possessed not only the biggest diamonds imaginable, but also possessed the worst taste imaginable, was a difficult task. As far as Gianni knew, the necklace was the reason for the meeting with Kir, but Kir knew that Gianni was the connection to Gabriella Antonelli.

*"Ciao, amico mio, come stai?"* Gianni Bruni rose from behind his desk and kissed Kir enthusiastically on both cheeks.

*"Non c'e male."* Kir was genuinely happy to see his friend. Gianni was an outgoing, genial man, handsome and charming, with a zest for life that was infectious. They had done business together for years, but it was always secondary to their friendship.

"Michael, this is perfect timing! I have a great surprise planned. Tomorrow we are all going to my villa in *Toscana.* We will drink good wine, eat well, and you will tell me what you have been doing." Gianni winked and smiled broadly at his friend. "About *le donne.*" Then, chiding him, Gianni said, "My friend, you work too hard, you never play."

"It sounds great, Gianni. And you're right, I have really been busy." Kir thought to himself, this is not the right moment. I'll have to ask Gianni about the girl later.

"It has been much too long since I last saw you, a year?"

"About that, Gianni."

"So where have you been?"

"My God, Gianni, if I start to tell you where I've been these past twelve months, we will be here all

126

night. Anyway, with that tan you have, I am sure you've been to much more enjoyable places. Where have you been?''

"A little beach town called Gaeta—very safe and secluded. And only about two hours from Roma.'' Gianni smiled and added, "Gaeta has become very chic.''

"No doubt,'' Kir replied. "Where Gianni Bruni goes, the rest follow.''

Gianni smiled, acknowledging the truth.

"Michael, shall we look at Prince Al bin Yami's wife's diamond?''

"Yes, Gianni. When did it arrive?''

"Let's see, perhaps four days ago. It is a beauty, Michael! You are an extraordinarily resourceful man, my dear friend. You always turn up the most perfect objects. And I am not only talking about gems,'' said Gianni smiling, as he got up and walked over to a small safe recessed into the marble wall. He opened it, then slid out a tray on which was resting a brilliant diamond. Gianni brought the tray to his desk and both men leaned over the fiery gem. Resting on the rich brown velvet was a 6.79 karat pear-cut diamond, the clarity and the cut enhancing the rare blue-white color of the stone. "Michael, it is fabulous. You amaze me how you are able to find these stones. This one is flawless!'' exclaimed Gianni. "Amazing to find no inclusions in such a large diamond.''

Michael nodded. He, too, was very pleased with this stone. All the searching he had done to find it had been very time consuming, but he had to do it to keep up appearances. If Michael Kir had suddenly dropped out of the diamond business, people would have become suspicious. By still buying for select customers, he was able to keep his cover. And it was the least he could do for Prince Al bin Yami, who was one of his best customers. For the Prince, price was no object—and he always insisted on the best. Finding a perfect diamond was a challenge that Kir enjoyed. It was just too bad that this stone wasn't for Prince Yami's English mistress, thought Kir. She was a woman who had exquisite taste and lovely hands; for her, this fabulous diamond could have been set simply, to its best advantage. Unfortunately, the diamond was for the Prince's favorite wife, and she would want everything but the kitchen sink set around it.

Michael had orders from Prince Yami to create something that the Princess would love. It would be a hard act to follow, after the two-million-dollar Rococo-ish diamond and emerald pendant Kir had delivered to her last year.

Gianni picked up the unset diamond and put his loupe, his jeweler's lens, to his eye. With the loupe, Gianni could see the pear-shaped diamond enlarged ten times and to his trained eye he could see no inclusions whatsoever. "Loupe-clean!" He let out a long-winded whistle. "It is flawless." Gianni put down the stone. "Now, Michael, tell me, what does the *principe* have in mind? You should know," Gianni said.

"Gianni, he wants it as a surprising gift for his wife, Princess Nuri. She just bore him another son. There would have been no gift if it had been a daughter."

"Yes, I know," said Gianni, shaking his head. "The Prince contacted me and told me that you would be able to help me with the setting. You know what the Princess likes, *vero?*"

"Yes, I have been giving it a lot of thought, and this is what I've come up with. Tell me what you think," Michael said. He took a pencil and paper from atop Gianni's desk and began making a quick sketch. Gianni leaned over his shoulder, watching.

"My suggestion, Gianni, is that you design a sixty-centimeter necklace, with the pear-cut diamond in the middle, and graduated baguette-cut sapphires at 1.5-centimeter intervals. Sad to say, the Princess is no beauty, but her eyes are beautiful—the color of sapphires. It would be a good compliment."

"O.K., *amico*, I'll take your advice."

"Gianni," Kir said, putting his hand on Gianni's back, "that is why I brought the diamond to you. You are the best."

Gianni smiled. He wasn't one to argue. It was the truth: he was the best.

The intercom buzzed. Gianni leaned over and spoke into it. "Fine, send her in," he said.

She breezed into the room, ripples of silk and perfume trailing after her.

"Michael, I'd like you to meet my dear friend, Gabriella Antonelli."

"Very nice to meet you," Kir said, mesmerized by her beauty. Even if she had not been the one Kir was searching out, she still would have been unforgettable. She was a striking beauty. If her parents had meant to name her in honor of the Archangel Gabriel, they had made a mistake. There was nothing angelic about her. She was a *diavola* with fire in her eyes, and a body that seemed as if it had stepped out of an inferno, smoldering with sexuality. Michael Kir couldn't believe his luck! He had never expected that Gabriella would be in Rome in early September, when half of the Italians were still at the beach.

"Oh, you must be here for Gianni's party," Gabriella said. "Everyone is here, we've all come back from the beach for Gianni's party. Everyone wants to celebrate the anniversary of his liberation." She squeezed Gianni's arm affectionately. *"Non è vero, caro?"*

That's right, Kir thought, tomorrow will be five years to the day that Gianni was set free by his kidnappers, after spending forty-five harrowing days locked in a dark cellar. Kir remembered back to those days. He had used all his connections in Iran to try and get the Rome SAVAK bureau to help out the bumbling Italian police, but SAVAK, which, officially, did not exist in Italy, refused to collaborate. But as a favor to Kir a top-ranking SAVAK general, Parvis Gazvini, ordered the SAVAK office in Rome to carry out its own separate investigation. SAVAK's information was slow in coming and the Bruni family went ahead with the ransom payment. The Italian police swooped down on the farmhouse where Gianni was being kept and apprehended the three kidnappers, killing them all instantly during a bloody shoot-out. But it was suspected that a fourth person was involved, one whose intimate knowledge of Gianni Bruni's comings and goings had assisted in the abduction of Gianni. The police had interrogated the servants and employees, but the list of such persons was long, and no one fit the bill as accomplice to the kidnapping. The theory of a fourth person was abandoned, and the file closed.

However, the SAVAK investigation had turned up the name of a possible person. The information was given to Kir, but it had come too late. By then, Gianni was safe at home and trying to forget about the horrors of the past months, so Kir decided that it was best to let things be. Kir had decided to keep that little gem of SAVAK information, and now it was paying off. Gabriella Antonelli had been the fourth person, and now she would have to do Kir's bidding—or else.

"Michael," Gianni said. "It's so rarely we get to see each other these days, my friend. Let's go out tonight! I know a new place, good food, and it's very safe, only tourists go there. Anyway, all the kidnappers are at the beach," Gianni said. "How about it, Michael, *va bene?*"

"*Mi dispiace*, Gianni, but I've made plans for tonight."

"No problem, tomorrow at three I'll pick you up and we'll drive to Tuscany, talk business and pleasure on the way up. Where are you staying, the Hassler?"

"Yes. I'll see you tomorrow, I'm looking forward to it." Kir turned to a slightly pouting Gabriella. "*Ciao*, Gabriella. See you tomorrow, too," he said, kissing her lightly on both cheeks. "Gianni, I've got to run."

"O.K., I'll walk you out." As they walked through the store, Gianni confided to Kir, "You know, Michael, that Gabriella, she's a crazy girl— so jealous. And we aren't even lovers anymore." He shrugged his aristocratic shoulders and raised his eyebrows; it was the same gesture every Italian, from the barman to the Pope, used to express, "It's out of my hands."

Kir remained silent. It would have killed Gianni to have known the truth about *cara* Gabriella. But Gabriella wasn't a dangerous woman, just a greedy one.

"Tomorrow then, Michael, three o'clock?"

"*Benissimo. A domani, Gianni. Ciao!*"

The next morning Kir awoke late, refreshed and in a good frame of mind. He had spent the evening in Parioli, the best residential section of Rome, with the beautiful ex-wife of an old CIA friend and her two equally beautiful and entertaining daughters. As he lay in bed he thought about the night before. It had been a pleasant evening talking about old times, better times.

The last year and a half of Kir's life had been so hectic. He had been constantly on the move, his social life consisting only of people who could do something for him, people he could use, and the whole time, hanging over his head, was the constant worry that he may run out of time, run out of money, run out of luck. After last night, laughing and joking with old friends, putting business out of his mind for a few hours, he realized that he was becoming totally involved in the plan: he was living it. Michael Kir realized he was becoming colder, harder, more ruthless as time went on, but he knew he had to keep going. He had to be able to deliver the girls by mid-September. He must not let up, he could not. Gabriella would be there in Tuscany today, and he had to make his move. He had to get her today, and get moving again. He had to be in Rio by Friday night. And after that, work would only be beginning.

Kir spent the morning making long-distance phone calls, checking with Mark in Washington, his various contacts elsewhere, and placating his employers. Anyone tapping his phone would have sworn that Mr. Kir was the most frivolous of men, talking about paintings, women, and vintage wines—his code language—to people all over the world.

Michael did not notice that Gianni was late. He was engrossed in Gabriella's file, trying to absorb more information. She lived in a very expensive apartment in Rome. She didn't work. Her parents, who had been dead ten years, had left her a small estate, but she had a continuous string of very well-to-do lovers who had kept her in the style she preferred. He closed the file. It was already four o'clock. The phone rang. Only an hour late, not bad for a Roman, thought Kir, as he picked up the phone.

"*Pronto*, Gianni, I'm on my way downstairs."

As Kir walked out of the Hassler lobby, he

shaded his eyes from the sultry Roman sun. He spied Gianni's burgundy Alfetta GT. *"Ciao,* Michael." Gianni leaned over and opened the passenger door. "Get in."

*"Dio mio,* it's hot today," Gianni said, wiping the imaginary sweat off his clear patrician brow with the back of his hand. "Being an *americano,* you probably want the air-conditioning on, right, Michael?"

"No, it's O.K., let's just open the sun roof instead."

As the car sped down the road, Kir leaned back and let the sun and warm wind rush in.

"So, old friend, tell me about your life and loves," said Gianni. "I've missed you."

"Traveling, as usual. I haven't spent more than a month in total in New York over the past year. I've been to Bangkok a number of times, and I thought of you and me, the times we spent there together." Both men smiled at the memory. Gianni's father had insisted that he learn the business from the bottom up, and in his mid-twenties he had been sent on buying trips to learn the ropes. It was in Bangkok that he'd met Michael Kir. They had become fast friends, and had enjoyed many an adventure together. While Gianni, the playboy, searched endlessly for the most perfect girl to fit his needs in that most obliging of places, Bangkok, Michael had searched for the perfect emerald, along the way teaching Gianni the fine points of jewelry buying in the Orient. One hand washed the other. Michael learned about the most indulgent, exotic sex imaginable, and Gianni, much to the relief of his father, learned about emeralds.

"In those days, the emeralds were only an excuse for going to see the girls," Gianni sighed. "And now tell me about some of your beautiful girls."

"Actually, Gianni, I've nothing to tell. I've been so busy that they just seem to flash by me like the scenery from this car window." He thought of Victoria, beautiful Victoria.

"In that case, my old friend, you should get married. If girls no longer linger in your memory you may as well get married."

"As good a reason as any," Kir replied, smiling at Gianni's quite serious comment.

They drove north, up the *Autostrada del Sole*, Highway of the Sun, the scenery becoming more beautiful as they neared Siena, as they traveled into the heart of Tuscany. The greens seemed to become deeper, darker, richer, and the trees more delicate, those long, elegant cypresses casting needle-like shadows over russet-colored stone farmhouses, their terracotta roofs gleaming in the late afternoon sun. The beautiful province of Tuscany had the most sublime power over people. It had inspired the most glorious period in Western civilization—the Renaissance. From these small farms, these precariously placed hill-towns, had come men like Leonardo da Vinci, Botticelli, Michelangelo, and Machiavelli. The feeling that the hands of man had molded every inch of land, but with an exquisitely gentle touch, a touch that had caressed, rather than changed the landscape, permeated Tuscany. A timeless place in a world of flux, thought Kir, as he looked out of the thick, bulletproof glass of the Alfetta.

"It is beautiful, isn't it, Michael?"

"Beautiful beyond words. There is something magical in the air. I feel like I've gone back in time."

"It makes me feel the same way. Have you ever been to my *vigna*, my vineyard?"

"No, I haven't."

"My place is about seventy-five kilometers

farther on. It's after Siena, actually very near San Gimignano. My land produces some of the best grapes and olives in all of Chianti country. But I'm selfish, I keep all of the wine and olive oil for myself and my friends. You'll see what I mean soon. My country place is beautiful," Gianni continued. "It's a fourteenth-century farmhouse, with a magnificent view. On a clear day, I can see Florence." The Alfetta turned abruptly off the *autostrada* and raced through the undulating hills covered with rows of vines, laden with plump, shiny grapes, ready to be picked.

"Gianni, you drive this road like you're in the Grand Prix of Monaco," Kir said, as the car sped around another curve.

"I learned to drive like this at an antiterrorist training school in Germany. After my release from the kidnappers, no one could believe I wanted to go to a school like that. But it's my life, and I want to know how to protect it." Gianni unconsciously gripped the steering wheel more tightly. His knuckles, exposed by the fashionable antelope driving gloves, gleamed white.

"You know, Gianni," Kir said, "the chances of you being kidnapped ever again are very, very slim. Law of averages, probability theory, and all that. No one gets kidnapped twice. Not even in Italy."

"There's always a first time, especially in Italy. I just like to be prepared. You know, Michael, you can't trust anyone."

The irony of that statement made a wry, barely perceptible smile cross Kir's face. Poor Gianni, Kir thought. It would break his heart if he knew the truth. If he only knew that his dear Gabriella had set him up for the kidnapping.

"I guess you're right," Kir said.

The car climbed up a steep incline and turned a

135

sharp corner. In the distance loomed the four-teenth-century hill town of San Gimignano, world-famous for its thirteen medieval towers. Jutting out against the clear sky, the tall, narrow stone towers proudly rising straight into the Tuscan sky seemed like a picture from a fairy-tale.

"My house is only a few minutes from here," Gianni said. Gianni turned the car abruptly to the right, onto a narrow, rough road, flanked on both sides by the silvery trunks of ancient olive trees. It was a bumpy ride, and Gianni turned right again, onto an even narrower, rougher road that seemed more like a pathway than a road. They drove a few hundred meters until reaching a high, stone arch-way, above a heavy iron gate. The car screeched to a halt. Gianni got out of the car, walked over to the gate, switched the intercom on, and spoke into it.

Then Gianni got back in the car and waited. A few seconds later the heavy iron gate opened. A heavyset elderly man, wearing a corduroy cap and carrying a shotgun over his shoulder, inclined his head and tipped his cap as Gianni drove past him up the gravel path, up into a dirt and pebble court-yard.

The Alfetta raised clouds of dust in the court-yard, causing the fat chickens to scatter noisily. They ran for cover beneath the parked Jaguars, BMW's, Lancias, and Alfa Romeos. Kir laughed at the incongruity of the clucking chickens scratch-ing at the earth near the tires of luxury automo-biles.

"Seems like everyone is here but me," Gianni said as he pulled up right in front of the four-teenth-century stone farmhouse.

*"Buona sera, Signor Gianni,"* shouted an armed guard from the side of the large wooden doorway.

*"Buona sera,"* Gianni said. Gianni patted the two German shepherds that had run up to greet him.

Gianni and Michael walked across the gravel courtyard. Kir's eyes appraised the crumbling stone farmhouse. It looked like it had seen better days—better centuries.

"How old is this place, Gianni?"

"Six hundred years. She looks pretty good for such an old lady, don't you think?" Gianni pushed open the weatherbeaten door. "Come this way," Gianni said as he led Kir into the ancient kitchen. Bits of straw stuck out of the rough whitewashed walls.

An old woman, red-cheeked and rotund, came out from behind a long table, wiping her hands on her apron. *"Signor Gianni!* How are you? We have been worried, you are late!" The bristly gray hairs of the woman's moustache moved rapidly as she talked. She turned away, shouting orders to an old man sitting on a stool.

Gianni put his hand on Kir's shoulder. "Since we're the last ones to arrive, we should join the others. Follow me."

Gianni led the way through a small anteroom, then through a dark narrow hallway that connected the kitchen with the rest of the farmhouse. Gianni opened the green wooden door to an immense, inviting room. Only the wooden beams across the high ceiling belied the room's true vintage. The room had been gutted from floor to ceiling. The high walls were painted pristine white, and the floor was covered with polished terracotta tiles. The furnishings were Italian *modernissimo* style; beige leather couches, Barcelona chairs, modern bronze sculptures on marble rectangular pedestals. About twenty-five people were gathered in the room.

A short bearded fellow of about forty was the first to sight Kir and Gianni standing on the threshold to the room.

*"Ciao, Gianni,"* he cried. Other heads in the room turned and faced the doorway.

Rome's *dolce vita* crowd of the 1980s was gathered at this country retreat to spend a pleasant evening with dear Gianni. Most of these trim, impeccably groomed people had been friends of Gianni Bruni's for years. They remembered the black saga of his kidnapping and, after six long weeks of captivity, his release. They were glad that, five years later, they could be with Gianni to celebrate the anniversary of his release. And how fortunate that Gianni's country estate was in the most beautiful part of Tuscany.

As Kir and Gianni chatted about the latest Bertollucci movie with its star, a pale, blond, French actress, Kir suddenly felt a cool hand on the back of his neck. He turned around, and found Gabriella edging her way between Gianni and himself. Gabriella, her hand still on Kir's neck, spoke to Gianni.

"Gianni, *caro,* I see you brought your *bellissimo* Signor Kir to the party. How very nice." Kir could feel her smooth enameled nails graze against his neck as she spoke. The combined effect of her touch, the dulcet sound of her voice, and the musky scent of her perfume made the hairs on the back of his neck stand up.

Gabriella turned slightly to face Kir. "Gianni tells me that the two of you have been friends for many years. Then you must have known him when that terrible thing happened to him. *Dio mio,* I prayed every night that they'd find the place his kidnappers had taken him to, and rescue him safely. It was a miracle he got out safely, especially when you think what happened to those kidnappers." She shuddered theatrically to emphasize her point. "All three of them, shot dead, and Gianni unharmed. An absolute miracle." She looked up at Kir earnestly with her wide, olive-green eyes. With her strong Roman features, golden flawless skin, and thick, chestnut hair, there was no doubt that she was a beauty, and she knew it.

Kir returned her gaze. A miracle for you that you were never caught, he thought. Kir's eyes betrayed no trace of the thoughts behind them.

"Yes," Kir said. "It was a real miracle. I'm glad that Gianni's friends are here to help celebrate the anniversary of his release."

"Excuse me," Gabriella said, moving away. "There's Sara. I must say hello." She walked quickly, for a European. She was of medium height, trim, but with full breasts. Her legs were exceptionally shapely, and the straight silk skirt she wore, with a provocative slit up the back, emphasized her great ass. Kir was glad she had approached him. That would save him the trouble of approaching her.

For the next few hours, Kir mingled freely and easily with the guests. Most of those present were Italian, but there was a sprinkling of foreigners. A couple of times, as he was chatting with a statuesque redhead, he saw Gabriella staring at him from across the room.

Around ten o'clock, dinner was served. The long refectory table was completely covered with bowls and platters of food; a smaller side table had been set up nearby to hold the plates, silver, and glassware the guests would need for the sumptuous buffet dinner.

Fantastic aromas wafted from the long table and permeated the room. The guests made favorable comments and gave appreciative glances at the table. The Italians' love and appreciation of food was one of the things that Kir liked best about Italy, and Italians. He smiled as he watched the guests hungrily eye the table as old Maria, still in her kitchen garb, put the last trays and plates on the table.

It was an enticing table, Kir thought hungrily. There were plates of *crostini*, thin oval slices of crusty Italian bread, spread with ham and provolone cheese, then baked until the cheese was bubbly, or spread with fresh chicken liver pate, or slender strips of anchovies. A silver tray was heaped high in its center with mounds of peeled figs and slices of cantaloupe, surrounded by slices, so thin they were nearly transparent, of *prosciutto di cinghiale*, wild boar ham. Gilt-edged trays of slices of sausages, flanked by rows of black olives and marinated mushroom caps, were on either side of the table. In sharp contrast to the silver and gold trays were the earthenware bowls of *fagioli*, white beans cooked in olive oil, seasoned with garlic and bits of *peperoncini*, sharp red peppers. In the center of the table was a huge round, wooden board, on which were perhaps three dozen roasted quails, pigeons, and pheasants. For those who preferred something more substantial than fowl, there were stacks of charcoal grilled beefsteaks. Wooden bowls of bright green salads, loaves of round and oblong bread, plates of small, ripe cheeses, and hand-woven baskets overflowing with shiny red apples, clusters of purple grapes swollen with juice, and russet and chartreuse pears completed the sumptuous repast.

"Please, everybody, take a glass of wine. I'd like to make a toast," Gianni said loudly from the far end of the room. When Gianni was satisfied that everyone present had a glass in his hand, he began addressing the group.

*"Amici,"* he said, "thank you for being with me on the anniversary of the happiest occasion of my

life. Five years ago tonight I was released from my captivity. My abductors had held me for six weeks. I thought I would never be released, never see any of you again."

Kir moved forward a few feet, until he was standing right behind Gabriella. He rubbed against her shoulder lightly, causing her to look up and smile at him.

"But, *grazie a dio*, I was released," Gianni continued. "And it was the happiest moment of my life. I am glad that you, my dearest and oldest friends, could join me tonight. To all of you, to friendship!" Gianni said, raising his glass in the air.

"To friendship! To Gianni!" The guests toasted. The room was filled with the sound of clinking glasses. *"Viva* Gianni!"

Kir moved closer to Gabriella so that his chest was pressing against her back. "Gianni would be heartbroken if he knew that you had set him up," Kir whispered softly in Gabriella's ear.

She didn't move, but Kir could feel her body stiffen.

"Gabriella, why don't we go outside for a walk? No one will miss us during dinner," he whispered to her. Without facing him, she nodded.

Gabriella followed Kir through the narrow hallway leading to the kitchen. Maria, slicing a loaf of bread, looked up at them as, arm in arm, they walked through the hot kitchen and out in the cool night air. Gabriella was glad that the servant had seen the two of them leave together. That way, if some terrible fate should befall her at the hands of this handsome stranger who knew too much, someone would be able to point a finger at him.

"We're going into the vineyards for a walk," Kir said to the guard standing in the courtyard. Kir took Gabriella's arm. He felt her arm muscles

141

tense, but he did not relax his hold on her forearm.

A gravel path led out into the vineyards. A full moon, bright and silvery, illuminated the low, softly rolling hills of Tuscany. The gravel path dissolved into a soft dirt trail between the rows of vines. The air was cool, but heavy with the perfume of grapes.

Gabriella's high-heeled shoes caught in a vine tendril, causing her to falter. Only Kir's grip on her arm kept her from falling.

"Grazie," she said. She stooped and unbuckled the thin straps of her Ferragamo shoes. She held both shoes together in her left hand. "Now, where are we going?" she asked Kir, her voice forcedly calm.

"Let's continue on a bit, toward that shed over there." Kir pointed to an old stone shed, perhaps three hundred meters in the distance.

All around them were endless rows of grapevines. Weather-beaten wooden sticks, bleached nearly white by time and the elements, gleamed semi-iridescent in the moonlight. These slender pieces of wood supported the thick, entwined vines. The large, dark grape leaves curled about the pendulous bunches of ripe grapes, swollen to near-bursting with juices. The grapes were still on the vines, awaiting the late-September harvest.

Gabriella suddenly stopped in her tracks, and faced Kir.

"What do you know? What do you want from me?" she said.

Kir replied by moving his hand from her forearm to the small of her back. He pulled Gabriella toward him. "You're lovely," he said. "I can see why Gianni was so enamoured of you." With his free hand, Kir gripped Gabriella's right shoulder. He moved his other hand up her spine to the back of her long neck. "But he'd probably have your lovely throat slit if he knew you set him up for his kidnapping." Kir kissed her throat.

"You don't know what you're talking about. You're crazy," Gabriella whispered.

"I know," Kir said. "But no one else has to." Kir led the way into the vineyard. In only a minute, they were standing beside the small stone shed, long since abandoned to the fate of storing rusting farm tools. The vines grew practically right up to the walls of the low building.

Gabriella leaned against a wall. Before she knew what was happening, Kir was pressed up against her. Gabriella put her arms around Kir's neck. If he wanted to make love, she was in agreement; so did she, and had since she first was introduced to this sexy, virile-looking man in Rome. He didn't have to try to blackmail her into submission. But, although Gabriella hoped that her body was all Kir wanted, she knew, from the awful, true, words he had spoken to her, that there was something more in the offing. She pressed her pelvis against him, confident that any man could be softened by a good bout of love-making.

Kir placed a strong hand on each of her hips and pushed her back against the wall.

"Gabriella, I know that you set Gianni Bruni up for his kidnapping five years ago. You had direct contact with all three kidnappers, you supplied them with the information about Gianni that they needed to succeed. Luckily for you, all three were killed in the shootout during Gianni's release."

Gabriella didn't answer for a moment. Then she said, "I don't know what you're talking about. You're making up lies. Why? What do you want from me?"

"I have proof, Gabriella. Written proof, that would hold up in any court."

Gabriella didn't know how it had come about,

but she was trapped. She believed that this beautiful Michael Kir did know about her past. She forced a few crocodile tears from the corners of her wide eyes.

"They promised me that they wouldn't hurt Gianni. They told me that they only needed the publicity and the money for their underground political group. I knew that Gianni's family could afford the money. I . . . I never knew it would turn out the way it did. Thank God Gianni escaped unharmed. I only did it for the money they promised me. I never wanted anything to happen to Gianni." A few more tears trickled down her cheeks.

"Tell that to Gianni. And to the *Ministero della Giustizia*," Kir said coldly.

Gabriella looked up at Kir.

"All right, what do you want from me? I don't have any money to speak of. If you know so much about my past, you know that I was never given the money they promised me."

"Gabriella, who could possibly want money from you? You have something far better to offer . . ." Kir's voice trailed away as he crushed his mouth against hers. He pulled her pelvis toward him, rubbing his torso against her, pressing her so hard against him that she let out a muffled cry of pain.

He unzipped his fly and pulled out his erect penis. He roughly took Gabriella's right hand from around his neck and placed it on his cock. She gasped. In response, he pulled up her dress to her waist. As he had expected, she was not wearing panties. Without any preliminaries, he started fingering her cunt. She moaned as his fingers moved in and out of her. She tried to guide his pulsing cock into her, but he resisted the insistent pressure of her hand, and hot magnetism of her slick cunt.

144

Kir pulled her to the ground. Despite her costly silk dress, she offered no resistance. I'll give her what she wants, Kir thought cynically. The two of them rolled around on the ground, still masturbating each other furiously. Abruptly, Kir pulled away from Gabriella and got into a kneeling position. He unfastened his belt and his pants; they dropped to the ground. He pulled his briefs down to his knees. With his cock sticking straight out in front of him, he pulled Gabriella up from the ground by her shoulders, bringing her face to his organ. She sucked at it while he continued to finger her cunt. She threw her head back in ecstasy as she came.

"Kneel," Kir commanded her. "Get on all fours and kneel. With your ass facing me."

Gabriella did as she was told. Her dress still bunched around her waist, Gabriella got into the classic doggy position, supporting her weight on her elbows and knees, her magnificent smooth haunches bathed in moonlight. Kir gripped her firm, tight buttocks, pulling her toward him into position. The tip of Kir's cock slightly parted the crack between her buttocks. Gabriella lifted her hips higher, expectantly, to make it easier for Kir to enter her pussy. He pulled her roughly toward him and rammed his cock into her ass. She screamed, her voice lost in the dark silence all around them. Kir was in her up to the hilt, his balls hitting her buttocks as he moved in and out of her tight ass. The momentary shock and pain quickly subsided, and Gabriella found herself moving in rhythm with Kir. She enjoyed the way he was fucking her, and welcomed the touch of his fingers on her clitoris as his right hand moved to her cunt. He rubbed her clit between his thumb and forefinger, and she came furiously, Kir not missing a stroke as she did so. He rammed into her with such force as he came that she lost her balance and collapsed onto the earth, Kir on top of her.

They remained motionless for a few minutes, their heavy panting gradually returning to normal breathing. Kir rolled off of Gabriella onto his back.

"Gabriella," he said.

She propped her head up on her arms and looked up at him. "Yes?"

"I have a proposition for you. I need you for a period of approximately seven months. I can't tell you where you'll be going, or anything more about it, except that your salary will be one hundred thousand dollars; half in advance, half when your employment is completed. Of course, all your needs—accommodations, clothes, et cetera—will be provided for. What do you say, Gabriella?"

"Well, *caro*, I don't really have much choice, do I?" The salary appealed greatly to Gabriella. Only the unspecified nature of her duties disturbed her.

"No, you don't," Kir said.

"Can't you even tell me what I'm supposed to do? And what should I bring? Will I need my *pelliccia*, my fur coat?"

"You don't need to bring anything. You'll be provided with a new wardrobe. And don't worry about your duties; I assure you they'll be easy. You start next week. You must be in Paris on September 10. I'll have a first-class plane ticket, along with additional instructions, delivered to your apartment in person. Your address is Via Arno 60, Interno 5, right?" Kir knew that the address he had for Gabriella was correct, but he just wanted to emphasize to her that he had a lot of information about her.

"Yes," Gabriella said softly. The thought of what she would do with the money counteracted her fears and apprehensions.

"And one more thing. It is essential, absolutely essential, that you tell no one about this. No one. You're a clever girl, Gabriella. You can invent some story about where you're going for the next seven months. We'll even help you out, later on."

"We'll?" Gabriella asked. "Who is we?"

"My business associates," Kir said calmly. He looked at his gold watch. "Now, shall we go back to the party? The others might miss us if we don't rejoin them soon."

Gabriella stood up. She brushed the dirt off of her legs, arms, and face. She combed her hair with her fingers as best she could, and tried to smooth her rumpled, dirty, dress into shape. Kir stood up and began fastening his clothes, as he watched Gabriella try to wipe the dirt off her face. He pulled a clean handkerchief out of his pocket and wiped her cheeks with it. He gently kissed her on the nose.

"Is my face still dirty?" she asked.

"Yes," he said smiling. "It's hopeless, but you still look beautiful." He picked up her shoes and handed them to her. "Let's go," he said. Gabriella, her shoes in her hands, followed Michael Kir up the path toward the farmhouse.

The two walked in silence.

# CHAPTER NINE

Michael Kir looked out the window of the Varig 747 as it made its approach into Rio de Janeiro. It was nightfall. As the plane passed over the Bay of Rio, the landmark Sugar Loaf Mountain, *Pão de Açúcar*, was barely visible, just a dark silhouette against the ink blue sky. From the air, the city of Rio de Janeiro was an open jewel box, its jewels spilling out into the bay. Flickering lights of cruise ships and small boats anchored in Guanabara Bay were more discernible as the plane continued its descent.

Kir was not looking forward to the task ahead of him; he hated digging up old memories. Lost in thought, he stared out into the darkness until the jolt of the wheels touching down at Galeão Airport brought him back to reality.

The stewardess handed Kir his coat as he left the plane. The cold blast of air greeted him. September was the coldest month of the year in Rio and, although Kir had expected it to be chilly, especially after the heat of Rome, it came as a bit of a surprise to him.

Kir's taxi pulled up to the Nacional Hotel, a tall, sleek, circular tower situated on Gávea Beach. Kir hurriedly checked in. He could not get to his room fast enough. The hectic schedule he had been keeping this week—Houston, London, Rome, and the long flight to Rio—had left him absolutely exhausted. He followed the porter down the carpeted hallway on the nineteenth floor to his room.

Undoing his tie, Kir walked over to the frigo-bar and took out a large cold bottle of *Tatuzinho*. He opened the bottle and took a long drink of the familiar, distinctive Brazilian beer. Michael Kir visited Rio fairly often. He had a number of important clients there, and also in Sao Paulo. But this trip was business of a different nature.

Wearily, he unlocked his briefcase and began poring over his files as he drank his beer. Abruptly, he closed the dossier he was studying and locked it back in his case. It was too painful; the opening up of old wounds, ones that should have healed a long time ago. Kir had been in love just once. It had been the first time, and the last time. It was as if he had been immunized against ever getting that disease again. Yet he had never really gotten over her. Reading the file is ridiculous, Kir thought. He already knew what he needed to know about Manuela. It's better to just do it and get it over with. Forget about the old ghosts of love, he told himself sternly. There were enough other ghosts haunting his thoughts these days.

He felt weary to the bone. He needed to sleep for a couple of hours, before he called Guillermo. He lay back on his bed, falling into a fitful sleep.

Michael could hear a shrill, impatient ringing. Groggily, he rolled over and looked at his watch. It was 10:00 p.m. The ringing continued, seemingly shriller. His head was thick with sleep. He was disoriented. Which hotel room was this, in which city, on which continent? His body felt cold. Was it summer or winter? The telephone continued to ring, and the curtains billowed as the cold air rushed in from the partially opened balcony window. Shaking the cobwebs out of his head, he answered the phone.

"Hello?"

A booming voice on the other end of the line jarred Kir out of his drug-like stupor. "Michael, it's me, Guillermo! You devil, why didn't you call when you got in?"

"Guillermo, hello. I just got in a couple of hours ago. Look, I'm sorry, I fell asleep. I was just going to call you."

"That's no excuse, you can't sneak into this town, Michael Kir. News travels fast. Anyway, we were expecting you."

"Sorry, I was a zombie when I got off that flight. You know that Rome-Rio flight is murder."

"You're forgiven, this time, Michael."

"About Manuela, is it arranged?" Kir asked a bit too eagerly.

"Of course! Michael, you really are the ultimate Don Juan. From Rome to Rio is a long way to come to meet a girl. Look, I know you have business here, too, but Michael, she is just a woman." Guillermo, the world-renowned playboy, said scoldingly. "It must be love," Guillermo added sarcastically.

Kir was silent as Guillermo continued to bellow into the mouthpiece. "I have everything arranged. I'm giving a little intimate party for a hundred or so tomorrow night. She has been invited. And don't worry, she'll be there. She travels in our circle, Rio's best," Guillermo said haughtily.

"Thanks, Guillermo, I knew I could depend on you." You asshole, thought Michael to himself. He had never liked Guillermo, a pompous idiot. Michael Kir did not suffer fools gladly, but Guillermo served a purpose.

"You're right, you old devil. Everyone loves your parties. She wouldn't miss it for the world."

"Michael, tell me something, my friend, can't a handsome man like you get laid in Europe? All the way to Rio . . ." Guillermo's voice trailed off. Kir had to smile. That slob Guillermo was something else. As a film producer, Guillermo was serviced by all the eager young starlets, but, thought Kir, that pig probably even believed that the reason he got screwed so often was because he was such an irresistible stud.

*"Ciao*, Michael. I'll see you tomorrow evening, ten-thirtyish."

Michael hung up the phone. He was wide awake now. The room was icy cold. The uneasy feelings that had haunted him all day would not leave him. He could not shake the sense of foreboding that had welled up inside him. He returned to his files, glad that he had the next day to rest.

At precisely 10:30, Michael Kir pressed Guillermo Diaz's ornate brass buzzer. His handsome face reflected in the mammoth ebony door.

A butler in white threw open the doors. Kir was led through a short entrance hall into a large room, noisy and crowded with the elite of Rio. The floor of the room was shiny rainforest hardwood, reflecting the high-heeled, well-heeled Brazilian beauties displaying more luminous skin than clothing, moving their supple bodies to the throbbing Latin beat of a tuxedoed five-man band. The ceiling was low and mirrored, imbedded with fat lines of colored light, pulsating through fluorescent tubes which lay in parallel rows in a chevron pattern. The crowd was dazzling: rich, desirable, hedonistic *cariocas* at play, flashes of white teeth against perpetually tanned faces, silver-haired aquiline-nosed patrician gentlemen with their young, beautiful wives, or their old, still-beautiful wives. Walls of door-to-ceiling windows displayed

Rio at night. The lights of the city sparkled in the distance, competing with all the glitter, the prisms of multicolored light, the sequined flashes contained in the dark crowded room of Guillermo's penthouse apartment.

"Michael!" a voice boomed over the din, as a large orange silk caftan floated across the room.

"Guillermo, you old devil, a party for one hundred, like hell. All of Rio is here!"

"All of Rio that counts," replied Guillermo, kissing Michael on the cheek.

Michael scanned the room quickly.

"Don't worry, Don Juan, Guillermo has delivered the goods. Take a look around, Manuela is here somewhere, somewhere in this crowd," he said, throwing his arms wide open. "Come on, you need a drink!" Guillermo snapped his fingers at a passing waiter carrying a large tray covered with glasses of champagne and canapes. Guillermo's pudgy hand reached out for a triangle of toast thick with caviar; he wolfed it down greedily. Screwing up his fleshy face, he exclaimed, "God, this is awful! Just look at these dry beady little eggs," he said, gesticulating at the tray. "What I wouldn't give for some good Beluga fresh from the Caspian Sea! You can't buy good caviar anymore."

"I have a friend who deals in caviar—black market, of course. I'll give you his number. He'll be able to get you the best," Kir said.

"That would be a relief. I mean, I entertain so much and I absolutely refuse to buy this crap anymore," said Guillermo indignantly. A henna-haired, cantilevered starlet latched on to Guillermo's spongy arm. "Enjoy the party, Michael."

Kir made his way through the crush of people. In his navy blue suit, perfectly fitted, the sharp line of his strong shoulders tapering down to narrow hips and long legs, Kir was a darkly elegant figure that cut into a sea of vibrant colors—hot spicy reds, iridescent blues, brilliant fuchsias, shimmering gold lamé. The sleek, bronzed bodies were dramatically wrapped and revealed by shocking, sexy, outrageous fashions— clothes that defied their owners to wear them.

"Michael, darling!" Kir turned to see who had grabbed his arm. He looked down at a tanned, heavily jeweled talon clutching his sleeve. Kir instantly recognized the magnificent Burmese twelve-karat square-cut emerald on one of the woman's fingers. He knew it would be easier for him to place the owner's name by this one-of-a-kind gem, than by her face.

"Enrica!" Kir turned to her and flashed her his most devastating smile.

"Michael, *caro!* You could tell it was me by my touch! You do not forget!" she said playfully. "Dance with me, darling," said Enrica, leading her prize, who was at least ten years her junior, onto the crowded dance floor. She danced close to Kir, within a hair's breath, moving seductively to the rhythmic Santana beat, pressing her soft, voluptuous form against his hard body. Her sparkling fingers crept along the edge of his fine handkerchief-cotton shirt, sliding between the buttons, long cool fingers touching his chest, threading through the thick curling hairs.

"Really, Enrica, Antonio is dancing near by! You are a devil," Kir said, without really meaning it.

"Michael darling," she cooed in his ear, "my husband doesn't give a damn. His little hard-on is for that sweet young thing he has crushed against his fat belly." She edged her thigh between his legs, moving her body closer to him. "Tell me, darling, is yours for me?"

Enrica adored Michael, although he was the

only one in a cast of thousands that had come her way. Promiscuous was an understatement in describing Enrica's sexual bent. But this man, Michael Kir, she remembered. He was what she considered a great lover; he was a lover of women, a man who truly enjoyed women. And she wanted to be reminded of that feeling. "Michael, can I steal you away from all this?"

"Enrica, you know there is nothing that I would prefer more," he said as he pressed his lips to her glittering hand, "but tonight is unfortunately a case of business before pleasure."

"Michael, darling, you really must try to get your priorities straight," Enrica said good-naturedly. She blew him a kiss as she sauntered toward her husband. She tapped the young would-be starlet on the shoulder and cut in, leaving her husband Antonio standing in the middle of the dance floor as she danced off with the bemused starlet.

That crazy Enrica, Kir thought to himself, smiling, as he made his way through the crowd, nodding at acquaintances—old clients—still searching for Manuela.

Suddenly, he heard a deep, throaty familiar laugh. He turned to see a woman throw back her head of shiny black hair, as her finely molded shoulders shook gently. Kir knew it was her. That laugh, the mannerisms as her hands cut through the air. He knew them so well.

A series of steps separated Michael from the sunken floor where Manuela stood, holding court to a group of admirers, obviously entertaining them with some amusing story. He could only see the top of her head, so thick and tight was the cluster of men and women around her. Yet, from the way the men looked at Manuela, her story need not have been either witty or amusing to have held their attention. He knew that. Once, he too had been under her spell.

Kir descended the steps. Manuela's back was to him, exposed. The deep V of her dress displayed the long soft indentation of her spine and the supple movement of her back as her body helped to animate her story. He studied her, her sleek black dress, a stark contrast to the peacock plumage that fought for attention on every side of her.

As she switched her focus from one man to the next her profile came into Kir's view. His stomach tightened violently. What he saw made his blood run cold. He turned his eyes away.

Michael Kir was not prepared for what he had just seen. Still, it was the profile he had expected to see. He knew it like the back of his hand, perhaps better. The reconstruction of Manuela's face had been set before him in a series of medical drawings. He had seen numerous photographs of her new face, the face of Manuela. Kir had anticipated that seeing Manuela in the flesh would be difficult, but he had never imagined it would be as chilling as this.

Perhaps it was the little nuances that he had just seen, like the evocative way she talked with her slim, graceful hands, that made her so unmistakably Mitra, not this new person, Manuela. It was as if the person he knew was wearing a mask. Kir's heart beat wildly as he drained his glass. He tried to calm himself, so that he could approach her. He felt guilty, horrified to think that it had been partly his work, to change Mitra to Manuela. But that had been to save her life.

The noise level in the room was rising and the people around Manuela were laughing. She nodded her head toward them, smiled as she gave an exaggerated bow, then walked away from the group, toward the bar.

Three tall bartenders stood behind a long, gleaming brass-and-mirrored bar. Back-lit soft amber, brilliant red, and sharp-green bottles of liquor, aperitifs, and liqueurs lined the wall behind the bar. Michael Kir stood at a distance as he watched Manuela bend forward slightly as a barman lit her cigarette. She inhaled deeply. Michael waited until the bartender moved away and she was alone. He approached her from behind and, in a voice barely loud enough for her to hear, he called her by name. "Mitra."

She turned around violently, the trembling tip of her cigarette glowing red, her eyes wild. Neither one spoke—Manuela because she was staring at someone she recognized, and Michael because he was looking at someone he did not. After an endless frozen silence she gasped, "My God, Michael?" as she reached for support on the brass rail running along the bar.

Kir could not think of what to say. Haltingly, he said, "I'm sorry, Mitra, to have shocked you like this, but I feared you would not have seen me, alone." He came closer, guided her to the stool and sat next to her. He could see by her eyes that she was afraid. Facing Michael Kir, all her elaborate and painful deceptions were now stripped bare like raw nerve endings exposed to the air. His voice quavered as he spoke. "Mitra, don't be frightened. I am not here to harm you. I need your help. Please, no one else knows about your new life. No one. Please, please, don't be alarmed. Remember, it is me, Michael." Instantly Kir felt embarrassed by his last remark. Although she looked completely different to him, her eyes saw a familiar face.

"What are you doing here, Michael?" she whispered uncertainly. "How did you find me?"

"We cannot talk here. Come dance with me. This

156

way." Michael took her hand, but her body was unyielding. She had thought she was safe, that no one would ever find her. It was the first time she had heard her name, her real name, in five years. She looked up at Michael searchingly.

"Come," he said softly. His hand was on her arm, and she felt goosebumps rise on her arm. His touch was gentle but firm. He took her in his arms. The feel of his body so close to her brought back a flood of bittersweet memories. Her large black eyes took in his face. He was as devastatingly attractive as when she first laid eyes on him, over twenty years ago. Almost instinctively, without even realizing what she was doing, she reached up and touched his face, as if to assure herself that it really was Michael.

As Manuela looked into Michael's eyes, she could feel how tumultuous his emotions were at this very awkward moment. She knew that he could not reconcile that she was the girl that he had been in love with twenty years ago, in Iran. The two of them had grown up together, and one summer in Tehran, when she was fifteen and he was eighteen, they had been in love, twelve incredibly feverish months of youthful passion. But all too soon it had been time for Michael to go to college in the States. He had promised to return, that they would one day marry, but Mitra had begged him either to stay or to take her with him. Mitra had confidently told all her friends that Michael loved her so much that, even against his family's wishes, he would surely take her with him, or that he would not leave at all.

But Michael did leave, and without her. Mitra was devastated, humiliated, destroyed. Kir's public abandonment of her caused her to "lose face" before her friends, and even her family. She was now, in the eyes of her community, the proverbial seduced and abandoned young girl, no longer suitable marriage material. Mitra suffered her heartbreak and disgrace in silence, barely venturing outside her home for months after Kir's departure for the States.

It was during the terrible days of her depression that Mitra first met Parvis Gazvini, a man more than twenty years her senior, a man who was also one of the most powerful and feared men in all of Iran. With a vengeance, Mitra set out to captivate Parvis Gazvini, second in command of SAVAK, the Shah's dreaded secret police. Mitra knew that Parvis had the power to destroy anyone—including Michael Kir. But Mitra's childish, vengeful rage soon dissipated, replaced by the high life into which she was brought by Parvis. Mitra soon had all the power, position, and privilege that came with being the mistress of Parvis. She was showered with expensive gifts, people kow-towed to her —her every wish was obeyed. She appeared to have everything. She was now Tehran's golden girl.

Mitra Tabrizi came from a well-respected and wealthy family, her father was once ambassador to Portugal, and she spent much of her youth in Europe. She was a clever girl, too clever for her own good, some had said. She studied medicine in England during the first seven years of her affair with Parvis, and he had treated her like a pampered, spoiled child. Life was easy for her in London, and Parvis was happy to have a pretty, petulant plaything at his disposal during his frequent, lavishly hedonistic trips to London. The life of the starving medical student had been an experience Mitra had happily missed. Her specialization was plastic surgery, but when Parvis asked her to come back to Iran and be with him, she forsook her career and became a permanent fixture in Parvis's life. Mitra's life with him was almost too encompassing to allow for a profession, but Parvis did have a family and, when he was with his wife and his children, she needed something to take up her time.

How Mitra finally put her years of study to use came about by accident. Mitra's friends would come to her, bemoaning the fact that they had just found the perfect man—rich, inordinately rich— and the marriage had already been arranged, but there was a slight problem. This man, this enormously wealthy man, thought he was getting a virgin, and he would not be very happy if he realized that the merchandise had already been used, so what was a poor girl to do, they would ask Mitra. It had been years since the bride-to-be had been a virgin, but this catch was just too lucrative a deal to pass up. Could she please help them, they asked Mitra. After all, she was a plastic surgeon and it was a simple operation, and the famous revirginizer of Tehran's fairest maidens, Dr. Osanman was often out of town, so could she—for a friend?

Mitra, who had set up her practice in the plush Aryamehr Medical Center in north Tehran, and who had hardly set foot inside the door of her office except to check the color of the silk wallpaper, decided to help out her friends. Mitra's office was soon crowded with Tehran's upperclass blushing virgins-to-be. Ordinarily, no Persian woman of consequence would bother going to a plastic surgeon in Tehran for major plastic surgery; that, they did in the privacy of a clinic in Switzerland. But for emergencies—a rush job revirginization before a lucrative marriage— it was sometimes necessary to get a quick fix-me-up in Tehran. And Dr. Mitra Tabrizi was the one they went to. Mitra's profession gave her a sense of independence that elevated her status even more among the budding, liberated, young Iranian women she knew. Mitra was the envy of all Tehran. But she never forgot, she never forgave, and she never stopped loving Michael Kir.

It was several years until she saw Kir again. It was at Club Privé, a very private, very posh dining and dancing club, thirty kilometers outside of Tehran. Michael must have been twenty-four or twenty-five then, Manuela thought as she pressed herself closer to Michael, oblivious to the crush of people around them on Guillermo's dance floor. Clear memories of that night flooded her mind: the cool, clean night air of the desert, the endless expanse of brilliant stars overhead, the candlelit tables around the phosphorescent-blue swimming pool. Mitra was at Privé with Parvis and his entourage. Bored with the conversation between Parvis and his hangers-on, she looked away from her table and saw Michael sitting with his friends. Her heart caught in her throat. He was now more handsome than ever.

Michael Kir's reputation had preceded him back to Iran. He was from a very good family, rich, well-educated, worldly, and sophisticated—a man all her school-girlish friends were in love with. But although she could not take her eyes off Michael Kir, Mitra's hand slipped under the linen table cloth onto Parvis' knee. Michael Kir, young, handsome, and wealthy as he may have been, was no competition for a man like Parvis Gazvini. Mitra was still powerfully attracted to Michael, but she was more attracted to Parvis' own sexual aura—his power. Mitra knew she couldn't have both. She chose Parvis Gazvini. It was a mistake she lived to regret.

Mitra's life had been truly enviable until one day in 1977, when Parvis had taken her to Evin Prison.

From that day on, her life changed. It was too horrible to think about. She would not think about it, she could not.

She buried her head on Michael's shoulder. Manuela felt so safe in his arms, so secure. She could feel his strength. She could not deny her feelings. Although she had hated Michael with a passion, Mitra had never stopped loving him. As he held her gently in his arms, the sexual longing that she had felt so acutely years ago was now, once again, unbearable. It could have been so perfect, she thought. But it hadn't been. Mitra was dead, and now it was Manuela, only Manuela, who looked up at Kir. His intense green eyes, even the dark shadows beneath them, made him incredibly appealing. But it was something more than that that made Manuela want him. She remembered the touch of his hard, beautiful body, and she wanted him inside her. She wanted him now.

The Brazilian music serenaded the couples crowding the dance floor of Guillermo Diaz's penthouse apartment. Michael held Manuela close to him, his hand resting lightly against the small of her exposed back. He wondered what their lives would have been like if they could have stayed together. But Mitra Tabrizi had been a headstrong girl who had demanded all or nothing. Michael's choice had been nothing. His responsibilities to his family, and his overpowering ambition had simply been too great; he left her behind. He had tried to explain to her what he wanted out of his life, why he had acted the way he had, but she had refused to take his calls, answer his letters. But when he finally returned to Iran, Mitra was lost to him. She was the unapproachable mistress of Parvis Gazvini. Now, as Kir looked at the beautiful but unknown face, he did not know what he really saw, or what he felt. But try as he might he could not reconcile this breathtakingly beautiful woman with the girl he had loved so many years ago. He reached over to kiss her. Her warm lips touched his skin as the smell of her perfumed sweetness overwhelmed his senses. Was it Mitra or was it Manuela who kissed him so passionately?

"My love, it's been so long. I want to be with you. Alone," he murmured.

"Michael," she said so softly that her throaty voice was barely audible. It was all she could do to keep her voice from wavering. Only the fierce pounding of her heart betrayed her terror—she had been discovered.

"How did you find me?"

Her body trembled almost imperceptibly. He held her close to him.

"I'll explain everything to you when we are alone." He kissed her tenderly. "Let's go," he said, firmly taking her by the hand and leading her off the dance floor.

The liveried butler opened the hall closet, revealing fur coats of every length and description. The temperate Rio weather hardly warranted fur coats, but the one or two months a year of cool weather were reason enough for the well-heeled *cariocas* to buy luxurious furs. And Manuela Ferrara, good *carioca* by adoption that she was, was no exception.

The butler turned to Manuela. "Yours, Dr. Ferrara, is the . . .?"

"The white fox," she said pointing to the Norwegian blue-white fox jacket.

As Michael helped Manuela on with her jacket, Guillermo came rushing over. "Trying to sneak out on us, you two lovebirds, eh?"

"Well, you know how it is," Kir said, putting his arm around Manuela's waist.

"You two must have a lot of catching up to do. I

remember, Michael, that you said you hadn't seen Manuela for absolutely ages. Where was it that you saw each other last?" Guillermo asked.

"Tokyo, in '77, I think. So we do have a lot of catching up to do," Kir said. Manuela smiled and nodded, although she had never been to Tokyo. She realized that Kir must have arranged to meet her at the party, telling Guillermo some vague, concocted, long-lost lovers story that bore no relation to reality.

"Tah, tah, darlings," Guillermo said, ushering them out the door. "Have fun."

They drove to Manuela's apartment in Petropolis, an exclusive suburb of Rio, three thousand feet above the city.

The tortuous mountain road was dark. For a while they drove on in silence, Manuela behind the wheel, Kir beside her. Finally, she took a deep breath, and spoke.

"How did you find me?" she asked.

Kir placed his left arm lightly around the back of her neck. His fingertips gently stroked her velvety skin. "Manuela, let's talk about this later. Please. Let's just spend some time together, be with each other, enjoy each other first. There will be time later on tonight."

She considered his words for a moment.

"All right," she said. "But you will tell me, Michael?"

"Yes," Kir said. Manuela gave him a sidelong glance. The pressure of his fingers on her neck increased, sending shivers down her spine.

"Yes," Kir repeated.

Manuela turned left, onto a long, winding road which led up to her apartment building. She removed her right hand from the steering wheel and placed it on Kir's thigh. He lifted her hand and pressed it to his lips.

# CHAPTER TEN

The key turned silently in the last of the three locks on her front door as Manuela ushered Kir into her apartment. The door opened into a monotone of white and beige, ultramodern and stark. A bit unreal, thought Kir. A bit like Manuela herself.

"Can I get you a drink?" she asked, as she dropped her fur over the sofa.

"Please," Michael replied, watching her turn and leave the room.

Michael walked around the room. There were no framed photographs, no knickknacks, no little objects d'art brought back from vacations—nothing. Nothing but large, dramatically lit canvases, slashes of vibrant color relieving the pristine sterility of the room. The apartment gave no hint about the person who lived there, thought Kir, as he leafed through a magazine, oblivious to the fact that she had re-entered the room.

"Michael."

He turned, expecting to see someone else— Mitra. But, no, it was Manuela. Of Mitra, only the beautiful voice remained.

"Michael, are you all right? You look like you've seen a ghost," Manuela said, half-jokingly. "Well, I guess you have," she added. "Come, sit down, and let's have a drink."

She motioned for him to sit beside her on the couch.

They sat on the long, white couch, not knowing

quite what to say to each other. Manuela could feel Michael's uneasiness; she understood. He was the first person who, having known her as Mitra, was now faced with the shock of Manuela. She hoped he would be the only one. She, herself, had gotten over the change from Mitra to Manuela long ago. She was a doctor, and thought of the metamorphosis quite clinically. Her new face was beautiful, more beautiful than she'd been before, and she liked it. She had no choice.

She bent forward and opened a small silver box on the glass table and hurriedly pulled out a cigarette. Kir reached for the enameled lighter next to the cigarette box. The flickering light caught the smooth planes of her face and the flame was reflected in her dark eyes. Their eyes did not move from each other's gaze.

"Come," she whispered.

The bedroom was dimly-lit and exotic, like a lair in the heart of the jungle, with its lush greens and rich shades of brown. A thick carpet covered the floor and, against one wall, on a raised platform, was a large bed covered with numerous Rousseau-jungle print pillows. A wall of mirrors covered the length of the opposite wall.

Manuela stood in front of Kir. She helped him off with his jacket. Slowly, she undid his dark silk tie. Then, taking his hand, she undid the button on his right shirt sleeve, then the left. Her hands moved across his chest, reaching the center, and ever so slowly she undid the buttons of his shirt. She pushed the shirt away from his chest and ran a long blood-red enameled fingertip very gingerly up his rib-cage, up to his hard brown nipple. Her other hand moved along his smooth, well-muscled back. She turned her eyes, flashing in the half-dark room, to him.

165

Kir felt an uneasy yet strong desire in his heart for a Mitra that no longer existed, but the lustful urge that was coursing through his veins was for the magnificent Manuela before him.

Manuela kissed him gently and lingeringly. She ran her finger along his jawline, and in a low, velvety voice said, "Relax, Michael, my love, and I'll do the rest." Then, like a geisha, she undressed him, removing his clothes, piece by piece, over what seemed like an eternity.

He lay back on the cool bed. In the half-light, Manuela faced him. Slowly, she pushed the thin straps of the black dress off her shoulders. It slid off her like honey off a spoon. Her naked body was narrow and lithe, her skin smooth and luminous, highlighted by the long line of her collarbone, the glow of her rounded full breasts, the narrow line of indentation that ran down the center of her gracefully muscled stomach to the shadowed triangle between her long legs. She knelt at the edge of the bed. Her hand moved up his thigh toward his pelvic bone. Her lips pressed against the inside of his knee and continued up the inside muscle of his leg. The feel of her hot, feathery breath, her soft lips, and the sensation of her cool fingers exploring his body made Michael's skin shiver in waves.

His penis was throbbing. Engorged and erect, it ached for her touch. Kir bent his torso forward slightly, his hands straining to caress her thick, luxuriant hair, but Manuela firmly but gently pushed him back on the cool, soft pillows.

Slowly, she raised her head upwards. Her warm, wet tongue brushed against his balls, the pressure of her tongue increasing as it moved up the back of the shaft of his hard, aching penis. Her soft mouth enveloped it. Her smooth red lips tightened, encircling his cock, moving up and down its full length, her bare shoulders rising and falling rhythmically.

Michael held her hair behind her neck, caressing the nape with his fingers. His body was moving against hers, the pressure building up inside him. Her hands teasingly stroked his balls. Manuela slid her mouth off his penis until only her tongue moved in circles around its head, her heavy breath cooling the wet, burning skin.

Kir moaned as Manuela moved her mouth over his bursting organ, moving up and down its taut length. Her tongue pressed firmly against the back of the shaft, heightening the tension, the pain, and the pleasure until he could stand it no more. One hand cupped his balls, while her other hand pressed against his hard, muscular stomach that contracted convulsively as he came inside her hot, wet mouth.

She kept his momentarily *fatigué* penis inside her mouth, flicking her tongue around it, sending shudders through Michael's body. Manuela lifted her head. Her supple body moved lightly along the length of his supine form until her head was at his shoulder. She kept the weight of her body on her elbows and knees as she rocked back and forth. Only their glistening skin touched; Manuela's breasts rested against his chest, her softly rounded stomach touched his hard, flat torso, her smooth legs entwined in his.

Michael admired her. She sat up, straddling him, pulling back her hair off her damp face. She was superb. In the *chiaroscuro* light her body gave off an aura of innate sexuality. He pulled her down to him, kissing her fragrant hair, her face, her open mouth. His hand moved along the space between his body and hers, cupping her breast in his hand. Manuela could feel his penis growing, lengthening, pressing against her. Her rose-petal lips were damp, and at the heart of the flower she felt a congested, hot aching. With a touch as light as a breeze, her mouth moved over his chest, brushing against his hard small nipples, as her other hand moved down his body to his tumescent penis. Manuela rubbed her body against it, languidly like a cat's sensual rubbings against the hard leg of a chair. Slowly, she began to open herself to him. Then, half-impaled, she brought herself upright and, with her hands behind her, pushed him deeper inside her.

He watched her body, glowing in the light. Her spine arched backwards, her stomach convex, her head thrown back, her lips parted, her breasts jutting outwards. Manuela's graceful body undulated before his eyes, her erotic moans increasing in intensity as she rocked harder, faster. He felt her body shudder as she let out a gasping cry. She bent toward him, her lips passionately crushed against his mouth. Her tongue voraciously explored his mouth, while the inside of her hot sex pulsed against his throbbing penis. Michael held her tighter, moving his powerful body against her. He moved with increasing urgency, their bodies in perfect synchronization. Their sensations climbed toward a crescendo. Waves of pleasure overwhelmed everything. With violent cries, they reached orgasm together.

"*Janam*, my love, *janedelam*, love of my soul," he murmured, his voice cracked.

"*Janedelam*, *azizam*, my dearest," Manuela answered.

As Manuela lay in Kir's arms, she was shocked at how effortlessly those words of Farsi had come out of her mouth. She had not spoken one word of Farsi in five years; she had vowed that she never would, from the day she became Manuela Ferrara.

Six years ago, her entire life had changed. Until then, as Dr. Mitra Tabrizi, she had led a happy, carefree, and privileged life in Iran. She was rich, had a medical practice, and, most importantly, was the mistress of Parvis Gazvini, the number-two man in SAVAK. Then, one early summer's day in 1977, Parvis asked Mitra to accompany him to Evin Prison, the notorious prison in north Tehran where thousands of SAVAK's political prisoners were kept locked away in underground cells.

By 1977, SAVAK's reputation for torture, terror and brutality had made it infamous around the world. A group of observers from the Red Cross and Amnesty International were planning to investigate the allegations of torture within the walls of Evin Prison. The two groups had specified certain prisoners that they would want to see during the investigation of the conditions of the prisoners held in Evin Prison. Parvis needed someone he could trust to perform the plastic surgery on the prisoners. Who better than his devoted young mistress, who just happened to be a doctor?

But the day Mitra went to Evin Prison changed her life. Manuela trembled in the warmth of her bed, recalling the haunting memory of a day years ago.

She could never forget that day when Parvis Gazvini took her with him to Evin Prison. At times the memory seemed clear and vivid, as if it had only just happened, while at other times it seemed much farther back in time than six years. It was a hot day in early June 1977. Parvis had offered her no explanation when he asked her to go to Evin with him. Mitra's curiosity was whetted, for Evin Prison was notorious as the SAVAK prison, where most of Tehran's political prisoners were kept. SAVAK's worst torture chambers were rumored to be in Evin. In the air-conditioned Mercedes, on the way to Evin, Mitra bluntly asked Parvis, "What really goes on at Evin?"

"We'll be there soon," he said, patting her hand.

What Mitra saw that day altered the course of her life. Beneath Evin Prison, three floors underground, accessible only by secret elevators, was a maze of cells, rooms, and torture chambers. The low-ceilinged, cramped, stone cells and the hideous instruments of torture seemed medieval, only worse. In the "interrogation" rooms, prisoners were suspended by chains from the ceiling upside down, beaten and kicked while hanging, and broken bottles shoved up the prisoner's anus. There were special metal devices for pulling out fingernails, and multithonged whips. The rooms were damp, from being constantly hosed down to wash away the blood and bits of flesh. In other rooms were the infamous "hot beds," narrow metal racks where a prisoner would be strapped down, spread-eagled, and fires lit beneath him. There were chairs a prisoner would be chained to, while electric shocks, increasing in intensity, were applied to the testicles and penis. For female prisoners, the shocks were applied to the breasts, before they would be mutilated. Prisoners' bones were broken and left unset; wounds from beatings, lacerations, and burns left to fester.

After being led through this chamber of horrors, Mitra was taken to a small, brightly lit cell. In the cell were several prisoners, all horribly mutilated and deformed, the obvious results of torture. One man's face was so severely scarred that Mitra winced just looking at it. The entire left side of his face was misshapen and scarred, and he was blind in one eye. Another prisoner had huge patches of red scar tissue covering his back and buttocks, the result of burns. One young man, who could have been no more than thirty, had a twisted, immobilized appendage for a right arm; a round, open wound on his collarbone still oozed pus. Hideous welts and fresh scars covered the spine of a man who could not walk; Mitra noticed that the nail-less stubs of his fingertips curled inwards. A teen-aged girl grimaced continually, her teeth permanently exposed by jagged remains of her lower lip. Yet, shocked as she was by the sight of the prisoners, what horrified Mitra the most was the fact that they did not speak, or even seem interested or capable of doing so any longer. SAVAK had succeeded in crushing and dehumanizing the prisoners. Mitra felt a searing pain in her chest and throat as she looked at the pathetic human beings before her.

"Well," Parvis Gazvini said. "Can you fix them up?"

"What do you mean," Mitra said, not quite comprehending what was being asked of her.

"Can you repair their faces, their hands, the scars on their backs, their legs? Can you make them look like normal human beings again?"

"Why? What? I don't understand."

Parvis came over to Mitra and took her hand in his, as if they were alone, and not in Evin Prison, underground, with a group of prisoners and guards around them.

"Mitra," Parvis said, "can you disguise the fact that these prisoners were tortured? An international human rights inspection committee has the names of these prisoners. When they visit this prison they will want to see these prisoners—alive."

Parvis's touch made Mitra's blood run cold. Panic and confusion gripped her, and she knew that Parvis sensed her fear.

"These prisoners," Parvis said, nonchalantly looking around the room, "what happened to them, it was a mistake. Some overzealous guard just trying to do his job." Manuela nodded, pretending to believe him. She knew what she would do, she knew what she had to do. But that would be later, the next day, or the day after. Now she had to get out of Evin Prison, without letting Parvis know how she felt, without letting him fathom the horror and revulsion which filled her.

"Parvis, I'll need a few days to arrange things. But, please, let's go now," Mitra said.

She had seen, for the first time, the horrors committed by SAVAK. But even more horrifying to Mitra was her own involvement, for eleven years, with Parvis Gazvini, a man who, Mitra now realized, knew about the torture, allowed it, and condoned these crimes against humanity.

Mitra realized she could no longer be a part of, nor support, a system that perpetrated torture. Mitra did not do what Parvis asked of her. Only a few days after her trip to Evin Prison, plagued by conscience, Mitra left Iran, ending not only her life there, but her life as Mitra.

She covertly left Iran, went to Amnesty International in London, and divulged all she knew about SAVAK, telling everything she had seen and heard. Her statement created such an international scandal that the Shah jailed—only temporarily —Parvis Gazvini. Mitra knew that she would never be safe again, for Parvis now hated her with as much passion as he had once loved her. He swore to track her down, and extract revenge. Mitra, with the help of Amnesty International, faked her own death, and then assumed a new identity. This way, Mitra's family, too, would be safe from Parvis's revenge.

No one knew that Mitra was still alive, that she lived in Rio. Even her family thought she had died, five years ago, in a boating accident off the southern coast of France, near Cannes.

Mitra's family was her one link to her former life that still caused her pain. She knew that they mourned her, that her supposed death permanently blighted their lives. Mitra's only consolation was that they were not in any danger. Like most Iranians, Mitra was closely bound to her family. Most of her family—her parents, her maternal grandmother, her two brothers—had been living in France for years before Mitra turned against Parvis Gazvini and SAVAK. In 1977, when Mitra decided to leave Iran, only a few aunts, uncles, and cousins remained in Iran, and these relations were too far removed from Mitra for even the notorious SAVAK to retaliate against.

But even outside Iran, Mitra knew, Parvis and SAVAK could seek revenge and strike at her family in Cannes. Living outside of Iran was little protection against SAVAK's vengeance. Hundreds of Iranians, perhaps more, in England, France, West Germany, and the U.S., had been murdered by SAVAK. Mitra knew that Parvis Gazvini would not hesitate to murder her family—as a means of striking against her—before he tracked her down and killed her, too. But Mitra knew that if she were dead, or if Parvis Gazvini thought she was, he would not harm her family. Her death would wipe the slate clean. Her family would live in mourning and sorrow, but they would be safe.

When Mitra Tabrizi died, Manuela Ferrara was born. Amnesty International had arranged everything for her; the surgery, the documents, and her new country. Once Mitra had assumed her new identity, once she had become another person, her face completely changed, she longed to see her family, especially her mother. But she could never go back—she dared not—knowing that Parvis still had the family home near Cannes watched. Although Parvis appeared to have accepted the story of Mitra's death, he would take no chances. Parvis's agents watched the Tabrizi family, just in case Mitra should one day rise from the grave and want to contact her family. Mitra was sentenced to a life alone. Even when the Revolution toppled the Shah's government and many of the high-ranking SAVAK officials were executed, Mitra was not given a reprieve. Parvis Gazvini escaped to Paris and had cunningly managed to elude the Revolutionary death squads that had hunted him. Through Amnesty International, Manuela knew that Parvis was said to be in South Africa. But Manuela knew that as long as Parvis Gazvini was alive, Mitra must remain dead. She knew that Parvis would continue to have old SAVAK agents keep her family under surveillance. Mitra knew that this was easy for Parvis to do, as he had enough money in Swiss bank accounts to outfit a small army.

Parvis greatly missed not having been able to extract revenge on Mitra himself. Had he been able to, Parvis Gazvini would have killed her with his bare hands. Mitra was sure that Parvis had not forgotten her and what she had done to him, nor, she was sure, would he ever. But as Manuela Ferrara, she did not feel particularly threatened. Parvis was on the other side of the globe and, besides, her tracks were well-covered. Mitra had had such extensive plastic surgery performed on her face and body that no one would ever have recognized her as Mitra. Her new identity was backed up by all the proper identification. She became Manuela Ferrara, and for the past five years she had lived in Rio as Manuela Ferrara, an emigre from Portugal and a successful, affluent plastic surgeon. Her new life had taken on a semblance of normality, but Manuela guarded herself against close friendships. Instead, she cultivated a large number of acquaintances, but never let anyone get too close. Her life was a deception, a story that she lived as if she truly believed it.

And now, after all this time, she had so easily spoken words of love in Farsi, almost as if the last five years had never happened. The naturalness with which the sweet Farsi words had flowed from her mouth disturbed her. She tried to brush it off, rationalizing to herself that being with Michael Kir again had brought the Farsi words out of her. But still, it disturbed her, because she always kept herself under tight control. As with everything in her life, with sex, Manuela could feel the sensations, but no emotions. The trials of her life had erased them. Her emotions had dissolved with the scars—or so she had thought. But now, Michael was back in her life, making her vulnerable again.

Mitra could feel Michael's warm even breath on her neck as they lay beside each other, his body lean, hard, and strong.

"Can we talk?" Michael asked her, finally breaking the silence.

But it was not easy to talk. Neither one knew where to start, what to say. They could not, rather, she *would not*, talk about old acquaintances. For Manuela, her past life was a book that was closed forever. She skirted his questions that referred to Mitra, answering only as Manuela. She talked as if her life in Iran, as Mitra, had never existed.

Manuela pressed Michael about himself—his life, his business, his travels. Kir tried to bring the conversation back to her, to explain to her what he wanted of her. He would have preferred doing so without delving into her locked past, but it was the past that was the key to Mitra's helping him. It seemed as if she had locked the doors to that life and had thrown away the key.

There was a strange tension between them. A number of forces were fighting each other. There were two competing levels of intimacy: familiarity, as lovers twenty years ago, and new lovers, of just thirty minutes ago. Michael was trying to continue where they had left off those many years ago, and Manuela was fighting to start things anew.

"Please, Mitra, we must talk," Michael said. "We must talk about what happened to you in Iran, about SAVAK, about Parvis . . ."

"I beg you," she pleaded. "Michael, please understand. I cannot. It is over. And please, do not call me Mitra. I am Manuela Ferrara. What do I care about some man named Parvis Gazvini? And what could he care about me? To me, neither Mitra nor Parvis exists."

"But, Parvis does exist and he is alive," Kir said. "He is here, in South America." Michael watched as Manuela's eyes widened in terror.

"Where?"

"Parvis is in Paraguay. My sources say he is hiding out with Tabeti, some of the Pahlavi family, and the usual assortment of old Nazis." Manuela's face was white. Kir reached out his hand to comfort her.

"Manuela, your secret is safe with me. No one else knows about you. Or your whereabouts. And there is no way Parvis will ever find out about you."

Manuela abruptly turned away from him. She sat up in bed, turning her back to him.

Michael could hear the tearing of cellophane as Manuela opened a package of cigarettes. She got out of the bed, and paced back and forth as she smoked her cigarette. She stubbed her cigarette out; naked, she turned to face Kir.

"Let's just forget the whole thing. I want to hear

no more about these demons from my past."

Kir could see that the conversation was effectively ended. The hint of hysteria in Manuela's voice made that clear to him. Looking up at her he said, "All right, Manuela, we won't talk about it anymore."

She sat herself down on the edge of the bed. She pressed her lips to the back of Michael's head in a gesture of truce. Suddenly, she rose, wrapped a red silk kimono around herself, lit another cigarette and walked toward the window.

Manuela, her back to Kir, stood at the window. She stared out into the black night, her arms wrapped tightly around herself.

Michael went over to her and put his arms loosely around her neck. He wanted to comfort her, but Manuela wanted no comfort from him. She was used to taking care of herself. She had left her friends and family behind, and had been forced to bear all her burdens alone, for five years. That was how she preferred it—alone. Alone she shared no secrets, alone no questions were asked, alone she had become Manuela. And now Michael Kir had discovered her, and Parvis was near. A sense of panic overwhelmed her. It was as if a hole had been blasted through the fortress she had built around herself. She felt that Michael would never expose her, but the thought that after all the elaborate and painful deceptions she had gone through to become Manuela Ferrara, Michael Kir had been able to find her, terrified her. If Michael could find her, then a cunning man like Parvis could, too.

She looked at Michael's handsome face, and wondered what was behind those green eyes. "Michael, how did you find me?" she asked.

"I never lost track of you. I've been in contact with Amnesty International from the beginning of your involvement with them, ever since you informed on SAVAK, back in 1977. I've kept close tabs on what was happening to you."

"How is that possible? Amnesty International would never allow you access to that kind of information. Michael, what is your connection with Amnesty? Tell me!" she demanded.

"I gave Amnesty International the money for your plastic surgery," he replied quietly.

"Why?"

"How could I not, after what had been between us? Besides, I knew what kind of man Parvis was. I had to make sure that you would have the best, that you would be safe. I never lost track of you."

Manuela was silent as she tried to fit all the pieces together. Manuela thought back to those long months of convalescence after her surgery in Switzerland. Everything seemed to fall so easily into place for her new identity: documents and professional and social leads for her life as Manuela Ferrara had been arranged for her while she waited in a secluded home outside of Geneva, like a caterpillar awaiting the right moment to emerge from its chrysalis as a butterfly, to be born again. She had had the best medical care and had wanted for nothing during her months of recovery. Now, as Manuela looked at Michael Kir, things seemed to fall into place.

"Thank you, Michael," she said.

He took her hand. "Come to bed, Manuela. It's late."

She pulled away from him. "In a moment," she said. Kir walked toward the bed.

Manuela trembled in the darkness. She could not shake the image of Parvis from her mind. She tried to be rational, to tell herself that she was as safe as she'd been during the past five years. Parvis's presence in Paraguay didn't mean he was

178

planning to surface. Probably, it was simply that Paraguay, with its long history of sheltering internationally wanted criminals, was a safer haven than South Africa. Parvis' move had nothing to do with her, she told herself, but fear still gripped her soul. Mitra had never been truly able to leave Evin Prison completely. The horror of those wretched prisoners and the soullessness reflected in the eyes of Parvis were visions which haunted Manuela. An involuntary shudder wracked her body.

Michael took her gently in his arms, stroking her hair. His reassuring presence pushed her thoughts of Parvis and Evin Prison away. In Michael's comforting arms, Manuela felt as if she had found a safe haven, but an unsettling question still clouded her mind. She was glad that Michael was in Rio, but she wondered what he was doing in Rio, why he had come to fnd her—now, after so many years.

Manuela looked into Michael's eyes. "Michael, why are you here in Rio?"

"I came for you," he replied.

She looked at him searchingly.

Kir took her hand in his. "Manuela, I need you for a period of seven months, starting next week. I'm working on a special business arrangement, and I need your help. I can't tell you anything more about it. Except, of course, that you'll be safe. You'll be paid one hundred thousand dollars and also . . ."

"You know I don't care about money," Manuela said angrily.

"You'll need to be in Paris by Wednesday, at the latest. That should give you enough time to close your office, settle your professional affairs. Naturally, I'll provide assistance for taking care of these matters, and provide the necessary cover

179

story to explain your absence. Can I count on you, Manuela? I need you."

Manuela looked at him, seeing both the Michael Kir of twenty years before, and the one who faced her. It was difficult for her to distinguish between the two. One she had loved, the other she had just made love to. Kir took her hand in his. She knew she owed him something. He was the one who had helped her escape Parvis' death warrant, and now she knew she must help him. But she would not do it unconditionally, there was something that Manuela wanted from Michael as well.

After several minutes of silence, Manuela spoke, "Yes, Michael. I'll do it. But there is one condition. You must promise me something."

"What is it, Manuela?" he said.

Manuela bent forward, and whispered in his ear. Kir leaned back and stared at her, as if seeing her for the first time. He nodded his head.

"Yes, I promise," Kir said, reaching for her body.

The first rays of the morning sun were lighting up the sky as Kir and Manuela drifted off into sleep.

# CHAPTER ELEVEN

As Victoria Graham stepped out of the black Citroen on Rue de Faubourg-St. Honore, in front of the gold and white House of Dior awning, she looked upward at the gray clouds enveloping the Parisian sky. The air was still and close. It looked like rain.

It was September 16, and Victoria had been in Paris all week. Since her arrival, she had been escorted, followed, and generally hounded by Gino, some lacky of Kir's or, as Gino put it, a "personal assistant to Mr. Kir." Victoria had hoped that, once in Paris, the mystery assignment Kir had hired her for would be made less mysterious. Victoria had expected to see Kir in Paris. She wanted to talk with him, to ask him some questions that had been left unanswered during their one and only meeting, that day in London less than two weeks ago. Gino had refused (albeit politely) to answer any of her questions, so Victoria had resigned herself to doing the rounds of the Paris shops and salons, as per her appointment book.

"What time does the plane leave tonight?" Victoria asked Gino, who had been standing attentively by her side as she scanned the sky.

"Midnight."

Victoria quickly mentally reviewed all the appointments that had been scheduled for her today, all the last minute details to attend to before she set off on her mystery assignment with Michael Kir tonight. Well, she thought, that's what Gino is for, to help me out. Victoria glanced at the short, curly-haired man beside her.

"Gino," she said, placing her hand on Gino's shoulder, a shoulder considerably lower than her own. "I'll be here at Dior for about an hour. That should give you enough time to pick up my purchases at Hermes and Mark Cross. And could you stop in at a *parfumerie* and get some Orlane sunscreen?"

"Will do, Victoria," Gino said as he smiled up at her. He opened the door to the couture house for her, then turned and got back into the Citroen, directing, in thickly accented French, the chauffeur to Hermes. The beak-nosed chauffeur curled his lip in disdain and drove off.

Victoria entered the elegant cream and gold Dior salon. A uniformed attendant took her light cashmere sweater. Madame Claudette, the Dior head *essayeuse*, was impatiently waiting for her.

"Right this way, Miss Graham," Madame Claudette said. Victoria followed behind the bird-like figure in black to the dressing room. Victoria did not relish the thought of what lay ahead; standing on her feet for what seemed like hours, while Madame Claudette pinned and poked.

"This should fit *à merveille*," stated Madame Claudette proudly as she found a hole in the masses of rustling blue moire-taffeta and slipped it over Victoria's head. Victoria stood perfectly still as the fitter scrambled around her, making last minute adjustments on the elegant taffeta dress.

"Ouch!"

*"Pardon, Mademoiselle Graham."*

"Please, hurry it up," ordered Victoria, annoyed

182

at the tedious task at hand. Then, smiling to herself, Victoria thought of how most women would die to have St. Laurent, Lagerfeld, or Givenchy personally design their wardrobes, telling them they looked divine, that this dress or that had been made just for them. To have a *carte blanche* at Cartier, picking out gold and enamel jewelry, gold-mesh evening bags and suede clutches. To buy silk blouses and scarves at Lanvin, fantastic sweaters from Sonia Rykiel, hand-tooled Hermes luggage, Missoni dresses, elegant Andre Laug evening dresses, outrageous Maud Frizon shoes, *sportif* Claude Montana clothes, and Gianni Versace *alta moda*. Or to have makeup artists and hairdressers at Carita and Alexandre fuss over them. Well, thought Victoria, I guess I would love it too, if it wasn't for that nagging fear that I'm being plucked and dressed, only to end up in the roasting pan. The fitter's cold dry hands startled Victoria. Madame Claudette, her mouth full of pins, unzipped the dress and motioned to Victoria to step out of it. Victoria dutifully obeyed her, as she watched an assistant bring in a rainbow silk chiffon that she knew had to be tried on once again.

"I think we have got that little problem fixed with this marvelous gown," said Madame Claudette triumphantly. Victoria sighed as she lifted up her arms, while the fitter and the assistant maneuvered the narrow waistband over Victoria's breasts. Victoria cursed the fashions for 1983, especially Dior's tight-fitting "Return-to-Romance" styles. With her body finally poured into the tight-bodiced dress, Victoria looked at her watch; it was 11:30 a.m.

"I hope to be out of here by noon," Victoria said coldly.

Madame Claudette nodded perfunctorily, as her

attention focused on the magnificent dress, not the beautiful woman inside it.

Gérome, the *premier* hairdresser at Carita, looked at his watch; it was eleven-thirty. She was a half-hour late. He'd done her hair a few days ago, and that trollop had been late then, too, but not this late. "Where is that Roman *puttana?*" Gérome hissed, as he continued to chainsmoke his Gauloises.

*"Ciao, caro!"* Gabriella rushed into the salon. *"Mi scusi, caro,"* she said to Gérome as she flashed him a brilliant smile. "Mark and I were at Gianni Versace's Boutique, and I was so busy shopping that I didn't notice the time."

Gérome bitchily eyed the tall, lanky American with Gabriella. So, this is what has happened to gigolos, Gérome thought. Obviously, the distinctive écru gabardine jacket and the double-pleated taupe linen pants that the towering, square-jawed American was wearing were from Versace. And the way that Gabriella ordered everyone around, it was obvious that she was running the show. Gérome drummed his fingers on the sharp pelvis bones of his narrow hips as he waited impatiently for Gabriella to get into the chair.

"You will forgive me, won't you, darling?" she asked sweetly, patting Gérome on the hand.

Gérome swiveled Gabriella around in the chair and began brushing her long, chestnut hair.

"Gérome, darling, I need a henna rinse."

*"Chérie,* no you don't," Gérome said flatly, exercising his prerogative for having the final word on hair. After all, he was the expert.

"Mark, come here," Gabriella ordered. She motioned with her arm to Mark Rowan, who was standing in the least conspicuous corner, uncomfortable in his itchy new clothes, and doubly so in the close, perfumed environ of a woman's beauty salon.

"Come, talk to me," she coaxed, as Mark cautiously approached the chair.

"Gabriella," Mark asked, "how long will it take to get your hair done?"

"It is not just my hair, Mark," Gabriella replied. "I want a manicure, pedicure, and a facial, and, Gérome, I want that new treatment, *manteau de paraffine.*"

"What is that?" Mark asked.

"That is when they wrap your body in warm paraffin wax. It is absolutely marvelous for your skin," Gabriella said.

"How long will all this take, Gabriella? Remember we have a plane to catch tonight," Mark chided her.

"Perhaps four hours," Gérome replied.

Gabriella took Mark's hand. "Gérome, what kind of haircut should we give Mark? He needs something new, don't you agree?"

Gérome looked up from Gabriella's long head of hair that he was combing and looked at Mark's blushing face and thick, blond, unruly hair.

"Definitely," Gérome said drily.

Mark started to back away from the chair. "Look, Gabriella, I've got to run. I've got a million errands to do. I'll be back in three hours, is that O.K., Gabriella?" Gabriella nodded. "Well, see you in a little while then. Nice meeting you, Gérome," Mark said as he hurried out the door.

The wooden floor creaked as Manuela made her way along the narrow rows jammed with books in the *Librairie anglaise*, the English Bookstore, a small centuries-old shop tucked away behind the Champs Elysees. A tall, blond, curly-haired man, his arms laden with books, followed close behind her. Manuela handed Andreas another book. He scrutinized the title, then piled it on top of the rest. He gave a disdainful look, and pushed his black glasses up on his nose. Manuela caught his look of disapproval.

"What's wrong, Andreas?" she asked, picking up the heavy medical tome. "Have you read this? Isn't *New Trends in Rhinoplasty* any good?" she asked jokingly.

"Well, no, not exactly. It is just that, well, how should I say . . ." Andreas continued to search for a polite way to say to Manuela that her reading material was boring. "It's just that all your books are the same. You need a little variety in your reading matter."

"Perhaps you are right, Andreas. It was just that I thought your insistence that I buy a lot of reading material before we leave Paris tonight would be a perfect opportunity for me to catch up on my journals and textbooks."

"That's a good idea, but still, you should have some light reading."

"All right, Andreas, help choose some books for me," Manuela said. "What do you suggest?"

"Follow me," said Andreas as he walked to the front display area of the bookstore.

Manuela smiled, thinking of the past four days in Paris. She had thoroughly enjoyed herself. Once back in Europe, she was reminded of just how behind the times things were in South America; fashions, hairstyles, everything was a few years out of date. It was great to be back in Paris, and she had been treated to the latest designer clothes, makeup, films, books—everything she wanted. It reminded her of the days when she and her girlfriends would fly from Tehran to Paris for a couple of weeks, on a shopping trip. What fun they had had! How they had squandered money foolishly, had quick affairs, had champagne breakfasts after nights at Crazy Horse and Regine's. After the close scrutiny of Tehran society it had been great fun to go wild in Paris and the south of France every once in awhile. Those days were gone, but still, even with the constant chaperon that Michael had provided for her, she felt freer here than she did in Brazil.

Manuela knew that her enthusiasm for Paris was partially because she was so glad to be away from Rio de Janeiro. After Michael had left, during those last few hectic days when she was closing up her office and referring her patients to Dr. Gomez, she was constantly looking over her shoulder. The news that Parvis was living in Paraguay had completely unnerved her. Even if Michael had not asked her to leave, she probably would have begged him to take her away from Brazil. She tried not to think of what the future held in store for her. Andreas had told her that tonight they would be leaving Paris for somewhere else. Being on the move felt good. Manuela felt elusive and she liked it. And Andreas was very protective of her; he clucked over her like a mother hen. Michael Kir had selected a very agreeable chaperon, or "personal assistant," as Andreas referred to himself. Andreas was tall and handsome and, just as he had promised her in his cavalier way when he had met her at Charles de Gaulle Airport, her every wish was his command. He had arranged all her fittings, her beauty appointments, had made sure she had enough clothes, the right clothes. They dined together every night at the best restaurants in Paris: Maxim's, La Tour d'Argent, or Fouquet's. He was with her constantly, except at night when he would retire to his room adjoining her suite. He was a perfect gentleman.

"Manuela!" Andreas called to her. "I've found

some interesting books for you," he said, carrying a stack of books in his arms.

"Andreas, what is this?" Manuela asked as she lifted up a heavy, glossy hardcover book.

"*Esperanto Made Simple?*" Manuela said, laughing. They really did have different interests. Yet, to her, Andreas was a fascinating man. He was an adventurer, an insatiable traveler, and a bit of a dilettante. He had taken a degree in chemical engineering from the University of Zurich; then he did an about-face and completed the course of study at the most prestigious hotel management school in Switzerland. In addition, he was an accomplished photographer. With his expertise in these three very different fields, Andreas von Elfensleben began traveling the world. In Iran, he had opened up a number of exclusive restaurants at various casinos throughout the country. In Kenya, he had been a wildlife photographer. He had been *maitre d'* at the Peninsula Hotel in Hong Kong, and head chef at the Jasper Lodge in Canada. Andreas traveled the world with a backpack and a Louis Vuitton suitcase. When he planned to do some exploring in the Himalayas he would check his suitcase somewhere, and go off for a month or two roaming through Nepal, Kashmir, and other lofty environs. Arriving back in civilization, he would pick up his Louis Vuitton suitcase which contained his tuxedo, dinner jacket, and expensive suits, and head for a job at the palace of an emir of an oil-rich sheikhdom or at a luxury resort in any of the far corners of the world. He was the quintessential traveler, although he joked with Manuela that he was just an "international hobo." Manuela wondered what Andreas's connection was with Michael. Andreas's explanation was that this was the perfect job for him—a beautiful woman, an undisclosed destination, and an unlimited expense account.

But whatever they were about to embark upon, Andreas knew more about it than she did—Manuela was certain of that. She had questioned Andreas in every possible way, she had tested him thoroughly. But he gave away no secrets. He was a man Michael could trust. Manuela admired that.

When Manuela and Andreas had met for breakfast with Michael this morning, in Michael's suite, both men had been very businesslike—employer and employee. Manuela had been a bit annoyed because that had been the first time she had seen Michael since arriving in Paris. She hadn't had a chance to see him alone, even for a few minutes after breakfast, but Andreas had explained to her that Michael had a million loose ends to tie up before they left tonight. That may have explained Michael's rather remote attitude at breakfast, Manuela thought.

"Manuela," Andreas's voice interrupted her thoughts. "Would you like anything else?"

"No, I've selected all the books I want."

Andreas stood at the cash register, waiting as the clerk added up the bill. Manuela wondered where she would be going with all those books. By tomorrow this time, I'll know, she thought.


It was 9:15 p.m. Michael Kir sat in the small bar off the lobby of the Ritz, the most ostentatiously smart hotel in the world. The Ritz, with a staff of four hundred to serve a maximum of two hundred and fifty guests, was a place where, in the humdrum world of chain hotels, a guest was still treated as a guest, an honored guest.

Kir's eyes took in the dark, understated elegance of the bar: the deep rich paneling, the bordeaux leather chairs. Small yellow-shaded lamps on the round tables provided the intimately muted light. Kir took a sip of his vodka and lime and leaned back in his seat, reveling in the brief moments of solitary relaxation. He motioned the waiter over to his table and ordered a scotch for Gino, who would be arriving at any moment. Kir smiled to himself as he thought of short, dark Gino escorting the tall, blond Victoria around Paris. Gino must have been in his glory, thought Kir.

Gino Barakat was Iranian. His real name was Homayoun Barakat, but during his years at the University of California at Berkeley, he had started calling himself Gino. He was short, with dark brown eyes and hair, and a full moustache. With his dark, pleasant looks, many American girls had thought he was Italian. So, Homayoun renamed himself Gino—he found he got more girls that way. Gino was a distant cousin of Michael Kir's, related on Kir's father's side. Gino had come from a poor family, and Kir's father had taken a special liking to Gino and had supported him since he was a child. Gino had spent about half his childhood in the Kir home in Tehran. It was Michael's father who had sent Gino to school in the States. After graduating from college, Gino stayed on in the U.S. to complete a pilot's training program, and became a fully-licensed pilot. Gino realized that he owed all of this to Michael's father. But Kir's father had died suddenly, while Gino was in his last year of pilot's training—before Gino had a chance to repay him for all his kindness.

When Gino returned to Iran in the early 1970s, he took a job with Air Taxi, the largest private airline company in Iran. In 1978 he went to Dubai, to work for British Petroleum as a helicopter pilot, ferrying people and equipment to and from the offshore oil rigs in the Gulf. When Michael had called him in February of 1979 saying he needed help, Gino was willing. He rented a small plane, and flew Michael in and out of Iran—in the middle of the Iranian Revolution. Then, a year and a half later, Michael had asked Gino to work for him.

Kir needed a good pilot and, more importantly, someone he could trust. He knew he could trust Gino; Gino was family, and had loved Kir's father as if he had been his own. Gino, although knowing the dangers involved, agreed to work for Michael. Gino knew this was his chance to repay the debt he felt he had to Kir's father.

"Hello, Michael," Gino said, sitting down next to Kir. He was wearing a steel-gray double breasted Ted Lapidus suit, obviously new.

"Is everything on schedule?" Kir asked.

"Right on the nose. Gabriella and Mark left for Orly at nine; Manuela and Andreas just left. Victoria is finishing packing, I just left her suite."

"She'll be ready to leave at ten?"

"Yes. The car is waiting, with most of her luggage already loaded."

"Then I'll leave at 10:30, as planned. That should give everyone ample time to board the plane and settle in before I arrive." Kir glanced at his Baum-Mercier watch, then rose from his seat.

"If you'll excuse me, Gino. I'd like to stay and have another drink with you, but I have some calls to make before leaving."

"Of course, Michael. I have to join Victoria shortly, anyway."

"Fine," said Kir. "See you on the plane."

Carrying only a sleek cordovan briefcase, Kir walked swiftly through the brightly lit terminal building, toward the first class check-in lounge.

*"Bon soir,"* said the Air France ground hostess sweetly as Kir approached her. She smiled at him coyly.

Kir looked around the blue, red, and white futuristic room. Except for himself and the Air France woman, the lounge was completely empty.

Everyone must have boarded by now, thought Kir. Everything was on schedule.

"I'm Mr. Kir," he said softly to the hostess. "I believe I'm the last passenger."

The woman consulted the clipboard, flipping through to the passenger list for the private aircraft, Flight 144, to Dubai. "Yes, you are, Mr. Kir," she said, neatly drawing a line through his name with a pencil. She picked up her two-way radio and spoke into it.

"Mr. Denier, please. *Vite!*" she ordered.

Moments later, a diminutive, efficacious airport escort, Mr. Denier, appeared.

"Have a nice flight," the ground hostess said, as Mr. Denier whisked Kir through the noiseless automatic doors and on through passport control and security to a waiting VIP minibus. The Boeing 707 was parked on a distant parking apron.

Through his thick hornrim glasses, Mr. Denier was studying this last VIP passenger that he was escorting out to the private 707. During the past hour, he had made three such trips, each time escorting an exquisitely beautiful woman and her companion to the plane. The brunettes were each accompanied by a blond man, the blonde by a dark-haired man—nice touch, thought Mr. Denier. They certainly were an exotic group.

Mr. Denier was glad that he had become friendly with that German who had boarded the plane earlier with the beautiful Brazilian woman. Andreas von Elfensleben explained to Mr. Denier, very confidentially, the whole story as they shared a coffee in the galley of the aircraft. Yes, thought Mr. Denier, he could hardly wait to give the other top-rank Orly personnel the story on Flight 144.

Andreas had explained that the women were call girls who had been hired by an immensely wealthy sheikh, who lived in one of those desert kingdoms.

Andreas had said that he couldn't remember which one—they all sounded the same to him. Mr. Denier couldn't agree more. He could just imagine it: an oil-rich sheikh, in his flowing white robes, with a falcon on his arm. Many times he'd seen those ugly, vicious birds shitting all over the first class lounge. Mr. Denier's imagination ran wild. He conjured up the image of an opulent, but *declasse*, palace in the desert, the solid gold Cadillacs, and, yes, a harem full of veiled women, the many wives of the sheikh. And probably fat and smelly under all their veils, thought Mr. Denier. And now the sheikh had bought—perhaps leased was a better word—these three beautiful additions to his harem. They would make love to him as he lay on a low couch covered with pillows and a hubble-bubble pipe at his side. Mr. Denier was digging into his fertile imagination. He always wondered if those sheikhs wore underwear under those long robes of theirs. These girls would soon find out, he thought.

Mr. Denier's reverie turned sour as he thought of how he had been forced to sell his beautiful red Peugeot last month. He could not afford to drive it. What with the price of gasoline, it was just too expensive for him to drive it anymore. Mr. Denier smiled for just a moment, thinking of the humorous ad that he had seen in *Paris Match* this morning, the *Moet et Chandon* Champagne House ad saying that they were developing a more fuel-economic car, one designed to run on champagne. Very funny, he thought. And we have those filthy Arabs to thank for this. They still fly around in their private jets and screw white women. *Merde*, he thought to himself.

The minibus pulled up in front of the floodlit, unmarked Boeing 707. The Pratt and Whitney turbofan engines were humming, and the service trucks began pulling away from the aircraft. Mr. Denier preceded Kir up the metal passenger stairs to the rear door.

*"Bon voyage,"* Mr. Denier said above the noise of the engines, as Andreas opened the door. Denier descended the stairs, and the ground crew pulled them away.

The interior of the aircraft was quiet and dimly lit. Kir followed Andreas from the narrow entranceway into a large stateroom. Kir set his briefcase down on a beige leather chair, and sat in another one.

"Any problems?" Kir asked.

Andreas shook his head negatively. "No," he replied. "The girls haven't seen each other. They are each in a separate section, with all doors locked. Gabriella and Mark are in section one, Victoria and Gino are in two, and Manuela is in three. Each of the girls has already had a drink, with a light sedative in it. To help them relax."

"Good," Kir said, adjusting his tie before the full-length mirror. "Prepare everyone for takeoff." Andreas left the room.

The 152-foot Boeing 707-320B had been completely outfitted as a luxurious private flying ship. Decorated like an ultramodern penthouse apartment, the interior of the aircraft had been divided into several rooms and sections, all of them providing complete comfort and privacy. The master bedroom (the stateroom) and an on-suite bathroom occupied the aft of the plane. A stainless steel galley flanked the mid-section area, which was divided into three separate sections decorated in shades of turquoise and cream, and furnished with sofas that turned into comfortable beds. Fully-equipped bathrooms separated the sections. Beyond the mid-section was the forward lounge and dining area. Beyond this plush playground, in the cockpit, the pilot, copilot and navigator prepared for takeoff.

An atmosphere of cool concentration prevailed in the dimly lit cockpit. The crew checked the more than one hundred and fifty instruments lighting up the central console, overhead switch panel, and flight engineer's panel. The radio crackled. "Alpha Delta one-four-four, cleared to line up and hold on runway two-four-right," said the voice coming from the Orly control tower. The push-out tug vehicle attached to the nosewheel of the 707 began pulling the plane out of the parking bay.

In the stateroom at the back of the plane, Kir studied his reflection in the mirror. He had been maintaining a whirlwind pace, but his face did not truly reflect his fatigue. Sitting down on the edge of the king-size bed which occupied much of the stateroom, Kir caught a glimpse of his briefcase, still in the chair. Only then did he realize that his arm felt incredibly light, that he felt momentarily free. The briefcase had been an intrinsic part of his life for many months.

Kir lay back on the bed, still staring at the rich dark brown leather case. It contained all the information he had needed to get the three women to do his bidding. Inside the briefcase were the infamous I-S files—the SAVAK top-secret files.

General Nasseri, chief of SAVAK for fifteen years, had held his own personal secret files, the I-S files, over the heads of everyone, even the Shah. They were said to contain the most incriminating evidence about everyone and everything concerning Imperial Iran, and the rumor was that if anything untoward should ever happen to Nasseri, his lawyers in Switzerland would disclose the truth about SAVAK's most clandestine activities, implicating even the Shah himself.

These were the rumors about the secret I-S files, but no one really knew if the files truly existed. No one, that is, except for General Nasseri and his second-in-command, Parvis Gazvini. Kir looked at his briefcase, remembering how the I-S files had come into his possession and how they had, through an incredible series of events, led him here, to this plane at Orly Airport.

It had started in Paris nearly five years ago. Kir was in Paris, in his usual suite at the Ritz, watching the news about Iran. The Regency Council— the Shah's interim government led by Bakhtiar— and the Shah's mighty army had fallen like a house of cards. The world, in shock, watched as the Revolutionaries, led by an enigmatic old man, Khomeini, took control of Iran. Kir was surprised when, early one morning, he received a call from Parvis Gazvini; Parvis asked Kir to come to his apartment on Avenue Foch. On the telephone, Parvis told Michael that he wanted some information on investing in diamonds, but when Michael Kir arrived at Parvis' luxury apartment that morning, Kir was shocked by what he saw.

Parvis was in a state of extreme agitation. He looked drawn and pale as he showed Kir the pictures in the newspapers of the dead General Nasseri, executed by a Revolutionary firing squad in Tehran.

"I knew it, I knew this would happen," Parvis said. "Michael, I escaped from Iran only two days ago. I was in hiding at a friend's house in Tehran when I received news that the U.S. Embassy had been seized. That day I decided to get out of Tehran. I knew that the situation was bad, very bad, and I would soon be hunted out and would have quickly ended up like poor General Nasseri, murdered by those madmen!" Parvis lit another cigarette and continued pacing back and forth across the opulent room with its silk walls, gilt moldings, crystal chandeliers, and precious Persian carpets. "Michael, I escaped by the skin of my teeth! It was just lucky I had some money left in Iran—nothing substantial, but it was enough for me to buy my way out."

"How did you manage your escape?" Michael asked, as he sipped his Scotch. "How guarded are the frontiers, Parvis?"

"It is absolute and total anarchy in Iran. Everyone is armed, but if you can make it out of Tehran, past the roadblocks, then you can fly out easily. That country is a mess, but Michael, it won't last for long. Mr. Khomeini will be out of there soon enough. Just wait and see."

"What do you mean, Parvis?"

"I have word that General Pakdal and his Immortals, who were forced to flee during the fall of Bakhtiar, have gone into the countryside and are regrouping, planning to attack Tehran any day now." Parvis poured himself another stiff Scotch. With the silver tongs still in his hand, Parvis put the lid back on the ice bucket and continued speaking. "Michael, I hear that you have been making inquiries into going back to Tehran, something about retrieving that valuable Faberge egg collection of your grandfather's?"

"You're right, Parvis." Michael's voice registered no shock, but he was surprised that Parvis knew. The inquiries that Kir had been making into the possibility of an illegal flight into Tehran had been extremely discreet. "I commend you on your sources. Yes, I am thinking about flying into Tehran."

"Well then, Michael, I have a proposition for you. I'm sure you can understand that I left

Tehran in somewhat of a hurry." Parvis laughed nervously, speaking in an almost flippant manner. "I was unable to pick up some documents of mine, and I would much prefer that I have these personal papers here with me, in Paris, rather than left in Tehran. I think you understand me, Michael. I can be frank with you. I expect that when these rabble-rousers are put down I will probably be asked, by the Shah, to take command of SAVAK. And," he said, shrugging his shoulders, "these documents that I am talking about contain some information that I would not like to be made public. Just the usual kind of things, you know—payments for assistance I gave to certain foreign corporations for services rendered. Nothing out of the ordinary, but Michael, you must realize that a man in my high public position cannot be fallible like the common man."

Kir nodded, but said nothing. He let Parvis continue.

"So, Michael, what I would like to ask of you is that you see if you can retrieve these documents for me while you are in Tehran. Of course, I'll compensate you for the inconvenience—let's say, one million U.S. dollars."

As Michael had been listening to this conversation, he suspected that these "documents" that Parvis wanted involved more than just a few incriminating bribes that had come his way. The million dollar pricetag that Parvis had put on these documents seemed to confirm to Kir that these were a lot more important than Parvis had led him to believe they were. It was the idea of the secret I-S files, in the back of his mind, that persuaded Kir to agree.

"All right, Parvis," Michael said, "I'll see what I can do. I can't guarantee anything, but tell me where they are and I'll try and get those documents for you. But, Parvis, if the situation is too dangerous, you'll understand if I come back empty-handed."

"Of course, Michael. No problem," Parvis said. "Now, let me tell you where the documents are. Do you know where the *Mina* apartment building is?"

"Not off-hand," Kir replied.

"It is on Amanyeh Hill, down the street from Dumah Apartments. *Mina* is the most famous *jende-khune* ..."

"Oh, yes, of course, the most famous whorehouse in Tehran," Kir said smiling. The *Mina* building had become infamous in Tehran. It housed a brothel full of European and English girls who came into Tehran for a three- to six-month tour of duty, made their money, and left.

"I keep a small apartment there," Parvis said. "I bought it under a false name and it is there, in Apartment 2B, that I keep my documents."

"But Parvis, why there?" Kir asked incredulously, *"Mina*, of all places."

"Think about it, Michael," Parvis said, smiling. *"Mina* was the safest building in all of Tehran. The police at the local *gendarmerie* spent more time hanging around *Mina* than at the police station. *Mina* had around-the-clock protection."

Kir smiled, but he suspected that Parvis not only owned that apartment, but the whole building and whores in it. Kir listened carefully as Parvis told him where the documents could be found, and then gave Kir the key to his *Mina* apartment.

Kir told Parvis that he would do what he could, but he had no idea what the situation in Tehran would be like when he got there. Kir would soon find out.

That very day, Kir flew from Paris to Dubai.

Gino Barakat was waiting for him there, having already arranged for the Piper Cheyenne they would use to fly into Iran. That same evening, taking advantage of the chaos in Iran, Kir and Gino were able to slip into Iran undetected. Gino landed the plane on a hard-packed strip of ground in a deserted area outside of Tehran. At dawn, Kir, dressed in a threadbare shirt, old, greasy jeans, and a moth-eaten sweater, walked out to the nearest roadway. With an Arab *kuffiya* wrapped around his head à la Yasser Arafat, and carrying an M-16 automatic rifle, Kir looked like any of the millions of jubilant Revolutionaries roaming the cities of Iran. Kir quickly hitched a ride into Tehran. Rifles braced outside the windows of the beat-up Peykan car, Kir and the five other Revolutionaries cheered and raised their clenched fists for victory as the driver honked the horn at the other passing cars.

Let off in the northern part of Tehran, Kir made his way to the exclusive suburb of Elahieh. Nestled in the poplar-treed hollow of north Tehran were the walled-in mansions of the rich, and the residences of the foreign ambassadors. Kir walked along the *kuches,* small streets, until he reached the gate to his family's home. For years only the servants had lived in the house, ever since Kir's mother had died. Kir let himself in. The place was totally deserted; the servants had all gone back to the relative security of the countryside. The large house was full of antiques and precious carpets, but Kir took only his grandfather's rare collection of small, delicate, jeweled eggs created by the master Russian jeweler Faberge. Then, taking one of the dusty Peykans from the garage, he carefully hid the jewelry in the car, and drove to Amanyeh Hill to see if he could get up to Parvis Gazvini's *pied-a-terre.*

Always in the back of Kir's mind was the story that Parvis had told him about the documents. The strange hiding place, plus the million dollar recovery fee, made Kir sure that it was the secret SAVAK I-S files he would find in *Mina*. It was the myth about those files that made Kir risk his life to go to Parvis's apartment. And it was the thought of those files that made Kir think to put a jerry can of benzine in the back of the Peykan.

Traveling along Jordan Avenue, Kir could see Dumah, the landmark brown-and-beige apartment building at the top of Amanyeh Hill. He was amazed at the state of total anarchy in the streets after the fall of the government of Shapour Bakhtiar. Chaos reigned supreme in the streets of Tehran as Khomeini's rag-tag Revolutionary soldiers, twelve-year-old children, *chador*-clad women, newly-released political prisoners and hardened criminals alike, brandished Kalashnikov rifles, Israeli-made Uzi machine guns, American M-16s, all "liberated" from Imperial Iranian Arms Depots. A few times Kir found himself caught in crossfire, as different factions fought for control of a certain intersection, or people practiced with their newfound weapons on life targets. On every corner there were road blocks manned by armed men, bandanas masking the lower part of their faces, cartridge belts strapped over their shoulders—Che Guevara style—looking for enemies of the Revolution.

With his M-16, the weapon of the Revolutionaries, a picture of Khomeini pasted on the windshield, and sporting a two-day growth of beard, Kir was waved through the roadblocks without event. He finally reached the steep road leading up to *Mina* and drove the hundred meters to the deserted green-tiled *Mina* building. He entered the second floor apartment belonging to Parvis, and quickly found the documents under the parquet floor. He hurriedly opened the thick package of papers. Inside the package Kir found what he had been hoping for, SAVAK files on microfiche. Kir wasn't sure that they were the infamous secret I-S files, but there was no way to find out until he had safely spirited the material out of the country. He put the package of documents and files against his chest, under his sweater. Quickly, Kir poured gasoline from the jerry can, saturated the apartment thoroughly, and set it on fire. He hurried out of the building and drove off down the road. As he drove down the expressway, on his way back to the waiting plane in the desert, he could see, in his rear-view mirror, the smoke coming from the hill as *Mina* went up in flames. Gino was waiting for Kir when he arrived at the plane. They took off immediately, and by flying over the vast uninhabited deserts of eastern Iran, they made it back to Dubai without incident.

Kir flew immediately to Switzerland, and examined the microfiche. They were the infamous I-S secret files of SAVAK. They were everything that Kir had imagined—and more. They contained incredible documentation on every facet of Iranians' lives and deaths. Michael Kir was sure that these files probably contained more information on Iran and the Shah's regime than all the history books in the world would ever have within their pages. And considering the incriminating evidence in these files, to some people they could be more valuable than the *Kour-e-Nour* diamond in the vaults of Bank Melli. Kir deposited the I-S files in a Zurich bank vault for safekeeping. He decided to wait and see just how valuable the I-S files could be, and to whom. When Kir returned to Paris, he went immediately to Parvis' apartment.

"Well, Parvis," Michael said. "When I got to Tehran I was told that *Mina* had been burnt down. I went to see for myself. It was burnt to the ground."

"What the hell . . ." Parvis said.

"Well, Parvis, everyone knew that *Mina* was a *jende-khune*, so the religious zealots set it on fire. Everything had gone up in smoke," Kir reassured Parvis. "But, Parvis, the incriminating evidence had been destroyed. Isn't that what you wanted?" Kir asked as he closely watched Parvis's face for his reaction.

Parvis belied no hint that he may have suspected Kir. "That is perfect, Michael, and," Parvis said, putting his hand on Kir's shoulder, "I'm glad that you got out of that mad country safely."

Kir kept the files, not knowing quite what to do with them, until, many months later, the information in the I-S files became invaluable to Kir himself. On one of the last pieces of microfiche was the story of the smuggling of Mr. Yusef Tabeti's important collection of artwork out of the country by Iran Air stewardess Victoria Graham. Another story, one that Kir already knew, but had not been able to substantiate, was about Gabriella Antonelli's involvement in Gianni Bruni's kidnapping.

These were the kind of girls that Michael Kir needed; beautiful women, women who could be forced to do his bidding. Kir knew that the taking of the I-S files had sealed his fate to the path he was on. Although Kir felt that by keeping the files secret from Parvis, and by using the women as he wanted, he could be able to control his fate, a nagging feeling kept coming back to him. Parvis was now one of his employers, and Michael Kir couldn't help wondering if he had been doing Parvis's bidding from that very day, nearly five years ago, when Parvis had sent Kir to fetch his documents at *Mina*. Parvis Gazvini was not a man to underestimate. He had had nearly infinite power before, and he wanted that power again—of that, Kir was sure.

Kir winced as he imagined Parvis Gazvini making love to the beautiful Mitra. Then his thoughts shifted to the magnificent Manuela, only yards down the corridor.

Kir made his way out of the stateroom and went to the galley. "A bottle of Dom Perignon '71 in section three, please." Michael Kir walked forward as the plane waited in line for its turn in the holding bay.

What a strange turn of events my life has taken, thought Michael Kir, as he walked toward the front of the plane, waiting for takeoff at Orly Airport, about to embark on the biggest, boldest adventure imaginable.

Kir opened the door to section three. At the far side of the lounge sat Manuela.

"Mind if I sit beside you, Manuela?" Michael asked. She motioned for him to sit down next to her.

There was a knock on the door.

"Come in," Kir said.

"Mr. Kir, your champagne," the steward said. "Shall I open it for you?"

"No," Kir said. "Just leave it." The steward set the tray on the table beside Kir and left.

Kir untwisted the thin wire around the cork, working the cork out until there was a muffled pop. Manuela watched as Kir poured the champagne from the smoking mouth of the frosty green bottle.

"To promises made," Michael said, smiling warmly at Manuela.

Her glass was shaking as the plane accelerated

down the runway. Manuela looked at Michael Kir.

"To promises kept," she said.

The plane climbed steeply away from Paris. As the landing gear was trundled into its well in the fuselage, and the aircraft began to level off, Michael undid his seat belt.

"I must go greet the other guests," Kir said to Manuela.

"The other guests?" Maneula asked. She was under the impression that she was the only person on the plane, except for Andreas, Kir, and the crew.

"I think it is about time we all met," Kir said.

Manuela nodded, perplexed. She had seen no one else enter the plane.

"This way," Kir said as he led her to the forward lounge.

Gabriella and Mark were already seated in the forward lounge when Kir and Manuela entered the stylized black-and-white room.

"Mark, Mark!" Gabriella nudged him with her elbow. "Look!" Before Michael and Manuela were within hearing range, Gabriella hissed, "What is *she* doing here?" Gabriella thought she'd be the only woman, and now here was this gorgeous girl stealing her thunder. *"Che puttana,"* she muttered to herself.

"What?" asked Mark.

"Hello, Gabriella, Mark," interrupted Kir. "I'd like you to meet Manuela."

Mark stood up, and Gabriella gave Manuela her best Roman-bitch look. As much as Gabriella hated to admit it, the raven-haired woman was *bellissima*. Michael threw Gabriella a steely glance and said, directing his words to Gabriella, "We are all going to be together for quite a while, so we may as well all become fast friends."

"We all . . . ?" Gabriella started, but was inter-

205

rupted by the appearance of Victoria and Gino, closely followed by Andreas. Kir politely introduced everyone.

"*Ciao*, Manuela," Gabriella said, as she took Manuela's cold, almost lifeless hand and squeezed it energetically, hoping that the blood would start circulating. She wondered why such a healthy-looking girl should have such a cold-blooded handshake. She didn't wonder long, however, because she was too busy giving Victoria the once over. I wonder if she is a natural blond, thought Gabriella, appraising Victoria's luminous tresses.

Michael Kir reached for the cabin interphone. "Steward, we'd like dinner, please." Kir stood up and motioned toward a round table set with gleaming silver and crystal. A large bowl of white gardenias formed the centerpiece. "Shall we go to the table?" Kir suggested.

The men pulled out the chairs for the women as a steward poured ice water into the goblets. Another steward wheeled out a tray full of hors d'oeuvres. He served Gabriella first. She daintily pointed to the *dolmeh*, the stuffed grapeleaves, and then to the fried red and green peppers. "*Basta, basta,*" she whispered frantically to the steward as he slipped an extra sliver of pepper on to her plate. She had no intention of eating those slimy oily peppers. Gabriella was a master dieter. She filled her plate so as to give the appearance of having indulged in a full meal, when in fact she had had only eight hundred calories, exactly.

While Gabriella played interior decorator with the food on her plate, and Manuela left her plate untouched, Victoria studied the two stunning women.

Gabriella daintily plucked the stem out of a fresh strawberry. "Michael, *caro*, how many more hours to Dubai? Isn't that where you said we were going, Mark?" Gabriella asked, turning to Mark seated on her right.

Manuela looked at Michael.

"Oh, about five and a half or six hours," Michael said. "You'll have a chance to rest after dinner, unless you care to see a movie?"

"I'm absolutely exhausted," Victoria said. "I'll pass on the movie."

"I'll have a *digestivo*, and then get some sleep. I'm tired," Gabriella said.

"How about you, Manuela?" Kir asked.

"Really, I'm tired, too. I think I'll just rest, the combination of the food and wine and the hectic day have caught up with me." Manuela looked at her watch. "No wonder I'm tired, it's one-thirty, Paris time." Manuela got up from her chair. "You'll excuse me?"

"There are beds made up for each of you in your own sections, ladies," Andreas said.

"Good night, everyone," Manuela said.

The air conditioning in the plane was on full blast, feeding pressurized air into the room. Manuela, nude, shivered under the cool, crisp sheet, wishing that she had put on a nightgown before retiring. She lay awake, listening to the hum of the engines as the airplane pushed on into the black night.

There was a light rap on the door and a shaft of light fell on the carpet. Manuela pulled the covers up around her and sat up. She recognized the tall silhouette at the door.

"Michael, is that you?"

"Yes, Manuela. I am sorry to have disturbed you, I just wanted to check and see if everything is all right. I really haven't had a chance to talk with you since Rio."

"Yes, everything is fine, Michael, except that I am very cold. Could you get me a blanket, please?"

"Sure, I think they are in here." He went over to the cupboard and opened it. "One blanket is enough?"

"Yes, thank you."

Michael put the heavy wool blanket on top of her and tucked it in. "May I?" he asked. She nodded, and he sat on the edge of her bed. "So, Manuela, how did things go with closing up your office? Dr. Gomez was able to take all your patients?"

"Yes, as I mentioned to you in Rio, it was very fortunate that I was not in the middle of any major facial reconstructions. Dr. Gomez was more than happy to take my patients. He is hoping that all my wealthy patients will stay with him. He is hoping that I won't come back from Portugal."

"So that is where you told your friends in Rio you were going?"

"Yes, I said that I had to go back to decide what to do with the family property. The Portuguese government frowns on absentee landlords, and the government might decide to expropriate all the land of the Ferrara family, and give it to the farmers who have lived there for generations."

"A very good story, Manuela," said Michael.

In the semidarkness she could see his handsome face. He was still dressed in his suit, his jacket open and his tie unloosened. She sat up in bed, slowly, the sheet slipping away from her body as she moved closer to him. The sensual contours of his face blurred, as the masculine scent of his cologne enveloped her in memories of their night together in Rio only eight days ago. Her lips moved to his. He pulled his head back slightly, but her fingers reached into his thick hair and she drew him toward her and kissed him passionately. His lips were hard and cold and he pushed her away from him slowly. The sting of his brusque rejection made her feel as if he had slapped her in the face.

She looked at him questioningly, but he seemed to stare past her. Manuela was speechless as he kissed her quickly on the cheek, before walking out the door.

Manuela slept fitfully, disturbed by the distance Michael had seemed to want to put between them. She awoke and looked at her watch. She had only slept four hours. It would soon be time to get up. As she lay in bed she could hear muffled voices from the forward lounge and could see a crack of light through the door. She listened carefully and discerned the voices of Michael and Mark. They must have stayed awake all night, she thought.

The steward carried in a tray with a small silver pot of steaming coffee and a glass of freshly squeezed orange juice.

"Good morning, Miss Ferrara. Breakfast is being served in the forward lounge. We will be landing in an hour and a half." He put down the tray on the coffee table and then excused himself.

Manuela took a sip of orange juice and then got out of bed, wrapping a robe around herself. She went to the bathroom, showered quickly, and dressed.

The aroma of strong coffee greeted Manuela as she opened the door to the forward lounge.

"Good morning," Mark said, spooning sugar onto his corn flakes. "Sit here, Manuela."

"Where is everyone else, Mark?"

"Oh, Gabriella is coming, just late as usual, that's all. Michael is waking up Victoria." He lifted the silver coffee pot. "Coffee?"

Michael Kir appeared at the table, and pulled out a chair at the breakfast table for the tall, sleepy-eyed blond who had entered the lounge behind him. Gabriella, her hair tousled but her face made up, was the last to arrive at breakfast.

As Victoria ate her piece of toast she watched the others at the table. She noticed the hollow-eyed look of both Kir and Mark and could feel the controlled edge of excitement to their voices as they exchanged niceties with the women at the table. Manuela was evidently not very hungry as she only sipped her black coffee. Victoria smiled as she watched Gabriella flirt unabashedly with both men. Even at the crack of dawn, Gabriella looked like she had "available" written in six languages across her forehead, Victoria thought.

As soon as the breakfast dishes had been cleared away, Kir spoke. "Just as a precaution, I think we should each have a smallpox inoculation."

"What for?" Manuela asked.

"Just a precaution," Kir said abruptly. "Gabriella, how about you going first?"

*"Va bene,* but do it on the inside of my arm," she ordered, "I don't want a scar."


After everyone had been inoculated, Manuela returned to her mid-section seat by the window. She was becoming more suspicious with every passing minute. Where were they taking her? The World Health Organization reported that small-pox had been eliminated several years ago. But she remembered reading in a recent medical journal that there were still rumors of inter-mittent outbreaks of smallpox in Iran. A feeling of panic gripped her. "Iran! My God, no!" she exclaimed aloud. She looked out the window and could see the eastern edge of the Saudi Arabian Peninsula and the waters of the Persian Gulf. But why would Michael be taking them to Iran, she wondered. She looked out the window again, as the plane slowly began making its descent. It was a clear day and, even at 18,000 feet, she could see the bright orange flames from the offshore oil rigs off the coast of Kuwait and Saudi Arabia. The plane continued to fly southeast, in the direction of Dubai. Manuela relaxed a bit. Dubai, the most important port in the Gulf, probably had a number of Iranian black-market traders. The smallpox shot was probably no more than a precaution.

Manuela continued to stare out the window. The vast expanse of water was blue-green, mottled with indigo, and was in vibrant contrast to the jagged yellow coastline of the United Arab Emirates that hugged the eastern coastline of the Arabian Peninsula. The 707 continued its descent, following the coastline. Then it banked sharply left and began flying away from the coast, directly north, crossing the Gulf, all the while still continuing to lose altitude. Immediately, Manuela realized that they were no longer flying to Dubai. They were flying away from Dubai—northward. "What the hell is going on?" she said to Andreas, who was peering out the window, on the opposite side of the lounge.

"We're making our descent," he answered.

"Not to Dubai, we aren't!" she said furiously. "Get Kir!" she yelled. Manuela continued to look out the window, hoping to catch a glimpse of land. The water was getting closer and closer, and there was no land in sight.

The pilot was now talking with the airport controller. Kir sat in the jump seat, listening to the crackle of the radio conversation as the controller gave an update on weather conditions and described the approach to land to be taken by Flight 144. "Winds calm, visibility unlimited, temperature on the ground, 32 degrees centigrade."

"Alpha-Delta, one-four-four, passing four thousand to three thousand," said the pilot.

"Roger," replied the controller, now guiding the

aircraft in its final descent.

The pilot spoke to Kir. "Nine miles out, Mr. Kir. It's a beautiful day on the ground."

The Boeing 707 continued its descent on a shallow glide path. The pilot lowered the landing gear and extended the flaps, slowing the aircraft. The runway was coming up fast. As the plane crossed the runway threshold, the copilot read off the ground distance.

"One hundred feet, fifty, forty, thirty, minimum."

"Landing," the pilot said, as the 707 touched down smoothly on the runway.

Manuela peered out the window, her eyes straining to see something she recognized, or something that would identify the place where they had just landed. Manuela knew that they were not at Dubai, but she couldn't figure out where they were.

"Michael," Manuela yelled to Kir as he walked through the cabin. "Just where the hell are we?"

"Look again," he said, lightly guiding her head to the window. Unable to believe her eyes, Manuela read the words on the gleaming sign aloud: "Welcome to Kish Island."

# CHAPTER TWELVE

The doors to the plane opened. Gabriella took one last look in her hand mirror and put it back into her shoulderbag. Hot, humid air seeped into the aircraft, and Gabriella felt her silk blouse start to adhere to her back. She quickly collected the rest of her belongings, anxious to see where they were. She'd heard Manuela shouting about not landing in Dubai, so obviously they were some place other than Dubai. Well, I'll soon find out where we are, Gabriella thought.

Stepping out of the airplane was like stepping into a sauna bath, yet there was not a cloud in the azure-blue sky. Gabriella immediately shielded her eyes from the bright sunlight, searching frantically in her bag for her Ray-Ban sunglasses. From her vantage-point at the top of the stairs, Gabriella looked all around. The peacock blue ocean was just a few hundred meters from the plane. A few palm trees were growing on the strip of gleaming white sand that separated the sea and the runway.

Once standing on the hot tarmac, Gabriella looked to the end of the runway, as far as she could see, past the flat shimmering gray concrete to the peaks of whitecaps on the choppy blue water.

A tall, beautiful building, the airport terminal, dominated the landscape. It was an ultramodern structure, triangular shaped, with a squared apex.

The front of the terminal building jutted out in a peak, like a bow of a ship. Large, turquoise-blue ceramic panels, divided by narrow ribbons of white concrete, covered the building. In the bright morning sunlight, the building sparkled like a rare, exotic jewel.

Low bushes of white, pink, and magenta flowers banked the terminal building, but other than these, there was no greenery. From the sun, the sea, the sand, and the heady scent of unfamiliar flowers, Gabriella had thought she was in a tropical paradise. But the landscape beyond the airport was stark and barren. Instead of the expected lush vegetation, only a few scrub bushes and palm trees dotted the rocky sand.

Gabriella noticed a large white jeep pull away from the terminal building and head toward the plane. Gabriella began to wonder where, exactly, this Kish Island was located. I should look on a map, she thought. No, better yet, I'll just ask Mark.

"Mark, *caro*," Gabriella cooed. "Could you tell me something about this island? Where are we?"

"Kish Island is a small island in the Persian Gulf. It is located near the mouth of the Gulf, not far from the Straits of Hormuz. One hundred miles to the south, across the Persian Gulf, is the United Arab Emirates."

"The United Arab Emirates?" Gabriella asked.

"The UAE is a confederation of seven sheikhdoms, of which Abu Dhabi, Dubai, and Sharjah are the most well known."

"Isn't Bahrain one too, Mark?" Gabriella interrupted.

Mark shook his head. He pointed his arm southward, then, moving in a westerly direction, said, "It's the UAE, Qatar, Bahrain, the east coast of Saudi Arabia, Kuwait, and Iraq at the head of the

Persian Gulf. And, everything up there," Mark said, sweeping his hand northward, "is Iran."

"How close?" Gabriella asked worriedly.

"Don't worry, Gabriella," Mark said reassuringly, "It may only be seventeen miles away, but that section of southern Iran is fairly deserted. Only a few small villages, and most of them are much too interested in their own survival to be interested in us."

Gabriella looked in all directions. "How big is this island?" she asked.

"Kish is only a small island, eight by fourteen square miles, but it has everything that you could want."

"Yes, it looks nice enough," replied Gabriella politely. She was unconvinced by Mark's words. The island looked dead. Not a soul in sight; not her style at all.

The first Range Rover sped past them and pulled up by the cargo door on the underbelly of the fuselage. Three Oriental workers in white overalls leapt out of the truck and began unloading the luggage.

"Our car is on the way," Kir called from the top of the stairs, at the aft door of the plane.

Another white Range Rover pulled up in front of the group waiting on the tarmac. Written on the side of the door was the sign "Gulf Island Resorts, Inc." Mark grabbed the handle and opened the door.

"Come on, girls, get in," Mark said. Inside the car it was refreshingly cool. The air conditioning whirred noisily. Victoria pulled her silk dress away from her damp thighs and pushed her thick hair back off her neck. She watched out the window as Michael Kir hurried down the stairs. It was the first time that she had not seen him in a suit and tie, yet he still looked incredibly sexy, dressed in faded jeans, fitted to his narrow hips and long legs, and a cool cotton shirt, casually rolled up at the sleeves and unbuttoned at the neck. Just looking at his virile body stirred something inside her. She quickly pushed the vague erotic feeling out of her mind. Her attention was captured by the déjà vu familiarity of Kish Island.

Victoria Graham had been to Kish before, several years ago. She was curious to see how it had changed. She had been under the impression that Kish Island had been boarded up long ago and forgotten. It was a white elephant, a very expensive white elephant left over from the Pahlavi Dynasty. And now here we are, she thought.

Kir got in the front of the car. The Range Rover, with Mark at the wheel, sped along the tarmac, past a newly built hangar. Victoria did not remember seeing that building before. She noticed a Falcon executive jet and a white Beechcraft parked on the runway.

The luxurious, bustling terminal building, as Victoria remembered it, now looked deserted and, as they drove past the front of the terminal, she noticed that the once refreshingly attractive fountain and reflecting pool were dead, bone dry.

The Range Rover continued along the two-lane asphalt road that led away from the airport, first traveling inland through the dry, stark landscape, then returning to the sparkling water's edge. On the driver's side was the seemingly endless blue water, while out of Victoria's window only the hot desert landscape could be seen.

We should soon reach the hotel, thought Victoria. She had been on Kish Island several times before with Mr. Tabeti.

It had been in the winter of 1977, Kish Island's one and only season of full operation as the most luxurious gambling spot in the Middle East, probably in the whole world, for that matter. No expense had been spared on Kish. The finest materials were used, the world's most prestigious firms contracted to ensure that absolutely everything on Kish Island, down to the last detail, would exude wealth and luxury. It was to be the resort to end all resorts. All the buildings on Kish —the airport terminal, the luxury two-hundred room hotel, the casino complex, the shopping arcade, with its famous-name boutiques, the several dozen fabulous private villas, the court ministers' villas, and the residences of the Shah and his family—all shared a cohesive uniformity of design. The dramatic design concepts incorporated into the buildings were sharply angled walls, precipitously sloped roofs, dramatic use of ceramic panels and contrasting white concrete, small reflecting pools, and the constant theme of an architectural element which had been designed specifically for Kish, the Pahlavi Arch—a sharply soaring arch, the point of which angled outwards, creating a third dimension. Kish Island itself was an effort to create a third dimension in the concept of a luxury resort, and the visual images of Kish's buildings accomplished that. Kish was an architect's dream, which harsh economic reality would have vetoed as being much too expensive to build. But harsh reality had had no part of this dream world.

The opulent haven for the oil-wealthy boasted every diversion that the idle rich could desire, but the most important part of all was the gambling casino, bigger than Monte Carlo's, where beautiful English croupiers in low-cut designer gowns raked millions of dollars off the green felt gaming tables. There were also sports for the more athletically inclined: horseback riding, tennis, sailing, scuba diving, swimming, and water skiing. And Kish offered the finest cuisine in the Middle East. Fresh food was flown in every day; smoked salmon from the icy rivers of Scotland, exotic fruits from India and the Orient, French wines, American beef, and even such mundane necessities of life as milk, eggs, and bread, all to be made into culinary delights by French chefs and served by Spanish waiters. Kish was a free port of entry and chic Paris boutiques—Cardin, Cristofle, Dior, Jourdan, and others—had outlets on the island. Everything was brought in to make one's stay on Kish more enjoyable. Madame Claude's high-priced call girls were ready to fly in at a moment's notice to satisfy whatever craving could not be fulfilled by the luxury goods and services already on the island. And one did not have to stay unsatisfied long—Concorde had a nonstop flight from Paris to Kish Island.

Yet, Kish had not been conceived of purely as a place for hedonistic delights. The idea had been to create an ultradeluxe playground for the super-rich in the Middle East—a place to spend their own petrodollars, rather than funneling them into London gaming houses and European casinos. Monte Carlo would pale by comparison—or, at least, that had been the plan. During Iran's boom years in the mid-70s, Kish Island Development Organization had seemed like a fantastic scheme. In retrospect, Kish seemed like a ludicrous idea, a wanton expense of so much to benefit so few.

As she looked out the Range Rover window, Victoria remembered back on the times that she had spent on Kish—what fun she had had! She and Mr. Tabeti had come to Kish Island a number of weekends that inaugural winter of 1977. It had been great to get away from cold, gray Tehran. Special Iran Air flights had flown groups of VIPs—high

218

rollers, influential men in government and business, the top society of Tehran—to Kish, hoping to entice those wealthy people who were not already members of the Kish Island Development Corporation to take out membership in this, the moxt exclusive of clubs in the Middle East. Tall, blond hostesses greeted the disembarking guests inside the fabulous terminal building. Membership passes and VIP guest cards were checked before the guests were whisked off to their private villas or deluxe hotel suites.

For Victoria, it had all been great fun, especially since she had a passion for gambling. Mr. Tabeti had always given her all the money that she wanted to gamble with. He did not care if she won or lost, or how much she won or lost. He was far too busy dropping small fortunes at the chemin de fer table. Victoria smiled to herself, thinking back on some of the amazing things she had seen on Kish Island.

She had watched men lose two million dollars at the roulette table. With every roll of the wheel the croupier would rake off seventeen thousand dollars in chips from the man with the stupendous losing streak of the evening. The unruffled loser would then telephone his bank in Tehran and request that they fly down another couple of million to bankroll his next evening's entertainment. When it came to "cool," the Iranians were the coolest gamblers around. They never blinked an eye whether they were winning or losing. With a look of studied indifference they would stack their skyscrapers of one-hundred-fifty-dollar chips on the green felt, waiting for the turn of the wheel or the luck of the cards.

Victoria had seen the cold-eyed Persian women, elegantly turned out, dip into their evening bags and pull out wads of ten-thousand-rial notes, which they quickly changed to chips. They would then proceed to gamble in a style that was similar to throwing money into a blazing fire.

Kish Island had been a microcosm of a certain stratum of Iranian society, the privileged elite, and the political elite: one and the same. It was a place where the rich could get away from the "cheap people"—"cheap people" being the upper class's description of the "low class." But, all too often, the upper class were reminded of how shallow were the roots of their modern society.

Many times, Victoria had seen it herself. Sitting between two elegantly dressed, reed-thin women, women from good families, rich, sophisticated, Westernized, would be a "cheap person." She was inevitably a fat, coarse-looking woman, squeezed into a loudly-patterned dress, huge rings on her stubby fingers, large clusters of diamonds and rubies on her fat ear lobes, with a designer scarf tied around her head in the style of a modified *chador*. Behind her would sit her fat little husband, dressed in his ill-fitting Tehran-made suit, lighting his cigarettes with a solid gold Dunhill lighter as he passed her more chips, which she would uncomprehendingly throw on the roulette table.

In their haughty way, the two women on either side of these "cheap people" would speak to each other either in French or English, confident that they would not be understood by the two seated between them. Perhaps they would comment on the revolting dietary habits of peasants, who ate too much sheep fat and rice. Their diet kept them obese and gave them a greasy, gamey smell that all the Charlie cologne in the world couldn't mask. The two women would snobbishly complain to each other about letting the riffraff into Kish. But they knew why the riffraff was let in: money.

As they continued to play, the women would speculate on how these particular "cheap people" got their money. Perhaps they had had a two-thousand meter lot on Pahlavi Avenue in Tehran, where they had lived in a small shack on the property with their chickens, washing their clothes and their copious amounts of rice in big aluminum vats outside their hovel, while their worm-infested children played in the dirt. These women would know. They had often seen such sights as they drove their Mercedes sedans to the Exir department store on Pahlavi Avenue to pick up their Clinique cosmetics and to buy skateboards for their Pierre Cardin and Courrèges outfitted children.

The incredibly inflated price of property in boomtown Tehran had created overnight multi-millionaires. Many peasants had sold their corner lot to a developer for four or five million dollars. Now, before the ink was barely dry on the deed of sale, they were here, on Kish. These were the nouveaux riches—literally. The gap between old money and new, chronologically, was merely a hair's breadth.

Iranians had a talent for conspicuous consumption that was unsurpassed by any other nation on earth. This was evident not only on lavish Kish, but in Tehran as well. As Tehran mushroomed, during the Shah's reign, the rich began building miniature Moorish castles, scaled-down replicas of Versailles, and gigantic white antebellum style mansions. Veritable smorgasbords of architectural styles were incorporated into single massive residences. Exceptional only as paragons of bad taste, these huge homes littered the foot-hills of the Alborz Mountains in north Tehran. These mansions—the Iranians' public face, their boastful monument to themselves—were not the only opportunity for conspicuous consumption. The interiors of these homes were crammed full of precious silk carpets lying next to turquoise and orange sheepskin throw rugs. Fine old oil paintings vied for attention with Keene wide-eyed waif paintings. Delicate and gracious antiques were interspersed among the pseudo-Louis XIV furniture, gilt, marble and hot-pink crushed velvet, and a de rigueur Lava Lamp. These Tehran living rooms would have made even the Sun King blush.

Besides their lavish residences, Iranians spent for show on cars and clothes. They had garages full of eighty-thousand-dollar Mercedes 450SLCs and one-hundred-thousand-dollar Porsche Carreras (the inflated prices due to a three hundred percent import tax on cars) and closets full of designer clothes. Iranians were elegant dressers, but it was hard to go wrong—you just matched up the initials. Their thin bodies were clothed from head to toe in Christian Dior, from the silk scarves on their necks to the CD on their pantyhose, or stamped with the gold horse-and-carriage Celine emblem, from the buckles on their shoes to the buttons on their blazers. The other favorite Iranian spend-for-show pastime was gambling, and Kish had definitely been a place to see and to be seen.

I wonder where all those people are now, Victoria thought, as she continued to stare out the window, lost in her own thoughts. Oh, how the tables must have turned on every one of those men and women that she'd seen on Kish only a few years before. Some had been executed; others, imprisoned—their vast holdings in Iran confiscated, their furniture, their clothing put up for auction, the graves of their dead desecrated. Some of these formerly "right" people had escaped with only the clothes on their backs, while others had prudently stashed away millions in Europe and the States, and were now living in luxurious exile. But they all had one thing in common; they were refugees, forced out of their homeland, unable to return. And these were the lucky ones. Many of Kish Island's most important members were dead. Was it only five years ago? Victoria thought, reflecting on all that had happened in Iran since then.

The Range Rover pulled up in front of the entrance to the five-story Kish Island Hotel. Mark got out of the car.

"Girls, Mike, I'll just be gone a few minutes. I have to check the dehumidifying system," he said. He walked quickly into the hotel.

The design of the Kish Island hotel was sleek and elegant. There was a rectangular central core, which housed the lobby, restaurants, discotheque, and conference rooms. The two hundred guest rooms were in the two wings—one emanating from each side of the central core—which flared out toward the sea.

Victoria looked up. She could see workmen, suspended from ladders all along the front of the hotel. They were cleaning the dull, dusty, tiled balconies that had once gleamed brilliant sea blue. She remembered the verdant grass that had carpeted the area in front of the hotel. Now, the grass was dry, sparse, and grayish-yellow.

"Just look at this place," Victoria said to Michael, as they waited in the car, the engine running and the air conditioning on. "It used to be so beautiful," she said, shaking her head in amazement. "I just can't believe what has happened here," Victoria said sadly.

Manuela and Gabriella looked at Victoria; they were surprised that she had been to Kish Island before.

"Yes, the ravages of time seem to work faster in the desert," replied Kir. "You should have seen this place when we got here. It looked as if people had just up and left at a moment's notice. Doors were left wide open. The sand blew in, covering the silk carpets. Thick layers of sand were banked up along glasses still sitting on the bar, swizzle sticks and all. The crystal chandeliers were so thick with dust and cobwebs that no light passed through when they were switched on. It seemed as if the desert was about to take up residence inside the hotel. We caught it just in time. We'll take you on a tour of the hotel, once you've rested from your flight. You'll be surprised what it looks like inside," Michael said proudly, as he pointed to the glass-doored lobby. "Good as new," he said.

Gabriella peered out the window. Indeed, the lobby did look like new. Through the sparkling-clean glass doors she could see the brilliant reflection of a large chandelier in the polished tile floor. Past the lobby area, she could see through another wall of glass doors to the other side of the hotel, to the crystal blue of the swimming pool, framed by a white patio, and blue-and-white striped umbrellas.

"Before and after," said Gabriella, as she looked first to the dusty facade of the hotel and then toward the gleaming interior.

"Yes," Kir agreed. "The workmen did a great job. The sand was moved back to where it belonged, the carpets were cleaned, the oxidized brass polished, the precious woods restored to their original luster, and the air conditioning and humidity control hooked up again. The hotel was in the worst shape of all the buildings on Kish. Some of the other buildings on the island were as good as new. It was like walking into a time warp; unread copies of *The Herald Tribune* from November 1978, and *Time* magazine with the

Shah's photo going up in flames on the cover were neatly stacked on coffee tables."

"That should have been a sign for everyone to get off this island—and fast," Victoria said.

"It probably was," Kir replied. "Everyone who was left holding the fort—the German engineers, the Swiss desk clerks, the American security men, and the French interior decorator—just up and left. We found telexes in the machines that hadn't been read."

The doors to the hotel opened and Mark came bounding out. He climbed back into the Range Rover. "Sorry to keep you waiting."

"How does everything look, Mark?" Kir asked.

"Looks good," Mark said.

As they were pulling out of the entrance, Manuela noticed a large sign being hoisted up to the roof of the hotel. She read the sign out loud: "Kish Island Sheraton—Opening 1984." She turned to Michael and sarcastically asked, "Michael, aren't we a bit early for the opening?" Kir just smiled at her.

The Range Rover drove past the dramatic six-sided casino near the water's edge. It was a glass and concrete building with thin, sharply-pointed walls that divided the six sides of the building, the effect being like that of an angular spider seated over the building. It, too, was empty, as were the luxurious court ministers' villas, farther down the road.

"What exactly has happened here?" asked Gabriella.

Michael Kir launched into a brief synopsis of the short, bittersweet life of Kish Island under the Shah. Victoria tuned the sound of Kir's voice out. She knew all too well what had happened to Kish. The winter of 1977 and early 1978 had been Kish Island's first and last season of operation. By midsummer of 1978, the death knell for Kish Island had already been sounded. The hint of scandal was in the air, and more important, Kish Island's pivotal figure, the Shah of Iran, was on thin ice.

Kish Island, with its gambling, liquor, high-life, and western ways, was symbolic of the decadence of the Pahlavis and Iran's elitist privileged ruling class. Kish represented everything and everyone that Khomeini and his Revolution hated most passionately. Victoria remembered those volatile days during the hot summer of 1978. It was Ramadan, the most religious month of the year, when good Moslems refrained from alcohol (a decadent Western indulgence), tobacco, and sex, and fasted from sunrise to sunset. The Iranians' xenophobia, their fear and hatred of Western ways, had reached a fevered pitch. Victoria, who had been in Iran at that time, felt the ominous tension in the air, and had accelerated her smuggling of Mr. Tabeti's calligraphy out of Iran. She had no intention of being in Iran when the pressure-cooker blew. She remembered that one of the things that added fuel to the fire burning under the Shah was the Kish Island scandal.

The beleaguered Shah, in a futile effort to start rooting out corruption, while at the same time loosening the restrictive bonds of censorship, had unwittingly unleashed the Kish Island scandal. It involved accusations of staggering sums stolen from the Kish Island Development Corporation by the corporation, and seven-figure payoffs. The press pounced on the story. There had been a natural backlash to the years of strict censorship of the press, and the shortlived free press of Iran screamed out tabloid-like headlines. Victoria remembered how the English newspapers, the *Kayhan* and *The Tehran Journal* had used disaster-height print almost daily for their scathing headlines. The Kish scandal was perfect for them. It was a story of corruption, Iranian style; a family affair, not unlike the Shah's own family problems at the time. It was a story of one family, the Zadeh family. Everyone in the Zadeh family—the wife, the relatives, the children, right down to the family Persian cat, almost—were awarded all the most lucrative contracts and concessions for the island resort and gambling operations. Then, to add insult to injury, it was said that the Zadeh family had "borrowed" the Kish Island Development Corporation plane to fly out the millions of dollars that they had emptied out of the corporate coffers.

More urgent problems soon took precedence in Iran, but the scandal caused irreparable damage to the Shah's already shaky throne. Kish Island had been one of the Shah's pet projects. It had been the site of his private winter retreat for many years, even before the resort complex had been developed. His name was linked closely with Kish Island, and the Kish Island scandal did not help his faltering popularity during those final months. It was in no way the only cause of the Shah's fall from his lofty pedestal, but it was the tip of the iceberg, a glaringly visible example of the corrupt elite. The whole iceberg had been full of holes, and, in the end, the Shah did fall through.

The Range Rover continued along the road, past beautiful private villas along the water's edge. Manuela, sitting silently in the back seat, noticed that, as they traveled farther along the road, the landscape was becoming greener, lusher. The vegetation obviously had been put there by man, then pampered and coaxed to grow in the harsh desert environ. The only natural vegetation was palms and scrub bushes, but along the road were neat plots of grass, dotted with vivid flowering bushes. Jasmine and oleander trees were scattered across the landscape as far as the eye could see.

227

In the distance Manuela could see a group of brilliant white buildings, standing on a slight rise of land, encircled by high walls. Rose bushes along the edge of the straight roadway created a dramatic entrance leading up to the white walls. As they drove closer, Manuela could see the imposing white gates and the familiar gilt lion and sun crest. Manuela knew they could be only in one place—the Royal Compound. Images of photos she had seen in magazines—the Shah and Empress and their four children posing for photographers in front of the residence; the smiling Shah walking along the white beaches of Kish with his black great dane; informal photos of the tanned, smiling Pahlavis picnicking under a large tree in the Royal Compound—immediately    flashed    through Manuela's mind.

The gates opened, and a swarthy guard nodded to Mark as he drove inside, up a slight incline. Manuela gasped. The Royal Compound was impressive to behold. A huge white ultramodern two-story villa stood at the end of the tree-lined road. The building was circular, with a slightly sloping turquoise-tiled roof that extended past the house, creating a shaded patio around the whole structure. Its dramatic simplicity was majestic—as befitted the Shah's residence. Interspersed among the lush, colorful gardens were four small villas, all white. They had dramatically soaring roofs, sharply angled walls, and were connected by walkways that were shaded by white Pahlavi Arches.

The Range Rover stopped in front of the Residence. Mark and Kir got out, and helped the three women out of the back seat.

"This place is fantastic, isn't it, Gabriella?" Mark said.

*"E magnifico!"* Gabriella replied, awestruck by her surroundings. She walked around to the other

side of the Range Rover, to where Michael and the two other women were standing. Gabriella opened her mouth, about to speak, but Michael ignored her, and addressed all three of them.

"I know you girls must have some questions to ask me, but I suggest you go to your villas, and relax. We'll meet for cocktails in the residence at seven-thirty. A little dinner party will follow. I will answer all your questions then." Michael turned away from the women, and called to three slight, Oriental figures standing on the shaded walkway.

"Boys!" Kir said, clapping his hands together.

At eight o'clock, Gabriella stepped out of her villa and hurried down the pathway to the residence. She stopped to pick a velvety purple flower, sticking it into the braided knot of hair at the nape of her neck. The sky was darkening, and the evening breeze was gentle and warm. Gabriella could hear the waves breaking on the beach. She was very happy. Things seemed to be working out just to her liking. She had a huge, beautiful villa and her own personal maid, who was absolutely marvelous. While Gabriella had slept most of the afternoon away, her little Filipino maid had unpacked her six suitcases. Gabriella had also called in the masseuse and the hairdresser. As she hurried through the fragrant gardens she felt refreshed and ready for the evening at hand. She knew she was late, but it had taken her so long to decide what to wear.

A uniformed butler opened the door and bowed. He turned and led her silently down the long mirrored hallway. The staccato sound of Gabriella's high heels clicked on the cinnamon-colored marble floor. She stopped and peered into a panel of mirrors, wanting one last look at herself before she made her entrance. She readjusted her flower so that just a hint of the purple petals accented her

229

sleek, neat head of hair. She was pleased, the color of the flower matched her dress perfectly. Gabriella knew that the competition would be stiff and she wanted to make sure that she would dazzle the guests.

She followed the butler toward the double doors at the end of the hallway. Gabriella could hear noise and laughter coming from inside the room. "A party, how marvelous," she said to herself. The butler opened the doors and Gabriella walked into the room. No one seemed to notice her, they were all too busy talking animatedly to one another, laughing and sipping their drinks. But where are the guests, she wondered. All Gabriella could see were familiar faces: Manuela, Victoria, Mark, Gino, Michael, and Andreas—no one else.

"Gabriella!" Michael Kir put down his drink and came over to greet her, kissing her lightly on the cheek. "We wondered what had happened to you, but Mark told us not to worry, that you are *sempre in ritardo*, always late," he said, chastizing her goodhumoredly. "Come, Gabriella," Michael said, taking her hand. "Say hello to everyone."

What everyone, just the same old faces, she thought with irritation. Gabriella naturally assumed that she had been given all the fabulous designer clothes for a reason. Obviously not, she thought, as she and Michael walked out onto the patio where everyone had congregated. The dramatically-set patio extended out over a twenty-foot drop to the water. A warm sea breeze blew in from the ocean as the surf pounded against the rocks.

"Good evening, Gabriella," Victoria said. "You look stunning!"

"Thank you," replied Gabriella graciously. "And you too, Victoria," she said, and she really meant it. Victoria had long, lovely legs and beautiful breasts. Both features were shown off to their best advantage by her clothing: a pair of narrow black raw-silk pants and a sheer black chiffon blouse embroidered with gold dots. A ropelike gold belt was twisted around her narrow waist. Gabriella took a quick look at Manuela, who was standing near the patio's edge talking with Mark. Her shiny black hair fell loose to her bare shoulders, and her ivory and plum dress clung to every one of her curves like glue. *The competition is stiff,* conceded Gabriella. *But competition for what,* she thought. Neither Mark nor Michael had acted like sex maniacs, so what was the point of all this? Why were they here? All these beautiful clothes for this —cocktail parties with *gli altri,* the others?

"All right, everyone. Will you all come take seats inside," Mark said, motioning for them to come into the room adjoining the patio. The three girls took their seats on the white wicker love seats across from the bar area. Michael Kir stood facing them, leaning against the bar.

Gabriella noticed that Andreas and Gino had discreetly left the room, while Mark, arms folded across his chest, stood at the back of the room. Michael looked at Mark and then began.

"I can imagine that you are eager to know about where we are, and what we are all here for," he said. "This island, Kish, belongs to Iran, but as you know, Iran has been experiencing extreme economic hardships for the past few years. A French corporation, Gulf Island Resorts, of which I am a representative, acquired a fifteen-year lease on this island from the Islamic Republic of Iran."

"Which Islamic Republic?" Manuela asked sharply.

"The government of 1981, the Second Islamic Republic. The lease was signed in late 1981."

Manuela nodded, satisfied, and Kir continued. "As I was saying, we were able to obtain the lease because of the government of Iran's acute financial troubles brought on by the pipeline sabotage and the subsequent cutoff of oil revenues.

Our corporation, Gulf Island Resorts, plans to develop this island into a resort area once again. As I explained to you on our drive in from the airport, Kish Island was once, very briefly, a fabulous gambling resort, but our corporation doesn't intend to develop it for the small, exclusive market that it was originally developed for. We have been fortunate that Khalaghani's government, the Third Islamic Republic, has continued to honor our lease, realizing the badly needed economic benefits they will gain. Because of a profit-sharing scheme which Iran insisted on, the Iranian government will receive thirty-five percent of the foreign currency profits that this gambling resort complex will generate. And we all know that Iran needs every dollar it can get."

"That doesn't seem to be in keeping with the Moslem fervor that rules Iran, does it?" Victoria asked.

"No, it doesn't, Victoria, but I don't think that you fully understand the ramifications of this project," Kir replied. "Iran was glad to disassociate itself from Kish Island. It conjured up too many images of the Pahlavi Regime, and anything that Iran could have done with Kish would have caused problems for the Islamic government. They had two choices; either let this place rot away, or make some money off this white elephant. And you all know that the latest government, the Third Islamic Republic of Iran, has clamped down even more on censorship of the press—or what's left of the press. They have a near-total news blackout within the country. So you see, the good Moslems of Iran know nothing about the 'den of iniquity' seething here in the Persian Gulf, only seventeen miles off their coast."

Victoria looked at Kir unconvinced. "So what was the big secret, Michael? Why the big mystery about where we were being brought to?"

"I was getting to that," he said curtly. "The

Iranian government insists that we keep this under wraps. We have agreed not to leak any publicity about this project until the final stages. The government was very strict about the conditions of the contract, but they are anxiously awaiting the flow of badly needed dollars, francs, and marks into their empty coffers. Naturally, the Iranian government has been curious about our project. Several times during the past year we have had the dubious pleasure of delegations of mullahs visiting the islands, observing our progress, reviewing our plans. They seemed to be able to overcome their religious convictions in the hope that perhaps Kish Island might be the first money-making scheme that Iran has embarked on in the past couple of years.

"As you know, there are acute food shortages on the mainland, even famine in some areas. Iran's share of the money to be realized from this lucrative gambling complex and the influx of tourist dollars could allow Iran to buy foodstuffs from the outside world, until it can either restore its agricultural lands to productivity or return its oil industry to a reasonable level of productivity." Michael Kir put his hands in his pockets and began packing back and forth.

"As I am sure you can appreciate, the cost of acquiring the lease on the island was formidable, and now we must attract the right echelon of clients needed to make this venture, Gulf Island Resorts, a success. We want companies that can provide the services essential to a luxury-class resort island, as well as people who will be able to direct customers to this island to make use of our facilities. We want to make Kish the convention center of the Middle East. As you have seen, the Sheraton is opening the hotel. We are currently working on a contract with Lowes for gambling concessions and another hotel.

Kir paused. "This is where you three come in." Kir's voice was hard, cold, and businesslike. He stopped pacing, and stood facing the seated women. "We want our very select prospective clients to see the potential that Kish Island has to offer, so that they will invest here. We want them to enjoy their stay here—in every way possible. We will have some very important guests here in the next few months, surveying the facilities, discussing terms, and contracts." Kir took a step closer to the women. "We aim to present Kish Island in the best possible light—as a true pleasure spot. You girls are here to help the guests —according to each guest's own particular proclivities—enjoy themselves completely. You are all sophisticated, highly intelligent women, who— I am sure—understand the situation and will entertain our guests admirably. I hope I have made myself clear."

Gabriella sighed inwardly. Indeed you have Mr. Kir, but for one hundred thousand dollars, what else should I have expected? At least now I know: I was hired as a whore. Well, "hired," isn't exactly the word—"blackmailed" is more like it, she thought angrily.

"But I want you girls to enjoy your stay here," Kir said emphatically. "Everything that you could want—sports, hairdressers, masseurs, and the like —is here for you on the island, and if you have any special requests, we will do our best to fulfill them. The only thing that is dangerous here are the sharks in the water. But don't worry," he said reassuringly, "there is a shark net for the beaches. Also, please be careful in the sun. It is still quite hot during the day here on Kish, but the weather will get cooler as we move into winter. Now, do you have any questions?"

"Michael," Gabriella said, still shaken from the threatening tone of his voice, "what I want to know, is..." She paused, having asked the question more out of nervousness than anything else, "I mean, what I want to know, why is all the help Oriental—the gardeners, the maids, the butler?"

"Very good question, Gabriella," Kir said, smiling at her. "We are trying to aim for top-quality service, at the most competitive labor costs. We have hired people from the Philippines —earnest, hard workers. They have come from small villages, so none of them speak much English. But they will understand anything you ask of them in their line of work. Andreas recruited them, and he has been on the island for most of the past month training them. We also have some Koreans, who service the planes and operate the airport and control tower. Our chefs have been trained in Switzerland. I think you will agree that Andreas has done an admirable job of organizing things on the island. If you have any complaints, suggestions, or requests, he'll be more than happy to help you out. Now, any more questions?"

There was complete silence in the room.

With his cold green eyes, Kir looked intently at all three girls. "I should emphasize that this is a project that we have been working on long and hard and we will allow nothing, I repeat, nothing, to jeopardize it."

Manuela was seething inside. Well done, Michael Kir, you liar, she thought to herself. You bastard. Something is going on here, and I'll get to the bottom of it. You aren't turning me into a *jende*, a whore, just to sell convention bookings.

The butler opened the double doors. "Dinner is served."

As Manuela walked past Michael Kir she gave him a venomous look, and through clenched teeth she whispered, "*Kos-khesh*, pimp."

# THIRTEEN

It was a gray October day in Tehran. The late afternoon sky was hazy, and the bone-dry air was cold. Ali-Reza drove away from Mehrabad Airport, after having spent an uneventful day at Civil Aviation Headquarters. He breathed a sigh of relief, glad the work day was over. He had important business to attend to. His breath condensed into a small, smoky cloud, then disappeared into the crisp cold air.

Ali-Reza turned right, driving past the boarded-up Imperial Flying Club. He passed the old Iran Air Headquarters, a chain securing the gate. Iran Air now worked out of much smaller offices at Mehrabad Airport, less than a kilometer behind him. Aliz-Reza's orange Range Rover was the only car on this access road to the airport. The once buzzing International Airport of Tehran was all but abandoned.

Ali-Reza turned onto the expressway that led into the city of Tehran. A few rickety trucks carrying half-rotten eggplants and other winter vegetables, and Datsun pickups, loaded down with scrap metal and scraps of wood, were the only vehicles on the road. Ali-Reza glanced over to where the Shahyad Monument had once stood. Now there was no graceful triumphal arch—the familiar soaring white structure that had once been the gateway to Tehran was gone. Only a mound of rubble lay scattered across the yellow grass. The Shahyad (literally, "Shah's remembrance") Monument had been torn down by order of Khomeini. Ali-Reza shook his head sadly. Nothing constructive had come out of the Islamic Revolution.

When a tactic was needed to divert the people's attention away from the problems of the Revolution, the mullahs ordered the destruction of all symbols of the Shah's rule. Topping the list was Niavarin Palace, the residence of the Shah. When the match was set to Niavarin Palace, the crowd at the palace gates cheered wildly. It was the best sideshow of the year, surpassed only by the seizing of the American hostages.

Shahyad Monument was next. The same jubilation and excitement that heralded the destruction of Niavarin Palace was generated when the wrecker's ball began smashing the white marble facing off the Shahyad Monument. Next on the list was the tomb that had housed the body of the deposed Shah's father in the town of Rey (the Shah had the foresight, before he left Iran, to remove Reza Shah's body). Also destroyed was the green Marble Palace in Tehran, which had served as a museum of the Pahlavi Dynasty. Mercifully, the destruction was halted before every Pahlavi-associated structure could be destroyed.

Ali-Reza continued to drive along the highway, keeping his eye on the few cars and trucks traveling into the city with him. The cars that now traveled the roads of Iran were strange hybrid vehicles. Since imported car parts had all but disappeared, and the latest model of the Iranian Peykans and Jyanes to have been produced in Iran was 1980, garages began creating their own mix-and-match designs. A BMW 320 passed along one side of Ali-Reza, its sleek design marred by a boxy, crude bumper from a utilitarian Peykan car. Ali-Reza passed a tinny French-styled Jyane, its bald tires adorned with Mercedes hubcaps, and bucket seats that looked like they had come from one of the popular Cameros or Firebirds that used to crowd the expressway.

Once a city with a population of five million, Tehran's population, by 1983, had been drastically reduced to just around a million people. After the Revolution there had been an initial surge to Tehran. The curious wanted to be at the center of the movement, to see Imam Khomeini in the flesh. Once the intitial excitement had worn off and the urban population realized that there was no work for them in the cities, the itinerant laborers, construction and road-crew workers went back to their villages and rejoined their hungry families, who were trying to eke out a living from the earth.

Then came the next blow; the capital was moved from Tehran to Qom, by declaration of Imam Khomeini. Qom, a small city of 250,000, a holy city of Shi'ite Islam, became the center of the Islamic government. All the government offices were moved there. A complex of government offices—buildings, residences for the clergy, and the headquarters for the *Pasdaran*, the Revolutionary Guards—were established. The official seat of government was the Madreseh-ye-Fazeyeh from which the ruling Ayatollah issued his edicts. There was a conscious effort on the part of the mullahs to move focus away from Tehran and to make Qom the model city of Islam. The only positive result of this policy was that there no longer was the unbelievable Tehran brand of deadly pollution, nor the equally infamous traffic jams.

Ali-Reza continued north, past the boarded-up Hyatt Regency Crowd Hotel. Immediately after the Revolution it was sacked, and seven hundred and fifty thousand dollars worth of liqour had been poured down the drains. The Hyatt, a symbol of Western decadence, was closed and boarded up. Nowadays, Ali-Reza's few-and-far-between alcholic drinks were out of cologne bottles—the standard, post-Revolution mickey flasks. No one went to a special celebration, such as a wedding, without a bottle of "cologne" in their glove compartment or purse. Eau Savage and Monsieur Givenchy were the drinks of the '80s in Iran. People in Ali-Reza's circles, the ones who had adopted Western ways, still tried to maintain some of their old traditions; they smuggled records into the country; made their own wine, smoked hashish and opium, and carried on occasional illicit affairs very illicitly. But what little novelty there might have been in getting around those things deemed *haram*, forbidden, by the mullahs had long ago lost its appeal. The lack of personal freedom was stifling, and the economic hardships made life in Iran in 1983 extremely difficult.

Ali-Reza continued along the expressway for another six kilometers until he came to the stoplight at the intersection of what had been called, before the Revolution, the Shahinshah Expressway and Pahlavi Avenue; now it was Mossadeq Expressway and Mossadeq Avenue. The Royal Tehran Hilton, to Ali-Reza's right, was still standing, but it was only the blackened shell of the former luxury hotel. The Hilton had been gutted by fire two years before. The few remaining foreign guests in the hotel had died in the fire. Arson was suspected, but never proved.

Ali-Reza's Range Rover sped down Mossadeq Avenue. There was hardly any traffic. Once honking horns and wall-to-wall cars and pedestrians had made Pahlavi Avenue (which stretched from the north end of Tehran to Rey, just beyond the southern outskirts of the city) one of the liveliest streets in Tehran. Pahlavi Avenue had been crowded with people buying the wares of the street vendors, who sold steaming-hot, purple-red beets in a sugary sauce in winter, and roasted corn in summer. Families stopped at Yaz *chelo-kebab* restaurant on a Friday afternoon and young people ate ice cream sundaes at Chattanoga Restaurant. Park Shahinshahi, with its polaroid photographers, artificial lake and boats, exotic birds in cages and hamburger stand was always crowded. The twenty kilometers of what was once Pahlavi Avenue, with its cinemas, clothing stores, furniture stores full of ugly furniture, Kentucky Fried Chicken, restaurants, hotels, banks, and businesses were now depressing and lifeless. Mossadeq Avenue was a street of boarded-up facades, empty shops, aimless wanderers, and filthy sheep.

Ali-Reza rolled up his window. Even on a cold day like today, the smell from the filthy *jubes* was overpowering. He leaned over and turned on the radio, more out of habit than interest. The radio only played—incessantly—the same monotonous chanting, prayers, and didactic monologues by assorted mullahs-cum-disc-jockeys.

"What a fucked-up country," Ali-Reza said in disgust, turning the radio off.

Ali-Reza turned left and headed down Raizan Street, a deadend street lined with withering, dusty poplars. He wove the Range Rover down the street, attempting to avoid the potholes that made up more of the street than did the pavement. He swung the car into the highway of his uncle's apartment building and brought it to a stop. Ali-Reza climbed out of the car, and walked toward the building.

The modern four-storey apartment building, owned by Ali-Reza's uncle, housed four apartments, one on each floor, plus a tiny subterranean apartment for the caretaker. Formerly, the floor-through units had been luxury apartments, complete with wall-to-wall carpeting, built-in washers and dryers, and sleek German customized kitchens. Well-to-do Iranians and foreigners had lived in these expensive apartments, but both the Iranians and foreigners had fled—during and after the Revolution. Shortly thereafter, squatters moved into the hastily vacated apartments. Rather than lose the whole building to squatters, Ali-Reza's uncle and his family moved into the third-floor apartment. But as time passed, and Tehran became more and more of a ghost town, even the squatters had left to go back to their countryside villages. Now, only Ali-Reza's uncle and his family remained.

Ali-Reza was about to enter the building, then changed his mind. He walked around to the back-yard to see if, perhaps, any wild roses still grew there. He wanted to have something to give his aunt. A fetid odor greeted him as he walked near the dry swimming pool. His uncle had, out of necessity, converted the pool into a makeshift barn; the few sheep were herded into the pool at night. These scrawny sheep were the only source of meat and milk for his uncle's family, and Ali-Reza's family was better off than most people.

Ali-Reza walked around the dead garden. There was not a single flower. He turned around and walked into the building.

The small entrance foyer was dark and cold. Ali-Reza hurried past the elevator; he knew that it did not work. It hadn't worked in years. He climbed the dimly lit stairs, two at a time. At the top of the third-floor landing he could hear voices inside the apartment. He hoped that his cousin, Hamid, had already arrived. Hamid, a chief engineer at the Abadan refinery, had finagled a travel permit to come up to Tehran, for medical reasons. It had been just over a month since Ali-Reza had last seen Hamid.

Ali-Reza tucked his shirt neatly into his jeans and finger-combed his hair before knocking on the door.

His aunt, a heavyset, pleasant-looking woman in her fifties, opened the door. She was dressed in an old black sweater and black skirt.

"Ali-Reza! What a surprise," exclaimed his aunt, giving him a bone-crushing hug.

Ali-Reza reciprocated, kissing his aunt on both cheeks, telling her that she looked beautiful. With his aunt, Ali-Reza always spoke English. She had studied in England as a young girl and liked to practice her English whenever possible.

"Come in, come in, my favorite nephew. I'm so happy to see you. How is your family?"

"Fine, auntie," replied Ali-Reza. "Just fine."

Ali-Reza's aunt looked sadly at him. "No one is fine anymore, both you and I know that."

Ali-Reza nodded in agreement with his aunt. He felt sorry for her. She hated the rule of the mullahs and had wanted to leave Iran from the day Khomeini had arrived back in Iran, but her husband was an opium addict, and preferred to stay in Iran, close to the source of his habit. He had friends in the western province of Azarbaijan who had farms on which they raised poppies: he was guaranteed as much opium as he wanted.

Ali-Reza did not need to ask where his uncle was; he knew that he was in another room of the apartment smoking opium with his cronies. Among the older generation of Iranians, opium smoking had been a well-respected habit. A man who smoked opium all his life became a sage. During the Shah's regime opium addicts were encouraged to register in a government program. In return they were given a monthly ration of the drug and the government was able to keep better controls on the illicit opium trade. Nowadays, the threat of death for opium smoking did not stop people such as Ali-Reza's uncle from smoking: illegal drugs were one of the few pleasures left. But among Ali-Reza's generation opium smoking was merely an occasional diversion from more popular drugs, such as marijuana and hashish. The fact that prolonged use of opium made one impotent was enough to curb Ali-Reza's appetite for it.

Ali-Reza's aunt beckoned to him, and he followed her into the kitchen. Taking a small metal teapot that was heating over a kettle on the stove, she poured a glass of tea for Ali-Reza. She apologized for not having any cakes to offer him, explaining that she had been unable to get butter or eggs for over a month. Ali-Reza did not bother to ask for sugar for his tea. He knew that sugar was just as hard to come by.

"Ali-Reza, why don't you leave Iran?" his aunt asked.

Ali-Reza looked at her, searching for a suitable answer.

"You're young, Ali-*jun*, why don't you leave? You should leave! This is no place for you. This is a dead country."

Ali-Reza changed the subject, inquiring about his aunts, uncles, and cousins.

"Hamid? Hamid is here!" exclaimed Ali-Reza's aunt. "He arrived from Abadan just today. He's with your uncle. He has been asking about you."

"Well, I should go and say hello," Ali-Reza said,

excusing himself.

Ali-Reza knocked on the door to the television room, except that now no one used it as a TV den. "Mullahvision" was no one's idea of entertainment. Ali-Reza smiled to himself, thinking that the television den had become an opium den.

Ali-Reza walked into the small room, thick with smoke. Blinking his eyes, he looked around the room. He greeted his uncle and his uncle's friends, who were sitting crosslegged in a circle around a rectangular brazier in the center of the room. Seated nearest to the door was Hamid. Ali-Reza sat down next to Hamid on a roughly-woven camel-hair cushion, a *pushtee*. Hamid smiled at his cousin, and gave him a nod.

Ali-Reza sat back and relaxed. He loved to watch the ritual of opium smoking, the measured sequence of steps, unchanged for hundreds of years. His uncle took a soft, malleable stick of opium from a wooden box. The opium stick was the size of a slender cigar, smooth and molasses-colored. He cut off a small piece with a pair of stainless steel clippers. Then, holding the piece of opium with a pair of pinchers, he heated it over the fire until it glowed red. Taking a long wooden-stemmed pipe with a porcelain bulb on the end of it, his uncle placed the sticky opium over the small, resin-stained hole at the top of the bowl, and sucked languorously on the pipe. The pipe was then passed around to all present, the piece of opium reheated as necessary by placing it next to the red-hot glowing coals in the brazier. Once Ali-Reza had partaken of a reasonable amount of opium to have appeared sociable, he motioned to Hamid. The two of them rose, bowed to their elders, and excused themselves from the room.

Ali-Reza followed Hamid out to the high-walled balcony just of the living room. The black night sky was only faintly illuminated by the stars overhead. A cold wind blew across the balcony. Ali-Reza shivered.

Hamid pulled a small knife from his pocket, cut open the lining of his jacket, and pulled out a large folded sheet of drafting paper. Ali-Reza did not bother to open it; he knew what it was. He unbuttoned his shirt, and placed the blueprints of the newly rebuilt Abadan refinery next to his chest. Whispering instructions to Hamid, Ali-Reza quickly buttoned up his shirt, pressing the paper close to his chest.

# CHAPTER FOURTEEN

The sun was beating down on the girls' well-oiled brown bodies. Clothed in bathing suits the size of postage stamps, the three girls lay by the secluded swimming pool of Victoria's villa, within the compound. Victoria took a sip of her tall, cool drink. "That Michael Kir really isn't the businessman he thinks he is. We've been here over three weeks, living in the lap of luxury, and he hasn't managed to dig up one client for this place," Victoria said.

The other two girls nodded and smiled.

"Yet, for some guy who hasn't managed to sell a rock off this island," Victoria continued, "he runs around like a social director on an ocean cruise."

"Yes, he looks run ragged," Gabriella commented. "I wonder where he flies off to every other day. Victoria, you've been in this area before, what else is there around here? *Mamma mia*, this island seems like it is in the middle of nowhere!" she exclaimed.

"Really, I couldn't guess," replied Victoria. "To Iran, perhaps?"

"Then, he really is *pazzo*, crazy," said Gabriella, looking up from her magazine. She shook her head. "You know, I hate to admit it, girls, but the boredom is getting to me. At first, I didn't mind the pampered life of breakfast in bed—at noon, the fitness instructors who almost do the exercises for you, and all this waiting on us hand and foot, but to be honest with you—I'm so horny I can't stand it! Frankly, I wouldn't mind it all that much if Michael Kir, the great wheeler-dealer, could manage to entice one of those 'very select prospective clients' to come here."

Victoria laughed. "God, I agree with you, Gabriella. Look, it's geting so bad that even Gino is beginning to look good!"

Gabriella laughed as she readjusted her mirrored sunglasses. "You know, I have a theory. I think that it is all those massages I take that are making me so horny—all that warm oil and friction."

"Darling, I think it is the caviar," Victoria said playfully. "A tried and true aphrodisiac. Dear old Mr. Tabeti swore by it. But a lot of good it did him."

"What do you mean?" Gabriella asked interestedly, male impotence being one of her favorite topics of conversation.

"Well, he smoked too much opium. After that, all the caviar in the Caspian Sea couldn't have helped him."

"I don't understand," Gabriella said, puzzled.

"Didn't you know, Gabriella, opium smoking makes a man impotent."

"Poor Mr. Tabeti," Gabriella said, pseudo-sympathetically.

"Mind you," retorted Victoria jokingly, "it didn't help that he was ninety years old."

Manuela lay on her back, her eyes closed, as she listened to the two girls giggling. Her bikini-clad bronzed body was perfectly still; she appeared to be asleep. Abruptly, she got up from the chaise lounge and dove into the pool, a quiet splash in the cool sparkling water.

"Look who's here," Victoria said as she pointed toward the entrance to the pool area. Gabriella squinted into the sun, recognizing Mark's gangly walk. She modestly reached for the top of her bikini and began doing up the strings.

"Hey, what's all the laughter here? I could hear it from around the corner. If it's a dirty joke, you should tell it to me." Mark pulled up a latticework deck chair and collapsed into it. "I need a laugh," he said.

"Poor thing," said Victoria. "Has Michael been working you too hard?"

"*Povero* Mark," echoed Gabriella. "Have a drink. You look like you need one." She handed him a frosty tumbler.

"I hate to say it, Mark, but you look awful. Does Michael make you work all night, too?" Victoria said.

"Just about," sighed Mark, taking a gulp of the drink.

The pool boy, dressed in white jeans and a rainbow-striped Gulf Island Resorts T-shirt, quickly brought Gabriella another drink.

"Girls, do you mind if I take my shirt off? I look like a ghost compared to the three of you." Mark pulled off his baggy T-shirt. His body was white and nearly hairless, but well-muscled, like a swimmer's. He positioned his chair to get the direct rays of the sun, then stretched out in the chair, his head back, facing the sun.

"Ah, this is the life!" Mark reached into the pocket of his pants, and pulled out a handful of postcards. "I almost forgot, could you girls please write a couple of postcards to your friends and relatives, so that they don't think that you've disappeared off the face of the earth." He handed them over in the direction of the girls. "Just take a bunch, O.K.?"

Victoria reached across and took them out of Mark's hand. "My, my, I wonder where I have just visited on my African safari? Oh, look at this Gabriella, we have just been in Kenya, Mombasa Beach."

"I was there last December," Gabriella said, looking over Victoria's shoulder. "It is beautiful. The Leopard Beach Hotel is full of rich and handsome Europeans. Only the best people go there, Victoria," Gabriella said in a low whisper. "Did I ever tell you about Count Egon?"

"Please, Gabriella," Mark said, "spare me the details."

"Later," Garbriella said to Victoria, raising her eyebrows.

"Could you please write these cards sometime today? We have to send them out to be mailed tonight," Mark said.

"Sure," Victoria said. She looked at the sky. "What's that I hear?" she asked. "A plane?"

"Oh, shit!" Mark said. "Excuse the language girls, but that must be Mike coming back."

"Coming back from where?" asked Victoria, pushing her sunglasses down her nose, looking directly at Mark.

"Flying lessons," Mark replied quickly. "Sorry ladies, I've gotta go," he said standing up. "You know I'd rather be here with you than there." Mark looked over to the residence, thinking wearily of the Communications Room on the top floor and of all the many late hours he and Kir had logged in there the past few weeks. Mark got up and walked along the pool's edge, watching Manuela in the water. "Very nice stroke you've got there, Manuela."

"Thanks, Mark. Leaving so soon?"

"Yeah, I've gotta get back to work. No rest for the weary, you know," he said smiling. "Oh,

Manuela, I left some postcards for you to write to friends and relatives. They've got to be ready by this evening, O.K.? We don't want anyone to get worried about you."

"Thanks Mark, but actually there isn't anyone. I'll give my share to the other girls."

"Manuela, I'm sorry . . ."

"Don't be," she said.

Manuela awoke from her afternoon nap. She automatically reached for the phone to ring for the maid, but decided against it. The clock beside her bed read 6:15 p.m.; she had time enough to get ready for dinner at nine o'clock. She got out of bed, slipped on her kimono and padded across the floor toward the balcony. The entire front wall of her bedroom was floor to ceiling windows, directly facing the water. She slid open the sliding-glass doors and stepped out onto the balcony. The sun was sinking below the horizon and the sky was turning dark shades of magenta. There was a chill edge to the evening air, and Manuela wrapped her silk kimono around herself tighter. She lit a cigarette with an enameled Cartier lighter, and inhaled deeply. It was quiet, there was only the sound of powerful waves breaking on the phosphorescent strip of beach below her. She looked at the lights of the other villas along the water's edge.

Each girl had her own house within the Royal Compound. The magnificent, luxuriously decorated villas were connected by fragrant flower-lined pathways. Manuela assumed, correctly, that her house had formerly been a guest house, whereas the other two girls lived in the houses of relatives of the Shah. Victoria's villa was the largest, the most luxurious; it had probably been the Kish home of Princess Ashraf, the Shah's twin sister.

Manuela remembered Victoria telling her how one day a faucet handle from the bathtub had come unscrewed, and when Victoria picked up the heavy handle, she realized that it was made of gold. Even Manuela, who herself had been part of the old, privileged Iranian upper crust, was amazed at the lavishness of Kish.

Manuela had seen Kish Island on horseback. Andreas had escorted her on these forays, always with a rifle slung over his back. They had ridden almost everywhere on the island—everywhere that was permitted. About half the island was off-limits—primarily the Arab village. Manuela had explored almost every building on Kish that she was allowed to visit, albeit under the watchful eyes of Andreas. She'd poked around the casino, where the workers were busy relaying the carpets, and explored the sumptuous private villas. Andreas had given her a tour of the desalination plant that had been built by the Israelis in 1971. She enjoyed looking around the shopping arcade, with its Ted Lapidus boutique and Cartier jewelry store ready to be stocked full of luxury items. But there were some places, even on the resort side of Kish, that were off-limits to her. Most days she'd been allowed to go into the hotel, but there were days when Andreas had steered her clear of it. She had been allowed to ride over to the airport and look inside the terminal, but she noted that she was never taken to the hangar. Other than that, perhaps the only other place that she had not seen was the inside of the Crown Prince's villa. It was situated next to the Royal Compound, and a short distance outside the compound walls. From its size and beautiful exterior, Manuela could tell that it must have been magnificent. But she was not allowed inside to visit it because it was being renovated, or so Andreas said.

Manuela couldn't shake the eerie feeling that she had about Kish Island. It was as if there was the appearance of activity on the island, but with nothing actually getting done. Inside the airport terminal was a scale model of the island, showing the stages of Gulf Island Resorts' development of Kish from the original buildings now standing, through Phase Three (expected completion date late 1985), with its new three-hundred-and-fifty-room hotel on the southeast corner of the island. There were planned additions to the casino complex, new tennis courts, and even an eighteen-hole golf course. There was also a large separate model of the Mid-East Convention Center, a huge complex to be built in conjunction with the new hotel. Everything was convincingly presented, yet Manuela was skeptical. It seemed like a very industrious undertaking, almost too industrious. She could not deny that something was being done. There was a hum of activity all over the island. Bulldozers leveled the ground for tennis courts; gardeners planted, watered, weeded; workmen were still busy cleaning the tiles on the hotel. Always something being done, yet, sometimes Manuela could swear that the Filipino workmen just wheeled their wheelbarrels back and forth, and the bulldozers just moved the dirt around.

The Filipino workers kept to themselves—whether by choice or because of orders, Manuela didn't know. They lived in the flat-roofed, white-washed, Moroccan-style dwellings across from the casino, which had originally been built to house the casino staff. The Filipinos seemed to be a content little community. Sometimes when she and Andreas would ride by, she'd see the women out in the gardens hanging out their wash. Andreas would stop and say hello, talk a bit with them, but little more than sign language passed between Manuela and those people.

Best of all, Manuela enjoyed riding her beautiful Arabian horse along the isolated white sandy beach on the southern side of the island. With the wind in her hair and the sun on her face, she would race Andreas to the end of the beach, toward the broken, rusting tanker that lay just offshore. The oil tanker was fairly small, and from its rust-eaten shell it must have run aground many years ago. The other ships she'd seen were small wooden *dhows*, Arab fishing boats that traveled around the point to the fishing village at the western corner of the island. Manuela had wanted to go see the village, but Andreas said that the Arabs living in the village would not approve of a half-naked woman on horseback. Manuela had countered that jeans and a T-shirt could hardly be considered half-naked, but Andreas had said that to the Arabs, accustomed to women completely covered by black veils and leather masks, she'd look like Lady Godiva.

Lately, Andreas had been too busy to take her riding, so Manuela had to stay in the compound, lounging around the pool. Manuela, Gabriella, and Victoria had become fast friends. Gabriella reveled in telling tales of her rich and famous lovers, and Victoria entertained them with stories of what Kish had been like in the days when she had come here with Mr. Tabeti. Yet, in spite of their friendliness, Manuela found it hard to become close to them; it was not her nature. She was used to keeping her distance, and it was enough that one person on the island knew her secret.

As for Michael, Manuela hardly ever saw him. He was gone most days with Gino in the Beechcraft, or with Mark, racing in and out of the compound in jeeps. Many times, late at night, Manuela, gripped by insomnia, would look out her window and see light coming from narrow slits on the second story of the residence. She knew that it must have been Michael in that room, but what was he doing, she wondered, and why was he neglecting her? The only time that she saw him was during dinner, in the company of all the others. After dinner they would often all watch a movie together, or play backgammon or chess, but Michael was always so distant.

A breeze rippled across the balcony. When it passed, Manuela lit another cigarette. As she stood on the balcony, smoking her cigarette, she looked northward, across the dark Gulf waters, to Iran. She was overwhelmed by melancholy. Sometimes Manuela thought that her night in Rio with Michael had never really happened. She felt abandoned by him, once again. Manuela went indoors, took a Valium, and dressed for dinner.

The eight of them sat at the table. Manuela was in a low-cut, spaghetti-strapped thin red dress. Andreas sat to her right, elegantly attired in a dark suit, and Mark was to her left. Victoria sat next to him, her shiny blond hair piled loosely on top of her head, tendrils of hair, like strands of gold, tumbling down her neck. Her dress was a brilliant cobalt blue and dramatically slashed to the waist. Next to Victoria sat Gino, almost hidden from view by a large centerpiece of flowers. He was dressed in a silk shirt and linen suit, rumpled as usual. Next to Gino sat Gabriella, resplendent in a tight cerise satin dress that looked as if she had been poured into it, the material mimicking every voluptuous curve of her body. Gabriella was engaged in an animated .conversation with the stranger seated next to her; he was the first guest on the island.

He had been introduced by Kir as Mr. Kalvani, the Middle East representative for a large hotel chain out of San Francisco. He was a man in his mid-thirties, with a strong, handsome face accented by a thin moustache. He spoke English with a faint Persian accent. Manuela eyed him suspiciously.

Silver platters piled high with saffron rice; savory stews; *khoresht-bademjun*, a mixture of eggplant, tomato, and lamb; kebobs of tender lamb and marinated chicken; plates of *sabzee*, greens, spearmint, peppermint, basil, scallions, radishes; and soft, crumbly, feta-type cheese covered the table.

At the insistence of Mr. Kalvani, Gabriella took some of the *fesenjun* stew that was being offered her. She eyed the thick, dark-brown, vile-looking substance lying on a bed of rice on her plate with great suspicion.

"What is it?" Gabriella leaned closer to Mr. Kalvani.

"*Fesenjun* is made from crushed walnuts, pomegranate juice and duck," Mr. Kalvani replied. "Try it, you'll like it," he coaxed her.

Gabriella gingerly tasted the strange mixture, pleasantly surprised that the sweet, nutty taste was palatable and actually good. She looked over at Mr. Kalvani, smiling sweetly. She took one more dainty bite and then put down her fork. One bite too many, and Gabriella knew that the satin sheen of her dress would magnify anything but the flattest of stomachs. Gabriella did not want that. She liked Mr. Kalvani, and she especially liked the idea that her period of celibacy was about to come to a close. Gabriella had flirted unabashedly with Mr. Kalvani all evening, and she was sure that tonight would be her night. In eager anticipation, Gabriella glanced his way again, this time looking below the belt. Mr. Kalvani's navy blue blazer was unbuttoned and what Gabriella saw made her gasp inwardly. A pearl-handled revolver was tucked into his belt.

Victoria surveyed the table heaped high with Persian food. Undoubtedly in honor of our guest, she thought. She had eaten too much and was sipping an ice-cold glass of *dougeh*. It had been years since she had tasted this yogurt and soda water drink that was so popular in Iran. It was an acquired taste, but once she was used to it, it had been the only thing to drink in the summer's heat after a big Persian meal. Tonight's typical Persian dinner reminded Victoria of the many times she had been to private homes in Tehran. Victoria had to smile, just thinking about what she had seen. At the opulent houses of the rich in Tehran, at tables set with Porthault linen, Sèvres china, and Waterford crystal, there were always those omni-present bottles of Coca Cola, Pepsi, and Canada Dry on the table, and those damned boxes of Kleenex. No table in Iran was complete without them. Victoria had always wondered about the Iranian Kleenex fetish. Every table, every car, in Iran had a prominently placed box of Kleenex. It must have meant something. Was it symbolic of their cultural advancement, proof that they'd made it into the twentieth century? Now they no longer wiped their asses and their noses with their left hand, but with a soft, powder-blue Kleenex? Well, thought Victoria, considering the mighty lurch backwards that the Iranians had taken these past five years, probably Kleenex boxes no longer grace their now-meager tables.

Well, no one will starve here on Kish, Victoria thought, as she watched a waiter carry in a large silver tray piled high with fruits, small cucumbers, and wedges of the famous Persian melon, *harbusay*. Victoria picked up a cucumber and began to cut away the bumpy, green skin. She wondered what, exactly, was Mr. Kalvani's business. She was surprised that Kir hadn't launched into his sales pitch yet, but it seemed obvious that it would be Gabriella who was going to "sew up the deal."

"Why don't we have coffee in the screening room?" suggested Kir, as the waiters cleared away the fruit plates.

"Good idea," Mark replied. "Go ahead, girls," he said, ushering the three girls out the door. "We'll be there in a moment."

Gabriella, Victoria, and Manuela walked down the long hallway to the screening room. There were about twenty overstuffed chairs in the dimly lit room. The three girls took their seats next to the pounded brass table, set out with dishes of *gaz*, a lightly floured candy made from fresh nougat and pistachios.

"Anyone care for a *digestivo*?" Gabriella asked, as she swiveled her chair around and opened the liquor cabinet.

"Is there any champagne in the refrigerator?" Victoria asked. "I feel like celebrating. After all, this is a big day for Gulf Island Resorts."

"I should say so!" Manuela added, sarcastically. "Our very first select prospective client and his proclivities."

"Then champagne it is," said Gabriella.

Mark hurried into the room. "Ready?"

"Ready for what?" Gabriella asked, expectantly.

"The movie."

"Where are Michael and Mr. Kalvani?" Gabriella asked.

"Oh, they have some work to do," Mark replied. "Business before pleasure." Mark handed Manuela a stack of cassettes. "Here are the latest movies, flown in especially for you. Now girls, I've got to run," Mark said, getting up from his chair.

"Just one second." Manuela gently but firmly pulled Mark back down to his seat. "We are all friends there. I think that you can tell us the story of Mr. X."

"What do you mean, Manuela," Mark asked innocently.

"What I mean is, what is protocol for 'entertaining' the guest?"

"Yes," continued Victoria, "do we pick him, does he pick us, do we draw lots, go in alphabetical order, what?"

"Don't worry, girls, Mr. Kalvani is here on business, purely business. He is checking out his company's holdings here on Kish. So, relax, girls, enjoy your movie."

Mark hurried down the hallway, walking toward the east side of the residence, a part of the building that was supposedly closed. He stopped at a locked door and pulled two keys out of his pocket. He opened the thick metal door, and stepped into a dark, very small, room. The room was empty, and had been intended as—or made to appear as—a storage room. Directly across from where Mark stood was another door. Before he could get the key into the lock, the door opened automatically. Shutting the door behind him, Mark climbed the white metal spiral staircase to the Communications Room.

The large room at the top of the stairs was brightly lit. Fluorescent lights harshly illuminated the metal desks, cabinets, telex machine, banks of scrambler telephones, closed-circuit television screens, and radio equipment. The pointed ceiling sloped downward to a junction with the walls that were only eight feet high. There were no windows in the room—only small, irregularly spaced horizontal slits.

Against one wall was a large map of the Persian Gulf and Iran, while set into another wall was a series of boldface clocks showing the time in various parts of the world: Seattle, Houston, Washington, London, and Tokyo. Seated next to a bank of twelve closed-circuit television screens was Michael Kir. Across the table sat Commander Kalvani.

"Take a seat, Mark," Kir said. "Commander Kalvani was about to describe the movement of his logistics support."

"Thank you," Kalvani said, as he stood up and strode over to the large map of the Persian Gulf, taking the pointer in his hand.

"We have approximately fifty dhows working the Persian Gulf area. From our base here on Kish, these boats carry goods from the port of Dubai, northward across the Gulf, past Kish and then eastward, traveling around the tip of Oman, through the Straits of Hormuz, closely following the southeast coastline of Iran. From the abandoned Iranian naval port of Chahbahar, the Baluchis pick up the goods and taken them into the mountains of Baluchistan. Another system of dhows travels from Dubai, angles off at Kish and travels northward, to the head of the Persian Gulf, to the province of Khuzistan."

Commander Kalvani paused. "I think you can appreciate that this operation has been much more sensitive than the one in Baluchistan. Baluchistan has virtually been abandoned by the central government in Qom. It seems that they do believe that cholera is still rampant in those mountains, so it is relatively easy for my men and me to slip in and out of that area. Khuzistan, on the other hand, is a different story. We were afraid that our logistics support system would have been easy to detect, but thanks to the thriving black-market trade across the Gulf, my job has been made a lot easier. We have been able to meld in with the rest of the dhows selling their contraband goods to Iran. And I must say," Commander Kalvani said, smiling, "we have turned a tidy profit in American cigarettes, jeans, and rock music cassettes."

On the blackboard, Commander Kalvani drew a quick sketch of a stout-bottomed wooden dhow, a cross-section showing a double hull. "The weapons are here," Kalvani said, pointing to the space between the two hulls.

Kir nodded approvingly. "Excuse me, Commander, but the plane is leaving this evening for London to pick up the Americans." Kir turned to Mark. "Would you send the telex to Phoenix now, Mark?"

"Will do," Mark replied, as he slid his chair over to the telex machine.

"Mark, don't forget to check Mr. Watkin's E.T.A. London. What's he flying?"

"Pan Am," Mark replied.

Commander Kalvani interrupted. "Why isn't the head of Bening Aircraft flying in a company plane?"

Mark turned around, "Well, sir, this trip is so classified that Mr. Watkins has given everyone the impression that he is off on a private visit to his ailing mother outside of London. Just a short visit to see the old lady and then come right back home." Mark turned and hunched over the telex, typing out the message expertly. He fed the tape into the machine and then sat back in his chair, waiting for the reply.

The telex machine began to clatter, and Mark's eyes followed the message being typed out. "Everything's fine, Michael," Mark said, pulling off the telex. "Mr. Watkins left Phoenix airport on Pam Am flight 195, and he'll be arriving London, Heathrow, at 0700 hours."

"Good," Mark said. "Now telex Houston, Texas, please, Mark."

"Right." Mark swiveled his chair around and typed out another message.

A message came rattling back. "Right on the nose," Mark said. "Mr. Connelly of Hall Helicopter left on Braniff 302. Estimated time of arrival at Heathrow, 0740."

"Everything will proceed as planned," Kir said. "Mark, you'd better get down to the plane. You should be leaving soon." Michael Kir turned to Commander Kalvani. "Mr. Rowan will fly to London tonight and meet Mr. Watkins and Mr. Connelly. They'll be flying back here immediately."

"Excellent," Commander Kalvani said. "I am glad to see you are taking good care of two of the most important men in the aerospace industry."

"I have a few other instructions for Mr. Rowan, so, Commander, would you mind accompanying us to the airport. Then I'll take you back to the Crown Prince's Villa.

"Fine with me, Mr. Kir. Besides, I am interested to see this luxurious flying ship of yours."

The Range Rover sped across the darkened tarmac toward the Boeing 707 waiting on the runway. Only the light that illuminated the shaft of the Kish Island control tower and the lights in the cab of the tower punctuated the night sky. Michael Kir stopped the car at the front steps to the aircraft. He hurried up the stairs with Mark, while Commander Kalvani walked around the underbelly of the plane, inspecting it with great interest. Kir opened the door to the cockpit and leaned

261

in. "Ready to go, Lucky?" he asked the pilot.

"Yes, sir, Mr. Kir," Lucky replied.

"You'll be picking up two Americans in London. Your E.T.A. in London is 0500 hours, London time, Wednesday. Am I correct?"

"Correct, Mr. Kir. 0500 hours," Lucky repeated.

"Mr. Rowan will accompany you on the flight. He'll greet the two guests and bring them to the plane."

"Roger."

"And, Lucky, give these men a good flight."

"Will do, Mr. Kir. I'll fly this baby as if it was made of eggshells."

Kir smiled. "See you back here tomorrow afternoon."

Michael Kir shut the door to the cockpit, and walked toward the back of the plane. Andreas was standing in the aft galley with Mark. He nodded to Kir, as he continued to read off a list to Mark.

"Let's see, capers, Sasso olive oil, smoked Scottish salmon, three kilos . . ." Andreas turned to Kir. "Just a few things I forgot to add to the grocery list for Harrod's."

"Andreas, I doubt if those retired military types will miss smoked salmon."

Andreas chuckled. "You're right, Michael. Perhaps I should increase the beer order."

"Good idea," Mark said.

"Mark," Kir said, "can I speak with you a moment? Excuse us, Andreas."

Mark and Kir walked toward the mid-section lounge. Kir spoke in a low voice. "Mark, do me a favor, watch the crew carefully. I don't want anyone abandoning ship in London, or trying to talk to the press. I don't want to read about it in the *Daily Mirror*—'Strange Happenings on Persian Gulf Island.' The crew will remain on the aircraft while it is on the ground in London. Mark,

I'd appreciate it if you'd feel them out. It seems that you've built up a rapport with them."

"I have," acknowledged Mark. "I've spent a lot of time with them at the hotel. They seem pretty happy screwing the little Filipino maids and lounging around the pool."

"Yes, we should all have it so easy," Michael said, placing his hand on Mark's shoulder. "Mark, I trust you to make sure that everything runs smoothly, no foul-ups."

"Don't worry, Michael, the pickup will go smoothly. See you back here tomorrow."

Kir drove the Range Rover along the dark roadway, only the headlights of the vehicle illuminating the road ahead. Commander Kalvani looked out the window of the car as it sped past the hotel. Some of the rooms facing outward to the road were brightly lit, but most of the rooms were in darkness.

"Commander, all the European staff and crew stay in the hotel, while the Filipinos live in the bungalows that were originally built for the croupiers, just across from the casino. There is virtually no interaction between the Filipinos and the Europeans. The Filipinos keep pretty much to themselves. Besides, we have kept their level of English very low."

"Ah, yes, Mr. Kir," Commander Kalvani said, smiling. "I can see that you subscribe to the old divide-and-conquer theory."

Kir nodded and answered firmly, "It is better to not let one hand know what the other one is doing, don't you agree, sir?"

"Completely, Mr. Kir."

Manuela's hand clutched the smoked-green brandy bottle. With a shaky hand she poured another stiff shot of Courvoisier into her glass, a few drops splashing onto her red dress. She slammed the half-empty bottle down onto the countertop of the white lacquered bar in her villa and reached across the bar for her Dunhills, knocking the brandy bottle to the floor. The sticky amber liquid seeped into the creamy-white carpet, matting the thick plush.

Manuela did not even bother to pick up the bottle. She was so distraught by Kir's behavior that she was on the brink of hysteria. She paced back and forth, tracking the sticky liquid over the living room carpet, anguishing over her fate. First, Kir had told her that she was to be a whore, then he had totally ignored her, and now he was trying to pass off Mr. Kalvani as a hotel representative. Throughout dinner, Manuela had had a nagging suspicion about "Mr. Kalvani." She knew that there was something familiar about Kalvani, something that a fairly mediocre plastic surgeon had not been able to disguise. He, too—whoever he was—must have had something to hide. Manuela knew she had met him before, but not as Mr. Kalvani, and not with the same face. She had spent the better part of a brandied evening reconstructing Kalvani's face as it must have been prior to the plastic surgery.

And now she wanted to know what the man who had once been the Shah's Navy Commander for the Persian Gulf was doing on Kish Island, posing as a sales representative of an American hotel chain? It was all too labyrinthian for Manuela's liking, and tonight she was going to get to the bottom of it. One thing was painfully obvious to her, Michael Kir cared nothing for her; she was just a pawn on his chessboard, and she feared that his unknown game would be a dangerous one for her. She spun around and picked up the nearly empty brandy bottle. Steadying one hand with the other, she took another drink of the heady liquor. Trembling, panic clouding her senses, she put down her glass and went in search of Kir.

Manuela's palms were sweating and she was breathing deeply from the exertion of her fast-paced walk from her villa to the residence.

As Manuela approached, a guard standing outside the residence stepped in front of the door.

"I want to see Mr. Kir," Manuela said.

"I believe Mr. Kir is unavailable," the guard said.

"I want to see him now. Tell him Manuela wants to see him."

The guard opened the door slightly, and he gestured to her to wait. The guard went to the far side of the entrance hall and picked up the telephone receiver.

"Just a moment, Miss Ferrara. Wait right there, please," he said, as he quietly spoke into the mouthpiece.

Manuela did not wait. She pushed the door open wide and stormed down the hall towards the east wing and Kir's private quarters.

A Filipino manservant stood at the entrance to Michael Kir's quarters. Manuela pushed her way past him and, without knocking, opened the door. Kir was in his king-size bed, reading. He looked up at the disheveled Manuela and dropped his papers.

In a flash, Manuela's dark eyes took in—for the first time—Kir's bedroom. It was furnished simply, but elegantly: charcoal-gray silk wallpaper, thick, gray wool carpeting, sleek cherrywood furniture.

"So this is the room where Michael Kir sleeps. Alone, since he is above sleeping with whores," Manuela said venomously.

"Manuela, what's wrong?"

She looked at him, then turned her head away in anger.

"Manuela, what is it?"

"You know exactly what it is, Michael. You and your goddamn lies, your deceptions," she said angrily.

"Michael, what is going on here? Tell me the truth," she continued, her voice verging on hysteria. "Tell me!"

"I cannot. I simply cannot, Mitra . . ."

"Don't you ever call me Mitra!" she said, her voice rising. Enraged, she approached Kir. "Ever!" Manuela repeated, her voice trembling with rage. As she came closer Kir could see the wild look in her eyes, her shaking body. She moved closer to him, and raised her right arm to strike him.

Instantaneously he grabbed Manuela's arm, causing her to lose her balance, tearing her dress as he tried to break her fall. He leapt from the bed, reaching for her. She fought back like a wild animal; he held her tightly, trying to control her rage. Finally, she collapsed against him in tears, her anguished sobs racking her slim body. Kir lifted her chin in his hands. Through the blur of her tears he could see the fear in her eyes.

"Manuela, please, I swear to you, you have nothing to fear. I'll explain to you . . ."

"What is going on, Michael? What is the Shah's Navy Commander doing here? What is happening on this horrible island?"

Michael Kir was shocked that Manuela had recognized the former Iranian naval commander. Momentarily stunned, he could think of nothing to say to her. He tried to press her even more closely against him but she broke free from his arms.

His heart ached as he looked at her kneeling on

266

the floor beside him, her hair tousled, her dress torn. He felt deep pain and guilt for the anguish he had caused her. As soon as he had brought Manuela to Kish he had known it was a tragic mistake to have done so. He loved her, and it devastated him to think of what he had brought her to Kish for, but there was no turning back—not now. Rather than deal with his emotional inner torture, his pain, he had closed himself off completely from her.

But now it was time to treat her more justly, more compassionately. He knew he owed her more than the cruel treatment he had subjected her to. He must tell her his plans, as much as he could.

Kir pulled her up to the bed, beside him. Slowly, Kir told Manuela what was really happening in the Gulf, that what she saw on Kish Island was merely a cover for something else. Manuela listened, amazed at the magnitude of his undertaking—and horrified at the associations Kir had been forced to make in order to achieve his goals.

As Michael confided in her his secret longings, his plans, his dreams, Manuela's mind wandered. In her own mind the question she dreaded to ask was rising up, pounding against her very soul. Everything Kir had said led her to believe that Parvis Gazvini, like a vulture circling overhead, must be close at hand. Finally, mustering up her courage she asked, "Is Parvis in this with you?"

Kir did not answer her, his silence incriminating him.

"Where is he?" she pleaded. "On Kish?"

"No, Manuela," Kir said, reaching for her hand. she yanked it away.

"No," he continued, "Parvis is not here."

"You liar, Michael!" she hissed. "Tell me," she said, the hysteria returning to her voice, "tell me the truth."

"Manuela, you have nothing to fear. Parvis knows nothing of your existence. Parvis is never going to see you. Believe me, you are not in danger. There is nothing to fear. I swear I would never let anything happen to you."

"You're lying, Michael," she said, her voice softer, calmer.

"For once I am not," Kir said, his voice heavy with remorse. "For once I am not," he repeated, this time in a low voice.

"Forgive me, Manuela," he murmured. "Forgive me."

"I love you," he said taking her in his arms. "I love you."

Manuela looked up into Michael Kir's face, searching for a semblance of the man she had known years ago, trying to see behind his handsome face, to believe the words he uttered. She desperately wanted to believe him, but the thought of Parvis did not leave her mind.

"Whatever you've been doing, Michael, you've been treading on thin ice," she warned. "You don't know Parvis Gazvini as I do; you may have overstepped your bounds. He is a very dangerous man." Manuela paused. "*I* know," she said, looking straight up at Kir. The tears started to well up in her eyes again. He kissed her throat tenderly; she did not resist. The hunger of their buried, unfulfilled passions was finally being satisfied.

# FIFTEEN

The midday sun was hot and bright. A light sea breeze blew across the runway, rustling the bushes around the terminal building.

Gino sat in the pilot's seat of the Beechcraft. He reached for his tinted aviator glasses and put them on. Gino slid the plexiglass window shut, glanced at Kir, and prepared for takeoff. The small plane hurtled down the runway, gaining speed, and lifting off, moving out over the water. Gino banked the plane portside as it gained altitude, and flew in a south-southeasterly direction. There was only the hum of the engines as the plane flew through the cloudless blue sky, three thousand feet above the Persian Gulf.

"It's a beautiful day, isn't it, Michael?" Gino said.

"Yes, it is," Kir said. He looked at his watch; it was twelve twenty-five. They would arrive by one o'clock. Kir opened his briefcase, pulled out some papers, and reviewed them.

About forty minutes later, the Beechcraft started its descent. The plane was now mid-way between Kish Island and the United Arab Emirates, a confederation of seven sheikhdoms including Abu Dhabi, Sharjah, and Dubai. Approximately sixty miles to the northwest was Kish Island, and an equal distance away was the Sheikhdom of Dabai. Kir and Gino watched as a small desert island, Abu Musa, appeared on the horizon. As the plane traveled closer, the island seemed to rise out of the water like a mirage. Gino circled the triangle-shaped island twice, as was his pattern.

Michael Kir put his papers back into his brief-case, and looked out the window at the island below. Abu Musa looked deceptively calm. It was an island of only six square miles, fringed by sandy beaches colored black and red by the eroding iron-oxide hills at the southern tip of the island. Near these hills was a small Arab village, since ancient times the home of perhaps a thousand fishermen, pearl divers, and gold smugglers. In more recent history these Arabs had become tradesmen, selling to the Iranian navy and marine commandos who controlled the island from November 1971, when the Shah, by agreement, took the island over from the Sheikh of Sharjah.

The Shah had made full use of Abu Musa. To relieve some of the congestion that plagued Iran's Persian Gulf ports, a huge cold-storage warehouse was constructed on Abu Musa. Ships were to unload at Abu Musa and their cargo stored in the cold-storage warehouse until smaller ships, dhows, could shuttle the cargo to mainland Iran. More importantly, a naval base was established on Abu Musa. Situated less than one hundred miles from the Straits of Hormuz, Abu Musa was a very strategic island. To protect this vital area in the Gulf, the Shah had installed several hundred marine commandos, as well as squads of navy frogmen, on the island. At the time of the Revolution, there were plans to install missiles and build a base for hovercraft patrol vessels. But with the fall of the Shah in 1979, and the subsequent disintegration of the Iranian military, the base at Abu Musa was slowly abandoned. With no one left to sell to, the Arabs, as well, gradually left

Abu Musa. The UAE, after repeated attempts by Iran to impose upon them the Iranian form of Islamic rule, retook the island in July 1982.

The Beechcraft circled low over a cluster of one-storey barrack-type buildings, and over the huge warehouse. From the air, Gino and Kir could see two dhows. They were moored alongside the breakwater that had been built by the Iranian navy in the early 1970s. The port and base now looked deserted, with only a few traders, fishermen, and soldiers wandering around.

The runway cut through the barren desert landscape. Gino brought the plane down and taxied to a stop near a sand-colored jeep. Two soldiers in khaki fatigues stood at attention near the jeep. In the distance, high on a pole, the green, blue, red, and white flag of the United Arab Emirates fluttered in the breeze.

Gino cut the engines, and Kir stepped out of the plane. As Kir walked across the windy runway to the waiting jeep, both soldiers gave him a sharp military salute. Kir and the soldiers climbed into the jeep. They wheeled off toward the military installation, a cloud of dust billowing out behind them.

The jeep came to an abrupt halt in front of the cold-storage warehouse. Two sentries, Uzi submachine guns at their sides, saluted Kir as he climbed out of the jeep. The heavy metal gray door slid open. A soldier inside the door escorted Kir down the long corridor. There was only the sound of their footsteps on the rough cement floor. Michael Kir's eyes were fixed on the door at the far end of the corridor, the door to Supreme Command Headquarters for Project Norouz.

The door opened automatically. Inside a large room sat the surviving generals of the Shah's armed forces—the generals who had escaped, who had not been executed. The six men greeted their faithful employee, Michael Kir, then beckoned him to take his place at the long table in the center of the room. The windowless, light-green walls were covered with large, detailed maps of Iran and the Persian Gulf area.

Tea in small glasses was quickly brought to the table. Seated around the conference table were the most famous—or infamous—generals from the Shah's regime. They were dressed in their Imperial Iranian Armed Forces uniforms. Michael Kir looked at their familiar faces and could feel the electricity in the air. The old soldiers were preparing for battle, preparing to regain the country they had lost.

Seated at the head of the table was General Vanak, a tall, massively-built man in his late fifties. His stern countenance and ramrod-straight posture suited the most professional of soldiers under the Shah's regime. He had been Chief of Police. He was rumored to have been responsible for the bloody Black Friday Massacre, in which two thousand persons were reportedly gunned down by the army during an anti-Shah demonstration. Vanak, who could be charming and gregarious in his private life, was reputed to be a merciless and cruel general. Nervous guests at the "eleventh hour" cocktail parties in Tehran during the winter of 1978 gossiped about General Vanak's counsel to the Shah regarding the holy city of Qom. "Bomb Qom," General Vanak had suggested to the Shah. "What do we need Qom for?" Did General Vanak really mean it? they had wondered. General Vanak had meant it then—and he still did—as he sat at the table on Abu Musa sipping his sugary tea.

Next to General Vanak sat General Asman. The Shah had installed General Asman as the Martial

272

Law Administrator for Iran, in a last-ditch effort to prop up the shaky Pahlavi Dynasty. General Asman was the quintessential military man, dour and dedicated to the idea of fighting to the bitter end. A true hardliner, he was thwarted by a vacillating and weak Commander-in-Chief. General Asman was unable to turn the tide of the Revolution by force, as he wanted to do. He had not accepted defeat well. General Asman had never forgiven the Shah for not allowing him to unleash Iran's military force upon the people. Now, sitting at the conference table, he stared out unblinkingly from behind his thick horn-rimmed glasses.

To General Asman's left sat Air Force General Pirayesh, a tall handsome man, as elegant as he was arrogant. He had been trained as a fighter pilot in Lubbock, Texas, and was reputedly one of the best pilots in the Iranian Air Force. His escape from Tehran after the fall of the Bakhtiar government in February 1979 was what one would have expected from him. At the height of a battle, General Pirayesh commandeered an F-4 from Doshen-Tappeh military base in Tehran and flew to freedom. When he landed at Jubail, Saudi Arabia, the Saudis gave him refuge, and agreed to keep the F-4 on Saudi soil until the situation in Iran stabilized. Now, nearly five years later, General Pirayesh was alive and well and coolly smoking his Gitane cigarette on Abu Musa.

General Mojat, sitting across from General Pirayesh, had a less exciting story to tell of his escape. General Mojat was the head of Army Aviation in Iran for a number of years, and had been at one time the Shah's personal pilot. Mojat had gone on vacation to the south of France in summer of 1978, as was his habit. When things began to blow up in Iran, he sent a telegram back to Tehran, saying that he wouldn't be back for awhile. He never made it back. Some said that clever General Mojat smelled a rat, while others said that General Mojat was a rat. He left Iran with eighty million dollars, but he was by no means the richest of the generals at the table.

Next to Mojat sat General Rujanian, once Minister of War and acknowledged as one of the most powerful and influential men in Iran. As head of procurement for the Imperial Iranian Armed Forces, he was said to be the man that foreigners courted and wooed to make sales of billions of dollars of the latest and most sophisticated weaponry. A tall heavyset man, he looked every inch the powerful and important man he once had been—and intended to be again in the very near future. General Rujanian hated the Shah vehemently. When the Shah departed Iran on January 16, 1979, he left his generals in Iran holding the bag. The generals were left to fend for themselves. The fortunate ones narrowly escaped from Iran. The consensus among the generals was that, instead of taking his damned pet dogs with him, the Shah should have taken his generals on his plane.

At the end of the table, rocking back and forth in his chair, was General Parvis Gazvini. Tall, trim, and distinguished-looking, with piercing black eyes, he had an aura of authority about him. As number-two man in SAVAK for many years, he had been one of the most feared and notorious men in Iran. He had also been the lover of Mitra Tabrizi.

Michael Kir set his empty tea glass down on the table.

"Generals," Kir said, "I have with me the revised versions of the agreements. They have been changed according to your recommendations at our last meeting. I have copies of both agreements for each of you." Kir opened his briefcase and took out twelve slim folders, six red, and six blue. He passed them out to the generals, one of each color to each man.

"As these agreements are the precursors of the actual contracts, Mr. Rowan prepared them in contract form. They should be be easier for the businessmen to deal with this way. The language of these agreements is, in places, highly technical. This is due to the nature of the agreements. If, after you have read them carefully, you have any questions or changes, I'll note them and pass them on to Mr. Rowan."

"Fine," I'm eager to see what they look like revised," General Vanak said, opening the red folder.

"We'll start with this one," General Vanak said, holding up the red folder. There was a rustle of paper as the other generals opened their folders and started reading intently.

Michael Kir looked at the generals. These were the men planning to run the new Iran, albeit an Iran not too different from the Iran they once ran. Kir thought back on how it had all began, how he had become involved in Project Norouz. Now, here he was, orchestrating the overthrow of the Islamic Republic of Iran.

After the Revolution in 1979, Michael Kir had kept in contact with General Vanak. As a matter of courtesy, he had kept up a formal friendship that had begun fifteen years before. General Vanak and Michael Kir had known each other socially in Iran. Michael had been the General's tennis doubles partner. At the Imperial Club where they played, they had been virtually unbeatable. General Vanak had picked Michael Kir as his partner because he was the best player at the club, and also because he could play for the high stakes

275

of those tennis games. A friendly little match on a Thursday afternoon for five thousand dollars was not unusual. And Kir knew that it did not hurt him to play with one of the most powerful men in Iran. General Vanak was acknowledged to be one of the Shah's most powerful officers, as well as a personal friend and confidant of His Majesty. Michael carefully cultivated his friendship with General Vanak, and as a result had made numerous large sales of jewels to most of the top-ranking generals in the Imperial Armed Forces. After the Revolution, when General Vanak was abruptly stripped of rank and influence, Kir did not abandon him.

In late 1979 and 1980, Michael Kir made visits to General Vanak. Whenever Kir was on business in Houston, which was frequently, he would drive to the General's guarded estate outside of Houston. After the fall of the Shah, General Vanak had been coolly received by the United States government and had been warned that if he wanted to stay in the U.S., he would have to keep a low profile. A quiet, low-key, lifestyle was what was expected of the Iranian generals, ex-generals, if they wanted to stay in the States. When Kir saw General Vanak for the first time after the Revolution, he was shocked. The man Kir saw in Texas was a far cry from the headstrong, arrogant general that he had known in Iran. General Vanak was an old, broken man in exile, a man without a country, and, more important, a man stripped of his power, a power that had been his lifeblood.

But by December 1981, when General Vanak again summoned Michael Kir to his Texas estate, the broken-spirited old man had disappeared, and in his place was a vital, khaki-clothed man strutting back and forth across the fake brick floor of his ranchhouse, full of fire and brimstone. General Vanak wanted his country back, and, more than that, he wanted his power back. He had been in contact with the other generals in exile. They, too, were miserable with their present ignominious lives, and they all agreed that something must be done to restore Iran to its pre-Revolutionary glory. The generals were tired of waiting for something to happen—they were going to make it happen. But this time they would run Iran without the Pahlavis. No longer would they be the servants, this time they would be the masters. The generals were all embittered men. They felt that the Shah had let them down: first, by refusing to allow them to use their awesome fire power; second, by abandoning them to live insignificant lives in exile.

General Vanak had devised a plan. From an island in the Persian Gulf, the generals would establish a base from which to make their move to retake Iran, establish a military government, and repress any resistance with force. The generals had the will and the financial means to do this, and General Vanak had thought of the way—Project Norouz.

But it was impossible for the generals to succeed alone. They needed an outsider, someone who knew the territory, Iran and the Gulf, and who was not associated with the Shah's régime. Someone who had all the right connections, yet could move about without arousing suspicion. And someone who had the cunning and savvy to pull it off. Michael Kir was their man.

When General Vanak approached him, Kir thought that the plan was just the paper dreams of old tigers. Although the staggering combined Swiss bank accounts of the generals would be made available to finance the endeavor, he was fairly certain that the generals' plan would go no farther than step one, which called for Kir to set up a dummy corporation and to acquire Kish

Island from the Islamic Republic of Iran under the pretext of building a resort center.

But the April 1982 oil pipeline sabotage caused catastrophic repercussions both inside and outside of Iran, and the Russian bear, sensing the weakness of the Iranian buffer, continued to move toward the Persian Gulf. Kir realized that, now, support by the United States, the Persian Gulf States, Egypt, and the UAE for a coup d'état in Iran by a pro-West junta might finally be forthcoming. The generals' plan no longer seemed so far-fetched. Any qualms the U.S. government might have had about the morality or the political advisability of sanctioning the return of a repressive military regime could be outweighed by the gravity of the crisis at hand. And Kir had reasons of his own to support Project Norouz.

Kir flew to New York City to see his friend, Walter Singer, a brilliant statesman, now a professor, who had served in the cabinets of two Presidents, and who was still, according to many, the most knowledgeable and one of the most influential men in international politics. After Kir presented the generals' plan to Singer, Singer promised to use his influence to secure support from the White House and the giants of American industry.

After spending a couple of months in the States, primarily Washington, D.C., Kir, at the suggestion of Walter Singer, took the opportunity to pay a visit to his friends in the UAE. Ostensibly, Kir had come to offer a collection of gems that he had acquired at an auction of a maharajah's estate in India. The palace doors of the sheikhs of the oil kingdoms were always open to Michael Kir, the famous diamond dealer. But on this occasion, at a private dinner party at the palace of the President of the UAE, in Abu Dhabi, the precious Indian jewels were hastily put aside when Michael Kir suggested to the sheikhs that a stable, pro-West, military government might return to Iran. The powerful rulers of the UAE, fearing Soviet expansion toward the Gulf and Iran's constant threats to their political independence, realized that it would be in their best interest to support the plan that Kir outlined to them. They agreed to take Abu Musa back from Iran, by force if necessary, and to make the island available as the generals' headquarters and nerve center for the military portion of the plan, far from prying eyes on mainland Iran, safe on foreign soil. In addition, they agreed to channel the generals' arms and supplies purchases through Dubai to Abu Musa and points north.

In August 1982, approximately one month after the UAE took over Abu Musa, Kir began one of the most delicate phases of the plan. Kir and his newly recruited corporate chief executive, Andreas von Elfensleben, flew to Tehran with their proposal to the Islamic Republic to let Gulf Island Resorts develop Kish into a convention center for the Middle East, and a winter vacation resort for frozen Europeans wishing to gamble away their Deutschmarks, francs, and pounds. Kir and Andreas flashed colorful diagrams and charts before the eyes of the beturbanned mullahs of the dug-out-of-the-mothballs Revolutionary Committee for Tourism and Information, and argued eloquently that European vacationers could be lured away from Africa, the Canary Islands, and far-off Bali, to winter on Kish. The mullahs agreed with the undeniable facts that Kish's winter climate was excellent, the beaches were sandy and white, the hotel and casino were already built. Indeed, they were persuaded that hard Western cash was just waiting to be raked up by the croupiers, then divided between the government of Iran and Gulf Island Resorts Corporation. And the projected size of revenues to be realized by the undertaking outweighed any moral objections that the Revolutionary Committee may have had to gambling, mixed bathing, and other corrupting evil Western ways. When Kir produced bank letters of credit evidencing the availability of the one hundred million dollars of private financing necessary to develop the project, the agreement was sealed. In September of 1982, the Revolutionary Committee leased the island to the corporation for a fifteen-year term, and Kir had his own headquarters from which to run the business operations of the plan.

Kir had then moved to the next step of Project Norouz: to obtain the military hardware for the coup. Under the Shah, Iran had been a lucrative market for the arms industry. As part of a nineteen-billion-dollar defense agreement with the U.S., Iran had, by 1979, made purchases of seven billion dollars in sophisticated military equipment from the United States, and at the time of the Revolution, another twelve-billion-dollars' worth of military hardware, such as F-16's and command and surveillance aircraft, were on line. When the Shah fell, the American aerospace industry suffered huge losses. The rough estimate had been nearly ten billion dollars in lost contracts, equipment, and outstanding bills.

Michael Kir had approached the heads of Bening, Chessman, Hall, Martin, Northern, Byrd, Aerospace National, and other U.S. aerospace giants. It had not been too hard for Kir to convince some of the arms and aerospace companies that a pro-West, military-based economy in Iran—an Iran run by the old hard-line generals—would be in their best interest. Kir offered these companies a chance to get in on the ground floor of a venture that would provide them with a highly profitable market. The package that Kir presented them was extremely attractive: in return for supplying hardware for the generals' coup d'état, these defense industries returning to Iran would have extremely lucrative contracts with the new military government. And, while certainly not all of the companies Kir approached agreed to participate in his plan, some—enough—did.

Agreements were made to ship aircraft and other military ordnance. Slowly the airbases outside of Cairo, Riyadh, and Jubail, on the Gulf; Al-Ain, in the interior of the UAE; and the newly constructed airbase at Dubai, in the UAE, acquired new AH-IS attack helicopters, AH-1T Sea Cobra choppers, F-14's, C-130 transports, S-61 big-lift helicopters, massive C-5 transports, 214ST super transport choppers, F-5's, and F-16's. By late 1982, Project Norouz had begun to stealthily tip-toe into the Persian Gulf. Project Norouz was underway, and there was no turning back.

Now that military backing for Project Norouz had been secured, the next stop, essential to the long-term security of the new régime, would be the revitalization of the economy of Iran as quickly as possible after the takeover. The return of the multinational oil consortium, that had controlled oil exports from Iran, was imperative. The consortium had been in the process of renegotiating its contract with the Shah at the time of his downfall. The new contract that Kir arranged with the oil consortium (to be effective upon its return to Iran, immediately after the generals' takeover) was the kind of contract that the consortium had wanted in 1979, only better.

During the latter part of 1982 and early 1983, Kir also approached the Japanese companies, some of which had had huge investments in the petrochemical industry in Iran during the Shah's régime, and the English, who had had a large stake in the auto industry in Iran, and who had supplied the Shah with many of the tanks and vehicles for his 460,000-strong army. Kir talked with an Italian conglomerate that had been involved in the building of roads and the refurbishing and building of ports in Iran, and a German industrial concern that had been building power plants and steel mills in Iran before the Revolution.

All these companies wanted to get back into Iran, especially since, this time, they could practically write their own terms and conditions. The generals were in no position to bargain. The generals needed the foreign backers if their coup was to succeed and their régime to survive. And, if many of the foreign corporations that had had the largest investments in Iran returned after the takeover, other companies would soon follow suit.

A lively discussion was in progress as Michael Kir watched the generals at the table. It was as if nothing had changed during the past five years. They may as well have been at the Chief of Staff Command Headquarters in Tehran. The discussion had moved from the agreements at hand to the generals' plans once the coup was completed. Kir listened to the tirades that he had heard so many times before: the generals' talk of crushing the insurgents, private vendettas, military strategies—their plans for a new Iran. The armed forces would come first—on that they all agreed. It was obvious that the need for internal order was the first consideration, and top priority would go to the military budget. Kir listened to General Rujanian argue for an even higher budget allocation than he had had under the Shah, when more than one-sixth of Imperial Iran's national budget was allocated for the purchase of military hardware and technical support.

Rujanian and the other Generals were discussing the reestablishment of ammunitions factories with the help of the Germans, the production of personnel carriers with the help of the English, the switching over of certain textile mills to the production of army uniforms, and the reestablishment of Bank Sepah, the Army Bank. These projects would all be high priorities, after the take-over.

The conversation turned to a discussion of the new repressive apparatus that would be needed. Parvis Gazvini explained that this time the secret police would not be publicly acknowledged as SAVAK had been. This time, he promised, it would be a truly secret police.

Kir could feel the energy level at the table rising. He knew that these once awesomely powerful generals were building up steam, that their confidence and determination increased with each passing day. The impending visit of the two Americans tomorrow was like a tonic for them. The generals spoke as if Iran already belonged to them, as it once had. Today, on Abu Musa, Kir remembered the generals as he had seen them in the 1970s: issuing orders from their Tehran offices; reviewing their troops; whispering into the Shah's ear at public functions, their uniforms heavy with gold braid and ribbons, proudly wearing their oakleafed hats. Then, as now, the generals were awesomely powerful figures.

An aide dressed in army fatigues entered the room. He saluted the generals sharply, then delivered a sheaf of papers to General Vanak. The aide saluted, clicked his heels together, and walked stiffly out of the room.

The generals had brought a small army of two hundred men with them to Abu Musa. These were dedicated career officers who had been plucked

283

out of the shambles of the Shah's armed forces. After the Revolution, the loyal career officers of the Imperial Iranian Armed Forces had either escaped from Iran, fearing for their lives during the midnight trials of the Revolutionary Council, or stayed on, hoping that the line of responsibility would not reach down as far as them. Those who had stayed on—and survived—quickly became disenchanted with the military under the Revolutionary Government. The Shah had supplied his officers with good housing, special PXs that stocked hard-to-find luxury goods, and other benefits above and beyond the means of average citizens. He supplied his officers with the best, newest, most sophisticated military equipment that money could buy.

After the Revolution, officers who stayed on were soon disheartened by the lack of discipline, lack of equipment, and lack of organization in the armed forces under their new commander-in-chief, the Ayatollah Khomeini. Soldiers sent to Khuzistan to put down the rebelling Sunni Arabs fought in rubber sandals, ignored their commanding officers, and lived in barracks that looked and smelled like latrines. Air Force fighter pilots sent to put down the Kurdish Rebellion in northwest Iran died in fiery crashes, the result of poor or nonexistent maintenance of their sophisticated American-built fighter planes.

Desertion was rampant, the entire system of military order and discipline was gone. A new, special military elite developed in Iran—the Revolutionary Guards, the *Pasdaran*—but military men who had been officers under the Shah's regime were not allowed to become Pasdaran. Bitter and disillusioned, the officers who could leave Iran, left.

Life for the officers who left Iran was difficult. "Former Imperial Iranian Army Officer, fifteen years' experience" on a résumé did not interest too many employers in the U.S., especially after the U.S. Embassy hostage crisis. U.S.-trained Iranian fighter pilots also returned to the United States, and tried to start new lives. But for former Iranian F-14 fighter pilots there were few opportunities in the field of commercial aviation. There were hundreds of displaced, disheartened officers in the U.S. and Europe. When the generals approached their old officers, these men were ready, willing, and eager to assist their once mighty commanders retake Iran.

Abu Musa was a model miniature military installation. Stationed on the island were the two hundred men recruited by the generals from the former Imperial Iranian Army officers in exile. They served as aides to the generals, hoping to upgrade their ranks in the new Iranian Armed Forces. They were the men who would accompany the generals on their triumphant return to Tehran and would make up the uppermost strata of the new army. But these were not the men who would provide the troop support for Project Norouz. That would come from a group of soldiers who had never left Iran.

The main troop support for Project Norouz would come from General Pakdal and his men in Baluchistan. These men were the Immortals. Carefully selected from the twelve-thousand-strong Imperial Guard, the elite of the Iranian military, the six thousand Immortals were the soldiers who had been personally responsible for guarding and defending the life of the Shah.

Even after the Shah was forced into exile in January 1979, the Immortals, on their wintery Lavizan base in north Tehran, pledged that they would shed their last drop of blood for the Shah. During those last days of Imperial Iran, in February '79, as the Bakhtiar government fell and

285

the Shah's mighty army crumbled, the Immortals were the only unit of the Iranian armed forces to fight back against the Revolutionaries. The Immortals, six thousand men, could not, alone, defend Iran. In the ensuing chaos of the Revolution, as the rest of the armed forces surrendered around them, the Immortals disappeared, seemingly into the wind. But that was not to be their last stand.

During the Revolution, the highest-ranking officer of the Immortals, General Pakdal, escaped into the desert. Those Immortals who were able to, followed him. Early rumors circulated that General Pakdal and his men had fled to Kurdistan, but they were never traced. Pakdal and his men eluded the central government, and went to Baluchistan. Over the next few years, other Immortals, who had been in hiding, filtered into Baluchistan. Pakdal and the Immortals participated in sporadic attacks on the Islamic régime, including the June 1981 bombing of the I.R.P. building and the Prime Minister's office a few months later. General Pakdal's men still pledged allegiance daily to *Khoda, Shah, Mihan*, "God, Shah, Country." These were the Shah's Immortals, the ones who would still lay down their lives for him. They could not forget.

Now, in October 1983, General Pakdal and six thousand Immortals were encamped in Baluchistan, in the southeast corner of Iran, guests of the Baluchis. The Baluchis, a two-million-strong tribe of nomadic, fiercely independent people, occupied the wild, mountainous area of Iran that bordered on Pakistan. The Baluchis despised the authoritarian, repressive government of the Islamic Republic. The Baluchis and the Immortals had a common enemy. General Pakdal and his men had been absorbed and protected by the Baluchis for four years. In return for harboring them, the Baluchis had received valuable medical aid during the cholera outbreak, and were well supplied with food, clothing, cigarettes, and most important, arms, all delivered by Commander Kalvani's dhow system.

The logistics support system for Project Norouz was directed by Commander Jamshid Kalvani, and was under the blanket protection of Islamic Navy Admiral Mahmoud. During the Shah's régime, both Kalvani and Mahmoud had been commanders of the Persian Gulf Fleet. Kalvani had been Mahmoud's superior. Both men had been under the direct command of the Shah's nephew, Prince Shafik, head of the Persian Gulf Fleet, headquartered at Kharg Island.

Kalvani and Prince Shafik escaped from Iran during the Revolution, but not before they had vowed to Mahmoud that they would return. Mahmoud was arrested and imprisoned by the Revolutionary government. His history and background as a naval officer were investigated, but no evidence of any wrongdoing by Mahmoud could be produced. During his interrogations, Mahmoud pledged love and allegiance to Khomeini and the Revolution. After six months in prison, Mahmoud was declared innocent, released from prison, and his record was cleared. By that time, Mahmoud was the only high-ranking naval officer with an intimate knowledge of the Gulf and the Gulf Fleet left in Iran. Mahmoud was named the new admiral of the Islamic Navy Persian Gulf Fleet.

But Mahmoud's cleared record and the statements he had made during his interrogations were no indication of his true loyalties. Although he performed his duties as Commander of the Persian Gulf Fleet well, Mahmoud was one hundred percent the Shah's man. He despised the

Islamic régime he worked for. He had acted the part of the loyal revolutionary only to get himself in a position of power so that, when the time came, he could make his move to help reinstate the monarchy. Mahmoud knew that, from France, Prince Shafik and Kalvani were plotting a coup d'état. Mahmoud was the inside man—he would allow Shafik's men to launch an attack from the Gulf. But Prince Shafik was assassinated in Paris in November of 1979, and the plans for the coup disintegrated. Still, Mahmoud carried on playing the part of the loyal admiral of the Islamic Gulf Fleet. He knew that the old chain of command would continue, and that, eventually, Kalvani would reappear with another plot for a coup to overthrow the hated mullahs.

In early 1982, the generals approached Kalvani, who agreed to participate in Project Norouz. Kalvani enlisted the help of former Imperial Navy officers, primarily marine commandos and navy frogmen living in exile in Europe and the U.S. When Kalvani approached his old officers, they were eager to return to their homeland any way they could. Even if that meant posing as Arab sailors, wearing a ragged *kuffiya* around their heads and loose-fitting shirts and baggy trousers while they manned the dhows, the navy officers knew that it was all a means to an end—an end they desperately wanted. Kalvani's men, disguised as Arab traders and black marketeers to avoid any suspicion, shuttled their dhows around the Gulf. They brought fresh mangoes to the resort on Kish Island; Levis, cigarettes, and rock music cassettes to the Arabs of Khuzistan; sugar, cigarettes, and medicines to the Baluchis. But the foodstuffs, cigarettes, and other black-market goods that Commander Kalvani dispatched throughout the Gulf provided the cover for more important cargo. Hidden in the specially-constructed double holds of the dhows were the arms and munitions to be used to implement Project Norouz. Admiral Mahmoud of the Islamic Navy Gulf Fleet ordered his men to let the dhows of the black marketeers operate peacefully back and forth across the Gulf—their goods were needed in Iran. Besides, they supplied the men of the Islamic Gulf Fleet with cigarettes and other luxuries.

"Mr. Kir," General Vanak said loudly, "these agreements are excellent. But tell me, in your opinion, what will the Americans think of the agreements? Will they want to sign them?"

"Definitely," Kir said.

Tomorrow, the heads of Hall and Bening would be coming to Abu Musa to personally discuss terms of agreements with the generals. The generals, in turn, would discuss the aircraft needed for Project Norouz.

Michael Kir looked at his watch. It was almost three o'clock, and he had to be getting back to Kish to greet the Americans.

"Gentlemen, do you have any questions about the agreements?" Kir asked.

"No, Mr. Kir, everything seems in order. What time did you say Mr. Connelly and Mr. Watkins were arriving?" General Vanak asked.

"This evening," Kir replied. He snapped his briefcase shut. "Mr. Rowan will accompany Mr. Watkins, Mr. Connelly, and myself here tomorrow for our meeting at 1130 hours." Michael Kir stood up, and gave a short bow, and walked out of the room.

The generals were in a jubilant mood. They agreed that things were moving along well, and they congratulated General Vanak on his choice of Michael Kir. He had done a good job.

General Vanak stood up, addressing the group. "A pledge of allegiance," he said. The other generals stood up and placed their right hands on their left breasts. They pledged allegiance to *Khoda, Mihan*, "God and Country." In previous times there had been a third part to the pledge, *Khoda, Shah, Mihan*. But this time the fate of the country would not rest on the strength of one man.

The generals sat down. General Vanak pulled up a chair next to Parvis Gazvini and took another glass of tea off the metal tray being circulated by a servant. He put a lump of sugar in his mouth and sipped his tea while he looked at a dispatch from General Pakdal acknowledging receipt of the M-16's. General Vanak turned to Gazvini and handed him the dispatch.

"It seems that Commander Kalvani is doing an admirable job of supplying General Pakdal with the necessary arms," Vanak said.

Gazvini nodded. "Yes, his dhow system works well."

"It's a shame about Kalvani," Vanak continued. "He is a good man, and a very able navy officer." Too bad he knew too much; too bad he, like Mahmoud, was still loyal to the Pahlavi Dynasty; too bad that he was one of the players in the uneasy coalition whose loyalties or political philosophies were suspect in the eyes of the generals who would comprise Iran's new military government. Kalvani would have to be eliminated after the successful completion of the plan.

"Too bad about Kir, also," Parvis Gazvini said. He crushed the lump of sugar between his teeth.

# CHAPTER SIXTEEN

Kir shielded his eyes from the sunlight as the Boeing 707 pulled up on the runway. The engines shut off and the stairs were quickly brought out. Mark opened the door of the plane, and out stepped two men, wearing sunglasses, dressed in open-necked leisure suits, and carrying brief-cases.

"Mr. Watkins, Mr. Connelly, how are you? Welcome to Kish Island," Kir said, shaking Burt Connelly's hand.

"Burt, call me Burt," Burt Connelly said. A man in his early fifties, his face showed the ravages of too many bourbons, unfiltered cigarettes, and the pressures that accompanied his position as head one of America's largest helicopter companies, Hall Helicopter Industries. His thinning head of hair was done in a classic Hank Snow pomaded hairstyle. Burt undid the button of his beige polyester jacket and surveyed the landscape. "Beautiful spot, isn't it, John?"

"Yes, very nice. Beautiful weather. Same kind of weather as in Phoenix in mid-October, but it's a bit more humid," John Watkins said. He was a big, tall man. The soft edges of his belly overlapped his belt cinched tightly around his girth, his dumplingish face was florid—hardly the imposing figure one would imagine as head of Bening Air-craft, one of the biggest aerospace companies in the world. A gust of wind lifted a crust of John Watkin's crisply hairsprayed sandy-blond hair. He quickly patted it down, then turned to Kir. "When is the meeting with generals, Michael?"

"Tomorrow at eleven-thirty. The Generals insisted that you have lunch with them. I hope you don't mind barracks food, Persian style," Kir said.

"Hell, no. I love that Persian rice. I just hate the thoght of all that goddamn tea we'll have to drink," Burt said.

"Well, gentlemen, Mark will take you on a short drive around the island, show you some of our facilities, and then take you to your quarters. I'm afraid I have some work to do. By the way, you'll be staying in the court ministers' Villas."

"The court ministers' Villas?" John said.

"Yes, when the island was originally developed, special housing was built for the ministers of the Imperial Court," Kir said.

"Then those villas must be something," John said as he got into the Range Rover. "Those guys used to do things in style."

Victoria took off her sunglasses to get a better look. "Human beings, or at least I think . . ." Her voice trailed off, as she watched Mark and two brightly dressed figures approach the pool.

"Where?" Gabriella asked, sitting up.

Mark waved to the girls as he walked toward the swimming pool.

Manuela lay face down on the blue-and-white chaise lounge. The sun beat down on her darkly tanned shoulders, sending tiny beads of Bain de Soleil-coated perspiration trickling down the curve of her back. A triangle of black cotton, string-tied at the hips, barely covered her firm rounded ass. The matte surface of the cloth was a sharp contrast to her glistening bronzed body.

Manuela turned her head slowly, opened her eyes slightly, and closed them again. "Where did they dig those two up?" she mumbled.

"Hello, girls, I'd like you to meet Mr. Watkins and Mr. Connelly. They're from the States," Mark said.

As if I couldn't guess, Gabriella thought, as she stared at the sky-blue polyester legs in front of her.

"Hi, girls. You sure are getting great tans," Burt said, eyeing the nearly naked bodies stretched out on the deck chairs. "You all look like you're having a great time here on Kish."

"Oh, yes, marvelous," Victoria replied.

"This sure is some spot, isn't it?" reaffirmed Burt, directing his attention to the blond Victoria.

"Beautiful," Victoria said.

"Beautiful is right!" Burt said referring to the close-range scenery of the golden-tanned Victoria, scantily clad in a minuscule sea-green bikini.

"Well, you girls sure beat the rush," John added, his pudgy frame blocking out the sun as Gabriella put down her *Vogue Italiana* and looked up at him.

"Yes," Gabriella replied, "this island is the most perfect resort that I have ever been to." She looked at Mark, expecting acknowledgment of her public relations work. Mark nodded and smiled at her.

"Hey, Burt, John," Mark said, as John moved to sit down in a deck chair next to Gabriella, "we'd better get going. I'd like to show you around Kish before the sun starts to go down; it's almost four-thirty. You'll have a chance to get acquainted with the girls at dinner."

"Nice meeting you, gals," John said. Both he and Burt waved back to the girls as they walked toward the gate leading out of the secluded swimming pool area.

Out of range, Burt let out a low whistle. "Lordie-me, those are some lookers! I didn't think that there would be girls on this island, especially gorgeous girls like those! Where did you get them? They are '10s'—all three of them!" Burt said excitedly. Then, realizing the impropriety of his statement, he asked, "Hey, are those your girl-friends?"

"If they are," John continued, "which one of you lucky bastards has two of them?"

"Hell, no," Mark replied casually. "They aren't our girlfriends, just good-time girls, if you know what I mean," he added confidentially.

"Really?" asked Burt incredulously.

"Yes, they're airline hostesses who like spending the winter lounging around Kish, having a good time."

"Uh huh," said Burt knowingly. "Stews." He winked at Mark.


"My, isn't this our lucky day," Victoria said as she watched Michael Kir walk toward the swimming pool. "So many visitors," she sighed.

He pulled up a deck chair beside hers and sat down.

"And to what do we owe the honor of this visit, Mr. Kir?" Victoria asked smiling.

"Oh, just a little discussion of this evening's plan." He looked at Manuela lying on her stomach, apparently asleep. "Manuela, are you awake?" he asked. She didn't respond.

"Gabriella," said Kir, "please nudge Manuela and wake her up. I have to talk to all of you. It is important."

Manuela opened her eyes and sat up.

"What is it?" asked Victoria.

"It is about those men you just met, the

Americans. It is imperative that this evening after dinner you seduce them. I don't care how you do it; two with one, all together, switching, just do it!'' Kir ordered. ''And the kinkier the better.''

Victoria sat upright in her chair. ''Kinky! You've got to be kidding! Those guys?'' she said incredulously. ''What if they don't feel like doing it?'' Victoria continued.

''Make them,'' Kir replied icily.

''You are *pazzo*, crazy, Michael,'' Gabriella insisted. ''Sure they probably wouldn't mind a little *amore*, but their idea of kinky is probably anything other than a missionary position.''

Manuela slowly took off her sunglasses and looked at Michael Kir. ''Tell me, Michael, what exactly did you have in mind?'' she asked. ''What exactly would you like me to do to these men, or have them do to me?'' Manuela was enjoying making Michael squirm. She knew it was hurting him to think that she was about to be screwed by someone else, and she was going to make the most of it. Manuela knew that Michael loved her—that he loved her as much as he could have loved anyone—that cold, calculating, son of a bitch. Manuela leaned closer to Michael. ''What exactly do you suggest, Michael? Your every wish is my command,'' she said sweetly.

''Yes, Michael, what do you want?'' asked Gabriella. ''B and S, M and D?''

''No, Gabriella,'' Victoria said laughing, ''it's B and D and S and M.''

''Oh, yes, that's right,'' Gabriella said smiling.

''I am dead serious,'' Kir said. ''You girls don't seem to understand.''

''That is right, Mr. Kir,'' said Victoria. ''We don't understand. Perhaps if you tell us exactly why we are here, and for what purpose, we might understand. I have the sneaking suspicion that you have not told us the whole truth, Mr. Kir. What exactly is going on here?''

Kir looked at Victoria stonily. "You are in no position to question me. You've been hired to do a job. Just do it."

Gabriella, now more serious after the sharp words between Victoria and Kir, asked, "But why is this kinkiness necessary? What has it got to do with these men?''

"Nothing in particular with these men. You are to be as kinky, as sexually creative as possible with all the guests that you'll service. That is the way heads of Gulf Island Resorts want it."

"What are you talking about?" asked Victoria, leaping up from her chair. "How would they possibly ever know what happens here on Kish?"

"It will all be filmed," Kir said calmly.

"Filmed!" cried the three girls in unison.

"The corporation likes to see what it is paying for," Kir said. "So you will be filmed with the guests, when you are, shall we say, entertaining them."

*'Non capisco,* I don't understand,'' Gabriella said, shaking her head slowly from side to side.

"Filmed! Why?" Victoria said.

"Don't ask questions," Kir said sharply. "You will be filmed. Now that you know, you will act accordingly. The kinkier, the more outrageous, the better. And do not ever mention, even insinuate, to any of the guests that they are being filmed."

"Just what the hell are you up to, Michael?" Victoria said furiously.

Kir glared at Victoria. In an icy voice, he addressed the three women. "I did not come here to discuss our plans with you three. May I remind you that Kish Island is a very important undertaking for Gulf Island Resorts, and we are deadly serious about it. Do not do anything to jeopardize it—anything. I am warning you. Just do as you are told, or you will be very, very sorry." Kir looked each woman straight in the eyes, turned on his heel, and walked away. Gabriella stared open-mouthed at Kir as he walked toward the residence.

Victoria watched silently as Manuela stood up, ran to the pool's edge, and plunged in. The cold water against Manuela's hot skin numbed her body. She wished the water would numb her brain against the thoughts rushing through her mind.

The candlelit table was set under a yellow and white striped awning on the patio outside Victoria's villa. The villa was the largest in the compound, with its own swimming pool and private gardens. Victoria sat inside the living room watching, through the tinted glass, the comings and goings of the waiters as they set the table. A large bowl of yellow and white roses from the garden were placed on the glass table. Three waiters brought out large ice-filled silver buckets, the gold-foil tops of the champagne bottles poking out of them.

Victoria admired the beautiful view; a classical Persian garden, completely surrounded by a high wall. It was a small, perfectly proportioned garden, full of rose bushes and trailing honeysuckle vines. Small lights dramatically illuminated the silvery poplar trees and rose-laden bushes. The swimming pool at the end of the garden was a luminescent turquoise. Victoria took another sip of champagne as she tried to block out of her mind the inevitable forthcoming events of this evening.

Victoria heard raucous laughter coming from just inside the garden. She looked up and saw two male figures, one slightly overweight, both poorly dressed, walking up the pathway with Manuela between them. Each had a can of beer in one hand, and escorted Manuela with the other.

Michael must have also suggested to Manuela what she should wear this evening—as little as possible, thought Victoria. Manuela was dressed in a pair of gossamer-sheer harem pants, slit up the sides and tied at the ankles. Her matching hot-pink chiffon top was also sheer, the bottom of the blouse falling to points in the front and back. The silver embroidery on the top hid little of her firm voluptuous breasts.

Victoria's outfit, too, left very little to the imagination. Her lemon-yellow silk dress plunged precipitously, the two paper thin pieces of silk that barely covered her breasts were tied behind her neck, and the skirt was slit high up her thighs.

"Entertain them as if they were the Shah himself," Victoria murmured, remembering Kir's last line before he left her to dress. "Now, that really is stretching the imagination," she said to herself softly, as she drained her champagne glass.

"Hi, Vicky," John said, poking his head in through the sliding glass door.

"Oh, hello, John," Victoria replied, smiling. "Come on inside. Let's have a drink while we wait for the others. Hi, Burt, Manuela," Victoria said, as she ushered them into the living room.

"What can I get you to drink?" she asked, as she pressed a button for the servant.

"Another beer," John said.

"Now, really, John," Victoria said, playfully chastizing him. "Beer? Tonight calls for champagne." Victoria sidled over to Burt and put her arm around his neck.

"A bottle of Dom Pérignon," Victoria said to the waiter.

"Ah, the Coors of champagne," Burt said with a smile. "Say, where is the other girl, that cute little Gab . . . Gabra . . ."

"Gabriella," Manuela said.

*"Eccomi!"* Gabriella breezed into the room. *"Ciao, caro,"* said Gabriella, kissing everyone as she flitted around the room.

"My, my, aren't we cheerful," Manuela whispered to her, as her lips brushed Gabriella's cheek.

"Diet pills," Gabriella said in a low voice. "They make me very cheerful."

"You certainly do look pretty," Burt complimented her, unable to take his eyes off her tight black bandeau dress that barely covered her breasts and clung to every sensuous curve of her luscious body.

*"Grazie, grazie,"* Gabriella replied in her whispery voice, as she gave a little bow and sat down close beside Burt, putting her hand on his knee.

"Shall we go to the table," Victoria said, wrapping her arm around John. "I know it's going to be a lovely dinner. I hope you like Kobe beef," she said, leading the way out to the torch-lit patio.

Through the tinted-glass sliding doors, Victoria saw Mark and Kir approach the beautifully set dinner table.

"My compliments to the chef," said John, as he scraped up the last of the burgundy remains of his Cherries Jubilee from his dessert plate.

"Great, absolutely great," Burt said, leaning back slightly in his chair. "You guys sure know how to live."

Michael Kir put down his napkin. "Ladies, Burt, John," he said, standing up. "You'll have to excuse me, but Mark and I have some paperwork to do."

"What time is the flight tomorrow, Mike?" John

asked.

"Ten-fifteen in the morning. A car will pick you up around quarter to ten."

"Goodnight, all," Mark said, as he and Michael walked away from the table.

"Those two guys really work hard," John said, shaking his head. "You girls must not get to see them much."

"Hardly ever," Manuela said. "We spend so many evenings alone," she added.

"But not tonight," Victoria said, smiling seductively at Burt, who was nervously straightening his slightly askew string tie.

"How about an after-dinner drink?" Manuela suggested as the waiter wheeled in a silver cart full of liqueur bottles.

"After all, the night is still young," Gabriella said cheerfully. "Let's have some fun." She raised her glass, clinking it against John Watkins's glass, and moved her chair closer to his.

"Yes," Victoria said, "I feel like having some fun!"

Burt and John nodded.

"Well, what the hell," Burt said, slapping his thigh. "Why the hell not?" He turned to John. "How about it, John, another drink before we hit the road?"

Victoria, a look of concern on her face, glanced at Gabriella. They both remembered what Michael Kir had told them that afternoon at the pool. Kir's hard voice: "I don't care how you do it, just do it!" echoed in their minds. They knew they had to seduce the Americans.

Manuela nodded to the girls as she poured a bourbon for Burt. She handed him the glass and stood up, her hands resting on the tabletop.

"I'm so light-headed from all the champagne," she said, smiling first at Burt, then at John. "I think I'll go for a swim. It will clear my head." Still standing at the table, Manuela slowly pulled off her shocking pink blouse. Her smooth shoulders, her firm round breasts and sleek, flat torso glowed in the candlelight. Naked to the waist, Manuela put her foot on a chair and began undoing the strap of her black velvet high-heeled sandal.

"John, be a dear," Manuela said, walking toward him. His face turning a florid pink at the scene he was witnessing. "I don't want to drown, so be a doll and come down and watch me while I swim." She sat on his lap, facing him, her soft breasts and hard nipples pressing against him. "Why don't you come swimming, too?"

John stood up abruptly, almost knocking Manuela over.

Burt drained his glass of bourbon as he watched Manuela, now dressed only in her sheer harem pants, walk down the stairs to the illuminated pool, hanging on John's arm. Burt glanced furtively at the two girls on either side of him. "Say, girls, how about another drink?"

As Victoria turned to pour Burt another bourbon, Gabriella bent over and kissed Burt Connelly hard on the mouth, pushing her tongue deep inside. She reached down and unzipped his fly, shoving her hand inside his pants. "I love American men," Gabriella murmured.

Victoria brought the glass over and placed it on the table. She took Burt's hand and squeezed it. She lifted his hand to her lips and kissed the fingertips. Then she quickly moved his hand up under her dress.

She sighed deeply, then whispered in his ear, "Burt, why don't you and Gabriella and I all go inside, where it is more comfortable?" Burt Connelly, as if in a trance, stood up and let the two women lead him into the villa.

The next morning at 8:15, Mark and Kir sat in the screening room in the residence, facing the large Advent video screen.

"Mark, will you please stop that!" Kir said, irritated.

"What?" Mark said, not lifting his eyes to the screen.

"That knuckle cracking! Look, if you don't like watching this video tape, don't! I can check it out myself."

"No . . . no . . . Michael," Mark said, mumbling, "No problem, really."

"Fine," Kir said, as they watched Burt Connelly's hand reach inside Victoria's dress as Gabriella undid the ornate silver belt buckle on Connelly's slacks, pulling out his flaccid penis. Expertly, she began manipulating his penis with her slender fingers and full wine-red lips as his half-opened mouth lunged for the soft-pink nipple of Victoria's just exposed breast.

"You want a cup of coffee?" Mark asked Kir.

"Yes, Mark, get me one," Kir said sharply, as Mark got up from his seat and rushed down the aisle.

When Mark returned, the screen showed Manuela and John Watkins also in the bedroom of Victoria's villa. Manuela and Victoria were working on the moaning Burt, prostrated on the moire bedspread, and John had Gabriella pushed up against the wall and was pumping into her. Her tapered plum-glazed fingernails dug into his fleshy freckled back as a look of disgust crossed her face.

"Christ! Look at that goddamn Gabriella," Kir said angrily. "If looks could kill, old John would be dead now."

John Watkins, the dimples in his lard-white rump contracting and releasing as he continued to pump away frantically, finally collapsed against Gabriella.

Gabriella, pinioned against the beige silk wall by John Watkin's huge bulk, cooed in his ear. "*Che schifo ... sei un maiale vero, caro. Sporcaccione mio, che culo di baleno, pisellino storto ...*"

"That bitch, Gabriella," Kir steamed.

"What?" Mark said, puzzled.

"The sweet nothings that she is whispering in John Watkin's ear are all profanities and insults."

"What exactly did she say, Michael?"

"Well, to give you a rough translation, she said: 'What garbage; you're a real pig, dear; my filthy one; what a whale's ass, and crooked cock.' Does that give you an idea about our Gabriella's love words?" Kir said, infuriated. "I'm going to speak to her later this afternoon, as soon as we get back from Abu Musa."

"So what if Gabriella said those things?" Mark said. "What does it matter? John Watkins never knew what she was saying."

"That is totally beside the point, Mark. The girls are paid to do their job. And they better do it right."

"Well, if you ask me, Michael, no amount of money could be payment enough for that," Mark said.

"Mark, you must remember: the girls are our insurance." Kir's voice was hard and cold. Kir gazed straight ahead at the screen. The film continued for another twenty minutes as the five naked bodies cavorted together.

Kir got up from his seat. He pressed a button on the remote control device he held in his hand. The screen went blank.

"Not bad, not bad at all," he said, as he switched

on the lights. "But I think we should move a couple of the cameras, to get a better angle."

"The Russ Meyer of Kish Island," Mark said to Kir.

As Michael Kir rewound the cassette, Mark eyed him. He was amazed at Kir's total lack of emotion. Mark knew what he was getting himself in for when he embarked on this project, but it was at times like this, when he saw what a cold, calculating, and heartless man Kir was, that he actually feared Michael Kir.

The Beechcraft headed toward Abu Musa. Mark sat in the front of the plane, next to Gino, busily going over his papers. Kir sat between the two Americans in the rear of the aircraft, chatting amiably with John Watkins.

Burt Connelly pulled a pair of photocromatic Ray-Ban sunglasses out of the pocket of his short-sleeved Perma-Prest shirt. The gradually darkening lenses shaded his bloodshot eyes from the bright sunlight.

Burt looked at Kir. "It must be kinda tough, running the show for the generals," Burt said. "They can't move mountains like they used to, like back when they were running the show in Iran."

"You're right," Kir said. "It hasn't been easy, but fortunately all the companies that were heavily committed in Iran before the Revolution have been receptive to the plan."

"You'd better believe it," agreed John. "And not just the Americans. The French, the Japanese, the Brits, the Germans, the Italians lost their shirts in Iran too."

"The Japanese are really hurting. They've got a couple of half-finished petrochemical factories in the south of Iran and, hell, the Japs used to get eighty percent of their oil from Iran. I'll bet they'll be as happy as hell to have some friends back in the driver's seat again soon enough," Burt said, lighting up a cigarette.

John Watkins looked at Kir. "I've been meaning to ask you, how are you keeping the lid on this?"

"Well, as you know, John, very few people know about this plan—only the heads of the corporations who'll be coming back in right away. You are one of a very select few."

"Not to mention a few heads of government," Burt said. "But they don't know nothing, if you get what I mean."

"You're right Burt," Kir acknowledged.

"I know, I know," Burt said seriously. "If this screws up, it is my head on a platter, and the White House doesn't know me from Adam."

"Granted, Burt, there is a risk," Kir said, "but with the fire power that the generals will have, they will succeed. Project Norouz will be a success."

"I'll tell you, I can't wait to see Iran get whipped back into shape by the generals. What a bunch of loonies those Ayatollahs are, threatening to annex other Moslem nations. The Islamic Government sure sounds menacing as hell," Burt said.

"Sure, it's the old Khomeini-style technique of directing vitriolic words to a scapegoat cause, in an attempt to turn the people's attention away from the problems at hand. And when Ayatollah Khalaghani started up again, threatening to export the Islamic Revolution to the monarchies of the Gulf, it worked to our advantage. Why else do you think Saudi Arabia and the UAE would be willing to let us use their soil as bases for our aircraft?" Michael said. "You see, the stakes are too high. None of the monarchs of the Gulf states wants to see what happened to the Shah happen to them."

John and Burt nodded in agreement.

Kir pointed out the window. "Gentlemen, directly ahead you can see the island of Abu Musa."

The six generals were waiting at the airport in a covered jeep to greet the plane. They greeted the Americans enthusiastically.

"Mr. Watkins, Mr. Connelly, how nice to see you," General Vanak said.

"General, it is nice to see you again," John Watkins replied.

"Gentlemen," said General Vanak, "shall we take a quick tour of the island before our meeting?"

Burt Connelly and John Watkins agreed, and the group of ten men climbed into the waiting jeeps and sped off in a northerly direction toward the port of Abu Musa. General Vanak and the two Americans rode in the lead jeep. The rest of the generals, Mark, and Kir were in the jeeps following behind.

The sun was rising in the cloudless blue sky, high above the convoy of three jeeps. The jeeps first circled the barracks that had been built by the Shah to house his marine commandos and frogmen stationed on Abu Musa. Now the barracks grounds appeared more or less deserted, and only a few soldiers in fatigues could be seen.

The jeeps traveled toward the docks. The dock area was bustling with activity as Arab fishermen and traders unloaded unmarked wooden crates, and burlap sacks of potatoes and rice from the dhows. Huge woven baskets piled high with limes, pineapples, and oranges lined the dockside, ready to be transferred onto the backs of sturdy gray-and-white donkeys.

As the jeeps continued along the water's edge, a

man dressed in baggy cotton pants and a long shirt, walking in front of a donkey loaded down with crates, saluted the generals in their passing jeeps.

"General Vanak," Burt asked, "was that what I thought it was? A salute?"

"Yes, Mr. Connelly," General Vanak said, turning around in his seat, "that was a salute." He smiled broadly. "Here on Abu Musa things are not what they appear to be. It is our little charade that the troops stationed on this island are from the UAE, and the fishermen and traders are Arabs. At least, that is what they appear to be. In actual fact, they are all loyal officers of the Imperial Iranian Armed Forces."

General Vanak took a handkerchief out of his pocket, wiped the dust and sweat from his neck, and continued. "Gentlemen, ahead of you is the Supreme Command Headquarters of Project Norouz."

Burt and John stared at the massive square building directly ahead.

"The building was originally a cold-storage warehouse, built by the Shah to store goods that could not be unloaded in the congested ports of Bandar Abbas, Bushehr, and Khoramshahr," explained General Vanak. "Of course, the interior was restructured to serve our purposes. Supreme Command Headquarters occupies only a small portion of the warehouse; most of the building is hangar space."

The three jeeps stopped in front of the warehouse. Huge gray metal doors stretched across almost one entire wall of the warehouse. Two armed sentries opened a small doorway into the warehouse. Burt, John, Kir, and the generals walked into the cavernous hangar. Inside this portion of the brightly lit, spotless hangar were six

F-4 fighters; Imperial Air Force markings were still on some of their silver fuselages.

"Holy shit," Burt said, whispering to Kir, "so this is where some of the missing F-4's ended up!"

General Vanak's voice boomed through the hangar. "These aircraft that you see here will be the ones used to make Project Norouz a reality."

"They look like they're in excellent condition," Burt said.

"Generals," John said, "how did you get hold of these aircraft?"

"Various ways," General Pirayesh replied. He walked across the cement floor until he came to an F-4E Phantom jet fighter. "This particular aircraft, Mr. Connelly and Mr. Watkins, is the one that I made my escape from Iran with during the fall of the Shah's government." His voice echoed through the high-ceilinged hangar as he told the story of his escape. "I flew this F-4 out of Doshen-Tappeh air base in Tehran on February 12, 1979. Running low on fuel, I was forced to land in Jubail. There, the Saudis offered me kind hospitality, and I left the F-4 stored at a hangar in Jubail. Then, I continued on to Paris, hoping to return to Tehran within the month. Unfortunately, things did not work out that way. These fighters and many other Imperial Iranian Air Force planes would have fallen into the hands of the Revolutionary Government, had my loyal air force officers not spirited them out of Iran.

"Many aircraft were flown to the UAE and Saudi Arabia, where they were stored and maintained, awaiting the time that we, the rightful rulers of Iran, would return to Iran to seize our country back from the mullahs. Because of the obvious space limitations here on Abu Musa, almost all of our aircraft are in the UAE and Saudi. We have two dozen C-130 transport planes.

In addition to these F-4's here, there are a couple of dozen F-4's and F-5's, but they are not in very good shape," continued General Pirayesh. "About ten F-14A's made it out, but we haven't been able to maintain them. You Americans are the only people who can keep those planes up. By the time we were able to get some American support, the planes were already deteriorated," Pirayesh said.

"Damned shame," John Watkins said.

"We fared much better with the helicopters. We have over two hundred helicopters: CH-47's, Sea Cobras, AH-1T's, 206's, 212's, and 214's."

"Where are the helicopters stored?" asked Burt.

"Most of them are in the UAE; some are in Dubai, others are in the interior town of Al-Ain. The rest are in Saudi Arabia, in the eastern port city of Jubail," General Pirayesh said.

"Are they operationally ready?" Burt asked.

"The majority of them are. The host countries are using a number of them, with their own markings, of course. Some of the helicopters need parts, however."

"I'm sure we can take care of that," Burt said amicably.

General Rujanian walked over to Burt Connelly. "Mr. Connelly, I'm interested to hear how the production model 214ST, the new Super Transport helicopter, tested out. I understand that the control tubes in the unboosted portion of the control system will be made of a new graphite and epoxy material. How is that superior to the conventional aluminum tubing?" General Rujanian asked.

"I see you've been doing your homework, General. I'll tell you and the other generals all about the 214ST at our meeting. I brought the specs on it, and some photographs, including some in-flight ones that are real beauts." Burt gave General Rujanian a friendly pat on the shoulder. He knew that General Rujanian, who had been his biggest customer, would soon again be in the position to procure another fleet of helicopters for Iran.

"Gentlemen, this way, please." General Vanak led the way through a metal door, down a long corridor, to the Conference Room.

Michael Kir sat at the long table in the Conference Room of Supreme Command Headquarters on Abu Musa. Small spirals of acrid smoke curled above the burning cigarettes—American and French—resting on the rims of large glass ashtrays. Glasses of tea, bottles of Pepsi and Canada Dry soda, and aircraft spec sheets covered the table. The meeting had been going on for three hours, interrupted by a short lunch break.

On Kir's left were Burt Connelly, John Watkins, and Mark Rowan. Seated across the table were Generals Mojat, Azman, Rujanian, Pirayesh, and Gazvini. General Vanak presided over the head of the table. The Generals were an imposing looking group. By contrast, the two Americans appeared unassuming in dress and manner.

Michael Kir watched with interest at the change that had come over the two gregarious Americans once they sat down at the conference table. Burt Connelly and John Watkins, who on the walk from the hangar to the Conference Room had been discussing golf scores with General Pirayesh—who had taken up golf during his period of exile in Marbella—became total professionals once they sat down to discussing business. And the generals knew it. They had done business with Watkins and Connelly back in the days of the Shah, and they knew that they drove a hard bargain.

Burt Connelly leaned back in his chair, and declined the glass of tea being offered him.

"Do you think I could get a cup of coffee?" he asked the orderly. "*Gaveh*," Burt said, recalling the Farsi word for coffee. The orderly nodded.

Connelly was pleased with the way the meeting was going. The Generals seemed much more pliable than they had been when they commanded the 460,000-strong Imperial Iranian Armed Forces, the best trained, best equipped army in the Middle East. In those days, the generals were second in power only to the Shah. They were feared and respected by their countrymen, and treated with kid gloves by the Western powers who sought Iran's business and political support. No wonder they're willing to make concessions now, Burt thought. The generals wanted it all back: the power, the privilege, the respect, and they wanted it badly.

The orderly returned with a small tin of Nescafé and a jar of Coffeemate on a metal tray. Burt smiled; it was exactly as coffee had been served to him at the Ministry of War office in north Tehran, where he had negotiated hundreds of millions of dollars worth of contracts. Burt poured a spoonful of instant coffee into the lukewarm water and added some Coffeemate. Some things never change; the water will always be lukewarm and the coffee always instant in the Middle East, he thought.

General Rujanian was discussing the equipment that would be needed to ferry the ground troops from Baluchistan to their striking positions within Iran. "In addition, we'll need at least ten more CH-47's to move General Pakdal's men out quickly and efficiently," General Rujanian said. Burt Connelly took notes on a small yellow pad.

"Also," General Rujanian continued," the AH-1T

helicopters we have stored in Dubai are all gun-ships which had been modified to TOW missile configuration. Can you arrange to send the needed TOW missiles through to Dubai?''

"I'm sure that will be no problem. Mark, what do you think?'' Connelly said.

"Nearly all of the ordnance for Project Norouz is being laundered through the UAE or Saudi Arabia. Since the UAE is scheduled to receive large shipments of FMS material in November and December, the TOW missiles can easily be slipped into the shipment,'' Mark said. "Mr. Connelly, you know who to contact State-side about this, correct?''

Burt nodded. Senator Joseph Sullivan's name had not been mentioned, but everyone present knew that Sullivan, through the Senate committee he headed, which handled Foreign Military Sales contracts, would make all the necessary arrangements.

"Mr. Connelly,'' General Rujanian said, "we're all very interested in these new 214ST's. Could you please tell us a few . . .''

"I was just about to,'' Burt Connelly said. "You beat me to the punch.'' Connelly stood up and opened his briefcase. "I have copies of the specs for each of you, and some photographs.'' He passed the specs around the conference table. "Generals,'' Connelly said, holding up a closeup photograph of the cockpit of a 214ST, "you'll notice that the vertical gauges. . . '' Burt Connelly launched into an involved, detailed explanation of the wonders of the new super transport helicopter.

"Gentlemen,'' General Vanak said, "if you'll all please turn to page three of the Hall agreement, the second paragraph, the escalation clause.'' An intense discussion of the terms of the generals' agreements with Hall and Bening ensued. Only Connelly, Watkins, and the generals participated in the discussion. Mark and Kir observed silently. Finally, General Vanak stood up and shook hands with Burt and John.

"I'm glad that we are in agreement, gentlemen. It is always a pleasure to do business with you. We look forward to your presence in Iran, once again," General Vanak said.

"That is some setup the generals have got there," Burt said, taking a drag on his unfiltered Lucky Strike. He took one last look down at Abu Musa, as Gino headed the Beechcraft west toward Kish. "Frankly, what shocked me most about the generals was how they had all aged. They sure looked rough. Revolution obviously did not agree with them."

"They may have looked rough, Burt," John said, "but they were sharp as hell. The generals are determined to succeed, that's for sure."

"Old soldiers never die, and these guys have no intention of fading away," Burt acknowledged.

"You are right," Mark said.

"Well, from what you briefed us on about the actual operation, Mark, it seems that the generals will do their 'generaling' from Abu Musa and leave the actual takeover to General Pakdal and his Immortals, and Commander Kalvani and his marine commandos," John said. He turned to Burt Connelly. "Burt, didn't you find the meeting with the generals a little spooky? It was just as if it were five years ago in Tehran, at Mehrabad or Bagh-e-Shah. God, even the food at lunch was like that right off the chow line at Bagh-e-Shah Base."

"Yeah, but I prefer my food this way, without the lead," Burt said. "Last time I ate *chelo-kebab* I was dodging bullets. It was February 10, 1979. I

313

was at Doshen-Tappeh, the air force base in south-east Tehran, with a few of my boys. We were trying to secure our equipment there, and burn the files. We knew that things were looking pretty shaky in Tehran, and the enlisted air force men looked as if they were going to take over the base in the name of Ayatollah Khomeini."

"Is that what was referred to as the Battle of Tehran?" Mark asked.

"That's right," Burt said, reminiscing. "It sure was ironic. The Imperial Air Force, the Shah's favorite branch of the armed forces, his pride and joy, they were the ones who did him in. Let me tell you, it was some scene there at the air force base the day the Bakhtiar government fell. It was a few rebel officers and the majority of the enlisted men against the loyal air force officers. And this was just what was going on inside the base! Outside the base, those crazy Eye-ran-i-ans were shooting up a storm with all those M-16's and G-3 rifles. It was a goddamn mess. It sure was a beautiful sight seein' that big baby, a 214 chopper, land on the roof and lift us out. Man, I was holding on to my can of Bud as if it was my last!"

"Could have been," John added. "You crazy old coot. I can't believe it, going into Doshen-Tappeh as Bakhtiar's government was collapsing, not to mention the whole goddamn great Shah's army."

Mark turned around in his seat. "You two must have seen some sights in Tehran during those last days before the evacuation."

"Do you want to know the sickest sight I saw? It was when Ayatollah Khomeini got out of his American-made Blazer on his triumphal ride back into the city of Tehran after his seventeen-year exile and got into an American-made chopper," Burt said, shaking his head. "Shit, that was one time I was praying for a main rotor failure." John Watkins laughed.

314

The Beechcraft landed on the Kish runway, just a few hundred feet from the parked Boeing 707.

"I see the plane is waiting for us," Burt said as he climbed out of the back seat of the small plane.

"Yes," Kir said. "Your bags are already on board, so you can take off immediately."

Kir and Mark walked Burt and John over to the forward door of the Boeing 707. Andreas stood in the open doorway.

"Goodbye, Mark, Michael," John Watkins said, shaking hands.

"Yeah, thank you for the hospitality. I really enjoyed my stay on Kish Island," Burt said, smiling broadly at Mark and Kir.

"Glad to hear it," Mark said.

"I'll be in touch with you next week about the FMS shipment to Dubai," Burt said, as he walked up the stairs. John followed, waving. The two Americans disappeared inside the aircraft.

# CHAPTER SEVENTEEN

Michael Kir took a glass of Mosel wine from the tray the waiter held out to him. He turned to the two men standing beside him.

"Mr. Kripp and Mr. Neumann, I propose a little toast. To your enjoying the rest of the evening on Kish Island," Kir said, glancing at the doorway, toward the three girls who had just entered.

"Thank you very much, Mr. Kir," Kripp said, his eyes transfixed by Manuela, dressed in a brilliant blue silk dress.

"Yes, very kind of you, Mr. Kir," Neumann said. The three men clinked glasses together. The two Germans quickly drained their glasses, and Kir motioned for the waiter.

Jurgen Kripp and Hans Neumann were the president and senior vice president, respectively, of one of the largest German industrial concerns. Besides owning steel mills, Kripp Industries owned one of the world's largest arms manufacturing companies. The men had arrived from Frankfurt that morning, and had spent most of the day on Abu Musa with the generals. Things had gone well on Abu Musa, and there was cause for the Germans to celebrate. Stepped-up shipments of ammunition via the UAE had been arranged. Final agreement had been concluded on a three-part deal that included supplying new furnaces to what had once been called the National Steel Company of Iran, the construction of a new steel mill in the south of Iran, and a concession for supplying all the coke needed by Iran. The stamp of approval on this agreement would come with the Bonn government's official recognition of the new regime in Iran.

Pleased with the package that he had arranged with the generals, Jurgen Kripp put business out of his mind, as he looked forward to a relaxing, enjoyable evening before heading back to cold, wintery Frankfurt early in the morning. He watched as the three women walked toward the bar. Kripp turned to Hans Neumann and smiled. Neither man had imagined that the three girls Kir had mentioned, who provided Kir and his associates with "companionship" on Kish Island, would be so spectacular-looking.

"Well, what do you think?" Victoria said to Manuela as she watched the bartender slip a wedge of lime on the rim of her tall glass of Campari and soda.

"About what?" Manuela said.

"Tonight's entertainment," Victoria said, looking at the two Germans. Manuela's gaze followed hers.

"Oh, no, dear, you've got it all wrong. We are the entertainment," Manuela said.

"Really, they're not bad," Victoria said, looking over at Kir and the two guests. Both men were in their late fifties, with good physiques, and they were well dressed.

"It's going to be another long night," Gabriella said. "And I'm still tired from those Americans three days ago. Burt and John kept us up all night."

"They certainly didn't look like they had it in them, did they," Victoria said.

"It's difficult to judge, just by looks. You never

know what to expect," Manuela said. She noticed Kripp eyeing her, and she smiled at him. Kir motioned to the two guests, and they put down their drinks.

"Oh, oh, here they come," Gabriella said.

Gabriella sat across from Hans Neumann at the dinner table. He stroked his goatee as his steel blue eyes undressed her. *Porca la misera*, what misery, this one likes me, she thought, bemoaning the fate that would be hers later in the evening. Germans had never been Gabriella's favorite types, especially in bed. Usually they made love with mechanical precision, every once and a while uttering some guttural *ich liebe dich* or *jetzt, jetzt, ich komme*. It was so distasteful, just like this awful German peasant food, she thought, as she stared down into her liver-dumpling soup.

A waiter entered the dining room, ceremoniously carrying a roast pig, complete with an apple in its mouth, on a silver platter. The waiter brought the roast pig first to Kir, who was sitting on Gabriella's left, for approval. Kir nodded, and the waiter took it away. Michael Kir leaned toward Gabriella and whispered, "And that, my dear Gabriella, is how you should feel—laid out on a silver platter with an apple in your gorgeous mouth."

"*Stronzo*, shithead," she muttered between her teeth, to Kir, all the while flashing a wide smile at the Teuton across the table from her. Gabriella turned a cold shoulder to Kir.

Only two days ago, Gabriella had had a tremendous screaming match with Michael Kir, and the animosity was still very much there. He had criticized her sharply for her bitchy performance with the Americans. "So what," she had indignantly told Kir. "Isn't it enough that I screw them, and royally, at that. Now I have to be nice to those pigs, too?"

Gabriella was still fuming at the thought of that *stronzo*, Kir. I'll show him tonight. For the camera, and the benefit of Kir, I'm going to give an award-winning performance, she thought. Gabriella was cheering herself up just thinking of acting on the "silver screen." When Michael Kir isn't so mad at me, perhaps I'll ask if I can see those films, thought Gabriella. She was very curious to see if her body looked as good in action as it did when she stood in front of the mirror. But, she wondered, worriedly, the camera puts on four or five kilos, and what if when that American was grabbing my ass, a couple of nights ago, the camera caught him squeezing some cellulite. Everyone is supposed to have it. Gabriella shuddered at the thought. For a moment, she even entertained the idea of asking Michael Kir how her body had looked in those films. Forget it, she thought. He'd probably lie and tell me I looked awful; just to spite me, because he is mad at me, Gabriella rationalized. Uninterested in her food, Gabriella looked around the table. Everyone seemed to be enjoying themselves.

Gabriella glanced toward Kir, who was engaged in a conversation with Neumann and Victoria. Manuela was laughing at a joke that Kir was telling her. Victoria and Manuela are probably in a good mood, just at the thought of getting nice, firm bodies, thought Gabriella. Gabriella remembered how Victoria and Manuela had laughed at the pool a couple of days ago, when she had said that she was afraid her fingers were going to sink into the doughy flesh of John's body and get stuck. Gabriella smiled at the thought.

"*Brava*, Gabriella," Kir said, leaning toward her. "It is nice to see a smile on your face."

Gabriella flashed him a dirty look, and turned away to assess the evening's entertainment. Neither of the two Germans was exactly handsome. Neumann had a goatee, which Gabriella despised. Still, he looked less menacing than the bald headed, barrel-chested Jurgen Kripp, who monopolized Manuela's attention as he told her an anecdote about his youth in Argentina. Gabriella looked over at Neumann, who was discussing the skiing conditions on the mountains in Germany this winter with Victoria. Not wanting to leave Gabriella out of the conversation, Hans Neumann turned to Gabriella. "Do you like to ski, Fraülein?" he asked staring at her cleavage.

"I prefer the *après*-ski," Gabrielle replied, smiling sweetly. Neumann laughed, his hand on Victoria's arm and his leg rubbing against Gabriella's under the table.

Yes, it's going to be Kripp with Manuela, and Neumann with me and Victoria. It's going to be a long night, Gabriella thought, sighing.

A breeze blew in off the balcony, causing the ruffled edges of the opened curtains to flutter. The smell of roses and jasmine, carried by the cool October night air, wafted into the room. Manuela inhaled deeply.

Jurgen Kripp lay in the center of a large bed in the master bedroom of Manuela's villa. Manuela stood at the foot of the bed, pulling off Kripp's Bally shoes. She knelt on the bed, unbuttoned Kripp's shirt, then unfastened his belt buckle. Kripp lay back quietly, his eyes closed, a slight smile across his lips.

Manuela undressed him quickly. She leaned on Kripp's chest and began kissing his face and neck gently, then more passionately. She spread the passive Kripp's legs with her own. Then, kneeling on the floor, Manuela licked the arch of his foot. Her tongue lightly, teasingly, grazed his skin as her parted lips moved up his well-muscled calf, her shiny black hair loose and trailing through the hairs on his leg, creating the sensation that they were standing on end. Her tongue sought out every erogenous zone on Kripp's body. She moved her hand up to his penis: it was still soft and calm.

Manuela stood before Kripp. Slowly, langurously, she began to move her clothing. She pulled her blue André Łaug dress up over her head.

"Ach!" Jurgen Kripp exclaimed. Manuela was wearing a black lace corset, black seamed stockings, and black patent leather high-heeled sandals. Diaphanous lacy brassiere cups, punctuated by a tiny red silk rose between them, covered Manuela's full, high breasts, pushed up even higher by the tight, boned, strapless corset. The gleaming tanned smoothness of Manuela's shoulders and round breasts contrasted sharply with the richly patterned lace of the corset. The corset tapered in at Manuela's narrow waist, then flared out at her hips. A tiny red silk rose marked the top of each of the four garter straps, two for each leg, that held up the sheer black stockings. Manuela's curly pubic hair touched the bottom edge of the lacy corset. The hair was as black as the tops of the stockings covering her long shapely legs.

Manuela turned around slowly, so that Kripp could admire her naked, round buttocks, framed by the edge of the corset, and the black lace of the garters.

Manuela turned, then leaned forward, bending down over the German's body, running her tongue lightly up and down Kripp's chest and abdomen as she manipulated his hard nipples between her fingertips. His nipples were hard, but his cock was not.

Manuela stepped back and faced Kripp, smiling seductively at him, enjoying her own performance, her play-acting. Emotionally Manuela had traveled to a point where she was now able to divorce herself from the sexual acts she was forced to preform and, in a way, she actually enjoyed the humiliations forced upon her. She was in that room with Jurgen Kripp only in body. She raised one leg and put her foot on the edge of the bed.

*"Schön,* .beautiful," Kripp said in a low voice. Manuela, encouraged by this word of appreciation, unfastened the garters on her raised thigh, and slowly rolled down her stocking over her ankle, she darted her head forward between Kripp's thighs and took his limp penis in her mouth. She manipulated it with her tongue, teased it with her teeth and lips. It soon became evident that Kripp's organ was not responding to her ministrations; she pulled back and lowered her leg to the carpeted floor.

Manuela kicked off her shoes, and, still clad in the corset and one stocking, climbed atop Kripp, rotating her hips and rubbing herself on him. She moved up, positioning her pussy directly over his mouth. He dutifully ate her, as Manuela's hand went to his cock. It began to stir slightly, only to wilt seconds later. Jurgen Kripp grasped Manuela's hips, and turned her around so her buttocks were over his face, her breasts grazing his abdomen, her face just over his cock. Kripp began kissing Manuela's smooth buttocks, moving closer and closer to the dark crack which separated the two round orbs. His tongue moved sinuously along the shadowy crevice, darting inside, then out.

Manuela methodically licked and kissed his soft penis. Kripp's tongue moved slowly down her inner thigh, until he reached the top of her stocking. He began nibbling and sucking at the firm flesh just above the top of the stocking; then, he lightly tugged at the garter strap with his teeth. Manuela could feel his cock starting to harden beneath her lips. So this is what he likes, she thought.

Manuela raised herself off to Kripp, and got out of bed. She retrieved her stocking from the floor. The stocking stretched out in her hands, her arms lifted above her head, Manuela rhythmically, sensually, undulated her hips. She trailed the filmy stocking over Kripp's face and body, then flicked him with it, at first lightly, then harder. She could see see his penis rising.

Kripp was still laying on his back, his legs slightly spread, his arms at his side. Manuela climbed into bed and lifted his arms up above his head, his hands resting on the pillow. She grabbed his hands and placed one atop the other. Holding his arms down with her knees, she tied his wrists together tightly with the stocking. She could hear his breathing becoming heavier. Manuela stood up on the bed and removed her other stocking. She knelt beside Kripp, and took his nearly-erect cock in her mouth. Then, abruptly, she lifted her head, and tied the other stocking around the base of his penis. Kripp moaned, and Manuela mounted his engorged, stiff prick. Kripp moaned as he felt Manuela's hot, tight pussy engulf his throbbing, hard penis. His hands bound above his head, Kripp writhed in pleasure as Manuela rode him furiously. She reached her hands back and began playing with his balls and anus. Kripp was moaning louder and louder, and his body was wet with perspiration. Manuela yanked the stocking tied around his penis tighter, and, with a violent scream, Kripp came.

The late morning sun, making its ascent,

appeared to follow the Range Rover as it raced along the water's edge toward the casino. Kir stopped the car under the canopied entrance to the Kish Island Casino and hurried through the front door. Kir stepped over the rolls of red carpeting, boxes, cables, and workmen's tools until he came to the pounded brass doors that led into the main room of the casino. As he entered the high-ceilinged room, Kir scanned the room, looking for Mark. The floor was covered in thick red carpeting, and the floor-to-ceiling windows presented a sweeping view of the Persian Gulf. Prisms of light from the enormous chandelier hanging from the center of the ceiling were reflected on the walls.

"Mark!" Kir called, as he stopped to let workmen carry a heavy carved wood gaming table across his path.

"Hi, Michael," Mark called from atop a ladder propped against the brass-paneled wall.

"What the hell are you doing up there?"

"Checking a problem with a ventilation duct."

"Mark, leave it for the engineer. Come on down. I have to talk to you."

Mark climbed down the ladder. "What's up?"

"It looks like Parvis Gazvini has decided to pay us a visit. I just received word from Abu Musa. His helicopter took off a few minutes ago. He should be here in twenty-five minutes."

"Shit."

"Nice surprise," Kir said sarcastically. "Mark, you go to the airstrip and wait for Parvis; I'll come as soon as I can. I'll get Manuela away from the Royal Compound, and take her immediately to the hotel. Even though Parvis could not recognize her, if Manuela saw him, I'm afraid she couldn't keep her cover. She is terrified of him. I'm going to get her right now. We don't have any time to lose."

Parvis Gazvini sat perched in the Bell Jet Ranger, surveying the expanse of sparkling blue water beneath him. The dun colored patch of land in the distance became visible as the helicopter flew westward Kish Island.

Parvis smiled to himself, imagining the flurry of activity his impromptu visit would be inspiring on Kish. He wondered what Michael Kir had been doing when he received word that General Gazvini would be arriving for a surprise "progress check." Had Kir been doing mundane paperwork, checking the military installations, talking to contacts in Europe or the States, or in bed with one of the imported whores? Parvis was all too well aware of Kir's reputation as a potent lover *par excellence*.

Parvis' musings stopped as his helicopter zoomed closer to Kish. Everything was going smoothy—perhaps a bit too smoothly for Parvis' liking. But things were not always as they seemed; that, Parvis knew from first hand experience. The other generals on Abu Musa were satisfied. They had no questions, no suspicions. Kir was performing admirably, and they were pleased.

Only Parvis Gazvini wondered. He knew Michael Kir well enough to know that he was capable of anything. And that was exactly what worried Parvis. The impromptu progress check was only an excuse to enable him to tour Kish.

Parvis wanted to find a mole—a spy—someone who was close enough to Kir to observe him, and who would report back to Parvis on Kir's activities. Perhaps one of Kir's assistants, or that little pilot, perhaps even one of the whores. Parvis was confident that for the right price, he could enlist anyone.

Kir gripped the Range Rover wheel tightly as he

drove toward Manuela's villa at breakneck speed. He knew that he had to tell Manuela that Parvis was coming to Kish. There was no other way he could explain keeping her in guarded seclusion, locked in the hotel for a day and a night. There was nothing he could tell her that she would believe. He had to tell her the truth. She would understand—she had to.

Michael dreaded seeing her face when he told her that the man she feared most in all the world would be so close to her. He could only hope that she would be calm, that she would listen to him. But he knew that she might resist him.

Accelerating, he turned off the main roadway, pulled up in front of the residence. Leaving his vehicle running, Kir ran into the residence, into his own quarters. He opened the top dresser drawer and grabbed a shaving kit off the top. He rifled through the small arsenal of pillboxes and jars, until he found what he wanted. He ripped open the box, pulled out a foil square, and jammed it into his pants pocket.

The Filipino maid who opened the door to Manuela's villa was surprised to see Michael Kir.

"Where's Manuela?" Kir said, entering the sunken living room.

"Miss, sleeping," the maid said, pointing in the direction of Manuela's bedroom.

"I'll go wake her—alone," Kir said. "Leave." He dismissed the maid with a wave of his hand.

Kir entered the darkened bedroom. Although it was nearly noon, Manuela was still asleep, tired from her night of entertaining Jurgen Kripp. Kir's eyes grew accustomed to the darkness. He could see Manuela's sleeping form, her dark hair fanned across the pillow.

Bending over her, Kir could hear her soft even

breathing, see her breasts rise and fall beneath the sheet.

"Manuela." She turned over onto her side.

"Manuela," he repeated, this time touching her face.

Her eyes opened immediately.

"Michael?" she said uncertainly. She looked at him with eyes more asleep than awake.

"Manuela, wake up. I need to talk to you. There's no time to waste."

At this last remark, she sat up.

"Get up, Manuela. Dress quickly, and throw whatever you'll need for overnight into a bag. We're leaving in five minutes."

"What? Where are we going?" Manuela said, pulling up the sheet to cover her nakedness.

"Manuela darling, it's for your own good. I just received word that Parvis Gazvini is coming to Kish to check something out. There's no need to be alarmed; he simply has to report back to the other generals. He should be arriving at the airport in about twenty minutes, and he'll be leaving tomorrow morning. Although Parvis would never recognize you I don't want to take the risk of you seeing him. I think it would be too traumatic . . ."

Manuela tuned out the sound of Kir's patronizing voice. Strangely, she felt no fear, only a detached curiosity, even excitement.

Kir took Manuela's cold hand in his.

". . . I want to spare you the pain," he said. "It's best if you stay at the hotel while Parvis is on Kish."

"No."

Manuela looked directly at Kir. "I want to see Parvis," she said. Her voice was hard and cold.

"It would be too emotional an experience for you. There is no reason for you to have to see Parvis. I'll take you over to the hotel now. You'll stay there, guarded—in case Parvis decides to do any snooping around—overnight, until he leaves Kish." Kir moved closer to her. "There is nothing for you to be afraid of," he said softly. "Come now, be a good girl, get up. We don't have much time."

"I'm not going to the hotel. I'll go join the other girls at the pool—I'm sure Parvis will want to see the *jende* here on Kish." She gave Michael an icy stare. "I want to see him, Michael. I want to see Parvis. He won't know who I am, but I'll know him—something poetic about that, don't you think? I must see him. I will."

"Manuela, don't be foolish. Get up. I'm taking you to the hotel—right now."

"I am not moving. There is nothing you can do to make me go." Her voice was filled with a strange combination of fear and determination.

Kir heard the sound of the helicopter overhead. There was no time to argue with her, and, at this point, it seemed like it would be a waste of breath. To threaten her also seemed futile. But he could not risk her seeing Parvis. There was only one thing to do. His hand went to his pocket.

He moved closer to her, and kissed her passionately on the mouth. She did not respond. He began covering her beautiful face and throat with kisses, as he whispered, "Manuela, darling, don't worry, I will not let anything harm you. We are in this together. You and me." He continued to talk softly, kissing her, caressing her. "Sweetheart, wouldn't you rather come with me? There is nothing to be afraid of, nothing, but it is better that you be secluded for a day. No one is going to harm you. Who would harm a beautiful girl like you, a beautiful body like yours." Kir tried to half pull, half coax Manuela out of bed, but she wouldn't budge. He knew what he had to do. He pushed her back. His strong hands fondled her naked thighs, keeping her pinned to the bed. He was becoming aroused, knowing he would have to take her by force. He began kissing her breasts. He unzipped his fly.

Manuela finally responded, not to the seduction, but to the rape. She began to fight, trying to push him off her. He crushed his lips to hers, and holding her wrists together with one hand, he moved his other hand under the sheet, surprised to feel that she was wearing panties. With one violent movement, he pulled the sheet off the bed. Then, yanking down her lace panties, his hand moved to her clitoris. The warm wetness was a relief to him. He ripped off her panties, looked at his watch, and pushed his hard penis into her. She gasped loudly, and his right hand moved to her mouth. He continued to push himself into her, harder, faster, unrelentingly. Kir reached into his pocket, and with his left hand, unwrapped the piece of foil. With the slippery white pellet in his hand, his hand moved along her buttocks. As Kir felt himself reaching a climax, his finger began playing with her anus. He could wait no longer, he did not have time for the niceties of mutual orgasm. As he felt himself about to come, he shoved the *Spasmo-Oberon* pellet into her ass, climaxing as he did.

Manuela screamed, the sound muffled by Kir's mouth pressed hard against hers. She had felt something being inserted into her, something smooth and cold, guided by Kir's warm moving finger. What was it, what had he done to me, she thought, thrashing wildly, trying to free herself from beneath Kir's hot sweating body. But within seconds her thoughts clouded, and her struggling subsided.

He stayed inside her for what seemed like a long time, caressing her, reassuring her, looking at his watch as he waited for the narcotic suppository to take effect. In a few minutes, the strong dose of codeine and barbiturate would relax her like a rag doll; then he could take her to Hades and she wouldn't care.

Kir looked at his watch again. He pulled himself off Manuela. The drug seemed to have taken effect. She lay motionless on the bed. Her torn lace panties were in a pile near her. Michael shook her; she did not respond.

Kir straightened his clothing before reaching for the telephone.

"Hello, Andreas? I'm at Manuela's villa. She won't be going to the hotel. It won't be necessary; she's staying right here. No, we won't be needing the guard."

Taking a comb from Manuela's dressing table he ran it through his hair. He picked the sheet up off the floor, covering Manuela with it up to her shoulders before he left the room.

From the window of the descending Jet Ranger, Parvis could see one male figure—the American, Rowan—on the tarmac. How small he looks, Parvis thought contemptuously.

Parvis stepped out of the helicopter and waved to Mark who was waiting for him at the far edge of the tarmac. Attired in a Pierre Cardin safari suit, wearing fine Italian loafers, Parvis bounded down the few steps from the helicopter to the ground. His gold Polo watch glistened in the sun as he smoothed his windblown, curly black and gray hair into place. He turned, glancing over his shoulder.

Kir's olive green Range Rover pulled up beside Parvis. Michael Kir jumped out, greeting Parvis.

"Hello, Michael," Parvis said, extending his hand. "I'm glad that you were able to meet me on such short notice. I hope my visit doesn't cause you any inconvenience."

"Not at all, Parvis," Kir said, giving Parvis a friendly pat on the shoulder. "No inconvience whatsoever. As a matter of fact, I welcome this opportunity to show you what we've been doing here on Kish. Right, Mark?" Kir said, addressing Mark, who had strode up to where the two men were standing. `

"Excellent," responded Parvis, nodding acknowledgement to Mark. "That is exactly what I'd like to see."

Michael Kir drove the Range Rover past the airport, along the roadway toward the Arab fishing village at the southwest corner of Kish Island. He turned to the man next to him. "Well, Parvis, what do you think so far?"

"Michael, I am very pleased. You have done a terrific job of keeping up appearances here on the island. Frankly, you almost had me believing those scale-models inside in the airport terminal! The resort concept proposed by your Gulf Island Resort Corporation looks so good that I'm going to suggest that, eventually, we do develop Kish Island as a resort."

"It wouldn't take much work," Kir replied. "All the facilities are always here."

"Yes, Kish could be a place where we could get away from the riffraff."

The Range Rover sped along the northern coast of Kish Island, eastward, toward the Royal Compound. They drove past the court ministers' villas.

Parvis stared out the window. "He should have taken my advice . . ."

"Who, about what?" Kir asked.

"His Majesty," Parvis said. His voice was cold and hard.

"What advice, Parvis?"

Parvis sighed heavily. "One day in early January 1979—those were terrible days, just before the Shah left Iran—I was with him at Niavarin Palace.

331

I was conferring with the Shah in his private quarters. I told him, 'Your Majesty, when you ascended the throne there were only eighteen million Iranians, now there are thirty-five million. Fight back, use your power. And if seventeen million are lost, so what? Leave the country with the same number of Iranians there were before you came to power—eighteen million.' The Shah looked at me as if I were crazy. But I'm sure that many, many, times before he died he wished he had followed my advice. What a pathetic end for him.''

Kir stared ahead at the road. He did not answer Parvis. They drove past the hotel and the casino. Some lights were on in the hotel.

"Who lives in the hotel?" Parvis asked.

"The airline crew, and the staff. Only part of the building is habitable, but repairs are still being done.''

They drove through the gates of the Royal Compound, and pulled up in front of the residence. Parvis and Kir got out of the car.

"Come on, Parvis," Michael said. "Let me show you two of the prettiest sights on this island.''

As Kir and Parvis approached the swimming pool area, Victoria and Gabriella were just collecting their things, preparing to go inside.

"Victoria, Gabriella, I'd like you to meet Mr. Gazvini,'' Kir said.

"Charmed,'' Parvis said, extending his hand first to Victoria, then Gabriella.

"Don't let us keep you, girls. We'll see you at dinner,'' Kir said. "Eight o'clock sharp, Gabriella,'' Kir called to the two girls as they walked toward their villas.

"So those are the two *jende*, whores, you mentioned to us a while back. Well, a man must satisfy his natural urges,'' Parvis said, watching

Victoria's rounded, bronzed ass, half-exposed by her minuscule bikini, until she disappeared around the corner. "And I'm certain the businessmen are very pleased to be entertained by those two beautiful girls," Parvis said. He plucked a delicate pink rose from a bush and held it to his nose.

"Ah, wonderful," he said, sighing deeply. "There is nothing like a Persian rose." He inhaled the rose's fragrance once more, then tossed it aside. "But tell me, Michael, aren't there three girls on Kish? Where is the third girl?"

"She's not feeling very well, I'm afraid. It's her, shall we say, special time, if you understand me."

"Yes, of course. I'm sure the girls need a few days of rest each month, anyway. They must work quite hard for you here on Kish," Parvis said knowingly. He gave Kir an strange look, at once accusing, questioning, envious, and leering. "It must be wonderful to be on this island with three gorgeous women at your disposal. Tell me, the third one, is she as beautiful as the other two? What does she look like?"

"She's every bit as lovely, Parvis, but in a different way, a different style. Variety is the spice of life. She's a Latin beauty—raven-haired, black eyed, perpetually tanned."

"She sounds wonderful. It's a shame I won't have a chance to meet her. But personally, I must say I prefer fairer coloring in women; I find those two who were sunbathing particularly to my liking."

"Parvis, they'll be most willing to entertain you after dinner," Kir said, as they walked toward the guest villa.

"You understand, Michael, what I would like after being on Abu Musa for so many months," Parvis said, looking Kir in the eye. His heart pounded with excitement, thinking of what pleasures lay ahead for him that evening. Just fantasizing about those two gorgeous women ministering to his desires made his loins ache.

Kir opened the gate to the imposing white villa.

"This is your villa, Parvis. Shall we meet for drinks, followed by dinner, at eight in the residence? We'll have an enjoyable evening, and leave business until tomorrow. You and I can have a breakfast meeting in the Conference Room so that we can review things before you return to Abu Musa."

"Fine, Michael," Parvis said. "I'll see you for drinks around eight." The butler opened the door of the guest villa for Parvis. Well, Parvis thought, I'll find my mole tomorrow; there will be time. Tomorrow, work; tonight, pleasure.

Manuela moaned groggily as she rolled off the bed in the darkness. The impact jolted her into semiconsciousness. She was cold, and her aching body felt like lead. Very slowly, as if in exaggerated slow motion, she pulled herself up and turned on the bedside lamp.

The malachite and silver clock on the table read two-thirty; whether a.m. or p.m., Manuela did not know. Manuela blinked, habituating herself to the strange feeling of her drugged stupor. The sight of her torn panties brought Kir's visit back to her in a flashflood.

Manuela dragged herself to the window and opened the curtains. It was night. So I've been out for over fourteen hours, she woozily calculated. My God, what did he do to me, she thought anguishedly.

Something shiny on the carpet near the bed caught her eye. She slowly stooped and picked up the crumpled piece of silver foil. As she smoothed it out between her fingertips the name—*Spasmo-*

*Oberon*—became visible. Manuela knew that the drug was a powerful knockout suppository; usually rendering a person unconscious for twenty-four hours.

Manuela's head was spinning. He had raped her, he had drugged her. This was the final degradation. She knew what she had to do.

She staggered over to her closet, her temples and medulla oblongata pounding. She pulled her black M.D. bag off the shelf. Squatting on the floor, she rummaged through the bag until she found what she was looking for. With her teeth, she pulled the aluminum cap off the small glass bottle. Holding the 10 cc bottle upside down, she inserted the hypodermic needle through the sterile rubber stopper into the bottle. She slowly, pulled the plunger back. The colorless liquid filled the syringe. She weakly extended her left arm. The needle pierced the tender flesh of her inner elbow. Slowly, measuredly, she pushed the plunger in, until all of the drug had been released into her bloodstream. She closed her eyes and waited.

Moonlight streamed in through the glass doors of the patio, casting an eerie yellowish illumination on the room. Parvis Gazvini was half-sitting, half-lying in bed, propped up by several large pillows. He reached out for his contact lens case. It was late and his eyes were sore. Parvis was exhausted after an evening of fantastically erotic sex with Gabriella and Victoria. Their function finished, he had sent the girls away. Parvis never liked sleeping with whores, only fucking them. Now that the women had left, there was no incentive to keep his vision razor-sharp. With a deftness perfected by years of habit, Parvis plucked the small gelatinous discs from his eyes. He put the white plastic contact case back on the bedside table, exchanging it for a cigarette.

Eyes closed, one arm folded and relaxed behind his head, Parvis lazily smoked a cigarette. Tousled sheets surrounding his body, a slight smile on his lips, Parvis contentedly reviewed the evening's events. First there had been a sumptuous dinner, equal to that in any four-star French restaurant. Then there had been the even more appetizing after-dinner indulgences.

It had been a long time since he'd had such an exciting time, with such skillful, sensuous women. Parvis sighed as he recalled the myriad pleasures of his sybaritic night. His mission in coming to Kish—find a mole—had not yet been accomplished. In fact, until this moment, the thought had been far from his mind, replaced by more earthly, carnal matters.

Parvis turned off the bedside lamp and sank down deeper into the kingsize bed. The musky, heady scent of sex combined with expensive perfume permeated the bed. The voluptuous scent, the scent of Gabriella, transported Parvis back to the events that had took place that evening. Thoughts of the two nubile and accommodating women, of the *ménage àtrois*, excited him once again. Much to his surprise, it was not the flaxen-haired beauty that had pleased him most; it was the fiery, proficient Gabriella. Parvis shuddered as he recalled the sensation of Gabriella biting his nipple. Parvis had thought that he was exhausted, totally spent, but he could feel his penis stirring. Parvis' hand reached down to his burgeoning organ.

Luscious images continued to flood his mind —soft, yielding thighs, smooth firm breasts, undulating waves of curves as he re-experienced the almost surreal sensation of being enveloped by two perfectly formed female bodies. Parvis' organ continued to swell; it was now fully erect. Reliving the excitement of the *ménage àtrois*, he imagined the delicious pleasure of Gabriella's oral ministrations; he wanted her back in his bed to service him again. The throbbing in his genitals increased. He moaned as his hand began moving up and down his shaft.

The sound of the glass patio door sliding open startled him. He looked up, vainly trying to focus in the direction of the dim moonlight.

A shadowy figure stepped into the room. Parvis saw that it was a curvaceous woman, walking slowly toward him. Her sent filled the room. Smiling at the woman, he pulled the satin sheet off his body. The shadow-shrouded figure returned his smile.

# CHAPTER EIGHTEEN

The sky was a gun-metal gray and the air was cold; a typical late December day in Tehran. Ali-Reza pulled up the fur collar of his short dark-brown leather jacket as he walked toward his orange Range Rover parked in front of the Administration Building at Mehrabad Military Base.

He quickly loaded the plastic jerry cans of gasoline into the back of the car. He put a couple of containers of water on the floor of the front seat. It was a tight fit, but all the containers were in the car. It was impossible to distinguish which of the jerry cans contained gasoline and which contained water. If he was stopped along the way by authorities or curious tribesmen who held dominion over part of the road he would have to travel, they would let him pass without searching every single container of water; at least that is what Ali-Reza hoped. If anyone found the gasoline they would, hopefully, just take it for themselves and not question why someone had enough gasoline to drive across the unpopulated Dasht-e-Kavir desert.

Ali-Reza covered the visible containers with blankets. He checked to make sure his automatic rifle was securely in place beneath the front seat and that the glove compartment that held his pistol was locked. This done, he re-entered the building through the back door. He walked the length of the corridor, down to the front entrance.

Upon seeing the guard, Ali-Reza nodded.

"You now," Ali-Reza said to the guard, "there are two desks here that would be very useful to me at my office. Would you be so kind as to help me load them into my car? They are upstairs."

"Yes, of course," replied the guard. They walked up the front stairs together to the Publications Department.

"These," said Ali-Reza, pointing to the two metal desks at the back of the room. "They're not heavy, I just need some help getting them down the stairs."

"A pleasure to help you, sir," the guard said.

Ali-Reza lifted up one side of a desk and the guard hurried over to help him.

They quickly loaded both desks into the Range Rover. The guard insisted that he open Gate 1 for Ali-Reza and ran ahead, while Ali-Reza climbed into the car and turned the key in the ignition. He leaned back in the seat, and breathed a sigh of relief. The precious containers of gas that he had hoarded over the past ten months and had secreted into the base were safely in the back of the car. It looked as if he was merely transporting two desks from one location to another. Ali-Reza had not dared to store the gasoline at his home; it would have been too risky. As an upper-level government employee, his apartment was routinely searched, and he kept no incriminating materials there. But using Mehrabad Base as a hiding place had worked out perfectly. Ali-Reza put the Range Rover in gear and drove toward Gate 1. He nodded to the guard who stood by the gate.

The dusty orange Range Rover sped along the road at a steady ninety kilometers an hour. Ali-Reza had left Tehran behind him about an hour ago. The winter sky was already starting to darken, and he wanted to make sure that he arrived at the Haraz Pass before it got much darker.

Ali-Reza was taking the long route to Tabas. There were two possible routes he could have taken. The first route, the shorter route, would have taken him south and slightly east, past the capital city of Qom, then farther south to the city of Isfahan. From there the road veered east, past the town of Nain, where women and young girls still wove the beautiful silk carpets known by the same name to the world; to the Zoroastrian town of Yazd; then north across the desert, until he reached the remains of the city of Tabas.

The second route, the longer one, led straight east from Tehran, over mountainous roads interrupted by the Haraz Pass, a covered pass that had been constructed by Reza Shah the Great just after the First World War, and was cut right through a mountain. The road went on to the holy city of Mashad, then south and west, through desert terrain, to Tabas. This route was nearly twice as long as the first one, but Ali-Reza had chosen it for one reason: safety. The first route, because it was the main road leading to Qom from both the north and south of Iran, was loaded with roadblocks set up by the Revolutionary Guards (the protectors of the Tomb of Imam Khomeini), and by the bands of thieves and hooligans who infested the road area. Often, it was hard to tell the two groups apart. A traveler risked the loss of his property and his life on that road. Ali-Reza knew that if he took this route, it was inevitable that some self-proclaimed roadblock group would stop him and search his vehicle. If he was lucky, he would be able to talk a good story and pay them off, but if he was unlucky, he would pay with his life, on the spot. Ali-Reza figured his chances of making it safely to Tabas via the southern, shorter road were so slim as to be nonexistent. He had no real choice but to take the longer route, much less popular with the bandits than the lucrative pilgrim route via Qom.

In spite of the dangers, Ali-Reza sang as he drove along. The mountains, huge imposing gray masses, were magnificent, the result of ancient cataclysmic bucklings and foldings of the earth's crust. With every turn in the steep, winding road, the landscape changed. First there were thick, tall pine trees as far as the eye could see, then, just around the bend, were deciduous trees, dominated by pistachio-nut trees. Ugly thatched-roof houses poked out from the vegetation and rocks every so often.

Incredible! All this greenery, and tomorrow I'll be in one of the most barren deserts in the world, Ali-Reza thought.

He pressed his foot harder against the accelerator. Daylight was fading fast, and he wanted to reach the pass before nightfall. In the old days an army guard detachment had closed the Haraz Pass every day at twilight, reopening it at dawn. The area just on the other side of the pass was so dangerous—frequent, sudden slides left huge rocks and rubble on the road, which motorists could not see at night—that the nightly closure of Haraz Pass was one highway regulation that had been obeyed by Iranian drivers. But, since the collapse of the Army, there were no longer any guards at the entrance to the pass, nor soldiers to clear away the debris of any slides. Every year, dozens of people who had risked going through the pass at night were killed on the road. Ali-Reza had no intentions of going through the Haraz Pass in the dark of night.

In spite of the road and the task that lay ahead of him, Ali-Reza was in a happy mood. The road reminded him of the road leading north from Tehran to the Caspian Sea, where he had spent many summers as a child, and, in the old days, many hedonistic weekends as a young man. The air was cold and crisp, and he enjoyed the solitary feeling of having the road to himself; he had passed only two small pickup trucks. If the road was this clear all the way to Nishapur, about an hour outside Mashad, he would arrive in time to have a good night's sleep before going on to the Tabas caravanserai.

When Ali-Reza agreed on the pickup point with Kir, he knew that getting there would present problems. He knew he would have to take the longer route, via Mashad, and that meant at least nineteen or twenty hours of driving. However, he had a safe place to stay along the way; a house of his own. Ali-Reza had inherited, from his father, an old farm house with some land, in the countryside outside of the town of Nishapur, now just a small town, but a former capital during the reign of the ancient Tamirid dynasty. From time to time his mother still went there in the spring or early autumn, bringing back jars of jams, dried fruits, and nuts. Ali-Reza hadn't been there in years, although he had spent a lot of time there as a child. Two old servants, Baatul and her husband Haddi, lived there; they had worked for his family and lived in that house ever since he could remember. He would spend the night there; the house was safe, and there was a small barn he could leave the car in.

He flicked the car lights on as he entered the Haraz Pass. The interior of the pass was covered with patches of red spray-painted anti-Shah graffiti. Ali-Reza vaguely wondered if the people who had written the graffiti were, in retrospect, sorry that they had done so. He doubted it; remorse was a development of the thought processes one step past the stage of revenge. Revenge, and only revenge, had been the standard fare in Iran for many years.

The sight of the headlights at the end of the long tunnel first startled, then worried Ali-Reza. As Ali-Reza approached the exit, the headlights blinked on and off, signaling him to stop. Ali-Reza could now make out that the other vehicle was an old army jeep, full of people.

His mouth went dry. Were the people in the jeep *Pasdaran*, or were they bandits who'd stolen the army jeep, Ali-Reza wondered. For a split second it occurred to him that perhaps they were simply motorists in distress, someone in need of help. But even if they are, he thought rationally, I can't risk it. Ali-Reza accelerated.

The jeep turned on its high-beams. Ali-Reza geared down, and zoomed out of the pass, leaving a sudden cloud of dusty exhaust and a spray of gravel in his wake. The jeep lurched backward, then spun around. The chase was on.

The staccato sound of gunfire filled the air. Ali-Reza ducked down in the front seat, his eyes just above the dashboard. The gunfire ceased, replaced by screaming and shouting coming from the pursuing vehicle. Ali-Reza lifted his head and looked back over his shoulder to see a jeep full of ragged men, arms raised, brandishing automatic weapons. Whoever they were, whatever they wanted, they were out to kill him.

Ali-Reza slammed his foot down to the floorboards, pushing the seven-year-old Range Rover to its limit. Bullets flew above the Range Rover, disappearing into the black gorge on the right, chewing up the wall of rock to the left.

Ali-Reza winced as he heard the metal-tinged ping of bullets ricocheting off the metal desks in the back of the Range Rover. The car swerved. Ali-Reza fought for control of the dark, treacherous mountain road. With its hair-pin turns, a sheer vertical wall of rock on one side and a precipitious gorge on the other, Ali-Reza concentrated totally on the road ahead, blocking out the gunfire so close behind. His head jerked up and down, sideways, as he simultaneously navigated the serpentine road and dodged the gunfire.

A bullet whizzed by the driver's side of the Range Rover, clipping the outside side mirror, shattering the glass, ripping off a large chunk of metal. Seeing a straight stretch of narrow road ahead, steering more by instinct than by sight, Ali-Reza leaned over and frantically reached for the glove-compartment latch. The sickening sound of grinding metal, the lurching of the car, catapulted him upright. Instinctively he pulled the wheel, narrowly having avoided smashing into the wall of rock.

He saw the glint of metal in the now opened glove compartment. Ali-Reza reached for the pistol.

Ali-Reza glanced backwards quickly; they were gaining on him. Pistol in one hand, the other hand tightly gripped on the wheel, he looked in his rear-view mirror, and decelerated ever so slightly. As he watched his pursuers gain on him he prepared himself. Out of the corner of his eye he saw the vehicle approach on his left. Instantaneously he pulled open his door, picked out the driver among the darkened faces and fired into his face. The windshield shattered, the face exploded, and vehicle careened, out of control, into the carbon-black gorge. Ali-Reza could hear the vehicle bouncing off the steep, razor-sharp sides of the gorge. Then it exploded. Imagining the searing orange ball of flames, the burning metal and flesh, Ali-Reza could almost feel the heat at his back.

A shiver rode up and down his spine. Pistol still in his hand, he pulled a Caron *Vetiver* bottle from beneath the front seat, and took a long swallow of vodka. The warmth quickly spread throughout his body, calming him.

Ali-Reza drove eastward, his pistol on the seat beside him. The landscape became more barren, more desolate. The road ahead of him was dark.

Ali-Reza finally pulled off the main road shortly after eleven p.m. He turned onto a winding, unpaved, bumpy path that passed for a road. He continued on this for a quarter of an hour until, straining his eyes in the darkness, he made out the rough wooden fence of his house. He opened the unlocked gate and drove up the gravel path leading to the house. By the time he stepped down from the Range Rover, Baatul was out of the house, a broom in her hands to beat off any trespassers.

"Baatul, hello! How are you?"

The hunched, *chador*-covered figure did not answer.

"Baatul, it's me, Ali-Reza. Don't you even say hello to me?"

"Sir, is it really you?" the old woman said incredulously. "What are you doing here, we didn't know you were coming." She hobbled down the few steps as fast as she could.

"Of course you didn't know I was coming. I just decided to yesterday," Ali-Reza said as he took the old woman's leathery hand.

"Come in, come in, it's cold out here," she said. "Haddi will take your things in. I see your car is full. Haddi!" she called into the house.

"No, no, that won't be necessary. I'm leaving tomorrow to go to Mashad."

Baatul eyed the two desks in the back of the Range Rover.

"I had these extra desks at my office and I knew

345

that my friend Assad, in Mashad, could use them," explained Ali-Reza.

Baatul grunted, accepting Ali-Reza's explanation.

"So don't worry about the car; I just want to leave it in the barn overnight."

Haddi, still in pyjamas, appeared at the doorway. The old man and woman exchanged some flurried words in their dialect. Haddi slipped on a pair of plastic sandals which stood by the door, and came over to Ali-Reza.

"Sir," he said, kissing Ali-Reza's hand. "Master."

Haddi opened the small barn. It was empty, except for some gardening tools and huge woven baskets, used in summer for gathering fruits. Ali-Reza drove the Range Rover into the barn. The two men locked the barn together, and went into the warm house.

Baatul had hot tea waiting for Ali-Reza. She poured the strong tea from the chipped ceramic teapot into a small glass and handed it to Ali-Reza. He put a lump of sugar between his teeth and sucked the steaming fragrant liquid through the sugar. Ali-Reza closed his eyes as he took the first sips of tea; only then did he realize how tired he was. Baatul alternated between exclaiming how glad she was to see him and besieging him with questions; how was his mother and brother and sister, how was Tehran nowadays, why couldn't he stay for a few days so she could prepare some of his favorite dishes for him? Haddi would slaughter a sheep in honor of the occasion. Ali-Reza explained he had to leave tomorrow because people were expecting him in Mashad, and no, he could not stop by on the way back because he had to hurry back to Tehran for business. Baatul tried to insist that he at least stay for lunch tomorrow, which Ali-Reza refused politely. She finally contented herself with planning to pack him a basket of the best dried fruits and pistachio nuts in the house, in case he got hungry on the two-hour drive to Mashad. She spread out warm bedding on a worn carpet near the gas heater for Ali-Reza.

"Baatul, I am very tired, so please let me sleep in the morning," Ali-Reza said, remembering that life in this house started at dawn. "But you must wake me by eight o'clock."

"Yes, sir. But I wish you would stay for lunch tomorrow, just the same."

"Baatul . . ."

"Goodnight, sir. We are very glad to see you again." As Ali-Reza stretched out on the floor, he felt relaxed and secure, more so than he had in a long, long time. Inside this house, with these old people who had helped raise him, it was as if things had never changed, as if life was the same as when he was a boy. The warmth from the heater permeated his body, and he stretched comfortably.

It's hard to imagine, he thought sleepily, the times as a young boy that I lay by this fire and dreamt of adventurous exploits, heroes and villains. Yet never in my wildest dreams could I have dreamt of an adventure like the one I am now involved in. Just before he closed his eyes, he saw Baatul silently set a small glass of tea on the floor, within reach. He drank it before drifting into a deep sleep.

That night, Ali-Reza had a series of dreams. At first he dreamt that he was a child again, standing in the kitchen of this very house, watching Baatul make rose-petal jam while she told him stories. At first, the roses were closed tightly; Baatul asked him to bring her some, and when he picked them up, they opened. Then he dreamt that he was in the

States again, but he did not know where. It was night. He was given a book, without a title written on it. When he tried to open it, he couldn't. Suddenly, it was bright daylight, and the book opened. It was blank. Then he dreamt that he was standing behind the podium in a large lecture hall, similar to the lecture halls at his university in the U.S. He was wearing a dark suit, and he no longer had his beard and moustache. The seats in the hall were filled, but he could not see the faces because that part of the hall was dark. When he started to speak, it was in English; he could not remember, when he woke up, what he had said.

Ali-Reza lay beneath the warm blankets, recalling his dreams, enjoying the vivid memories. Usually he did not recall his dreams so clearly. He dressed quickly, and went into the kitchen. He found Baatul preparing a breakfast tray for him.

"Ah, you're awake," Baatul said. "I was just going to wake you up. Here, have some tea. I'll bring your breakfast in the other room in a moment."

"No, Baatul, don't bother. I'll eat in here." Ali-Reza pulled out a carved wooden chair and looked around the room. It had looked exactly the same for as long as he could remember; a simple kitchen, with a worn marble floor, painted wooden cabinets, and a wood-burning stove.

Baatul placed the breakfast tray in front of Ali-Reza on the wooden table. Ali-Reza ate ravenously: *sangak*, the paper-thin, unleavened Persian bread, mounds of white goat's cheese, butter, honey, and *halvah*, a sweet paste made of ground pistachio nuts, all washed down with small glasses of tea.

"Did you sleep well?" Baatul asked.

"Yes, I did," Ali-Reza replied, taking another swallow of tea. "You know, Baatul, I had the strangest dreams last night, three of them; I remember all three. I dreamt . . ." and Ali-Reza told Baatul his dreams. When he finished speaking, she looked at him intently.

"Yes, I see," she mumbled, more to herself than to Ali-Reza.

"What?"

"Your dreams mean," she said, "that you will soon become a very important person. It will be before you are much older than you are now. You will have a very high position, an official one." She continued to look at him. "But when you were born, I told your mother that. It has always been your destiny."

"Baatul . . ." Ali-Reza began, trying to sound as if he didn't believe the dream interpretations of an old woman. But inside his heart was pounding. He knew that Baatul could read dreams, and the unerring way that she looked at him made him tremble inwardly. He did not like the idea of anyone being able to see inside of him, especially with secrets that he held.

"Really, Baatul," he said smiling, "you know that I don't believe in that sort of thing. Reading dreams is for grandmothers."

Baatul said nothing, she just smiled. Ali-Reza excused himself and went out to get the car from the barn. Haddi insisted on cleaning the front headlights with a cloth. Baatul gave him a basket laden with dried apricots, berries, and nuts. She also gave him a thermos full of hot tea.

"Baatul, I'm only going to Mashad. This is enough food for a week."

"You might get hungry," Baatul answered. "Besides, you are much too skinny." Ali-Reza nodded knowingly. Baatul always complained that he was too skinny. He thanked the two old people and got into the Range Rover.

"Have a safe trip," Baatul shouted after him as he drove down the dusty road.

The mid-morning air was clear and cold. He

would get to Tabas in plenty of time, with hours to spare.

Approaching Mashad, the road became busier; a few cars, small trucks, and horse-drawn wagons from the villages nearby, going into the city to sell their wares. Ali-Reza avoided the city, skirting its perimeter. The turquoise and gilt roof of the Shrine of Imam Reza gleamed above the low skyline of the city. Ali-Reza turned on to the road leading south. He stopped long enough to toss out the desks, knowing that someone would retrieve them and put them to good use.

South of Mashad, the terrain changed. The land was flatter, and even more barren. Ali-Reza was driving along the far edge of the Dasht-e-Kavir desert, the plain of salt, a vast dry land, one of the three deserts that composed over fifty percent of the land mass of Iran. As Ali-Reza drove on, the land became dustier and drier, then sandy. The vegetation, except for low shrubs and hardy desert plants, had disappeared. At first he saw occasional families walking or riding donkeys on the road, but by early afternoon, these, too, had disappeared. Ali-Reza had to watch the road closely and keep a moderate speed because the road was full of deep potholes; some of them seemed deep enough to swallow up half of the Range Rover. The wind increased; the sand blew across the road like dervishes spinning madly.

The paved road ended at Gonabad and Ali-Reza headed west. There was nothing around him, nothing, only vast expanses of barren land, for as far as the eye could see. The road was patches of asphalt alternating with smaller patches of gravel. Holes of all sizes peppered the narrow road. It was beginning to get dark. He had plenty of time; the plane wasn't due to arrive until midnight. Still, it was a good thing he had allotted himself plenty of time, because the trip was taking longer than he had thought it would. The road was becoming bumpier, almost impossible to drive on.

Once a verdant, palm-treed town—an oasis—Tabas, the "jewel of desert," had been leveled by a catastrophic earthquake in 1978. At least twenty thousand people had lost their lives in that earthquake, and Tabas was now only a ghost town. Ali-Reza had to choose another route around Tabas. Even if the road skirting Tabas had been passable, Ali-Reza preferred not to drive it; it was best to leave the dead undisturbed.

Ali-Reza stopped the car and switched on the overhead light. He reached into the glove compartment and pulled out his worn Imperial Iranian Geographical Society map. The worst part of the drive was coming up; after Tabas he had to leave the main road and begin his drive across the desert. Up until now, Ali-Reza had only skirted the fringes of the great inhospitable Dasht-e-kavir. He studied the map carefully. It was so easy to get lost in the desert; the monotonous landscape, the eerie desolation could so easily disorient a person.

Ali-Reza put away his map and started driving. It was getting darker. The sky was inky blue, the stars sparkling like bits of crystal high in the cold, empty desert sky. Ali-Reza looked at his watch; nearly ten o'clock, no wonder he was hungry. He poured himself some tea, with his eyes still on the road. Then he reached into the basket Baatul had packed for him and took out a handful of dried apricots.

The headlights of the Range Rover illuminated the sign that read "Tabas"; an arrow pointed east. The sign was on a tilt, but it was probably the only thing left standing after the horrible earthquake of five years ago.

There were no shoulders on the road; the road was separated from the desert on both sides of it only by the fact that it was slightly higher than its surroundings. Stone markers announcing the distance to Yazd, the city where this miserable excuse for a road ended, had disappeared kilometers back. Ali-Reza glanced at his odometer; it was just about the point where he was to turn off the road and into the desert. Ali-Reza gulped hard; his throat was dry. He took a drink of water from the canteen on the seat next to him. It was only fifty kilometers to the caravanserai, but a treacherous fifty kilometers over the salt-covered plain. He turned his wheels sharply right and headed deep into the dark desert.

The Range Rover's ride was surprisingly smooth, the shocks on the seven-year-old car still in amazingly good shape. There was a three-quarters full moon, and the sky was flooded with stars so bright that they cast a faint illumination on parts of the desert. In this vast barren expanse, everything seemed intensified. The headlights of the solitary Range Rover cut a path across the desert landscape. Ali-Reza checked his compass; he was still heading toward the caravanserai. The ruins of the caravanserai were out there in the darkness, ahead of him.

The caravanserai near Tabas was a fairly recent one, dating from the seventeenth century; it was one of the nine hundred and ninety-nine caravanserais erected by the Qajar ruler Shah Abbas. A number of caravanserais had dotted the Dasht-e-Kavir in bygone times; every fifty or sixty kilometers there was a caravanserai of some sort, offering lodging for the weary members of the camel caravans who trekked across the desert. The caravanserais were rectangular structures made of stone or baked brick. In the center of each caravanserai was an open courtyard with a well. Around the courtyard were rooms, stables, and a special area for harems that traveled with the *shahs*, kings. Most of these caravanserais were small and primitive, and, after years of disuse, crumbled away, just as the caravan trails across the desert had faded away. The caravanserai near Tabas, however, was quite large and constructed of stone. Although closed for nearly a century, its exterior walls were still standing. Because of the caravanserai's isolated position and the flat unfissured land around it, this ancient caravanserai had been chosen as the pickup point for Gino's rendezvous with Ali-Reza.

Ali-Reza drove along for more than an hour across the flat, empty desert. Then, suddenly, he saw the caravanserai walls ahead of him. He drove around to the far side of the caravanserai, and stopped the car in the back of the building, near the gate. He climbed out of his car, stretched, and relieved himself against the wall. He zipped his pants quickly. There was no time to lose, it was nearly eleven o'clock, and the plane would arrive at midnight.

Ali-Reza opened the back of the Range Rover and took out all the jerry cans full of gasoline and water, as well as the empty ones. He pulled up the carpet from the back and quickly began unscrewing a section of metal plate. After unscrewing the final screw, Ali-Reza lifted off the metal plate. In the space below were twenty battery-powered spot lamps, borrowed from Civil Aviation. He set them up in two rows, ten in each, fifty meters between each lamp in the row, thirty meters between the two rows. When they were all set up, Ali-Reza went back and turned them all on. The makeshift runway was bathed in white light. Ali-Reza paced the length of it, picking up large stones and tossing them aside. Now, the only thing left to do was wait.

Ali-Reza didn't have to wait long. A quarter of an hour after he had set up the runway, he heard the sound of an approaching plane. Ali-Reza picked up his large powerful flashlight, turned it skyward, and flicked it on and off repeatedly. The plane flashed its lights on and off twice in acknowledgment. It circled the caravanserai a couple of times, and began its descent. The Beechcraft made a smooth easy landing, dust billowing up around the lights. The door to the Beechcraft opened, and a dark-haired, moustached figure wearing an orange flight suit stepped out.

"Ali-Reza?"

"Yes," Ali-Reza replied.

"I'm Gino, Michael Kir sent me," Gino said, walking over to Ali-Reza. The two men shook hands.

"How was the flight? Did you have any problems?" Ali-Reza asked.

"None at all, except for about a half-hour of poor visibility down near Bam."

Ali-Reza nodded. "Usually at this time of the year there are high winds and dust storms in that area. Other than that?"

"No problems. It was easier getting here than I thought it would be. How about you?"

"I had one incident, but I'll tell you about it on the plane. Gino, can you help me put the lamps back in the car? I don't think that we should leave our runway out here."

"Sure thing, just let me turn the plane around so that I can take off the same strip of clean ground."

Ali-Reza turned the final screw on the metal plate and put the carpet back over the well that held the battery-powered lamps. He opened the rickety wooden gate that led into the interior courtyard of the caravanserai. Gino climbed into the driver's seat and drove the Range Rover inside. He flicked on the high-beams. There was an eerie emptiness in the high-walled abandoned courtyard.

Gino leaned out the window. "Ali-Reza, where do you want me to park this baby?"

"As close to the wall as possible." Ali-Reza was pointing to the spot against the wall.

Gino turned off the ignition. Ali-Reza opened the passenger side door and pulled out a small canvas bag from under the seat. The bag contained a fresh change of clothes and toilet articles.

"Ali-Reza, why did you bother parking your car inside the caravanserai?" Gino asked. "If anyone wants to steal it, they'll do it anyway. They'll carry your Range Rover off in pieces."

"What I'm hoping," Ali-Reza said, as he shut the rotting wooden gate, "is that any nomads who travel these parts won't bother looking inside the caravanserai. This place was picked clean centuries ago."

Gino nodded. "Let's go, Ali-Reza."

Ali-Reza climbed into the passenger seat of the small aircraft. The back seat of the plane was piled high with cartons of Winston, Marlboro, Kent, and Merit cigarettes.

"What is all this?" Ali-Reza asked.

"My cover," Gino replied. "If I was forced down on my way here, my story was that I'm just a black-market smuggler."

"Very good," Ali-Reza said, turning around to look at the cartons and cartons of cigarettes. "You have a small fortune here."

"Buckle up, Ali-Reza," Gino said, as he started the plane.

The small plane took off, heading south toward Kish Island.

# CHAPTER NINETEEN

Michael Kir was waitng for the Beechcraft when it arrived from the Dasht-e-Kavir, on the morning of December 23. The sky was still dark, and there was a chill edge to the early morning air.

"Good morning," Ali-Reza said, as he stepped out of the plane. Ali-Reza seemed bright and awake, despite the early hour. He shook hands with Kir, and the two men walked toward the car.

"Welcome to Kish Island, Ali-Reza. Come on, I'll show you to your quarters." They climbed into the car.

The car pulled up in front of the guest villa at the far end of the Royal Compound. The morning sky, now the palest shade of blue, cast a cool light on the stark white villa nestled in a garden of dewy oleanders and still-closed pink and fuchsia bougainvillea. The houseboy scurried out to the car and tried to take Ali-Reza's toilet bag, but Ali-Reza held on to it. The houseboy insisted, and a tug-of-war over the small bag ensued. Ali-Reza gave in and handed over the bag.

"He'll take care of your needs," Kir said. "Speak to him in English, but slowly."

"This is service," said Ali-Reza smiling.

"Gulf Island Resorts aims to please," Kir replied. "Ali-Reza, would you like to sleep for a couple of hours, or would you prefer to just shower, then meet for a working breakfast?"

"I'll shower and change, then we can meet."

"All right. I'll be at the residence; it's only a short walk from your villa. The houseboy will show you the way. I'll see you soon." Kir drove off.

The houseboy opened the door to the villa. He led the way, Ali-Reza close behind him. A series of wooden slatted ceiling fans created pleasant currents of air as Ali-Reza walked down the air-conditioned hallway. An intricately patterned mosaic floor composed of octagonal tiles of rust, turquoise, and gold led the way to an atrium at the end of the hall. The sound of trickling water spilling down the tiered fountain in the plant-filled atrium gave a sense of refreshing coolness.

The houseboy opened a door off the long hall-way, near the small square atrium.

"Your room, sir," the houseboy said, bowing slightly from the waist.

Ali-Reza was shocked by what he saw. Everything in the villa was so sumptuous—it seemed that no expense had been spared to create an ambience of total luxury. There was thick pecan-color carpeting, elegant leather Italian furniture, and dramatic arrangements of freshly-cut flowers. He walked over to the wide-screen television and looked through a number of cassettes stacked nearby. Dozens of the latest movies were here to be played on the video machine. In the crystal bowl were fruits Ali-Reza hadn't seen in years: plump bananas, fragrant pineapples, and crisp-looking apples. He walked into the brown-tiled bathroom. The counter was lined with expensive French soaps, shampoos, and toiletries for men.

Ali-Reza showered quickly and put on the beige velour robe hanging on the hook behind the door. Looking through his shaving kit, he pulled out numerous scraps of paper, and laid them on the desk. Pulling up a chair, he wrote out the notes for the reports that he planned to present to Kir during the meeting. The bits and pieces of papers on the desk contained important information that Ali-Reza trusted only to be delivered in person. Ali-Reza finished writing his notes and got up to dress.

"Did you know," Manuela said, "that the rays of the winter sun are equally as strong, and sometimes even stronger, than those of the summer sun? And the water," she continued, directing her words to Victoria, who was in the swimming pool, "increases the intensity of the rays."

"Well, if I don't swim, I'll start to get fat," Victoria replied.

Manuela looked at Victoria's trim, tanned form as she walked toward the diving board. "You have nothing to worry about Victoria, but you're right, we don't get enough exercise."

"That's for sure," Gabriella said, critically pinching her perfect body for signs of flab. "Those pathetic excuses for great lovers we have popping in don't give us any workouts."

"Although we certainly give them some," Manuela said, as she rubbed the peach-colored lotion over her sleek bronzed legs.

"Well, I'm still hoping for a gorgeous, masculine, well-built man—under fifty years of age—here on this island," Gabriella said, sighing deeply. Looking up, she suddenly caught her breath. There, standing only about ten meters away from her, was Kir, talking to just the sort of man she had wished for.

"He can't be for us," Gabriella murmured. "He's far too young and attractive. And he looks like he might be good at it."

The other two girls looked up to see who Gabriella was talking about. Kir and the stranger were walking slowly toward the pool area.

From the way he was dressed, Gabriella thought the new guest was Italian. He was wearing beige corduroy pants, and a beige-and-white checked shirt, unbuttoned at the collar. An olive green jacket was draped over his strong shoulders. The pants were tight and straight-legged, showing off his long legs. Gabriella couldn't help but notice his firm ass, as he turned to nod to Victoria in the pool. Behind Gabriella's mirrored sunglasses, her eyes zeroed in on his well-filled crotch. His large dark eyes were fringed with thick lashes, and his smile was warm and sensuous. He was very, very handsome. And he carried himself with the confidence of a man who knows he is attractive to women.

Michael Kir introduced the stranger as Ali-Reza Raissi.

"Pleased to meet you," Manuela said, extending her hand.

Victoria placed her palms on the pool edge, and pulled heself effortlessly and gracefully out of the water. She squeezed the water out of her thick blond hair as she walked toward Ali-Reza. "What do you think of Kish?" she said smiling.

"Beautiful," replied Ali-Reza, who was trying to keep his cool in this situation. It had been five years since he had seen a sight like this, beautiful women parading around in skimpy bathing suits by a swimming pool. And he had never seen women as beautiful as these. He looked at Victoria, her body still glistening with water, her eyelashes thick and wet, framing her azure-blue eyes. She had on a one-piece white bathing suit, cut high on the thigh, that made her long legs seem to go on forever. The top of her suit plunged almost to the navel. Ali-Reza turned his gaze, not wanting to appear to be staring. He had never seen a more beautiful woman, unless . . . unless it was the one lying on the chaise lounge in front of him.

"Gabriella," continued Michael Kir making the introductions, "Ali-Reza."

Gabriella lifted her sunglasses off her eyes.

"*Ciao, caro,*" she said in her most coquettish voice. "*Come stai?*" Gabriella sat up, and pulled off her wide-brimmed hat. Her long chestnut-colored hair tumbled out, the dramatic effect of which was not lost on Ali-Reza, who was amazed to hear Italian coming out of that pouty, pretty mouth.

"*Bene, grazie, e Lei?*" he said politely, showing his utmost respect by using the formal *Lei.*

Gabriella's hazel eyes lit up when she heard this gorgeous creature answer her in slightly accented Italian. This was too good to be true!

"Why don't you sit down and have a drink, you two?" ordered Gabriella in her least imperious voice. "Just a cup of *caffè* or something?"

Ali-Reza looked toward Michael. "Have we got time?"

"Sure," replied Kir, knowing that Ali-Reza was enjoying this more than anything else. "Just a quick one," he said, addressing Gabriella, who was snapping her fingers at the pool boy.

"*Va bene,*" she acquiesced, patting the end of her chair. "*S'accomodi.*"

Ali-Reza sat down, as Gabriella moved her legs over ever so slightly to give him room. He smiled as he watched her, admiring her lithe, luscious body, as she inquired as to what everyone wanted to drink. Gabriella was wearing a light purple bikini, its narrow top held up by tiny spaghetti straps. The bottoms, extremely brief, were tied tenuously together at the hips. Gabriella's legs were resting against Ali-Reza's.

"Are you Italian, Signor Raissi?" Gabriella asked, as she flashed Ali-Reza her most promising smile.

"No, I'm not. I'm Iranian, but I lived in Italy for a number of years," Ali-Reza said, looking at Gabriella. He was becoming more excited by the moment, both from what he saw in front of him and what he felt as Gabriella absentmindedly rubbed her leg against his thigh.

Gabriella sat up abruptly when the coffee came and presided over the serving of it. "*Cappuccino* for you, Victoria? And you, Manuela?"

"Yes, Gabriella," said Manuela, reaching over for the two cups of foamy white-capped coffee.

"*Espresso* for you, Michael, and you, Ali-Reza?" Without asking, she handed Kir his with one spoon of sugar, then she turned her attention to Ali-Reza. "*Zucchero?*"

"*Grazie, un cucchiaino,*" he said smiling at Gabriella.

Gabriella can be so charming when she wants to, thought Michael, stirring his coffee. When she wants to . . . when she wants something. Michael looked at Gabriella and Ali-Reza lustfully eyeing each other. It was obvious Ali-Reza found Gabriella, with her pouty, voluptuous, little-girl sensuality, the most appealing of the three magnificent women.

Michael Kir set down his empty espresso cup and stood up.

"Ali-Reza, we've got to be going. Please excuse us, girls. We'll see you at dinner."

"Very nice meeting you," Ali-Reza said to all three women, looking intently at Gabriella.

As soon as the men were out of sight, Gabriella started rummaging frantically through her pile of magazines, until she found the fashion magazine she wanted. She thumbed through the glossy pages, stopping only when she found the horoscope column.

"*Ecco!*" she said triumphantly. " 'This will be an

361

exciting week for you. Your job scene will be enlivened by a handsome new stranger . . .' "

"Oh, brother," Victoria said, doubling over with laughter. "Your job scene . . . I love it!"

Gabriella ignored Victoria's remark as she fished in her bag for her mirror. Gazing at herself, she continued, "I don't care about the whole week; a few exciting hours would be enough for me." She picked up the magazine again. "Either of you two want to know your horoscope for this week?"

"I don't need to, Gabriella. I know my future for the next three months: suntanning and screwing creeps," Victoria said.

"Manuela," asked Gabriella, now brushing her wavy hair, "What did you think of Ali-Reza? Isn't he gorgeous?"

"Yes, Gabriella, he is gorgeous, but I don't care for Iranian men."

"I hear that Persian men make the best lovers," Gabriella said.

"You'll find out soon enough," Manuela replied.

"I can hardly wait," Gabriella said, smiling broadly.

The sun was bright on the walls of the small Conference Room in the residence. Michael Kir got up and pulled the louvered blinds shut, blocking out the view of the glistening blue waters of the Persian Gulf. He turned as the door opened.

Mark entered the room. "Hi there," Mark said, walking over to shake hands with Ali-Reza, who was seated in a leather chair at the conference table.

"Mark, I'd like you to meet Ali-Reza Raissi. Ali-Reza, this is Mark Rowan."

"Pleased to meet you," Mark said, extending his hand.

"My pleasure," Ali-Reza replied. He was surprised that Mark Rowan looked like the kind of guy that arranged Lions Club meetings rather than armament shipments for Uncle Sam.

Mark sat down at the conference table.

"Ali-Reza, what is the status of the Zurkhaneh?" Kir asked, wasting no time beginning the meeting.

Ali-Reza looked at Mark Rowan, still shocked that someone as cleancut and young-looking as Mark was the United States government's representative—official or unofficial.

Mark sensed Ali-Reza's reluctance to discuss sensitive information in his presence. Intervention of a superpower in the affairs of Iran was against Ali-Reza's ideals, but he pragmatically realized that this way was the only way.

Ali-Reza walked over to the large map of Iran on the wall. "With this map, I can give you a better idea of our strengths and weaknesses," Ali-Reza said.

"What is the total number of Zurkhaneh in the country?" Mark asked, as he pulled out his own pen and pad of paper.

"The number of Zurkhaneh has remained fairly stable for the past year, around ten thousand. About ninety-five percent of the members are men, which means nearly all the members have done some sort of military service, and have a working knowledge of weaponry. As agreed upon before, General Pakdal will supply me with comprehensive specifications on the weaponry that the Zurkhaneh will be using during the takeover. The weapons that we managed to hide from the government forces during the roundup of arms in January 1982, plus the first shipments from you, are stored in the Alborz Mountains. We have a number of caches of arms in that area, and to get to them, and to train, we can travel undetected."

"Undetected?" Kir queried.

"Along with the skiers," Ali-Reza replied. "People still go skiing in the Alborz Mountains just north of Tehran, at Dizin and Shemshak. Of course, the lifts no longer work, but some people still go up there. My men pack up their skis and boots and travel up the mountain with the rest of the skiers. They spend their weekends familiarizing themselves with the weaponry in the secret depots, then, at the end of the weekend, they travel down the mountains just like the rest of the skiers."

"Very ingenious," Mark said.

"Let me assure you," Ali-Reza said, "we are training all the time. The Zurkhaneh will be ready when the day comes."

"You are the only member of the Zurkhaneh who knows of Project Norouz, the date, exact time, and the mode of the takeover? Is that correct?" Mark asked.

"That is correct," Ali-Reza replied. "And it will remain that way until very close to Norouz." He reached into his pocket, took out a crisply folded piece of paper, and handed it to Mark.

"Here is a list I prepared this morning of the top Zurkhaneh leaders in the major cities. They are without a doubt the most competent people in the country, and they are rabidly anticlergy. Death is too good for the mullahs, as far as they are concerned," Ali-Reza said.

Mark perused the list carefully.

"I see the Zurkhaneh have infiltrated everywhere, even the military. Let's see, the head of radio and television in Tehran, the assistant director of radio and television in Tabriz, the deputy head of Civil Aviation in Shiraz, assistant director of Rasht Airport, a few lieutenant-colonels in various cities. Very impressive, Ali-Reza." Mark continued reading the list.

"There are a large number of Zurkhaneh working for Civil Aviation in Tehran. How did you manage that? You don't have enough air traffic to warrant that many air traffic controllers," Mark said.

"You're right, Mark. Before the Revolution, when Mehrabad Airport was one of the busiest airports in the Middle East, Civil Aviation in Tehran employed a lot of technicians and air traffic controllers. After the Revolution, I kept many of these people on, because I knew their sympathies. Although there really was no work for them, I assigned them to positions I invented. These people have become the core of the Zurkhaneh and will be involved in one of the most important aspects of the plan—controlling the air space during the last stage of Project Norouz. Air traffic controllers and radar technicians, working for Civil Aviation in Tehran, will be on special assignments on the twenty-first of March. I'm sending my Tehran people out to all airports in the country to check the equipment. They're going to find something wrong with the equipment—especially radar equipment—at every airport. My men will render all systems inoperative, and take control of the airports."

"Excellent," Kir said. Mark nodded in agreement.

"Now, if you'll give me the maps of the major cities, I can update them by marking out the locations of the garrisons and arms depots of the Revolutionary Guards," Ali-Reza said.

Mark got up and took a sheaf of papers from a folder at the end of the conference table. He gave the papers to Ali-Reza.

Ali-Reza took a folded piece of paper from his shirt pocket and handed it to Mark.

"This is the detailed, up-to-date map of Qom you

requested, Mark."

"Thanks," Mark said, sitting down.

Ali-Reza looked through the maps, marking off Revolutionary Guard headquarters in the cities of Isfahan, Shiraz, Tabriz, Kermanshah, Mashad, Kerman, Bandar Abbas, Abadan, Rasht, and Ahvaz. "I can give you approximate numbers of Guards in each of these towns."

"Very good," Kir said.

While Ali-Reza was going over the maps, Mark handed Kir the list of names of Zurkhaneh that Ali-Reza had given him. Kir looked quickly down the list. He would check his own files upstairs after the meeting; he was sure the I-S files had something on all these people. Old information, but valuable, none the less.

"I also brought a couple of other things that I thought you would like to see," Ali-Reza said. He dug into his jacket pocket and pulled out a well-worn cassette and some leaflets. "Have you got a cassette deck here?"

Mark got up and slid a panel open. Behind the panel was a sleek Bang and Olufsen stereo and cassette deck.

"You certainly do," Ali-Reza said. "Here, stick this humble little tape in there."

Mark turned the machine on and the three men listened to the tape-recorded voice. Mark had a hard time decifering some of the words. Mark's Farsi was adequate, but this was a dialect that he was not too familiar with. Yet Mark could understand that this was a vehement diatribe against the ruling clergy. Kir, Mark, and Ali-Reza listened in silence to the tape.

"Excellent, Ali-Reza." Kir said, pleased by what he had heard on the tape. He turned to Mark. "The voice on that tape was speaking Turkic, so you probably had some trouble with it. The person on the tape was speaking out against the mullahs in Qom in a very forceful way, so reminiscent of those tapes that Khomeini had sent to Iran when he was in exile in Iraq and Paris. It is the same kind of nonintellectual, stilted outpouring of venom as were Khomeini's tapes."

Kir turned to address Ali-Reza. "I'm sure these tapes have been very successful in Iran, changing public sentiment, making the people receptive to a change of government."

"Yes, we have taken great pains to appeal to the masses in the tapes that we distribute—no high-minded ideals, just down-to-earth complaints against a repressive and unsuccessful system of government by the clergy." Ali-Reza smiled wryly, "And, I can assure you, it has not been hard to dig up complaints about the government."

"What really impresses me," Kir said, "is that this tape actually does sound like an ordinary, simple, religious Iranian complaining about how he got screwed by the government, not some Western-educated public relations/communications expert complaining—which I'm sure it was."

"Yes, it was. Two Zurkhaneh and I make all the tapes. A Zurkhaneh, who used to work in radio during the Shah's régime, made this one. He makes all the Turkic dialect recordings. They amount to a third of our recordings. Another third are in Farsi and the rest are made in the Kurdic and Arabic languages. We have distributed twenty thousand cassettes so far, but for every one we make, we estimate three or four pirate copies are made. We have also been redistributing the Bakhtiar tapes made in Paris a couple of years ago. Rather than get new ones, we fell it is better to use the old ones. Shapour Bakhtiar's message still gets across to the people, but we prefer to

367

keep him out of the picture—until just before Norouz. We plan a continually escalating blitz of pamphlets and tapes that will culminate just before Norouz." Ali-Reza handed some pamphlets to Kir and Mark. "These are some pamphlets that we have distributed through our different channels."

"Different channels?" Mark asked.

"We distribute both the pamphlets and tapes through the bazaar—the Tehran bazaar, and the bazaars in each town. We also distribute our information through the military. As you know, the discipline in the military has broken down completely, and the government does not pay much attention to the activities in and around the bases. The Revolutionary Guards are the only real military force left in the country."

Kir read one of the leaflets aloud. " 'Why must we suffer under the tyrannical rule of the government? In the name of Allah they pretend to govern us, but they are godless souls who have brought nothing but treachery and fear into our lives. They have corrupted our earth.' " Kir flipped through the pamphlets. "This one says:

My name, I will say, is Hossein-Ali Matlobe. I will not use my real name for fear of persecution. I was once a government employee; I worked on a road crew. The work was very hard, but I was rewarded with a salary that allowed me to buy the necessary food and clothing for my family. Now I have no job. I live with my wife's relatives on their land, and I must work very hard for enough food to feed my family. I am not my own master. I am a slave. If Allah is merciful he would not allow those imposters who call themselves Ayatollahs to. . . .

"Let me see," Kir said, searching for the right words, " 'keep us under their thumbs' . . . Yes, that would be the rough translation."

Michael looked over another pamphlet. "This one, Mark, is about women's rights; a complaint about their loss of protection that the Family Act of 1967 had given them, and an especially bitter complaint about concubinage."

"That's also mentioned on a tape," Ali-Reza said.

"I commend you, Ali-Reza, for using the same tactics that Khomeini used to convince the people of his cause, by sending tapes through the bazaar," Mark said.

"It worked once, it will work again," Ali-Reza replied. "We keep bombarding the people with these leaflets and cassettes. The government has confiscated a number of them, but they have blamed the Tudeh, the Iranian Communist Party, for them. Ironic, when you think about it. The Islamic government managed to wipe out Tudeh more thoroughly than SAVAK did. There really are very few Tudehs left in Iran, perhaps one or two cells."

"What about the other antigovernment groups in the country—the Kurds, the Arabs in Khuzistan, and the people of Azarbaijan? The Baluchis, well, we know about them," Mark said.

"Our support in Azarbaijan, especially the city of Tabriz," Ali-Reza said, pointing to the northwest corner of the map of Iran, "is extremely strong. Historically, Tabriz has always been a hotbed of revolt against the government in power. In the 1920s Azarbaijan tried to secede from Iran. The Shah had reasonable success with the people of Azarbaijan because he allowed them some degree of autonomy, as well as participation in the Tehran government. The Qom government, on the other hand, has suppressed the people with brutal force."

"Khalaghani's disarming the citizenry was an important move; it allowed the government to continue its policy of autocratic rule uncontested," Kir said. "But it has turned out to be to our advantage. It will make things easier for us after the takeover."

"You're right," Ali-Reza agreed.

Mark's eyes were fixed on the wall map of Iran. "How is the northwestern border area? Is it secure?" Mark asked.

"Completely. The Zurkhaneh are up there in full force. Only last week I hitched a ride on a flight up to the town of Bandar-Ansali."

"Bandar-what?" Mark asked.

"Bandar-Ansali," Ali-Reza replied. "It used to be called Bandar-Pahlavi. After the Revolution, Bandar-Pahlavi was changed back to its old name, the name it had before the Pahlavis. The naval base up there is in pretty good shape. Admiral Mahmoud, who is head of the Persian Gulf Fleet, is also the de facto head of the Navy. Mahmoud has made sure that the Caspian Fleet continues its patrols of Iran's water border with Russia. Mahmoud keeps those boats running at any cost."

"How are the military capabilities at Bandar-Pahlavi, I mean Bandar-Ansal?" Mark asked.

"About five hundred men stationed there. A fairly docile lot. Nothing much in the way of hardware."

"And the Kurds?" Kir asked. "What is the situation in Kurdistan?"

"The number of Zurkhaneh among the Kurds is very few. The propaganda we use to infiltrate Kurdistan—the tapes and pamphlets—is regionalized, focusing on the Kurd's grievances. The Kurds will support anyone who is fighting the Qom government. When push comes to shove, the Kurds will be with us; anything, rather than rule by the clergy.

"The Kurds are well armed," Ali-Reza said. "Once a month, in the town of Sanandaj, the

370

Kurds hold an arms bazaar. They have a motley collection of weapons—Russian, American, Israeli, German, and even some old French pistols."

"Where do the Kurds get the money?" Mark asked.

"Well, you'll never believe it, but the Kurds do a booming business in condoms—French condoms, American condoms, German condoms. Ever since the Islamic Republic outlawed all forms of contraceptives and made abortion illegal, foreign-made contraceptives have been big business. And the Turkish-Iranian border near Sanandaj and Rezaiyeh, to the north, is wide open for smuggling. The Kurds are Iran's condom sellers," Ali-Reza said, smiling.

Kir was taking notes. He looked up from the papers in front of him. "The Kurds and the Sunni Arabs in the southwest, in Khuzistan, are definitely the two groups that we must focus upon. How about the Zurkhaneh's strength in Khuzistan?" Kir said.

"In numbers, we are not that strong in the province of Khuzistan, but I have focused on the refinery in Abadan. I understand it will be the responsibility of Kalvani and Mahmoud to secure the oil fields and the refinery at Abadan. I have an inside line to information at the refinery. My cousin is the chief engineer there."

"The grand tradition of *partee*, connections, lives on, eh?" Kir said, smiling at Ali-Reza.

"Of course. Iran is still Iran. Anyway, my cousin has supplied me with the information concerning the oil fields, pipelines and refinery, and a blueprint of the refinery."

Ali-Reza spread the blueprint of the Abadan refinery out on the table. "The main control room is here. This entranceway has been blocked off; the southeast gate is now the only way in. Guards are

371

stationed here." Ali-Reza looked up from the map. "This is the latest information. I believe it will be useful to Commander Kalvani. Will I have an opportunity to meet with him today?"

"I'm afraid he is in Jubail. A shipment of TOW missiles arrived, and he is there supervising the loading of the Cobra gunships. We will pass your information on to Commander Kalvani," Kir said.

Kir looked at his watch. "Gentlemen, shall we break for lunch? After lunch we will discuss the Zurkhaneh in the central and eastern sectors of Iran, and the responsibilities of the combined strike forces of the Zurkhaneh and General Pakdal's men in securing the mjor cities of Iran during the final staging of Project Norouz." Kir rose from the conference table.

Ali-Reza twirled the *spaghetti bolognese* expertly on his fork. "It has been years since I've had some decent pasta. It's rough trying to make noodles without eggs, you know."

"I thought eggs were coming in from Turkey," Mark said.

"Actually they still come from Israel, the few that we get," Ali-Reza replied. "As you know, under the Shah's regime, most of the eggs in Iran came from Israel, but after the Revolution the mullahs said they would rather starve than eat 'Zionist' eggs. But I can tell you, no mullah has ever starved, and they do eat the eggs that are shipped from Israel. The few eggs that do make it to Iran make it to the tables of the ruling clergy. The average family gets no more than four eggs a week, if they are lucky."

"The situation must be very bad," Mark said.

"It is, Mark," Ali-Reza said. "You'd have to see it to fully comprehend it. In only a few short years Iran went so far backwards. Life is very, very difficult for the Iranian people."

"Do the people have any kind of social lives?" Mark asked.

"Mark, quite seriously, it is hard enough to keep body and soul together. The basic necessities of life are so hard to come by, that people don't have time to have fun, nor do they seem to have the inclination, anymore."

Ali-Reza took a sip of his wine. "Excellent Chianti," he said, holding the glass of ruby-red wine to the light. "Today I feel very privileged."

"It's a '79 vintage," Kir replied. "1979 was a very good year."

"Perhaps for Chianti," Ali-Reza smiled sadly. "But not for Iran," he said, as he put down his glass. "Shall we get back to work? I'm anxious to review the rest of the information with you."

A large map of Iran dominated the Conference Room.

"Moving inland," Ali-Reza's right index finger moved toward the center of the map of Iran, "toward Shiraz and Isfahan we are well covered; over a thousand Zurkhaneh in each of these cities. There is a high level of sympathy for the Zurkhaneh among the populace. In the city of Kerman we have several hundred Zurkhaneh."

Ali-Reza moved his finger upward on the map. "Our members in Qom are, for obvious reasons, scattered outside the city proper. In Mashad," said Ali-Reza, pointing to the northeast corner of Iran, "we have only about four hundred members, but they are all in key positions: government offices, radio and television, Civil Aviation, and the local police. I should mention that Mashad is in our pocket, if, immediately upon seizing power, we reestablish Mashad as the most holy city in Iran. Let's face it, with the tomb of Imam Reza, Shi'ite Islam's most venerated saint, Mashad is the most holy city in Iran and the Mashadites are mad

373

as hell that the ruling clergy in Qom saw fit to change the focus to Qom."

Ali-Reza paused. "The eastern borders with Afghanistan and Pakistan are General Pakdal's responsibility. With the airport and the city of Zahedan in the hands of the Baluchis, I have used mediation with the Baluchis holding the airport as an excuse to go to Baluchistan. I've flown into Zahedan twice, and I've met with Pakdal and discussed the coordination of our efforts."

"Ali-Reza, could we go over the status of the military bases in Iran?" Mark said. "What can the army of the Third Islamic Republic get off the ground or out the gates to confront us?"

Ali-Reza unfolded some papers, and handed them to Mark. "Here is some data that I wrote up this morning on the mobilization capabilities of the major military bases still in operation in Iran."

"Let me look these over, Ali-Reza," Mark said, leafing through the papers, "and then we will discuss supplies."

"Fine," Ali-Reza replied, taking a seat. He began listing his requests for the supplies, arms, and ordnance that would be used by the Zurkhaneh for Project Norouz.

It was mid-afternoon when Michael Kir placed all his notes inside his briefcase, including the sheets of paper given to him by Ali-Reza.

"I can't thank you enough, Ali-Reza. The information you have given us today has been invaluable. Now, I think that we all need a bit of a break. Mark or I can take you on a tour of the island, or if you'd prefer, you can go to the pool and relax. I would suggest that the three of us get together later on, around seven, so we can discuss any further questions that might come to mind."

"I think I'll just go to the pool," Ali-Reza said. "There are swimming trunks in my room."

"I'll walk that way with you," Kir said, picking up his briefcase. Kir and Ali-Reza left the conference room.

Once Mark was out of earshot, Kir spoke to Ali-Reza.

"Mark makes you nervous, doesn't he?"

Ali-Reza did not reply.

"We need someone like Mark. He is very capable. And, most important, he provides us with the link we need with the American government. Do you really think that the U.S. would enter into this—even unofficially—without the involvement of someone like Mark? There is a lot at stake here, and they don't want to be caught with their pants down. It comes down to a question of trust: the Americans trust other Americans, and without the backing of the Americans, Project Norouz won't stand a chance."

"I know you are right," Ali-Reza replied, as they stopped at the door to Ali-Reza's villa.

"Trust me," Kir said, "no one will overstep his bounds."

Ali-Reza remained silent for a moment, his hand on the doorknob. He looked directly at Kir. "I accept everything you are telling me, but just remember: the Zurkhaneh, ten thousand dedicated people, are in a state of agitation. They can be easily turned from one side to the other, by the right leader."

"I'll heed your warning, Ali-Reza," Kir said. He understood Ali-Reza's message clearly. At all costs, Kir planned to keep Ali-Reza on his side. The Zurkhaneh were the backbone of the new Iran.

Ali-Reza opened the door to the guest villa. "I'm going to get my bathing suit, and go out to the pool. What time shall we meet?"

"Before dinner," replied Kir. "Seven o'clock in the Conference Room. See you then." Michael Kir turned and walked back down the pathway.

"*Ciao, caro*," came a hushed voice, as Ali-Reza opened the door to his bedroom. The curtains had been drawn, and there was only the whir of the fan overhead and the heady smell of Tamango perfume in the room. In the semi-darkness, Ali-Reza could make out a figure lying on his bed. Gabriella slowly moved off the bed and walked toward Ali-Reza. She wrapped her arms around his neck and kissed him passionately. Ali-Reza felt every curve of her body through the thin flowered sarong tied around her.

She pushed herself away from him. "*Caro*," she whispered softly, "I just came from the swimming pool and I'm covered with suntan oil. I must have a shower, come." She spun around and walked toward the bathroom.

Ali-Reza quickly undressed and followed her into the bathroom. As Gabriella stood in front of the mirror pinning up her mane of chestnut hair, he came up behind her and kissed her salty neck. He untied the knot in her sarong, which fell to the floor, revealing her exquisite bronzed body punctuated by wisps of iridescent lavender. Ali-Reza slowly untied the bow at the nape of her graceful neck and the bikini top fell away.

In the mirror, Gabriella admired Ali-Reza's fierce, handsome face. His strong hands, sculptured as a pianist's, cupped and caressed her now bare breasts. She could feel his erect cock jutting against the small of her back. She turned around to receive and return his violent kisses. His hands moved to her hips and tugged at the strings on her bikini bottoms.

He looked in the mirror as the last bit of

lavender fell away. His hands caressed the smooth, shiny skin and moved to the curve of her tiny waist to guide her into the shower.

While the gentle torrent of warm water poured over them, Gabriella's expert hands soaped Ali-Reza's strong shoulders, and chest, and his tight ass, sliding over every inch of his muscular torso. He licked up and drank the warm liquid as he kissed every part of her delicious body. Gabriella massaged his long, hard cock with her soapy hand. She lifted her face to kiss his mouth, and their tongues began a fierce battle. He pressed her to him, gasping for breath, his stiff organ pressing against her scalding belly.

With water still pouring over both of them, he pushed her against the wall. She spread her legs, rising on tiptoe and tilting her hips forward so that he could enter her. Gripping her ass tightly, he bent his knees and then thrust his cock upward into her. They began moving in rhythm. Gabriella bit his neck, his shoulders, his chest as he moved in and out of her, thrusting faster and faster.

*"Sì, amore mio, sì, è così bello, ora, ora, vengo,"* she murmured breathlessly.

"Now," he cried, as he rammed into her, his taut balls pounding against her, and they came together in nerve-shattering waves.

*"Dio mio!"* Gabriella moaned, oblivious now to the water rushing over them.

Mark opened the door to the Communications Room.

"Hi, Michael. Where is Ali-Reza?"

"I left him at his villa about a half hour ago," Kir replied, not taking his eyes away from the computer printout.

"Find out any important information about the Zurkhaneh leaders on Ali-Reza's list?" Mark said.

"An interesting pattern is emerging about the Zurkhaneh leaders on the list—at least the ones I have checked out so far. Almost all of them had been under surveillance by SAVAK at one time or another. I guess that was to be expected, considering that most of the Zurkhaneh held positions of responsibility during the Shah's regime. But what is interesting is that in these cases SAVAK could not come up with any evidence of corruption or misuse of power. SAVAK had nothing to use against those people in case it was ever necessary to put them in their places."

"SAVAK always liked to have something on everyone," Mark said.

"Here are two people—typical Zurkhaneh—that SAVAK investigated," said Kir, picking up a sheet of paper. "Here is a guy who was the former managing director of an Iranian government industrial complex: Harvard-educated, graduated with honors, comments from his American colleagues like 'able,' 'dedicated,' 'could run an American corporation.' SAVAK said he wore Lanvin suits, and drank Chivas Regal scotch. Now he is a key Zurkhaneh in Tehran."

Kir picked up another sheet of paper. "Here is another Zurkhaneh: Educated at the University of Texas at Austin, geological engineer, likes country and western music, especially Waylon Jennings, and had a mistress during his Texas days. SAVAK says he continued to support her once he returned to Iran to work National Iranian Oil Company in Abadan. He is now a top Zurkhaneh in the southeast of Iran."

Mark picked up a number of other printouts on Ali-Reza's Zurkhaneh and perused them. "I'm impressed. It would appear that these are some of the most competent people in Iran. Ali-Reza has made good and sure that the new Iran will not be a rudderless ship." Mark put down the papers and looked up at the bank of closed-circuit television monitors. The monitor hook-up to Ali-Reza's bedroom in the guest villa was turned on. The monitor showed only an empty bedroom, with Ali-Reza's clothes in a heap on the floor.

"Ali-Reza didn't make it to the pool?" Mark said.

"No. It seems he had some company when he arrived back in his room."

"Let me guess," Mark said. "Our little Gabriella."

"Correct."

Mark looked up at the empty bedroom. "So where are they?"

"In the bathroom," Kir replied, without looking up.

"Here they come now," Mark said, watching the screen.

Ali-Reza and Gabriella, with towels wrapped around them, walked into the bedroom and fell on to the bed. Ali-Reza began pulling the towel off Gabriella, his mouth moving to her breast. Gabriella embraced Ali-Reza passionately.

"You can practically see the sparks flying," Mark said, looking at the two naked bodies on the screen.

"For someone who used to be rather shy about watching the videotapes, you seem to relish it now," Kir said.

"Vicarious pleasure," Mark replied.

"You know, Michael, I feel sort of bad about filming Ali-Reza," Mark said, turning to Kir.

"It is necessary. We don't want him to be able to become too powerful," Kir said.

"I know," Mark said.

"Just remember, Mark, no one in high places, in a position of power or influence, likes to be a porno star."

"You're right, Michael," Mark said, turning his attention back to the screen.

Ali-Reza's long, lean body covered the writhing Gabriella. Her hands ran up and down his back, her fingers grasping his thrusting buttocks.

Mark returned to reading the computer printouts Kir had given him, as Kir fed more names from Ali-Reza's list into the computer.

Michael Kir, Mark, and Ali-Reza arrived for dinner a few minutes late. Their meeting had taken longer than expected, partly because a detailed discussion of quantities of arms needed by the Zurkhaneh developed, and partly because Ali-Reza was exhausted—and not a little distracted—from his strenous afternoon with Gabriella.

The girls were already seated at the table when the men arrived. Ali-Reza took his seat between Gabriella and Victoria, and wine was poured for him.

Dinner was a sumptuous affair: ivory-colored hearts of palm peaked with tiny mounds of thick mustard vinagrette; roasted pheasants stuffed taut with savory wild rice, their golden breasts flecked with thin shavings of rich brown truffles; crisp green beans glistening with drawn butter; icy, pale-chartreuse endive salad, peppered with bits of garnet-red beets. Light, dry, but fruity Frascati wine sparkled in crystal glasses.

It was a pleasant dinner, full of light conversation and jokes. Gino seemed to be monopolizing the conversation, telling slightly ribald stories. Gabriella noted that Gino was not drinking. She guessed that he had a flight tonight, and she also suspected that Ali-Reza would be on it. When Ali-Reza had left her that afternoon, she hadn't thought to ask him how long he would be staying. Glancing at Ali-Reza's strong masculine profile, thinking that he would soon be leaving, Gabriella felt a pang of sadness.

As Ali-Reza cut into his steaming pheasant, Gabriella leaned toward him. "You are leaving this evening?" she quietly asked.

Ali-Reza looked into Gabriella's clear amber eyes. "Unfortunately, yes," he said, almost in a whisper. He set his silverware down and reached for Gabriella's hand under the table. He did not want to leave this adorable girl, and he could tell from the way she gazed at him that she felt the same way.

"But my plane doesn't leave until after midnight. I want to be with you until then," Ali-Reza said, stroking the top of Gabriella's hand with his fingertips. She nodded slightly, almost imperceptibly, and smiled at him—a slight, closed-lipped smile. Gabriella reminded Ali-Reza of a Raphael Madonna. He could scarcely focus on the conversation at the dinner table.

The waiters cleared away the dinner dishes. A silver bowl of lemon ice and a golden citrusy cake covered with a fine layer of powdered sugar, *schiacciata alla fiorentina*, were brought to the table. A servant served coffee in gold-rimmed white demitasse cups.

Gabriella took a sip of her coffee and looked up at Ali-Reza over the edge of the cup. He caught her eye and smiled. His eyes are the same color as the coffee, she thought, only deeper, more molten. She laid her hand on Ali-Reza's thigh; her heartbeat quickened.

Gabriella and Ali-Reza hardly touched their desserts. As soon as the others had finished, Gabriella, then Ali-Reza, stood up.

"We're going for a walk," she announced. "Ali-Reza can't leave without seeing the rose garden."

Gabriella took Ali-Reza's hand, and they left the dining room, hurrying down the hall and out of the residence.

Hand in hand, they quickly walked through the rose garden on the way to Ali-Reza's villa. Halfway through the garden, Ali-Reza stopped and pulled Gabriella close to him. One arm circled her waist as he gently pulled her head back by her long cascading hair. In the moonlight, he admired her beautiful face; the finely chiseled features, the glowing skin, the wide eyes framed with lush, thick lashes, the full inviting mouth. He inclined his head, and kissed her tenderly on the lips. But the smell of her perfumed skin, her hair, the warm smoothness of her body excited him, and his kiss grew more passionate. He slid his tongue into her already opened mouth. His strong hands moved up and down her trembling body. He pulled back, and laughing, said, "I guess, my love, we ought to try to make it to the villa, don't you think?"

The bedroom was dark and still. The musky odor of sex permeated the air above the kingsize bed where, for the past two hours, Gabriella and Ali-Reza had been making love. Now spent, they lay entwined in each other's arms. Their strong naked bodies were wet with perspiration, and the stickiness of love's aftermath. Gabriella pushed her damp hair off her face and nestled her head against Ali-Reza's shoulder.

"What time does your plane leave?" she asked.

"One a.m.," Ali-Reza replied. He raised his right arm and looked at the luminescent face of his Omega watch, the only thing he was wearing. It was a few minutes before midnight. "We have an hour," he said softly.

Gabriella did not reply but embraced Ali-Reza more tightly. The lump in her throat prevented her from speaking. Gabriella had known many men, and loved more than a few, but none had moved her the way Ali-Reza had. She did not know or understand what it was about him that made her feel so warm, so womanly, so loving, nor did she care to. It was enough just to have the feeling. Since she had left Ali-Reza that afternoon she had revelled in these new-found emotions. Now, the bitter reality of separation faced them.

Ali-Reza sensed her feelings, and, propping himself up on one elbow, he softly kissed her forehead, earlobe and cheek.

"Gabriella," he said. She turned toward him. He could feel her full round breasts against his chest.

"*Sì, caro,*" she murmured, brushing her lips across his chin. The hairs of his thick beard grazed her lips and face and she enjoyed the sensation. He stroked her face, her neck, her shoulders as she covered his throat with light short kisses.

He wanted to make promises, but knew he had no right to. If the plan succeeded, if all went well . . . then, perhaps, they could have a future together. But if the plan should fail, or not go as anticipated, then. . . .

"I want to see you again," Ali-Reza said. "I don't know when, I don't know where it could be. But I want to see you, and I will."

The two lovers were silent a moment but they could feel each other's hearts pounding.

"I want the same thing," Gabriella said, finally breaking the silence. "Perhaps I can come to visit you. I can leave Kish at the end of March. Could I meet you somewhere?"

"Trust me to make the arrangements," he said, kissing her passionately, yet tenderly, as he tried to capture this moment that he knew he would savor again and again in the difficult and dangerous months to come. She pressed herself against him as he moved atop her, to make love one last time before he left.

A sharp thunderclap shattered the black sky. Kir awoke with a start; his body was drenched in sweat. He had fallen asleep an hour or so after returning to the residence from the airport, where he had seen Ali-Reza off, and had slept about as long—an uneasy restless sleep. The creeping feelings of anxiety that had plagued Kir's waking hours these past few weeks seemed to have now invaded his sleep. A shiver ran down Michael's spine, as if the intangible demons deep in the back of his mind had crept onto the back of his neck. Thoughts of possible failure, of traitors to the plan, were luxuries of paranoia that he had thus far not allowed himself. He dared not. Yet, now it seemed as though these fears were surfacing on their own, against his will.

A shot of lightning, a strobe of light, flashed into the bedroom, freezing the room in a cold, unnatural white light for an instant. Kir counted the seconds between the flash of lightning and the thunder that would soon follow. Seconds passed and a booming roll of thunder shook the sky.

Laying in the dark room, Kir listened to the storm approaching, as the intervals between the lightning and thunder lessened. Michael switched on the bedside lamp and its yellowish light banished the darkness. He got out of bed, walked to the window, and opened the window, just a crack, letting in a warm, moisture-laden gust of air. Michael listened to the powerful waves crashing against the rocks on the beach. He gazed out at the agitated Gulf waters and dark sky, anxious for the safety of the small Beechcraft caught up in this unexpected storm. A jagged three-pronged fork of lightning stabbed the sky, with a roll of violent thunder following on its heels. Kir shut the window, then closed the blinds and the thick velvet drapes, cutting the room off from the tempest that was boiling outside.

The room was quiet. There were only muffled rumblings as the eye of the storm moved over the island, leaving bursting rainclouds in its wake.

Michael walked over to the sleek cherrywood bar and poured himself a stiff brandy and then sat down on the nearby couch. A selection of the latest magazines and journals had been artfully arranged by the maid on the travertine topped coffee table. Michael reached over, picked out a *New Yorker*, and began leafing through it. Unable to concentrate, he tossed it aside and reached for another magazine. As he leaned across the table, his arm outstretched, a sharp, splintering crash froze Kir's body. The sound had come from nearby, from inside the residence—or so it seemed. Kir hesitated a moment before moving. Perhaps it had only been the storm. But the thunder was now just a distant rumbling, and the only sound was the driving rain. Quickly, Kir got up, switched off the light and opened the door of his room. A line of dimmed track lighting, creating sections of shadow, then muted light, illuminated the hallway.

Michael's heart pounded heavily against his chest as he moved down the hallway, keeping as close to the shadowed edges of the wall as possible. He moved toward the Conference Room, the scene of the meeting with Ali-Reza earlier that day. He pressed his body against the door, stopping for a moment to listen. There was only the sound of the wind rushing through unknown cracks. Then, slowly, carefully, he slipped the key into the lock, and turned it until the lock was disengaged.

Gingerly, Kir pushed the door open. The light from the hallway behind him traced an arc across

385

the royal blue carpet; sparkling shards of glass littered the carpet. With a tight grasp on the handle, Kir pushed the door open all the way. He took in the whole room, and saw the shattered glass lamp lying on the floor—and the half-opened window with the curtains billowing around it. Kir rushed to the window, but as he peered out into the rainswept darkness he could see nothing, no one. He glanced back at the shattered lamp. It must have been the wind that knocked the lamp over, Kir thought. It was only the wind. But he remembered the window as having been closed when he left the Conference Room. Or had it been?

He took a closer look around the room—without turning on the lights. Someone could be watching from outside. There was nothing more that Kir could do tonight. Slowly he walked back to the door, unable to shake the uneasy feeling he had about the room. A wave of déjà vu flooded over his tangled thoughts, ebbing before he could capture it. Disturbed, Kir left the room, closing the door behind him.

As Michael stepped out into the hallway he suddenly realized what it was that had bothered him about that room. It was a hint of perfume, just the faintest hint, that he had smelled in the Conference Room. He opened the door and stepped back into the room. The fresh breeze billowing in from the open window seemed to have erased the perfume. Still, Kir was certain that he had smelled the lingering hint of a woman's perfume, now so diffused by the fresh air that his senses could not grasp it. But he had smelled it. He knew he had. Now there was nothing, no trace at all.

Michael stood in the middle of the room. He closed his eyes. He could smell the scent, but it was as if that hint of perfume was far in the distance—too far for him to reach it. He opened his eyes. The scent was gone.

# CHAPTER TWENTY

The clear morning light filled the Conference Room. The Filipino houseboy hummed to himself above the noise of the vacuum cleaner as he pushed it over the royal blue carpeting. It was only eight o'clock, but he had already been working for two hours. He did nearly all the cleaning early in the morning, since Mr. Kir so often worked late into the night or all through the night. The houseboy ran the Hoover repeatedly over the broken glass. The bits and pieces of glass made a rough brittle sound as they were sucked up into the vacuum.

Michael Kir, impeccably dressed in a blue-gray suit, entered the Conference Room. The circles under his eyes were a lighter shade of his suit color. Kir carried a steaming mug of coffee.

"What are you doing here?" Kir asked the houseboy.

"Cleaning, sir," the houseboy replied, bewildered. He cleaned the Conference Room every morning. Many times Mr. Kir had come in while he was still working, and he didn't understand why Mr. Kir should be asking him today what he was doing.

"Did you see that?" Kir said strangely, pointing to the broken lamp, still on the table.

The houseboy froze, terrified. Mr. Kir thought he had broken the lamp. It had been a very fine lamp, too. He would surely have to pay for it, they would dock his wages, and he needed the money to send to his family.

"Sir, I not break lamp," the houseboy said pleadingly. "I see it broken when I come in this morning. I . . ."

"I know you didn't break it," Kir said, realizing the houseboy thought he had been accused. The houseboy breathed a sigh of relief. "But how do you think it happened?" Kir asked.

The houseboy looked at him blankly. "Big storm last night, sir. Window open," the houseboy answered uncertainly. He moved to pick up the broken lamp.

"No—leave it!" Kir shouted.

The houseboy, now thoroughly confused, resumed vacuuming the shards of glass still on the carpet.

"That's enough," Kir said. "I have some work I have to do now. Leave everything just the way it is. I'll let you know when you should finish up in here." He shooed the houseboy and the Hoover out of the Conference Room.

Kir sat down at the conference table and took a large swallow of coffee. Commander Kalvani had just returned from a dhow transport mission, and was scheduled to meet with him at 9:00 a.m. Kir still had some notes to prepare before the meeting. He stared blankly at the stack of papers before him as he finished his coffee, mentally reviewing what he had to discuss with Kalvani. Kir still felt uneasy about last night's occurrences. He was nervous, and suspicious, but of what or who, he didn't know. He tried to tell himself that he was just being paranoid, that a strong gust of wind had simply blown a lamp over. But anxious thoughts kept coming back to him, tormenting him.

Kir suddenly noticed that the paperweight on the stack of papers was out of position. He always placed the marble rectangle carefully on the upper right corner of the paper, the outer edges of the paperweight lining up exactly with the paper. Now the paperweight was askew, almost in the center of the paper. Kir could feel his heart start to pound. He now feared that something was amiss.

Mark Rowan walked into the Conference Room.

"I have to talk to you right now, Mark," Kir said, before Mark even had a chance to sit down.

"O.K., Kalvani won't be here for a half-hour," Mark said.

"What I've got to tell you won't take that long," Kir said. He launched into a rapid-fire recounting of what he had observed in the Conference Room last night, and the latest discovery of the out-of-place paperweight.

"You can see for yourself," Kir said, indicating the glass on the floor, the broken lamp, the stack of papers. "I know there is the possibility that all of this may be just an accident."

"We can't take that chance," Mark said. "We'd better check things out. Kalvani will be here this morning, and you're going to Abu Musa this afternoon, right, Michael?"

"Correct. And Mark, when were you planning on going to Baluchistan to check on Pakdal and his troops?"

"Next week."

"Go radio Pakdal. Tell him you've had to move up your plans. You're going to Baluchistan tomorrow."

Mark looked out of the Beechcraft window as Gino flew eastwards across the Gulf. The December morning sky was cloudless. The sharp demarcation beween the azure water and the bone-white desert landscape on either side of the

Straits of Hormuz could be seen from the aircraft. To the south were the steep cliffs of Musandum Peninsula, which formed the tip of Muscat and Oman. To the north, the island of Qeshm, with its strange primeval lizards, and the ancient Portuguese fortress island of Larak. Gino's flight plan followed the shipping lanes through the Straits of Hormuz rather than traveling over Bandar Abbas and the sparsely populated areas surrounding that once thriving port city. As the plane flew east across the Gulf of Oman, Gino banked the plane slightly northward, still following the contour of the coastline of Baluchistan, the most southeasterly province of Iran.

Mark pointed to a tip of land jutting out into the Gulf of Oman. "Chahbahar?"

Gino nodded as the plane flew over the rocky limestone plateau, the site of the largest single construction project ever attempted, long since abandoned. The port of Chahbahar, planned for the Imperial Iranian Navy, was a seven-billion-dollar project. Chahbahar was to provide a deep-water naval base for the Imperial Iranian Navy destroyers that were to protect the Persian Gulf waterway—the most vital shipping lanes in the world. This mammoth undertaking was nowhere near completion at the time of the ouster of the Shah, and it was quickly abandoned by the Islamic Republic.

Gino flew the Beechcraft low over Chahbahar. The motor drive on Mark's Nikon clicked away as they flew over the desolate air and army bases on the sand flats behind the partially-constructed naval port.

On the ground below were three guards, Admiral Mahmoud's men, who stood watch over the deserted Chahbahar installation. One of the guards radioed a message to Gulf Fleet Headquarters on Kharg Island, reporting the overhead flight. A communications officer copied out the message, and an aide delivered the information to Admiral Mahmoud, Commander of the Gulf Fleet. The message reporting an unidentified plane over Chahbahar was placed on Admiral Mahmoud's desk—later to be filed in the wastebasket.

The Beechcraft headed almost due north, into the Makran highlands occupied by the Baluchis and their guests, General Pakdal and his Immortals. The harsh, mountainous terrain of Baluchistan and the independent spirit of the Baluchis made it nearly impossible for the central government to control Baluchistan. Communications had always been haphazard and the province's major airport, Zahedan, was under Baluchi control. Rather than fighting for autonomy, as the Kurds and Arabs had done, the Baluchis had simply retreated to their harsh, mountainous corner of Iran and continued on as they always had, a fiercely independent mountain people, heeding no government. And the terrible cholera epidemic of 1981 branded the Baluchis as "untouchables," contributing greatly to the central government's policy of nonintervention in Baluchistan. The mullahs in Qom wanted as little as possible to do with the cholera-ridden Baluchis.

Yet, things were not as bad in Baluchistan as the Baluchis had shrewdly led the ruling clergy in Qom to believe. True, there had been a cholera epidemic, but not on the scale that it had been reported back to Qom. The death toll was not nearly as high as it could have been, thanks to General Pakdal's intercession, at the beginning of the outbreak, in mid-1981.

The Baluchis had willingly allowed Pakdal and the Immortals to hide out in the mountains of

Baluchistan after they fled Tehran during the Revolution, but esteem for Pakdal grew during the cholera outbreak. Pakdal arranged for drugs and medical treatment to stem the epidemic which was killing hundreds of Baluchis. Doctors came from Pakistan, on Commander Kalvani's dhows. Drugs—ordered by Michael Kir—were flown in from Switzerland and secretly airlifted to Baluchistan. Hundreds of thousands of doses of cholera vaccine were brought into Baluchistan (again, by Kalvani's dhows), and the Baluchi children were immunized against cholera.

The Baluchis considered General Pakdal their savior, and they considered it their duty to protect him and his men from ever being discovered by the Islamic Government. In return for the protective wing that the Baluchis spread around Pakdal and his men, the regular shipments of food, clothing, and medical supplies that arrived in dhows to harbors along the deserted coastline, or arrived via parachute drops into the mountains, were shared with the Baluchis. Pakdal also supplied the Baluchis with rifles, rifles being a most important sign of manhood aong the proud Baluchi men.

"Damn!" Mark exclaimed. "This is the most godforsaken-looking place I've ever seen!" Mark looked out the window of the plane: for as far as the eye could see the land was a rusty purple. The jagged eruptions of mountains that pierced the crust of the barren plain were a deeper purple.

"Ugly as hell, isn't it?" Gino said.

"Actually," Mark replied, reaching for his camera, "I kind of like it. It looks like a moonscape, an environment too hostile for man."

"Yeah, I guess you're right," Gino said. "Only the Baluchis could love it." Gino glanced at Mark.

"Don't use up all your film, buddy. Mount Taftan is coming up."

Mark strained his eyes. In the distance, through the purplish haze, he could see the 4,000-meter-high semiactive volcano. Mark quickly reloaded his camera.

"Put on a longer lense, Mark," said Gino, looking at his watch, "I won't have time to fly in closer. It's breakfast in Baluchistan with General Pakdal, remember?"

Mark rested his camera against the seat, and as Gino flew past the triple-peaked cone of Mount Taftan, the camera clicked away furiously. "Spectacular, absolutely spectacular," Mark said.

"Maybe when we're coming back this evening we'll see it with the sun setting behind it. That is really a great sight."

Gino looked dreamily out the window. "Ah, yes, like a triple-dip from the Dairy Queen against the setting sun, melting into the cherry red sunset . . . Gee, what a sensitive guy I am," Gino said, grinning at Mark.

"A regular poet."

The mountains were getting higher and the peaks more jagged as the small plane traveled northward. Mark opened his briefcase and began reviewing the notes that he had made for his meeting with General Pakdal. Mark was making the trip to Baluchistan to arrange the logistics of aircraft, arms, and ammunition that were to be used in the final operations of Project Norouz, less than three months away. But there was another reason. The troops of the Makran Plateau, General Pakdal's Immortals, were the main troop strength of the whole project, and Mark had to check things out for himself. Kir expected a very detailed first-hand report.

Mark looked up from his notepad. "Jesus!" he

exclaimed. On either side of the plane were sheer rock faces.

"Relax, relax," Gino reassured Mark. "This is the pass that leads to the Makran Plateau."

Mark looked anxiously out the window at the rough-hewn cliffs, seemingly only a wing-tip away. Mark could see a dried-up river bed full of boulders below. Mark's eyes moved higher up the face of the rock, he saw that a small ledge ran the length of the pass. Mark watched the walls of rocks on either side of them. "Is that a road down there?" Mark asked incredulously.

"Yes, it is. The road through this pass, the Bamiyam Pass, is the easiest way into the plateau—the only way, actually," Gino said as he pointed downwards with his finger. "And that road is for friend, not foe. The Baluchis guard that road with their lives. Nobody, absolutely nobody, sneaks into the Makran Plateau."

The end of the tunnel-like pass was almost in sight. Mark could see blue skies ahead and in the distance another range of bluish-purple peaks that straddled the border between Iran and Pakistan. The morning sun was rising above their jagged edges. The little plane flew out from between the rocks, into a wide open space.

"Wow!" Mark exclaimed as he gazed at the deserted plateau, about ten kilometers by fifteen kilometers, completely surrounded by a ring of violet mountains.

The Beechcraft began its descent.

"The plateau looks deserted," Mark commented.

"It does appear that way, but both you and I know it isn't," Gino replied, as he brought the aircraft down on the hard-packed plateau floor.

Mark looked across the vast expanse of flat land, to the east and then west, to the mountains rising dramatically from the plateau floor, only one thousand meters from where they had landed. Mark quickly gathered up his papers and put them into his briefcase. He stashed his camera under the seat, and picked up the papers that had slipped off his lap onto the floor. Locking his briefcase shut, Mark looked up. The entire plane was surrounded by fierce-looking men: unshaven, swarthy figures, turban-like scarves wrapped around their heads, ammunition belts strapped across their chests, rifles in hand.

"Our welcoming party," Gino said cheerfully. Gino climbed out of the plane, and spoke quickly to the men surrounding the airplane. Poking his head back inside the plane, Gino yelled to Mark, "Let's move it, Pakdal is waiting for us at camp. These friendly-looking devils will drive us there."

Mark climbed out of the airplane and pulled on his down jacket. The morning air was chilly. A jeep was waiting nearby and Mark could see the morning fires of camps at the edge of the plateau. Gino climbed into the front seat of the jeep, next to the driver, and Mark climbed into the back. On either side of him were two armed Baluchis, one foot in the jeep, the other on the running board, their rifle butts resting against their hips. The jeep circled the airplane and sped off.

At the northern edge of the plateau the jeep began a steep climb up into the hills. The path was a dry, gravel river bed. The rock faces of the mountains were so close that Mark felt he could almost reach out and touch them. The jeep slowly wound its way through the mountains. Finally, after about a half-hour, they rounded a sharp corner. Before them on a patch of rocky but level ground was a Baluchi camp, buzzing with activity. The tribesmen standing guard waved the jeep through. Colorfully dressed children came out to greet them, their dirty faces peering intently and suspiciously at the two strangers in the jeep. The children followed the jeep as it drove slowly through the camp.

Mark looked around at the camp. It was a placid, picturesque scene. There were women squatting near a fire, turning the wooden spit on which a lamb was roasting. Other women, dressed in voluminous brightly-colored skirts, their heads tightly wrapped in scarves fringed with small gold coins, sat on carpets doing intricate embroidery work. Bits of the famous Baluchi embroidery lay on the ground: brightly colored, bold, geometric designs. Mark noticed that everyone in the village looked healthy and well-fed. Cartons of Winstons and a few cassette recorders were stacked near a tree, under which sat a number of men cleaning their rifles.

After passing through the Baluchi camp, the jeep traveled another fifteen minutes along a narrow road, the left hand side of it being a precipitous drop into a seemingly endless canyon. Mark chose not to look in that direction. The jeep rounded a bend and they arrived at a second camp, full of khaki-colored tents, nestled between the steep mountain walls.

General Pakdal walked out of a large tent. Pakdal was a tall, sturdily-built man of about forty-five. He had high cheekbones, heavy eyebrows, and a full head of black hair. His gait was brisk, and he carried himself with the bearing of a true military man. He was dressed in Imperial Iranian Army fatigues. Pakdal shook hands with Mark and led him to his tent.

Mark looked around the tent. The tent was outfitted with a plain army cot, a washstand, a metal cabinet, a Collins shortwave radio, a wooden table, and a spartan writing desk. An orderly brought in glasses of tea.

"Please excuse the simple surroundings," General Pakdal said. "We nomads have to travel light, you know." General Pakdal unrolled a large map of Iran and placed it on the rickety wooden table. He motioned for Mark to come over to the table.

"We are here," General Pakdal said, pointing to a spot on the map, "ten kilometers north of the Makran Plateau. My men are situated at various camps in and around the Makran Plateau."

Mark studied the map for a moment, noting the camps marked out by Pakdal. "Shall we start by discussing the transport aircraft that will be needed to lift your troops out of Baluchistan on March 21?" Mark suggested. He opened his brief-case and pulled out a notebook. "You'll have to excuse me, General, but all my notes are in code, so I will have to read out my information to you, sir."

General Pakdal pulled a chair up to the table for Mark. "Please, Mr. Rowan," General Pakdal said, motioning for Mark to take the chair.

"Regarding our discussion with General Pirayesh on Abu Musa last month," Mark said, as he looked at his notebook. "That was the meeting of November 29."

"Correct, Mr. Rowan."

"As per that meeting, the number of transport and attack helicopters you requested for the strike forces has remained the same?"

"Yes, Mr. Rowan," replied General Pakdal.

"Let me give you a rundown on the aircraft," Mark handed General Pakdal a sheaf of papers. "Comprehensive specs are listed here," Mark said. "We have about twenty-five C-130's; most of these were liberated from Iranian bases during the Revolution, and have been maintained in Saudi and the UAE, but seven of the Hercules C-130's we'll be using during our operations are new."

"Part of defense sales to the UAE?" General Pakdal asked.

"Yes," Mark replied. "About eight percent of the C-130's are in the UAE, at Dubai and at Al-Ain. The rest are in Saudi Arabia, at Jubail. A C-5, slotted for us, part of an FMS package to Saudi, is on the ground at Jubail. The other C-5, which the UAE will lend to us, is at Dubai. Both of the C-5's will come from Dubai for your men fully loaded with ground ordnance—M-60 tanks, M-113 personnel carriers, Pershing missiles with tow and launch vehicles. How will you be troop-loading?"

"Only partial capacity. I intend to send one C-130, at least, along with each C-5," Pakdal said.

Mark nodded. "The helicopter situation looks very good. Thanks to the large shipment of spare parts from Hall Helicopter, which arrived in the UAE about three weeks ago, about eighty-five percent of all the helicopters which were flown out of Iran during the Revolution are now operationally ready. Since the UAE and Saudi Arabia have been using a number of them as their own, these choppers will have to be painted; expected completion date for this is the last week in January.

"The military bases at Dubai, Al-Ain, and Jubail are crowded with helicopters. Roughly eighty percent of the helicopters are in the UAE: the rest are in Saudi Arabia. We have troop carriers and attack helicopters: sixty-five CH-47's, twenty AH-1S's, forty AH-1J's, fifteen 212's, twelve 214C's, and a few others. Twenty 214ST's are due to arrive in Cairo in late January; they'll be forwarded immediately to Dubai. Armaments for the helicopters are still coming in: one hundred percent of the helicopters will be operationally ready and fully armed by March 19."

"Excellent, Mr. Rowan. Before we discuss

comprehensive scheduling for the aircraft, I'd like to review command responsibilities for the final staging of the project."

"Fine," Mark said.

General Pakdal bent over the map of Iran lying on the wooden table. "The southwest of Iran, including Kharg Island, the Abadan oil refinery, and the oil fields are the combined responsibilities of Commander Kalvani and Islamic Gulf Fleet Admiral Mahmoud," Pakdal said. "Because of heavy Zurkhaneh infiltration in the Abadan refinery, and the fact that the vast majority of the men under Admiral Mahmoud's command are loyal to him personally, rather than to the Islamic Republic, I anticipate that the securing of these areas should go smoothly. The entire southern coastline of Iran already falls under the command of the Gulf Fleet, so Kalvani and Mahmoud will be responsible for securing and protecting this area during the takeover. I believe that the Navy will join forces with us almost immediately."

"That is the thinking of Commander Kalvani and Admiral Mahmoud, as well," Mark said.

"Yes," Pakdal said. "With the Navy on our side, responsible for the Straits of Hormuz, the southern coast, and the oil area, we will be able to devote our manpower and resources to securing the major cities and the borders."

"As concerns the securing of the major cities," Mark said, "Ali-Reza Raissi was on Kish two days ago. We discussed the plans for operations that will occur on March 21, and he said that you and he had coordinated efforts for the takeover at Tehran, Qom, and the other cities."

"Yes," General Pakdal said. "The securing of the major cities will be a coordinated joint effort of the Immortals and the Zurkhaneh. Mr. Raissi was here just ten days ago—he flew into Zahedan on the pretext of negotiating with the Baluchis for the return of Zahedan airport to the Islamic Republic's hands. Mr. Raissi and I had a very fruitful meeting. He supplied me with the latest information on Revolutionary Guard garrisons and strengths, and he updated my maps of the major cities. We discussed various aspects of Zurkhaneh-Immortals interaction and mutual support. Mr. Rowan, I have prepared a report for you on my last meeting with Mr. Raissi." General Pakdal went to his desk, unlocked a drawer, and pulled out a handwritten sheaf of papers. He handed them to Mark.

"Thank you, General," Mark said.

"All the information on our combined strike forces—men and equipment—are detailed here. But let me give you a brief rundown of the plan now."

"By all means, General," Mark said.

"Basically, the operations for the final staging of Project Norouz have been divided into three main areas of responsibility: the Gulf operations, under the command of Kalvani and Mahmoud; the Tehran and Qom operations, and the major cities operations, both under my command, and working in conjunction with the Zurkhaneh.

"As you know, Mr. Rowan, I have five thousand men in Baluchistan. Three thousand of these men will be sent to Tehran and Qom—fifteen hundred to each city—and will be deployed from the Makran Plateau. The other two thousand will be sent to major cities throughout Iran, and will be deployed from Zahedan airport. All of my men will be deployed by air—via C-130's, C-5's, and helicopters—to their destinations. Mr. Raissi and the Zurkhaneh will provide us with a radar blackout throughout Iran on March 21; I'm sure he discussed the details of this operation with you during your meeting on Kish."

400

"He did," Mark replied.

"The troops assigned to Tehran will be transported there by a combination of C-130's, and helicopters—CH-47's primarily, and AH-1J's. The C-130's will land at Mehrabad airport in Tehran, and they will support a large contingent of heavily-armed Zurkhaneh, under the command of Ali-Reza Raissi. They will assist in completely securing the international airport and taking over Tehran's military bases.

"Troop deployment to Qom will be entirely by helicopter. We wil be using all models to move on Qom: CH'47's, AH-1J's, 212's, 214ST's. I will personally lead the Qom operation, but will be in constant radio contact with my other troops. I'll be commanding from a RH-53 reconnaisance and surveillance helicopter."

"Coordination with the gulf operation should be excellent. Commander Kalvani will also be using a RH-53," Mark said.

"The third area of responsibility, the major cities operation, will be coordinated by Colonel Bahman, my best officer. The key cities in Iran involved will be Mashad, Tabriz, Kermanshah, Isfahan, Shiraz, and Bandar Pahlavi. Two thousand Immortals will be deployed, from Zahedan, to these six major cities."

Mark nodded.

"In forty-five days, Colonel Bahman and the two thousand men under his command will move out of the Makran Plateau, and start traveling toward Zahedan, they will be disguised as Baluchi tribesmen. They'll set up camp near the Zahedan airport.

"Excuse me for saying so, General, but isn't that a little dangerous?" Mark asked. "I know that Zahedan is under Baluchi control, but won't your men be easily spotted? Two thousand pseudo-Baluchis . . ." Mark's voice trailed off. Mark new that the Baluchis were a distinctive tribe, their language very different from Farsi, which was the language spoken by the Immortals.

"Mr. Rowan, I know you must feel it is dangerous to let my troops get so close to Zahedan, but they will pass as Baluchi tribesmen. Let me assure you that my men, after having lived with the Baluchis for some four years, can fool even a real Baluchi."

"Very good, General," Mark replied.

"To continue," Pakdal said, "the C-130's, the two C-5's, and some helicopters will land at Zahedan airport, and be troop-loaded there. One C-5, fully loaded with hardware and troops, will be sent to Tabriz, and another will be sent to Mashad. The men comprising both these two operations—northeast and northwest—are members of highly-trained, mobilized units whose sole responsibilities will be to guard the northern frontiers of Iran.

"My men will be deployed, mainly in C-130's, to each of the major cities, to support the Zurkhaneh. As Isfahan and Shiraz are fairly close to Zahedan, about half the troops assigned to Isfahan and Shiraz will be deployed there by helicopters—again, by CH-47's, AH-1J's, and 214ST's.

"In Shiraz, Isfahan, Kermanshah, and Bandar Pahlavi, my men will be working with the Zurkhaneh to take control of key parts of each of these cities—the airport, radio and television stations, Revolutionary Guard garrisons, and so on. In Mashad and Tabriz, however, the Zurkhaneh will be responsible for securing the cities; the Immortals will largely be guarding and securing the borders."

"The Zurkhaneh are very strong in both Tabriz and Mashad," Mark said. He looked at his notes. "Yes, from the information Ali-Reza gave us on the

Zurkhaneh in both those cities, it seems like they have done a thorough job of infiltrating key positions in Civil Aviation, radio and television, and military."

"The Zurkhaneh have done an excellent job of infiltration," General Pakdal said.

"And you, General Pakdal, have done an admirable job of coordinating your efforts with the Zurkhaneh. I'm sure that Michael Kir, and the generals, will be very pleased with this information."

The radio crackled, and Pakdal turned away from Mark. Mark listened as Pakdal spoke with General Vanak on Abu Musa.

"Excuse the interruption," said General Pakdal, returning to the table. "As you heard, that was General Vanak. He was inquiring about a parachute drop of supplies yesterday that had not been acknowledged."

"General Vanak seems to take a great interest in every facet of the project," Mark said.

General Pakdal shrugged his shoulders. "The generals are anxious that everything proceeds exactly as planned, and they want to take good care of their men, the men that will make up their new Iranian Armed Forces. As you know, Mr. Rowan, the generals can't help but feel a little anxious about the Immortals. The Immortals were the Shah's men, never theirs. But the generals know that my troops will follow me," General Pakdal said.

"Good," Mark said.


"Now," said General Pakdal looking at his watch, "it is time for lunch. I am sure you are hungry, Mr. Rowan."

No sonner had Pakdal spoken than two Baluchi woman pulled the tent flap open. They scurried

403

into the tent, carrying a large aluminum pot covered with a cloth, and bottles of Pepsi. They set the pot down. Taking a small rolled carpet that was propped against the wall of the tent, they unrolled it on the floor. The older woman flashed a gold-toothed smile at Mark. The younger woman stood shyly behind her as she handed the plates to the old woman, who piled the steaming rice pilaf, full of bits of lamb, raisins, dates, and grains of bright-yellow saffron rice onto the plates. The young girl, her eyes cast downwards, set the two plates on the carpet. Sheets of *lavash*, thin, unleavened bread, wrapped in an embroidered cloth were set out in the middle of the carpet.

"Eat," ordered the old woman, as she took a box of Kleenex from the metal cabinet and placed it on the carpet. The old woman grabbed the young girl by the hand and they hurried out of the tent.

As they ate, Mark discussed the agenda for the next meeting on Abu Musa that General Pakdal was expected to attend.

"General Pakdal," Mark said, "all of the generals will be reassured that you and your Immortals are working in such close conjunction with the Zurkhaneh. The generals have some doubts about the loyalty and effectiveness of the Zurkhaneh."

"Yes, but the generals were willing to make the compromise. They realized that internal support was necessary for the success of Project Norouz," Pakdal said. He paused for a moment. "It seems we have all learned to make compromises."

Mark nodded, but did not reply.

"Do you care for some more pilaf?" General Pakdal asked, noticing that Mark's plate was nearly empty.

"No, thank you," Mark said, taking a sip of his Pepsi.

"Oh, Mr. Rowan, isn't today your Christmas? Yes, but of course! How could I forget, December 25!" General Pakdal raised his bottle to Mark. "Merry Christmas."

"Thank you," Mark said. He looked out past the open tent flap at the towering mountains that surrounded this secret encampment of the Immortals hidden in the mountains of Baluchistan. Never in his wildest dreams had Mark thought that he would spend a Christmas in such a place.

The two women returned to the tent, bearing glasses of tea and a plate of fresh dates. Mark picked at the sticky amber-colored dates as General Pakdal collected his papers and locked them away in his desk.

"Come, Mr. Rowan, we must be getting down the mountain. I have some things that I would like to show you on the plateau."

The sentry saluted them as they exited from the tent. Gino was waiting for them at the jeep. Pakdal, Mark, and Gino climbed into the back seat.

The afternoon sun was low in the west and a shimmering haze covered the flat dry Makran Plateau.

As the jeep sped across the plain, General Pakdal explained to Mark that the arms caches were stored in natural tunnels in the mountainsides. Small arms and ammunition, as well as foodstuffs, were brought to the coast of Baluchistan via the dhow system, and choppers loaded with supplies sometimes flew in from Dubai and landed on the Makran Plateau.

The jeep passed a series of checkpoints, at each of which General Pakdal was given crisp salutes. Finally, in the shade of the high mountains, right at the mouth of a tunnel, the jeep stopped and Pakdal and Mark got out. The opening to a tunnel was guarded by a contingent of immaculately uniformed soldiers. The General led the way inside the cool, dark, tunnel. Mark could make out large wooden crates piled high along the walls. He recognized the markings on the crates—he had requisitioned them. An aide ordered a forklift operator over to where the General and Mark were standing. The tongs of the fork-lift slid into the wooden pallets on which the crates rested, and a few crates were brought down from the pile. An aide opened one box, pulling out shiny new Uzi automatic weapons, then opened another, full of J-3 rifles. He opened a number of other crates. The tunnel was full of arms, uniforms, boots, and ammunition. General Pakdal and Mark continued on to other strictly guarded sites, other tunnels, of arms caches and food supplies.

The bright sunlight hurt Mark's eyes as they walked out of the last tunnel.

"There is one more thing I would like to show you before you leave, Mr. Rowan," General Pakdal said. General Pakdal led Mark over to a small wooden reviewing stand. In the fading afternoon sunlight, Mark was treated to a brief display of the Immortals' military vigor. There, marching across the dusty Makran Plateau, were five thousand Immortals—the Shah's most devoted branch of the military. Dressed in army fatigues, their weapons flashing in the late afternoon light, the Immortals goose-stepped in perfect precision. It was a strange sight; here on this deserted plateau in southeastern Iran, to see the Immortals, in uniform, marching in review. The Immortals saluted, and placed their right hands on their breasts.

*"Khoda, Shah, Mihan,* God, Shah, and Country," they cried. Their pledge had not changed from the days when they had trooped on their parade ground at Lavizan Base. It was as if they were still on Lavizan Base, Tehran, in Imperial Iran. It was as if nothing had happened.

General Pakdal looked straight at Mark. "We will not fail this time, Mr. Rowan. If need be we will fight until our last drop of blood is shed."

Mark understood the determined and bitter tone of General Pakdal's voice. Project Norouz would truly be fought as General Pakdal's and his Immortals' last stand.

# CHAPTER TWENTY-ONE

Mark sat leaning over his sleek walnut desk in the Communications Room, busily writing in a spiral-bound notebook. Kir sat on a leather couch across the room, staring at the map of Iran on the wall. Mark hummed quietly to himself as he wrote.

"You know, Mark, you make me nervous writing everything down in a notebook," Kir said.

"Can't help it, Michael. It's my training. Walter always told me, 'Write it all down. There is no such thing as total recall.' And I've found he was right. I'm writing a couple observations that I made in Baluchistan, things I want to mention to Walter. But don't worry, Michael. No one could ever understand this code, except you, and, of course, Walter Singer."

"Great. When we see him today, I'll tell him you're doing your homework. What time is he due in?"

"Eleven," Mark replied, as he continued to write in his book.

Kir looked at his watch; it was only nine-thirty. He stood up and began impatiently pacing across the floor. "The one thing I can't stand about this room is that there are no windows. Just those tiny slits. You can hardly tell if it's day or night out, let alone what hour of the day it is when you're in this room."

"This Communications Room was the Shah's personal little fortress. In the event of a coup d'état against him, one of his contingency plans was to escape here to Kish. From this room he planned to recoup, retake Iran, and claim his destiny. Well, it sure didn't work out that way, did it?" Mark looked up, shaking his head.

Kir looked straight at Mark. "Destiny is still being determined from this room," Kir said.

Kir walked over to one of the tiny slits of light and- stared out. "The view from up here is beautiful. You can see the Persian Gulf, and, if you use your imagination, the mainland of Iran. I really do appreciate a room with a beautiful view. In my apartment in Cannes, there is a view of the sea from every room. I have a great view of the Palm Beach Casino, and that circular discothèque, the Sporting Club, and I can see that restaurant, the, hmm . . ., I forget the name of it, but you know the one I mean, the one with the best *croque-monsieur* in all the Côte D'Azur?"

"I've never been to Cannes," Mark said.

Mark's reply caught Kir momentarily offguard, although he knew it should not have. From the dossier that Michael Kir had on Mark, Kir knew Mark Rowan's complete background. He knew that Mark was of modest origins, from a very small town in Iowa. Mark had joined the ROTC while still in high school; it was his only chance of being able to afford to go to college. During his four years at the University of Iowa, where he majored in history, he stayed in the ROTC. After graduating from college, Mark joined the Marines, and went to Vietnam. His sharp intelligence soon brought him to the notice of his superiors, and he spent his three years in Vietnam in the Intelligence Corps; I-Corps. After the war, Mark continued on in military intelligence and counter-intelligence, reaching the rank of captain. Then, on the G.I. bill, he enrolled at Georgetown University, to pursue a Ph. D. in International Relations. While at Georgetown, Mark took three seminars in foreign policy from Walter Singer, the former Secretary of State.

Singer was impressed with Mark's keen, perceptive grasp of foreign policy. Mark had a far superior comprehension of global repercussions than any other student Singer had ever seen. Mark was gifted with what Singer called peripheral vision; he could see the "big picture"; he could keenly assess the geopolitical implications of foreign policy moves. Mark soon became Walter Singer's protégé.

Kir looked at Mark, who was still at work, in deep concentration. Singer's opinion of the guy is right, he is very sharp, Kir thought. Kir knew that behind Mark's easy-going manner was a very aggressive individual who had a sense of his own destiny—not destiny as a predetermined course of events, but something to be formed by the manipulation of events. Singer, too, believed that individuals could alter the course of history. It was a feeling that all three men shared.

The phone rang. Mark picked it up. "Yes, yes, fine, yes," was all Mark said. He hung up the receiver. "That was Singer."

"What did he say?"

"He can't make it today. His meeting in Cairo took longer than he had expected. He just arrived in the UAE this morning, so he has to double-up on his appointments there."

"When is he coming here?"

"Tomorrow evening. Today he had meetings with Sheikh Zayed of Abu Dhabi. Tomorrow he has bank business with the bank people in Sharjah, then he supposedly is going to visit some offshore Shell rigs. Our chopper is to pick him up at the Dubai Hilton helipad at seven o'clock."

Kir got up from the couch and went over to the file cabinet. "You said Shell rigs, didn't you, Mark?"

"That's right."

"I just want to be sure that we get our props right," Kir said as he pulled two large yellow Shell decals from the file cabinet.

"Come on, Mark," Kir said. "Let's go put the Shell markings on the 206 now."


It was 7:30 p.m. Mark and Kir were waiting outside the airport terminal building for Walter Singer to arrive. Mark was nervous; it was the first time Walter would see him in action on Project Norouz, and he hoped Walter would approve of the way things were going.

The noise of the chopper became audible, and Mark and Kir looked up into the sky. The helicopter was still far away, a noisy dark insect against the pale sky. As the helicopter approached, it seemed more like a tadpole, with its full, rounded cabin tapering, then narrowing, into an upturned tailboom. The black rotor shaft was barely visible under the blur of the whirring blades. The helicopter was directly overhead; a bright yellow Shell emblem could be seen on the cabin door. The noise and wind the chopper created were terrific, and Mark and Kir stepped back against the terminal building.

As the helicopter carrying Walter Singer landed, Mark looked at Kir. "Well, visit from Walter Singer or not, it is just you and me."

Michael Kir nodded knowingly. If the plan should fail, Walter Singer had covered his tracks so well that no one could implicate him. And Singer would not know Mark Rowan or Michael Kir ever existed. Walter Singer had not gotten to where he was by being a nice guy. Both Kir and Mark knew that.

Walter Singer, carrying a large brown briefcase, stepped out of the helicopter and walked briskly toward his welcoming party of two. He was a man in his early sixties, rather short, and somewhat overweight. He had the pudgy well-padded look that comes with sitting at countless conference tables and state banquets. Boating and women were the only sports he indulged in. Walter Singer's conquests of some of the most beautiful women in the world were as famous, or perhaps more so, than his reknown as an ocean-class racing yachtsman. Singer still had a full head of curly brown hair, peppered with gray, and his light-colored eyes provided an unexpected contrast to his darkly tanned face.

Mark moved forward to greet Singer first. "Walter, welcome to Kish Island," he said, energetically shaking Singer's hand.

"You look great, Walter. Younger every time I see you. That is some tan you've got," Kir said.

"I've been in Antigua. I hated to leave it. Sailing in the West Indies has been great this season. Sorry to have cancelled out on you boys yesterday, especially after I gave you such short notice that I was coming in the first place. Yes, Antigua was beautiful, but when the bank asked me to see some Arab investors in the UAE for them, I jumped at the chance—I knew I could sneak in a little visit to Kish. Then, at the last moment, I had to put Cairo on my itinerary. Mubarak wanted to talk to me about a couple of points on a loan I arranged, concerning work to be done on the port of Alexandria."

"How was Mubarak?" Kir asked.

"Fine, except he has itchy feet, awaiting Norouz. The sheikhs in the UAE are the same way," said Walter.

412

"Let's get started back to the Royal Compound," Kir suggested.

Walter Singer plunked his briefcase in the back of the Range Rover. He still carried the same boxlike heavy brown leather briefcase he had carried on all his shuttle-diplomacy missions. Singer's control of world events was less obvious now than when he had been Secretary of State, but he still exercised his will.

After leaving his post as Secretary of State, Walter Singer had retired from government service. For a few years he rested on his laurels, successfully defending his title in the Americans Cup yachting race three years in a row, and teaching International Relations at Georgetown University in Washington, D.C. Gradually, he took positions on the boards of a number of the most important coporations in the world. Political figures, as well as heads of corporations, still sought Singer's opinions on political, economic, and diplomatic issues. Walter Singer remained one of the most influential men in the world.

Singer stayed in the public eye because of his outspoken criticism of the present administration's foreign policy. He called it wishy-washy in public, and worse when among friends. Singer was especially critical of the way the U.S. had handled the Iran situation, both before and after the 1979 Revolution.

The Revolution, and the ensuing hostage crisis, had been a frightening, volatile situation for America, and Singer's warnings of one year earlier kept echoing back. The Shah of Iran had been a loyal and important ally of the United States for almost three decades, and in his time of greatest crisis he should have been supported by the United States, not undermined, Singer had said.

And the situation in the Persian Gulf region

continued to deteriorate. The attempt at a republican form of government in Iran failed miserably, as the mullahs refused to relinquish their control over the affairs of state. The Russian aggression in Afghanistan, the increasingly shrill threats of exporting Iran's Islamic Revolution across the Gulf, and the uncertain oil production in Iran constantly reminded America of the foreign policy blunders that had created this mess. But in 1982, when the whole system of Iran's oil pipelines was sabotaged, the U.S., along with the rest of the Western world, went into a state of shock.

It was shortly after the sabotage that Walter Singer first heard about Project Norouz from his friend Michael Kir. Singer agreed with Kir that support for the project could be forthcoming from the United States, Egypt, Saudi Arabia, and the United Arab Emirates, to name only a few countries that had been affected by Iran's instability. The Gulf states were anxious about their own security, and Egypt's long-abiding hatred of the lunatic Khomeini and his successors would make Mubarak a willing ally in this operation, said Walter Singer. Direct military intervention by any of these countries, or the industrialized world, was out of the question, but the once-powerful old Iranian generals on a Persian Gulf Island, plotting their return to power? Why not? It was still Iranians against Iranians. Singer was sure these countries would surreptitiously aid the project, acting as laundering agents for the hardware needed.

But Singer and Kir agreed that the project could be taken a step further. For that they would need the island of Abu Musa. Walter Singer had a plan. In June 1982 Singer suggested to Kir that now was the time for him to make that trip to the UAE he had been planning, to show the sheikhs of the UAE a fabulous collection of gems acquired from a maharajah's estate, and to convince the sheikhs of the political advantage of retaking Abu Musa—immediately. Singer had told Michael Kir that if he could manage that, if the generals could be separated from Kish Island, then the project could successfully go ahead on their terms.

Kir did go to the UAE. In July 1982, the United Arab Emirates retook the island of Abu Musa. Two months after the Abu Musa takeover, the lease for Kish Island was signed. Project Norouz had begun.

Walter Singer's part in the affair was like that of a consultant to Kir. Singer had no intention of getting his hands dirty. He did not get directly involved with selling the idea to heads of government and industry, but he did open the right doors and clear the right channels for Kir. Walter Singer commanded the respect and confidence of the most important international industrialists and heads of state. Singer put his connections to use, beginning with the White House.

In 1982, Kir and Singer convinced the U.S. of the advisability of supporting Project Norouz. Senator Joseph Sullivan, Head of the Foreign Relations Committee, and who was expected to be the 1984 Presidential candidate for the incumbent party, covertly assumed responsibility for Project Norouz. Sullivan felt its success could be the push that would definitely get him into the White House. When Senator Sullivan handpicked Mark Rowan as the sole attaché for this delicate top-secret mission, Sullivan did not know that it was Singer's man he had planted in this key position. Walter Singer and Joseph Sullivan shared an animosity toward each other. Walter Singer enjoyed the intrigue of secretly manipulating the man who would be the next President of the United Sates; he would have Sullivan in his pocket, which was exactly where Singer wanted him.

In the early months of 1983, when Kir was garnering support for Project Norouz, Walter Singer made himself available to the exact same people that would cross, or had crossed, Michael Kir's path. With his diplomatic finesse, Walter Singer had either smoothed the path for Kir, or allayed the fears of misgivings of those who were asked to participate in Project Norouz. Singer appeared to merely give advice when it was asked of him, but the truth was that Walter Singer was masterminding the scenario. With Project Norouz, Walter Singer was rewriting history.

The Range Rover headed toward the Royal Compound.

"When do you have to be back in Dubai, Walter?" Mark asked.

"Eight o'clock tomorrow morning. I have a meeting in Sharjah with the Sheikh."

"Then we'll try and make it a relatively early night. How does 8:30 sound for dinner?" Kir said.

Singer looked at his Royal Oak watch, a Rolex watch that had been designed especially for the Shah of Iran, and which the Shah, when he was still King of Kings, had given to all his old cronies. Most of those people who had received a Royal Oak watch had slipped it off their wrists when the Shah fell from power and became a pariah, but Walter Singer still wore his proudly.

"Actually, I'm not too hungry. If it's agreeable with both of you, I'd prefer that we talk first. Then have a light bite later on, just the three of us."

"Sounds fine to me," Mark said. "Michael?"

"Fine. And by the way, Walter, the girls are in their private villas. I know you don't want anyone to see you. They would wonder what Walter Singer was doing on Kish Island."

"That's the price of fame," Singer replied.

They drove through the gates leading into the Royal Compound, and stopped in front of the residence. Walter Singer got out and looked at the striking white buildings.

"This is all such a goddamn shame. I can remember back in 1973 when the Shah told me all about his plans to build this dream resort called Kish Island. He never could have imagined that six years later all his dreams and schemes would come crashing down around him," Walter Singer said sadly.

" 'The best laid plans of mice and men are often gone astray,' " Mark said.

"The problem was, they were not the best laid plans," Walter Singer said to Mark. "Let's hope your plans have been thought out better than those of the Pahlavis. Let's go inside."

"So this is where it will happen," Walter Singer said, as he walked around the Communications Room.

"This is it, all right," Mark said solemnly. "Michael, is there anything you'd like to say first? If not, I'll go ahead and brief Walter."

"No," Kir replied. "Please, go ahead."

Mark stood up and walked over to the wall map of Iran. "Walter," he began, "as you know Norouz, the Iranian New Year, always falls on the twenty-first or twenty-second of March, as determined by the solar equinox. The moment of the spring equinox is also the moment of the beginning of the Iranian New Year. The next Norouz will occur at exactly zero nine zero seven hours, March 21, 1984. At exactly that moment, the culmination of

417

Project Norouz will occur."

Mark unfolded a large sheet of paper and tacked it on the wall, next to the map of Iran. "Walter, this is an updated map of Qom. Ali-Reza Raissi, the head of the Zurkhaneh, provided us with this comprehensive map last month," Mark said.

"The blue line running across the city is the dividing line between the two sectors of Qom. When Khomeini declared Qom the capital of the Islamic Republic, the city was divided into two sectors: residential, for the ordinary people, and governmental, where only the religious leaders and their aides live.

"On Norouz morning, Iran's top religious and political leaders will gather at the Madreseh-ye-Fayzeyeh, the residence of the Head of State, to participate in the Norouz ceremony." Mark pointed to a spot in the governmental sector of Qom.

"The Madreseh-ye-Fayzeyeh is here. The Ayatollah Khalaghani will be leading the ceremony from the balcony of the Madreseh-ye-Fayzeyeh. The faithful attending the ceremony will be gathered in the large square in front of the Madreseh. The Norouz ceremonies will be closed to the public, as they were last year. Only mullahs, government officials, and specially invited guests will be allowed to attend the ceremony. About 150,000 people are expeced to show up in Qom for Norouz. Rougly 130,000 of these are mullahs; over ninety-nine percent of Iran's mullahs."

Walter Singer nodded.

"This year," Mark continued," the entire Norouz ceremonies will be broadcast live on television and radio throughout Iran. Everyone in Iran will be watching it. But the ceremony will never be completed. The TV and radio audience will never see or hear the interruption. What they will see and hear is: 'Due to technical difficulties . . .' "

"Is that Raissi's responsibility?" Singer asked.

"Yes, the National Islamic Radio and Television is completely infiltrated by the Zurkhaneh. Ali-Reza is responsible for all communications blackouts during the takeover, as well as airport closures."

"The Zurkhaneh sound well organized," Singer said.

"They are, Walter. Ali-Reza was here last week; he gave us a complete briefing. He provided us with all information concerning Iran's troop concentration, if you can refer to that rag-tag Islamic military as troops. He has also provided us with information on operationally ready military hardware inside Iran.

"In addition, the Zurkhaneh have provided us with well-documented data regarding the Revolutionary Guards' movements and strategic command posts. Walter, I have here a list of some Zurkhaneh members and some data that Michael has drawn up on them that we thought would be of interest to you." Mark handed Singer a sheet of paper. "So you see, there are still competent people left in Iran."

"And Commander Kalvani, working with Admiral Mahmoud, will secure the oil-producing region during the final staging of the project?" Singer asked.

"Yes, Commander Kalvani has fifteen hundred marine commandos, stationed here, who will secure the oil region."

"Stationed here on Kish?" Singer asked.

"Yes," Kir said. "They live in the Arab village on the southwest corner of Kish Island, and run the dhow support system."

Singer nodded. "At what stage are the pipeline

repairs in Khuzistan?" he asked.

"About ninety percent complete. By Norouz, the pipelines should be completely repaired," Kir said.

"And how is Pakdal?" Singer said.

"I was just with Pakdal a week ago," Mark said. "Everything on the Makran Plateau is going smoothly. After all, those are the Immortals, the only true soldiers that the Shah ever had."

"How do you think the combined efforts by General Pakdal and Ali-Reza Raissi will work?"

"The two of them seem to have coordinated their efforts well. Due to Zahedan airport takeover, Mr. Raissi has been able to fly down to Zahedan several times for meetings with General Pakdal. And a number of key Zurkhaneh have been sent to the Makran Plateau for training with Pakdal and his men."

"Mark, how is the morale of the Immortals?"

"When I was in Baluchistan I saw the Immortals on review. Walter, let me tell you, the Immortals are a finely-tuned fighting machine, and after four long years in the mountains, in exile, Pakdal and his men will fight until the bitter end. They want their country back, and badly. The same holds true for the Zurkhaneh. Of course, they are not the fighting machine that the Immortals are. But they are dedicated people, Walter, and they have been waiting just as long to regain their country. Together, they will be very effective."

"And now for the generals," Singer said. "Tell me about the most important cog in this wheel."

Kir turned on one of the closed-circuit televisions. The Conference Room at Supreme Command Headquarters, on Abu Musa, came into view. The generals were seated at the conference table, carrying on an animated discussion.

"The generals are fine," Kir replied. "They have

been pleased with the results of their meetings with the industrialists, and are now finalizing the agreement that they want to make with Martin Aircraft."

Walter Singer looked steadfastly at the television screen.

"Your view of the Conference Room is excellent. The cameras were certainly placed in the right locations," Singer said.

"Yes, they were," Kir agreed. Concealed cameras had been placed in the Conference Room on Abu Musa shortly before the generals moved to the island.

"The generals look well," Singer commented. "Although General Pirayesh appears to have put on a few pounds since I last saw him in Paris, shortly after the Revolution, nearly five years ago."

"Walter," Mark said, "I'd like to go over the results of some of the latest business meetings held on Abu Musa, particularly those concerning U.S. aerospace involvement in Iran after the takeover." Mark unlocked his desk drawer and took out a notebook.

As Walter listened to Mark, he was pleased by what he heard and saw. He was impressed with how Mark handled himself. Not that Singer expected anything else; he had trained Mark himself. Behind Mark's naive country-boy looks was the razor-sharp mind of a ruthless military strategist.

"Well, Mark, you seem to have covered every base. Very well done," Walter Singer said.

"Thanks, Walter," Mark replied. "I have you to thank for that, I learned my lessons well." Mark smiled. "I want to have your old job before I'm forty."

Walter smiled, but he knew that Mark Rowan

was not joking. Mark had learned all his lessons well. Mark's drive and ambition matched Walter's, when he was Mark's age. Mark would go far. His involvement in the project proved that he had the balls and the brains to not play by the book all the time. Looking at Mark Rowan and Michael Kir, Walter Singer got a vicarious pleasure out of watching these two men change the course of modern history, but Singer reminded himself that it was under his tutelage that Project Norouz had come into being.

Walter questioned Mark about the Hall and Bening meeting, the Chessman meeting, how the Germans reacted and what they would supply, what the Japanese were willing to set up, constantly checking and cross-checking. When Singer was finally satisfied that things were in order, he stood up.

"Things seem to be going smoothly," Singer said, addressing Mark and Kir. "Just keep your wits about you. Now, shall we have dinner?"

A cool night breeze blew into the guest villa bedroom through the partially-opened terrace door. Walter Singer unknotted his Brioni tie. He flecked a bit of food off of it, then hung it on the wooden valet at the foot of the bed. Unbuttoning the top couple of buttons of his shirt, he assessed his physique in the mirror. Maybe I have lost a few pounds, he thought proudly. I didn't overdo it too badly tonight. He recalled the light but elegant supper he'd just enjoyed with Mark and Kir at the Residence: *oeufs sardou* accompanied by a delightful 1978 Pinot Noir, followed by *mousseline de framboise* for dessert. Singer loosened the buckle of his alligator belt a notch.

Digging into his boxlike briefcase, Singer withdrew a thick manila envelope. He glanced at his watch; 11:30. He adjusted the arc reading lamp, then settled comfortably into the leather easy chair to read his papers.

Singer felt a sudden gust of air at the same time he heard the squeaky slide of the terrace door. He looked up.

"Mr. Singer, will you take a walk in the garden with me?" the honeyed feminine voice inquired softly.

"Certainly, my beautiful friend," Singer replied. "Wait for me just a moment, please."

Placing his papers carefully back in the envelope, Singer got up from the chair. His back to the waiting woman, he opened his briefcase and put the envelope back in. From the briefcase he pulled a .28 caliber Beretta, outfitted with a silencer, and put it in his inside jacket pocket.

He turned to face the woman. Gallantly taking her arm, the two steped out onto the terrace and disappeared into the black garden.

# CHAPTER TWENTY-TWO

On February 9, the Boeing 707 climbed steeply above London's Heathrow airport. The wheels trundled into the belly of the plane as it flew through the black sky on a southeasterly course toward Kish Island.

Joseph Sullivan was dozing peacefully, the tranquil and easy sleep that comes only to the very rich and powerful, who know that the world is theirs, or soon will be, as in the case of Senator Sullivan. Joseph Sullivan came from one from one of the wealthiest, most influential families in the U.S. His Welsh-American father had made millions in coal and railroads in the early 1900s, and spent his later life grooming his son for a public office of higher stature than the ambassadorial posts handed out to the elder Sullivan in gratitude for his less than honorable actions as a robber baron.

It was automatically assumed that, after taking a law degree at Harvard, Joseph Sullivan would enter politics, and that he did with the greatest of ease. His father had greased the rungs for his son, and Joseph Sullivan's moves up the political ladder had not been a long, hard climb. He'd taken the elevator. Now Joseph Sullivan, Republican, United States Senator from New York, U.S. Senate majority leader, was one of the most powerful men in America. The next step was inevitable. Sullivan was seeking the Republican Party's nomination for Presidency of the United States. It seemed very likely that, barring any unforeseen circumstances, he would win the nomination and the 1984 election.

Joseph Sullivan was risking this trip to assure himself of a piece of the political action that was happening on Kish and Abu Musa. He was jumping the gun, but Senator Sullivan was sure that by overstepping himself a bit, he would, on Inauguration Day in January 1985, have a very important ace in his deck—Iran. The fall of Iran had sounded the death knell for American prosperity, and Joseph Sullivan was sure as hell going to be in on the about-face.

"Wake up, Senator Sullivan," the steward said. "We'll be landing at Kish in a few minutes."

Sullivan opened his eyes and yawned. "What time is it?"

"Ten thirty-five. Would you like anything to drink before we begin our descent?"

"No thanks, I'll wait until I'm on the ground."

Mark and Kir were waiting for Sullivan when he stepped off the plane.

"Hello, Senator," Mark said, extending his hand.

"Welcome, Senator," Kir said. "I hope you had a nice flight."

"Hello, Mark, Michael. Good to see you both again."

Sullivan shook hands firmly, like a true politician.

"How was your flight?" Kir inquired.

"The flight was fine. I slept like a baby."

The three men walked to the lounge inside the airport building. Coffee, orange juice, and Danish pastries were served at once.

"This is some place," Sullivan said, admiring the surroundings. "And great weather. It has been cold as hell in Washington this winter. Not bad at all, boys. Nice, very nice."

"If you don't have any objections, Senator," Michael said, "I suggest that we go see the generals as soon as possible. They are anxiously awaiting your visit. We can go to Abu Musa directly from here."

"Fine with me," Sullivan said, taking one last sip of coffee.

The generals were seated at the conference table when Mark, Kir, and Sullivan arrived. The generals stood up as the three men entered Supreme Command Headquarters.

"Senator Sullivan, how good to see you. We are so glad you could make it," General Vanak said, making his way to the front of the room, so he could be the first one to greet the important American. Each general greeted Senator Sullivan individually, and then took his seat at the long conference table.

"Generals," Sullivan said, in his best speech-making tone, "let me tell you how pleased I am to be here. On the flight over here from Kish, Mr. Kir and Mr. Rowan informed me that everything was going according to schedule for Project Norouz. I am very pleased to hear this, and look forward to that day." The generals applauded.

"Our main concern, Senator, as you can appreciate, is what posture the United States will publicly take toward the new government after the coup d'état."

"Let me assure you," Sullivan said, "that your new government will receive diplomatic recognition from the United States once you have seized

426

power in the country. Naturally, the United States will disavow any involvement in the coup d'état, as will other Western countries.

"But once the United States officially recognizes the new government of Iran, our allies will follow suit. You can understand that our first dialogue with your new government will be cautious, rather than whole-hearted support. The only resistance to the new government that I can foresee in Washington is the fact it will be a military government. For most, the phrase 'military government' has a bad ring to it. However, Iran is a special case. The Islamic Republic of Iran has been such a repressive dictatorship that I believe the U.S. Congress will be of the opinion that any change will be for the better. Any problems with accepting a military government can be gotten around, especially since your new government will be strongly pro-U.S., and it will promise that Iranian oil will once again be reaching our shores. In addition, generals, I will be loudly and firmly supporting you."

"Thank you very much, Senator Sullivan. If I may speak on behalf of the other Generals as well as for myself," General Vanak said, "your words have greatly allayed any apprehension we might have had about U.S. support and recognition. We greatly appreciate having you, Senator, a most influential and respected man in American politics, on our side."

"Not only am I your friend on Capitol Hill, but I plan to be your friend in the White House." Sullivan smiled broadly. "Probably one of the worst-kept secrets in the world is that I have aspirations to the Presidency of the United States. The President of the United States will not, as he is in poor health due to advancing age, run for reelection. I think it would be safe to say that he and

427

I are the two most powerful and influential men in the United States and, since we are both Republicans, on this most crucial issue of the return of power to the proper hands in Iran, we see eye to eye. So, once your takeover is complete, the present administration's relations with your new government will be very close. And I will be my party's candidate for the 1984 elections, and I . . ."

While Senator Sullivan talked on, holding the group's attention with his booming voice and theatrical emphatic gestures, Parvis Gazvini slipped out of the room. He climbed into a jeep parked right outside Supreme Command Headquarters. He drove to the nearby Abu Musa airstrip, and pulled up alongside the parked Gulf Island Resorts aircraft.

Parvis scanned the area; save for a few guards at the far end of the airstrip, there was no one around. Parvis got out of the jeep, and opened the pilot's door of the Beechcraft. Bending over into the tiny cockpit area, he reached under the passenger seat, feeling the cushioned underside of the seat. It was there. Parvis pried the envelope loose, and, without even looking at it, slipped it inside his shirt. Parvis pulled a sealed white envelope and tape from an inside pocket of his uniform jacket. Swiftly, he taped the letter—instructions to his undercover agent on Kish—under the pilot's seat. His task completed, he got into the jeep and sped back to Supreme Command Headquarters.

Joseph Sullivan was still talking when Parvis returned to the meeting. Parvis was certain that no one suspected anything irregular about his brief absence.

". . . I pledge you my complete support," Sullivan said.

428

"Again, on behalf of all of us here, I thank you," General Vanak said. "Your support has been invaluable, and I hope that the relationship between our two countries will be friendly and extremely fruitful."

An aide brought a stack of folders to the table. "Now, Senator," General Vanak said. "Perhaps we could discuss some of the arms agreements with you, some of the terms and conditions. As these contracts will all be foreign military sales contracts, and you serve on the committee which must approve them, I believe you will find them interesting," General Vanak smiled, "and fruitful."

"Certainly," Sullivan replied.

The generals did not actually have very much to discuss with Sullivan about the agreements. The terms and conditions of the contracts were fairly clearcut, and had already been unofficially agreed upon by the businessmen and the generals. Sullivan commented favorably about the work that had been done toward the realization of Project Norouz.

The generals received assurances that weapons already on order would be forthcoming immediately, and that Iran would get priority treatment for military hardware orders once the oil revenues started coming in. In turn, Senator Sullivan was reassured that Iranian oil production would be brought up to pre-Revolutionary figures, 5.8 million barrels per day. The generals also agreed that upon their takeover, Iran would rejoin OPEC and be a moderating voice.

On the flight back to Kish, Sullivan relaxed in the back seat of the Falcon jet. "An excellent meeting. The generals seemed alert and in total control of the situation. Wouldn't you agree?" Sullivan said, glancing toward Mark who was seated next to him.

"Yes, indeed, Senator."

"The generals are just as we used to know them when they were the top brass of the Shah's Imperial Iranian Armed Forces," Kir added.

"Yes," Sullivan said, stretching his legs, "those old guys are tough nuts, but when it comes to Iranian-American relations we aren't going to have any problems with those generals. Just keep them in military toys," Sullivan said, smiling smugly. "The more oil they sell us, the more they will be able to buy!"

Sullivan paused a moment. "Of course, I know that the generals cannot neglect the rest of the economy in favor of the military. They won't. Are you kidding? They learned their lesson last time. They'll get Iran back on its feet a hell of a lot faster than any civilian government could. They may be hardliners but they are not stupid. We can all argue about the merits of General Howard—urging moderation—meeting with the generals in Tehran during the last days of the Shah's regime. But let's face it, if the generals could have used their arsenal of weapons to stem the anti-Shah sentiments in Iran, there would have been no Khomeini and none of the goddamn mess we are in now." Sullivan's voice was straining to its booming campaign pitch. Within the confines of the small cabin, it seemed to shake the plane. "I say, let the generals have their chance. Better late than never!"

"I agree completely, Senator," Mark said.

"Of course," Kir said. "I feel the same way." The plane began its descent.

"This has been a busy morning, Senator," Kir said. "Perhaps you'd like to rest for a few hours.

430

Then Mark and I will escort you on a tour of the island."

"Fine with me, Michael. I could use a few hours of sleep."

After dropping Joseph Sullivan off at the guest villa, Kir and Mark went directly to the Communications Room. Mark opened the drawer to his desk and got out his notebook, quickly recording the highlights of the meeting with the generals and Sullivan.

Kir turned on all twelve closed-circuit television monitors. "I want to make sure the television cameras in Sullivan's villa are in order."

"Everything should be O.K., Michael. I checked it out early this morning. We have him covered on all bases."

Mark pressed the button that turned on a camera, and Kir and Mark were treated to the sight of Sullivan sitting on the toilet, wiping his ass.

"Oh, Christ, Michael, do we ever have every base covered!"

Mark quickly pressed the button for the living room camera, and saw the houseboy setting a vase of fresh flowers on the low glass table. They pressed the buttons for the most important cameras—the three in the bedroom—and saw the entire bedroom, from the closet to the kingsize bed to the glass doors leading out to the balcony, in three split images on the TV screen.

"Perfect," Kir said. "There is no way we can miss a thing." He turned and looked at Mark. "Even the things I'd prefer to miss seeing."

"Hell, Michael, if you ask me, that bathroom shot proves what we've been saying all along. Sullivan is full of shit."

Michael Kir stopped by Sullivan's villa for a drink before dinner. Afterwards, the two men walked to the residence together. When they entered the lounge and patio area, they found Mark and the girls already there, sipping cocktails. Sullivan had not seen the girls yet, but they had been told that a very important guest would be at dinner, and that they were to devise an especially seductive and exciting scenario for him.

All three girls were dressed to kill. Manuela had on a white silk dress, strapless and elegant. Victoria was wearing a lowcut pink jersey dress, with slits up the side, and obviously nothing on underneath. Gabriella wore a beaded black and silver dress, the beading on the sheer black chiffon top barely concealing her breasts.

"I never expected this," Sullivan murmured to Kir. "They're gorgeous, absolutely gorgeous."

"Come, let me make the introductions," Kir said, escorting Sullivan toward the girls.

The waiter set iced bowls heaped high with tiny beads of glistening ivory—golden caviar—down on the candlelit table.

Michael Kir is really pulling out all the stops for Joseph Sullivan, thought Victoria. Golden caviar—the eggs from an albino sturgeon—was one of the rarest delicacies in all the world. Victoria looked across the table at Senator Sullivan, who was seated between Gabriella and Manuela. Golden caviar is not the only delicacy being served up to the illustrious senator this evening, thought Victoria.

Victoria observed Sullivan carefully. She remembered the photo of Sullivan on the cover of last week's *Time*. Senator Sullivan is much better looking in person, than in photographs, thought Victoria. She was actually looking forward to the evening's events. The three girls had something special planned for Senator Sullivan.

Shiny orange-red broiled lobster tails and small silver bowls of drawn butter were served with a flourish. Crisp lemon-yellow endive salad and golden-brown puff potatoes accompanied the delicate white meat. Copious amounts of Pouilly-Fuissé 1969 aided in enlivening the conversation.

Sullivan bit into a fresh strawberry tart as he smiled at Victoria. Victoria smiled back at Senator Sullivan, who seemed more interested in after-dinner treats than dessert itself.

Gabriella and Victoria leaned on Joseph Sullivan's arms, laughing as they weaved through the hallway of Sullivan's villa. They followed the trail of Manuela's white fox boa that dragged behind her as she pushed open the double doors to the luxuriously appointed living room. Carelessly dropping the boa on the white carpet, Manuela walked toward the chrome and lucite bar, as Gabriella and Victoria steered Sullivan toward the large off-white leather couch. The two girls, still laughing and whispering in his ear, began to slowly undress Sullivan. Victoria unknotted his tie as Gabriella slowly undid the vest of his dark pin-striped suit. As if in slow-motion, the two girls hovered around his body, not distracting him from Manuela.

Manuela had turned on the reel-to-reel tape machine and the exotic sounds of belly dancing music filtered through the four JBL speakers in the room. With a cold bottle of champagne in one hand, Manuela danced seductively in front of Sullivan's eyes, undulating her hips, throwing back her hair, shaking her shoulders and breasts until her strapless white silk dress was barely held up by her hardening nipples. The music switched to a throbbing Latin beat and Manuela stopped belly dancing and began to open the bottle of champagne.

Joseph Sullivan's cock felt like the champagne bottle—about to explode—but Victoria and Gabriella kept him firmly pinioned to the couch, allowing him only to watch Manuela as she played with the cork to the champagne bottle, trying to release the mounting pressure. The cork exploded like a missile, ricocheting off the mirrored ceiling. The champagne foamed out of the narrow neck, drenching Manuela's white silk dress until it was almost completely translucent, the wet fabric adhering to her hard brown nipples, her flat stomach, and clinging to her thighs.

Gabriella got up and walked out of the room silently. Then Victoria stood up, and Joseph Sullivan made a move to get up as he greedily eyed Manuela.

"Sit," commanded Victoria to the senator, as if giving her lap dog orders. He meekly obeyed, as he watched Victoria walk over to Manuela and take the champagne bottle out of her hand. Victoria poured some champagne into her cupped hand and then put her dripping hand to Manuela's luscious red mouth. Manuela drank out of Victoria's hand. Victoria pulled Manuela's dress down over her nipples and poured champagne over Manuela's breasts as she put her pink mouth to Manuela's now glistening wet breasts and lapped up the liquid.

Senator Sullivan rubbed his crotch as he watched the two girls. He moved to undo his belt. Victoria's head whipped around, and her blue eyes flashed. "Stop," she ordered him. "Just watch."

Senator Sullivan sat back again, beads of perspiration on his face, his engorged cock straining within the confines of his trousers, as he watched the two women performing for him.

Before his eyes Manuela continued to remain passive while Victoria, standing at her side, slowly pulled Manuela's dress down over her hips, kneeling as her lips traced the curve of Manuela's hip. Victoria's pink jersey dress was slit to the thigh, and as she crouched lower, Sullivan watched her bare ass make contact with the soft beige leather of her high-heeled shoes. Sullivan's attention flicked from Victoria's hand moving upward along the inside of Manuela's firm bronzed thigh to Victoria's blond pussy as she rocked back and forth on the heel of her shoe.

Gabriella, now naked, appeared out of one of the darkened rooms, carrying a small vial of white powder in her hand. Victoria continued to finger Manuela's pussy, moving more rapidly as Manuela's moans increased. Gabriella moved towards Manuela and put a gold coke spoon to Manuela's nostril. At the crescendo of excitement the potent white powder exploded in Manuela's head.

Victoria stretched out on the carpet, legs together, fondling her own breasts through the filmy fabric of her dress. Gabriella bent to the floor and pulled Victoria's dress up to her waist. Gabriella parted Victoria's legs and knelt between them, then stretched herself out atop Victoria's lithe beautiful body. She kissed Victoria's mouth, neck, breasts, and belly, then parted her legs, and moved her mouth to Victoria's blond pussy and began eating her, at first slowly and gently, then hungrily.

Joseph Sullivan's hand instinctively went to his engorged penis as he watched the girls on the carpet. "Stop," commanded Manuela imperiously. "You must watch!" Manuela knelt over Victoria's writhing body and pulled her dress off her. Then Manuela moved her body until her cunt was at

Victoria's mouth. Victoria began eating her voraciously.

All three girls turned on their sides, all licking and stroking each other's pussies in a daisy-chain. The sight of these beautiful naked women, stretched out on the carpet making love to each other, was too much for Senator Sullivan. He began to groan and masturbate. Seeing that Sullivan was at the point that they wanted him, Victoria called to him, "Come."

He hurried off the couch, tearing his clothes off as his mouth searched for one breast, then another. Victoria pushed Sullivan on his back and mounted him. Manuela, facing Victoria, squatted over Sullivan's face. Gabriella stretched out along side of him, caressing his sides and thighs while he fingered her pussy. As Victoria began to ride him faster, she and Manuela kissed and fondled each other's breasts, while Sullivan ate Manuela's pussy, all the while fingerfucking Gabriella as she licked and caressed him. The man and the three women developed their own rhythm, and Sullivan began to move with increasing urgency. He came in a wave of violent shudders, Victoria collapsing on his heaving chest, his fingers still working Gabriella's clitoris, and his tongue and heavy breath in Manuela's pussy.

Victoria pushed herself off Senator Sullivan's chest. She stood up and walked to the couch and retrieved her purse from under a pile of clothes. She opened her small black silk purse and pulled out a couple of new hundred-dollar bills and picked up the vial of cocaine from the table. Victoria pulled the drawstring of her silk bag shut and tossed it on the couch as she walked over to Sullivan and the two girls.

Sullivan was mounting Gabriella from behind. Victoria sprinkled a line of white powder into the palm of Manuela's left hand, and rolled a hundred-dollar bill into a tight, tube shape, as Manuela continued to finger Sullivan's asshole. Victoria inserted one end of the bill into Manuela's nostril; Manuela inhaled the cocaine in her hand quickly and sharply. Victoria poured out some more cocaine into the palm of her hand. Manuela put some of the white powder on her fingertip and then moved it toward Sullivan's thrusting buttocks. Victoria snorted the cocaine through the hundred-dollar bill, and crumpled it up and tossed it aside. She moved along Sullivan's thrusting body, and put her forefinger laden with powder to Sullivan's nose. He eagerly inhaled, pounding his cock harder into Gabriella.

Victoria lay down in front of the gasping Gabriella and put a pinch of powder to Gabriella's nose, spilling some of the white dust on her breasts as she did so. Gabriella then leaned over and licked the traces of white powder off Victoria's nipple. Gabriella kept her mouth to the hard nipple, biting it, as Sullivan continued to thrust deeper into her, harder and faster. As Sullivan exploded inside Gabriella's tight hot pussy, Manuela's cocaine-laden finger thrust deeply into his asshole.

Sullivan slid off Gabriella and lay outstretched on the floor, exhausted, his hands caressing whatever tit or piece of ass that he could grab and fondle.

"I'm dying of thirst," he moaned. Manuela reached over him. He put his mouth to her breast as she poured him a glass of champagne. Capitol Hill's stud extra-ordinaire was not finished yet.

"Holy shit," exclaimed Mark, his mouth wide open with amazement. "I can't believe it. Again!" He turned his eyes away from the screen as

Sullivan dusted Manuela's cunt with cocaine and bent his body over her, licking the powder from her clit as she writhed and moaned in pleasure.

Kir reached over and shut off the television monitor. "I'm sure we've got enough film here, Mark," he commented, "but let the cameras run."

"Boy, that Sullivan is really the stud that he is rumored to be in Washington," Mark said.

"He has been fucking the U.S. for nearly twenty years, so he sure as hell should be able to fuck three girls for three hours," replied Kir drily.

"That was no three hours," Mark said, looking at his watch. "Hell, it's been more like four or five hours, and he is no spring chicken. I've gotta admit, Michael, I've always wondered if Sullivan was the Lothario he was reputed to be. This sure as hell proves it, if you ask me."

"His sexual energy is in direct relationship to his ego, both insatiable. The guy thinks with his cock," Kir said, as he picked up his jacket and got up to leave the Communications Room. "Mark, we'll edit the film of the illustrious Senator and our three little whores tomorrow. I'm beat. See you tomorrow," Kir said wearily.

"Hell, Michael, if you think you're beat," Mark said, "think about Joseph Sullivan."

The sky was clear and the morning sun already warm at nine a.m. Joseph Sullivan turned down the window of the Range Rover as it made its way along the road to the airport. Mark, sitting in the front seat next to the driver, did the same.

"Beautiful weather here. I can hardly believe it is February. And it doesn't get too humid, like most islands. I bet you guys will hate to leave," Sullivan said.

"It is beautiful," Kir replied. "But frankly, Senator, we are very anxious to bring Project Norouz to completion."

"I, too, look forward to that day," Sullivan said.

"I hoped you enjoyed your visit to Kish, Senator," Kir said.

"Immensely, Michael. Kish is really a beautiful spot, especially as a winter resort. I have some connections with a hotel chain that I think we could interest in this property, seriously," Sullivan said, winking. "We'll have to see about developing Kish as such, maybe a meeting can be arranged."

"Why not? It is a beautiful place," Kir said affably. The car pulled up in front of the waiting Boeing 707. Mark and Kir accompanied Joseph Sullivan to the plane.

"I had a great time on this island. To me this place is paradise," said Senator Sullivan, flashing his famous smile. "And to me," he added, "paradise is any place where there are no media people around." The noise of the engines forced Joseph Sullivan to speak louder. "For once I didn't have a camera sticking in my face."

Andreas poked his head out of the door. "Senator, we are ready to leave."

"Coming," Sullivan said, shaking hands quickly with Michael Kir and Mark Rowan.

As they stood on the tarmac watching Sullivan climb up the stairs, Mark leaned over and said to Kir, "God, I almost cracked up when Sullivan laid that line on us about no cameras sticking in his face. Christ, if he knew that they were aimed at his ass, he'd shit!"

"He'd do a lot more than shit," Kir said, a broad smile on his face as he waved to Sullivan as the aircraft taxied past them.

# CHAPTER TWENTY-THREE

The telephone rang in Kir's bedroom. Surprised, Kir looked up from his reading; he was not expecting anyone. He reached out to answer the bedside telephone.

"Yes?" Kir said into the mouthpiece.

"Miss Ferrara is here to see you, Mr. Kir," the houseboy said.

"Send her in," Kir replied without hesitation, rememebering his last tryst with Manuela, only a few days ago. But Kir was surprised at Manuela's unexpected visit. It was not like her to just drop by without a set rendezvous—especially at one in the morning. He hoped that nothing was wrong.

The light rap on his door brought Kir off his bed. He tucked his cotton shirt neatly into his jeans. He opened the door.

"Michael," Manuela said breathlessly, rushing into his arms. She pressed her head against his chest, and embraced him. "Oh, Michael," she murmured. "I'm so glad to see you."

He laid his hand on her shoulders and gently pushed her back. She was wearing a simple black dress. Kir cupped her chin with his hand and looked at her; she was wearing very little makeup, and her hair was loose around her face. Kir thought she looked distressed, but ravishing.

"Manuela, what's the matter?"

"I was sleeping, and I had a terrible nightmare—about Evin prison, about Parvis. It disturbed me terribly."

Manuela slipped from Kir's hands and went to sit on the edge of the bed. She let out a deep sigh. Elbows on her knees, face in her hands, she cast her eyes upward to him.

"It's not just the nightmare, Michael. I feel so upset. I don't know. I feel the tension increase as Norouz draws nearer. Today's March 8. Everything will soon be over. Norouz, and the plan, you and I being together will be over," she cried agonizingly. "I don't want it to end for us."

Kir rushed to her, to hold her, to comfort her. As he embraced her, she fell back beneath his strength. He looked down at Manuela's face, only a few inches from his own. He gently kissed her lips.

"I love you, Michael. I've always loved you, I never stoped, never, not even for a minute. Now that I'm with you, I can't bear the thought of losing you again. But I'm afraid of what will happen after Norouz, I'm afraid I'll never see you again and. . . Michael, I love you."

"I love you, too. Completion of the project won't be the end for us. We can be together. We will be."

Kir could feel Manuela trembling.

"There's something else I'm afraid of, Michael, more than anything. I'm afraid of Parvis," Manuela said softly. "My life has been so horrible, Michael, you don't know the pain." She turned her head to the side. He tenderly kissed her throat.

"My beautiful darling, I promise you, no harm will come to you. I will never let anything harm you. I love you, Manuela." He kissed her lips, her ear, and buried his face in her hair, inhaling her intoxicating perfumed odor. He was suddenly aware of her body beneath him.

Kir could feel her breasts rise against him as she exhaled. He pressed his torso against her. She let out a gasp as she felt his hardness.

"I will keep my promise that I made to you in Rio. I love you," he whispered. Michael could feel Manuela's heartbeat quicken as she heard his words. She stared up at him, and he nodded affirmatively. She lifted her chin and opened her mouth for Kir to kiss her.

He responded quickly, covering her inviting mouth with his until she gasped for breath, embracing him. He hungrily kissed her face, her throat, as his hands caressed her breasts. She responded to him with a passion equal to his.

Manuela moved quickly, opening Kir's shirt, unzipping his jeans. Her hands caressed his muscular body, his hard cock. Running her hands tantalizingly over his entire body she pushed and pulled his clothes off.

Naked, Kir sat up and pulled Manuela up to her knees. He lifted her dress up over her head. He undid her black lacy bra and covered her now naked breasts with kisses, as his hands reached for her bikini bottom, pulling it down over her firm, round ass.

Kir bent lower, pulling her tanga bikini panties down her sleek thighs. Manuela could feel his warm tingling kisses on her thighs slowly moving inward, upward. Her hands caressed his thick dark hair, grasping tighter as his tongue probed deeper into her aching pussy.

He gently pushed her back on to the bed and continued his oral ministrations. His strong hands continued to caress her writhing body, stroking her breasts. He slid his hands under her ass, bringing her closer to his mouth. He brought her to orgasm once, twice with his mouth. Kir pressed Manuela tightly to him as shudders of pleasure wracked her body.

He moved slowly up her body, kissing her stomach, the soft underside of her breasts, her hard nipples. His mouth met hers, muffling her gasp as he entered her.

She wrapped her arms and legs around him, and their wet, open mouths crushed against each other, devouring each other with ardent kisses. Kir started to moan.

"My love, my love," he whispered, as his moans increased in intensity.

"Michael," Manuela whispered breathlessly, "is what you said to me really true? Will you keep your promise that you made to me in Rio?"

"Yes," Kir said, his heavy breath coming in waves, as he moved in and out of her rapidly. "Parvis will be killed."

Manuela screamed in ecstasy as Kir's orgasm ignited her own.

It was the morning of March 13. Victoria lay on her back, against the cool satin sheets. The early morning sun streamed through the open windows of her bedroom. Lord Wilson leaned across her naked lithe body, groping for his pince-nez glasses on the night table.

With his glasses on, he looked around the room for his white Gieves and Hawkes boxer shorts. He spied his Saville Row shorts hanging in a rather undignified manner from a lampshade, and hurried out of bed to retrieve them.

As he pulled his shorts up over his sizeable belly, he stared down at the woman lying on the rose-colored sheets, waves of shiny blond hair framing her beautiful face. He admired her body that had given him so much pleasure the night before. Her creamy smooth breasts, her firm buttocks, her sensuous lips, and her tight pussy were a far cry from Lady Wilson in her flannel nightgown and sagging everything.

Victoria slowly opened her eyes, aware that she was being watched. She looked up to see Lord Wilson looming over her.

"Good morning, my dear," he said.

"Good morning," Victoria replied, smiling as she stared at the half-dressed British Lord. She watched him as he buttoned his shirt over his gray-haired paunch. My dear Lord of the Realm, Victoria thought, biting her lip, if you only knew how silly you look standing there in your baggy Saville Row knickers and black stockings and garters. Put a man in his underwear and the status that he enjoys in public life—fully clothed—flies out the window, thought Victoria, who had seen more than a few of the most important businessmen in the world in their underwear during the past six months on Kish. Now here was Lord Wilson, one of England's leading industrialists, head of Hilland Motors, and as stodgy an aristocrat as had ever sat his blue-blooded buttocks in the House of Lords, looking downright ridiculous in his underwear.

Lord Wilson, now dressed, adjusted the chain on his waistcoat and stood over Victoria. "My dear," he said, admiringly, "you are truly Botticelli's Venus." He bent down, his jowls sliding forward as he kissed Victoria on the forehead.

The three girls sat in the swirling waters of the Jacuzzi. Manuela rested her arms along the blue-tiled edge of the round pool next to Gabriella. Victoria held a *Fortune* magazine up above the swirling water, half-listening to Gabriella and Manuela discuss the two men that they had serviced the night before.

"You know," Gabriella said, "It is true what they say about the Japanese."

"They really do have the smallest cocks in the

world," Manuela said, finishing Gabriella's thought.

"Victoria," Gabriella asked, "why weren't you included in last night's little *ménage à quatre?*"

Victoria looked up from her magazine. "I think it was because I was busy showing old Lord Wilson the time of his life."

"Which one of those *vecchi rimbambiti*, old farts, was a Lord?" Gabriella asked.

"Rodney," Victoria replied in her best English accent. "Darling, you remember Rodney, white-haired, fat old fart with the pince-nez."

"Oh, yes," Gabriella said, "the one that retired into the library with Michael for port and cigars after dinner."

"And then retired to my room," Victoria added.

"So tell me, Victoria, how did you know Rodney was a lord, Lord Wilson?"

"His picture is in *The London Times* frequently. He is a member of Parliament and the head of Hilland Motors. His wife, Lady Wilson, is on the board of the Trust Houses of Britain. If you look through an issue of *Country Life*," Victoria said, pointing to a large stack of magazines at the tub's edge, "I'm sure you'll see a picture of Lady Wilson in her sensible wool tweed skirt and Pringles cashmere sweater, standing outside the family home of Wickhamshire with her beagles."

"So, Victoria," Manuela asked, smiling, "tell me, my dear, how did you show Lord Wilson the time of his life?"

"I am sure that March 13, 1984, was the first time Lord Wilson had gotten it up since V-Day back in 1945." A smile flashed across Victoria's face. "It was probably the first time that anyone has given him proper head. Although I always thought that the prune face of Lady Wilson's might have been the results of years of tireless blow-jobs on Lord Wilson." Victoria laughed, as did the other two girls. Victoria picked up the *Fortune* again as Manuela and Gabriella continued with their discussion of the Japanese guests of the night before.

"Girls," Victoria said, "you are not going to believe it!"

"What?" Gabriella asked.

"You know *Fortune* magazine puts out a list of the five hundred biggest corporations in the world, and girls, we have screwed much of the first page."

"Let me look," Manuela said as she reached for the magazine. She studied the magazine for a moment. "Yes, indeed, you'll be pleased to know that we've screwed almost everyone in the top twenty."

"Not bad," Victoria said, laughing. "Not bad at all."

"Bad, very bad," Gabriella countered. "Most of them were very bad."

"Who do you think was the worst, Gabriella?" Victoria asked.

Gabriella looked at the magazine. "Well, let's see . . . Number 5 was pretty bad, but then Number 8, with the funny bend in his penis and the staying power of a limp celery stalk, was awful as well."

"I agree with you, Gabriella," Victoria said. "That head of the oil company with the crooked cock was unbelievable. His picture is in this magazine. Here, take a look," Victoria said, showing the glossy photo to the two other girls.

"Who'd imagine that beneath that pin-striped suit was the most bent-out-of-shape cock in the world," Manuela said. "That cock of Winthrop Lowell's reminded me of an arrow that could point the way out of a labyrith."

"And who do you think was the top man on the list of bad Very Important Person fucks?" Victoria asked Gabriella playfully.

"My vote goes to the Japanese last night. To know them is not to lust over them. They go down on you like pilots on a kamikaze mission." Gabriella said, doubling over with laughter. "I can't believe this conversation. I don't know about the rest of you, but after almost six months on this island I am losing my grip on reality."

"It's not *losing* your grip on reality, Gabriella," said Victoria, "it's *lost* your grip on reality. The moment you set foot on this island you lost any contact with reality. This is not the real world," Victoria said emphatically.

"Well, since we are on the subject," Manuela said, "who do you think has been the best VIP fuck?"

"Well, it has hardly been stud farm material that we have been dealing with," Gabriella said, "but my vote goes for the American arms man. He thought his penis was an extension of his F-14. He attacked me like I was a tactical target on the ground."

"Oh, yes, how could I forget him, and the gentleman from Northern. Their idea of a dream vacation was going to Africa and being mercenaries. I'm sure they were kidding," Victoria said.

"Don't count on it," replied Manuela.

"Well, my vote goes for the Italian industrialist," Victoria said. "He was very smooth. He had the polished patina of a count."

"Cont von Sacher-Masoch," Manuela retorted.

"Now, that's not really fair, Manuela. Personally, I think he was more of a sadist, than a masochist," Victoria said, as they discussed the sexual quirks of Giovanni Agnellone, one of

Europe's leading industrialists.

"No, he was definitely a masochist, Victoria," Manuela said. "Anyone who likes to have a scarf tied around his neck until he is almost strangled is definitely a masochist."

"Well, from the bite marks on my bottom, I would say that Signor Agnellone was of the other persuasion," Victoria replied.

"Frankly, girls," Gabriella said, "they have all been so bad! All I can say is I don't know how all these men made it to the top of their corporations, but I can guarantee you that they didn't do it by screwing their way to the top."

"Oh, what I wouldn't give for a nice young guy, with a full head of hair and an erection that doesn't have to be coaxed into place. I am tired of these guys with one foot in the grave and the other on a banana peel," Victoria said.

"Me too. What I want is a *pezzone*, a real piece," Gabriella sighed, thinking of Ali-Reza.

"Save your dreaming, girls. Our sojourn on this island will soon be over," Manuela said.

When Kir walked into the Communications Room, he found Mark already there, seated in front of the radio. Mark took off his headset when he saw Kir.

"That was Abu Musa I just talked to. Parvis is on his way here. It seems he was up all night reviewing the industrial purchase contracts, and he wants to discuss the currency devaluation clause with you. That bastard really likes to surprise us, Michael."

"Did he say how long he's staying?"

"He didn't specify. But I'd assume overnight—he certainly enjoyed himself last time."

"I'll take him to see the commandos," Kir said, planning aloud. "We can discuss the contracts tonight."

"Mike." Mark hesitated, then asked the inevitable question. "What do you want to do about Manuela? The girls are all at the pool together."

"Nothing." Kir recalled the ugly experience of drugging Manuela. He knew there was no way he could bring himself to repeat that performance. And, he felt, at this point in time, she could handle seeing Parvis. "Just leave her be," Kir said. "I guess I'd better go to the airport to meet our visitor."

"Parvis is coming by helicopter. Since our airstrip is crowded, I told him to land at the north beach helipad."

"I'll see you later," Kir said, walking out of the Communications Room.

Parvis and Kir sat together in the front of the Range Rover, driving along the narrow beach road.

"How fortunate that the five hundred elite commandos are on Kish now. When did they arrive?" Parvis asked.

"Two days ago, from Egypt, where they had been training in the desert," Kir said.

"I'm anxious to see them as soon as possible," said Parvis as he flipped open his gold cigarette case and pulled out a cigarette.

"Would you like to see some of the latest aircraft arrivals first?"

"Of course, Michael," Parvis said, taking a long drag on his just-lit cigarette.

Kir turned left, into the airport area. He drove across the shimmering tarmac, pulling up in front of the hangar entrance.

"Parvis, the four Ah-IS helicopters started arriving here on Kish, each separately, on the tenth of February. A few more are still due in." Kir and Parvis stepped over a number of cables trailing out of one of the camouflage-painted single-engine Huey Cobra helicopters in the process of being TOW missile-loaded by a group of technicians.

Kir pointed to the narrow-profile, low-silhouette Cobra gunships to the left of where he and Parvis were standing. "These Hueys will be equipped with M-197 twenty-millimeter turret cannons, with seven hundred fifty rounds of ammunition," Kir said. He then directed Parvis toward the RH-53, a large command and surveillance helicopter.

"This will be Commander Kalvani's command post during the Gulf Operation. The majority of his men will be deployed in Wellington hovercrafts, which will come from Kharg Island the night of March 20. Kalvani and Mahmoud are responsible for securing Kharg Island swiftly, so that it can be used as a staging base for the 214's and AH-1T SeaCobras that will carry the elite units being sent to the oil refinery at Abadan and the oil fields."

"Very good," said Parvis. "The generals will be very pleased."

Michael Kir drove the Range Rover past the airport, along the roadway toward the Arab fishing village at the southwest corner of Kish Island. He turned to Parvis. "Well, Parvis, what do you think so far?"

"I'm impressed," Parvis replied, as he stared out at the bone-dry, barren desert landscape flashing by.

They drove down the unpaved road leading to the water's edge and the village.

"Michael, give me the rundown on the men stationed here."

"Commander Kalvani has stationed fifteen

hundred former marine commandos and navy officers here in this old Arab fishing village. But not all the men are presently in the village—they are out on Kalvani's dhows that travel the Gulf waters with supplies and arms. The elite unit of five hundred men that arrived from Egypt, where they were training in secret, are all former top Imperial Iranian Navy commandos. They are the men who were hand-picked by Prince Shafik during the late 1970s for the Persian Gulf Fleet's elite units, which were responsible for the operations concerning the vital oil fields, pipelines, and refineries."

"The commandos trained by the Israelis?" Parvis said.

"Correct, Parvis."

"The Israelis did some work on Kish, isn't that right, Michael?" Parvis asked. Kir glanced at Parvis, and before he could answer, Parvis said, "A desalinization plant, isn't that correct?"

"That's right," Kir said. He turned the wheels of the Range Rover sharply right, down the unpaved road that led to the Arab fishing village. The sparkling blue water could be seen in the distance as the Range Rover wound its way down the dry, barren terrain, to the water's edge. A small cluster of buildings came into view.

The Range Rover drove through the narrow, dusty streets of the small Arab fishing village, once the home of pirates who controlled the Gulf waters. Parvis looked out the window of the jeep, watching the busy activity on the streets and at dockside as men dressed in their *kuffiyas* and *dishdashas* went about their business with a purpose.

"So this is the Kish Island naval installation. One would never know that the ragged fishermen in these villages are not Arabs, but former members of the Imperial Iranian Navy," Parvis said, "except for the fact that there are no women around."

"That's true," Kir replied as he brought the jeep to a halt by the dockside. "But maintaining appearances is mainly for the benefit of any aerial reconnaissance flights—by anyone."

Parvis stepped out of the jeep, and took in the view around him. "Arabs," speaking Farsi among themselves, were loading crates into dhows. Low white buildings, made of sun-baked mud covered with whitewash, rose from the dusty, unpaved streets. Delicate chimneylike wind towers, the ancient method of air circulation for cooling the interiors of Gulf houses, cluttered the rooftops. Several hundred meters down from the docks, Arabs were setting up cement ramps along the beach; the long slabs of cement extended out into the sea, and up onto the barren beach.

"For the hovercraft?" Parvis asked Kir.

Kir nodded.

"Is Commander Kalvani here?" Parvis asked.

"Yes, follow me, Parvis." Kir led the way down a close, crooked street. They turned left, and then left again. The streets were quiet and still. Only a few Iranian commandos, dressed as Arabs, passed them on the streets. As Kir and Parvis exited the street, they faced a square of high white walls, enclosing a large area. A simple but commanding tall dome rose from within the walled space.

"Kalvani is in the mosque?" Parvis asked.

"He's conducting a briefing with the five hundred newly arrived commandos," Kir said.

Parvis chuckled. "As good a meeting place as any," he said.

Two sentries, their flowing white Arab robes moving slightly in the breeze, stood guard at the wooden gate, cut into one of the walls, that led into the mosque area.

Kir and Parvis walked through the gate and entered the courtyard. Encircling the mosque was an arcaded walkway, a series of columns and pointed Arabic arches that provided shade for Kir and Parvis as they walked toward the mosque. In the center of the courtyard was the mosque—a large, simple, almost stark building, its high imposing dome stretching up toward the clear blue sky. The mosque was pure white, devoid of any decoration.

A uniformed sentry stood at the entrance to the mosque. Kir spoke with him, and went inside the mosque.

A moment later, Commander Kalvani appeared at the door of the mosque. He was dressed in uniform.

"General Gazvini, Michael, very good to see you," Kalvani said, shaking hands with the two men.

"How fortunate to catch you on Kish, Commander Kalvani. I know how much traveling around the Gulf area you do," Parvis said.

"Yes, especially now," Kalvani said.

Parvis nodded. "I would like to see the new arrivals, and even have a few words with the men. The other generals back on Abu Musa would be pleased to have a first-hand report from me."

"Certainly, General Gazvini. It would be a great honor for the men. The men of the elite strike forces are assembled in the mosque. We had just started a briefing," Kalvani said.

Parvis and Kir followed Kalvani into the mosque.

The interior of the mosque, a large open area, was crowded with the five hundred uniformed commandos. The focal point of the mosque's interior was the *kibla*, the wall which faced toward the most holy Moslem city of Mecca in

Saudi Arabia. In this particular mosque, the *kibla* was the western wall. The entire wall was covered with glazed ceramic tiles, richly decorated with arabesque designs and intricate geometrical patterns, all interweaving and seemingly flowing into one another. The vivid blues, greens, turquoises, and gold of the ceramic tiles contrasted sharply with the stark white of the rest of the mosque. All of the uniformed commandos stood facing the *kibla*.

In the middle of the *kibla* was a large niche, the *mihrab*. This was the prayer niche, toward which all worshipers focused their attention, so that they would be facing Mecca as they prayed. In front of the *mihrab* was a long wooden table, on which Commander Kalvani had his papers. To one side of the *mihrab*, a series of maps illustrating various areas of the Abadan refinery was attached to the wall.

"If you'll excuse me," Kalvani said to Parvis and Kir, "I was reviewing the layout of the Abadan refinery with my men."

"Of course," Parvis said. Kalvani walked briskly up to the *mihrab* and, standing behind the wooden table, addressed the commandos assembled before him.

Parvis and Kir listened and observed with interest. Kalvani concluded his briefing and introduced General Gazvini to the assembled men.

The eyes of the commandos followed Parvis Gazvini, once one of the most powerful and feared men in all of Iran, as he made his way toward the front of the mosque.

The late afternoon sun was waning as Kir and Parvis drove out of the Arab village.

"The generals will be very pleased," Parvis said. "The elite commandos are a formidable unit, and the other fifteen hundred men are equally well

454

prepared. They seem very anxious for Norouz."

"We all are," Kir said.

"We are going to stun the world, my friend," Parvis said.

"We will," replied Kir. "We will."

The Range Rover drove through the gates of the Royal Compound.

"What a brilliant sunset, and the weather is so lovely! I feel like walking a few paces," Parvis said.

They parked near the court ministers' villas. The two men walked toward the residence, discussing terminology to be used in the upcoming contracts. A loud splash, followed by feminine laughter, interrupted the conversation. Parvis and Kir looked to their left, beyond the shrubbery.

Manuela was in the pool, her maillot-clad body brightly illuminated by the underwater pool lights. Victoria and Gabriella were stretched out by the pool, chatting and laughing, the last bit of the day's sun casting shadows on their lithe bodies. Parvis looked at the three women dispassionately for a moment, then walked on.

As Kir and Parvis entered the residence, Parvis said, "Don't bother sending any women to me tonight, Michael. I've got too much on my mind."

The low, heavy sound of galloping hooves hitting sand was drowned out by the breaking of the waves on the beach. The white horse, with a long-tressed woman astride it, raced northward along the beach under the starlit sky. The lone figure on horseback cut a dramatic silhouette against the dark landscape of sea, sky, and sand. A parked helicopter in the distance was the only other object on the horizon.

The woman's hair billowed in the wind as the horse sped toward the helicopter. Reaching her goal, the woman jumped down. She ran to the helicopter and jerked open the passenger side door. Crouching low, she thrust her hand beneath the seat. With her long vermillion-lacquered nails, she pried the note loose, and slid it into her jeans. Using his mane to pull herself up, she mounted the stallion and rode off into the night.

"You look beautiful," Parvis murmured to her. They were standing on the high-walled terrace outside the bedroom of the guest villa. She was wearing a demure peach silk dress, high-collared, with a row of tiny buttons down the front. The wind blew her hair across her face. Parvis gently pushed it behind her ear. His forefinger traced the delicate folds and curves of her ear, his fingertips felt the fine particles of sand adhering to her skin.

"Let's make love here, under the stars," she whispered, eyeing the thickly cushioned chaise lounge.

He slowly unbuttoned her dress, and pulled it off her shoulders and arms. Her full, round breasts were cupped in two tiny triangles of pale peach silk and creamy lace, held together by thin strips of peach satin. His left hand moved down the length of her body, caressing the curve of her hips, her waist, moving up to her breast, his thumb moving over her silken, erect nipple. Parvis moved his index finger under a delicate satin strap. She felt his hand at the top of her breast. He pushed the strap off her shoulder, and the thin piece of silk rolled off her breast, revealing a dark pink nipple. Parvis moved his mouth toward it. It hardened under the feel of his firm tongue. His kisses were warm, wet, and biting, and her body ached for him. His lips moved away from her nipple, to the soft creamy underside of her breast, as the fingers of his hand slid inside the silk that covered her other breast.

She could feel the warmth of his hand, pressing against the small of her back. He moved his finger deftly, releasing the clasp of her brassiere. The filmy fabric fell to her waist. He cupped her naked breast in his hand. He leaned toward her, holding her against his chest. Then, with one hand supporting her back, he gently pushed her down onto the chaise lounge. She reached out and clasped her arms around his neck.

Her long, stockinged legs wrapped around his body, the heels of her high-heeled sandals indenting the muscles of his back. He reached down and pulled at the last string of silk that encircled her waist. She wore a garter-belt of the same peach silk, and her panties were a mere wisp of peach and cream. He moved his hands down to the slight indentation of her hipbones and ripped the satin strings that held her panties together. They fell to the ground, bits of silk and lace lying on the terracotta-tiled floor.

With the thumb of one hand lying in the valley between her two cheeks, pushing her up toward him, his other hand moving over her breast, he bent over and pushed his sharp, hot tongue into her warm, wet, garden of earthly delights.

Her hands grasped at his salt-and-pepper hair as her body writhed on the slippery fabric of her dress beneath her.

Pieces of fabric still covered parts of her body, like pastel icing on a creamy cake, the peach silk garter-belt straining against the movement of her body as his mouth ate up her sweet sex. She uttered small moans, and her long vermillion nails pressed into his neck. Like a trapped animal her body writhed under his hot breath as he brought her closer and closer to orgasm. He held her tighter as her body stiffened. Then she shuddered again and again.

Parvis slowly lifted her up to him, moving his

hand up and down the long smooth curve of her back, her delicate breasts pressed against his cotton shirt. Her hand slipped between his thighs and through the fabric of his trousers she could feel his hard penis. She undid the zipper of his trousers. Then, with her hands against his shoulders, she pushed away from his chest and moved on top of him. Now she was in control. Parvis was caught in a vise, her thighs pressed tightly against his hips, delving deeper, moving faster, bringing him close to a climax, only to move slower, her body caressing him and her cool finger running up and down the back of his hard, throbbing penis, applying an isolated, excruciating pressure to his enflamed organ. The fingers of her other hand were pressed spread-eagled against his chest, her breasts moved in front of him, tempting, tantalizing, glistening, her swollen hard nipples brushing against his lips with the rhythm of her movements. She was in total control, bringing him to the brink, then ebbing away, then bringing him back, once again to the edge of the abyss. She moved harder, faster, with passionate intensity, synchronizing their movements until she knew they could stand it no longer. He seized her by the waist and thrust himself deeply into her.

Her body crumpled as her head fell against his shoulder, her thick hair spread across his black shirt. Outwardly smiling sweetly, inwardly laughing demonically, she lay still as he caressed her face.

# CHAPTER TWENTY-FOUR

"Fool!" shouted General Vanak, as he slammed his fist on the table.

As Kir brushed a few drops of splattered tea off his shoe, General Vanak berated the servant who had dropped a metal tea tray on the floor of the Conference Room. Tempers were frayed; everyone was becoming increasingly anxious as the time drew nearer.

Kir looked around the conference table at Supreme Command Headquarters. Everyone was present—the six generals permanently stationed on Abu Musa, as well as General Pakdal and Commander Kalvani, both of whom had flown to Abu Musa for the final meeting before the culmination of Project Norouz, only twenty-four hours away.

There was a break in the meeting, and Kir leaned back in his chair and rubbed his tired eyes. The final weeks of preparation for Project Norouz had been extremely hectic. All helicopters, transport aircraft, and arms had been covertly moved into the Gulf area, and now were armed and ready for deployment.

"Gentlemen," General Vanak said. "Today is the twentieth of March; Norouz will soon be upon us. As this is our last meeting before the realization of Project Norouz, I would like to review the mobilization schedule with you. And I shall call on

General Pirayesh, Commander Kalvani, General Pakdal, and Mr. Kir for additional information."

Kir looked at his watch; it was exactly 9:00 a.m.

"Mobilization of aircraft and troops will begin at zero three hundred hours on March 21, exactly eighteen hours from now," General Vanak said. "And only twenty-four hours from now, at zero nine zero seven hours, Project Norouz will be realized."

General Vanak turned to the former head of the Shah's Imperial Iranian Air Force, General Pirayesh. "General Pirayesh, Air Command Coordinator, will discuss the scheduling of the aircraft." General Vanak sat down, giving the floor to General Pirayesh.

General Pirayesh stood up and strode to the head of the table, to a map of the Persian Gulf area and Iran. He stubbed his cigarette out in the ashtray and began speaking.

"In front of you is the timetable of comprehensive scheduling of the aircraft," said General Pirayesh, referring to the folders in front of each of the men.

"With the assistance of Commander Kalvani and General Pakdal, I have arranged the scheduling of the aircraft so that all aircraft will arrive at their designated destinations at 0907 hours, March 21, the exact moment of Norouz. All aircraft will be able to slip into Iran undetected, due to a radar blackout that will be in effect from midnight tonight. I'll give the floor to General Pakdal, who has been arranging this radar blackout."

"Thank you, General Pirayesh," Pakdal said, as he stood up and walked over to the map. "As of midnight tonight, all of the airports in Iran will be closed. As the head of Zurkhaneh is one of the highest-ranking men in Civil Aviation, he has arranged that the airports in the key cities in

Iran—Tabriz, Mashad, Bandar Pahlavi, Kermanshah, Isfahan, Shiraz, Tehran, and Qom—will be suffering from malfunctioning equipment. Teams of Zurkhaneh air traffic controllers and technicians are being dispatched from Tehran to these cities today. All radar facilities, will be totally controlled by our men during the movements of our aircraft into Iran.

"At this moment, Colonel Bahman is in Zahedan with his troops. From Zahedan, his men will be deployed to the farthest key cities. Aircraft to transport these men will be arriving in Zahedan all night.

"The C-5's, one on the ground in Jubail and the other in Dubai, will be loaded with heavy hardware prior to taking off for Zahedan. At Zahedan the C-5's will be troop-loaded with the special border patrol units for Tabriz and Mashad. Once in Tabriz and Mashad, these units will secure the northwestern and northeastern borders, respectively.

"Strike forces for Bandar Pahlavi, Kermanshah, Isfahan, Shiraz, and counterinsurgency rangers assigned to Tehran will be deployed from Zahedan, via the C-130's and various model helicopters that will be arriving tonight from Al-Ain and Dubai. Colonel Bahman will leave with the last unit out of Zahedan; he will go to Isfahan.

"Helicopters from the UAE will be arriving fairly continuously all night at the Makran Plateau. From the Makran Plateau, I will be supervising the pickup and deployment of the strike forces to Tehran and Qom. I shall personally conduct the Qom operation. Immediately upon receiving confirmation of the Qom strike, I will proceed with my mission. Commander Kalvani will now brief you on the Gulf operations." General Pakdal returned to his seat at the conference table.

"Thank you, General Pakdal," Commander Kalvani said, rising to his feet. He walked over to the large, very detailed map of the Persian Gulf area and discussed the combined responsibilities of Admiral Mahmoud and himself for the Gulf region: the securing of Kharg Island, the Abadan refinery, the oil fields of Khuzistan, the Straits of Hormuz, Iran's southwestern border with Iraq, and the major cities of the southern coast of Iran.

"With the exception of our elite strike units in the SeaCobras that will be deployed from Jubail to the Abadan refinery and the oil fields, the majority of my men will be deployed by Wellington hovercraft, and by AH series attack helicopters, some of which will be TOW missile-loaded. You have the specific information listed in front of you, generals.

"Admiral Mahmoud, who is on Kharg Island, will dispatch the hovercraft from Kharg to Kish tonight. Iraqi intelligence has already been alerted that the Islamic Republic of Iran's hovercraft fleet will be beginning night exercises in the Gulf tonight, so they will not view the movements of the hovercraft in the Gulf waters as anything out of the ordinary. The hovercraft will arrive at Kish, be loaded with my commandos, and will depart Kish at 0545 Hours for Kharg Island. Their arrival at Kharg will coincide with the Qom strike at 0907 Hours.

"Now, generals, and Mr. Kir, you must excuse me. I must get back to Dubai. Preparations for the loading of the C-5's have begun." Commander Kalvani gave a sharp salute and walked quickly out of the room.

General Vanak continued the briefing. "We aim to have all cities secured by nightfall tomorrow, and we anticipate announcing our new government tomorrow night. Securing the vital points quickly will be made considerably easier by

462

the fact that no communications will be coming out of Qom. And the final briefing on that I shall leave up to you, Mr. Kir."

"As concerns media coverage of the takeover," Kir said, "my contact in National Islamic Radio and Television in Tehran has informed me that everything is ready to roll with them. NIRT will be televising the Norouz ceremonies, so there will be live, on-the-spot coverage from Qom. Everyone in Iran will be glued to the TV or radio. NIRT will begin televising the Norouz ceremonies from the Madreseh-ye-Fayzeyeh at 7:00 a.m. NIRT headquarters are within the governmental sector of Qom, as you know. When the broadcasting from Qom goes dead, NIRT in Tehran will immediately take over broadcasting to the country. A 'Due to technical difficulties, this program has been interrupted' announcement will be broadcast on the television and radio. Special programming will continue until the curfew is announced. You, generals, will be able to announce your new military government to the people of Iran upon your arrival in Tehran."

"Excellent, Mr. Kir," General Vanak said enthusiastically. "We have come a long way, Mr. Kir, since the day I first formulated the idea of Project Norouz."

"Indeed we have," Kir said. "A brilliant plan, General Vanak, and you will soon be where you rightly belong. As will all the rest of you great generals," Kir said.

"Generals," Kir continued. "As we discussed before, the formal signing of the business contracts will take place immediately after the successful completion of Project Norouz. The nine most important businessmen involved in the project—the heads of Chessman, Hilland Motors, Martin, Agnellone Industries, Kripp Industries,

463

Mitsutanaki, Bening, Hall, and the oil consortium representative—will be arriving in Cairo tonight. Mr. Rowan will be flying to Cairo later today to meet them. The businessmen will arrive on Kish late tonight. They are scheduled to arrive on Abu Musa tomorrow morning at eleven o'clock, to sign the contracts prior to your departure for Tehran."

"Eleven o'clock is fine," General Vanak said.

"Very good," Kir said, smiling. "Then after the final meeting with the businessmen tomorrow, the show is all yours, generals," Kir said, closing his briefcase. "Now that all these months of preparations are drawing to a close, well, frankly, generals, I need a vacation," Kir said.

"Yes, I'm sure you do, Michael," Parvis Gazvini said smiling, knowing that Michael Kir's usefulness was coming to an end.

The wind was howling across the flat, deserted plain on the southeast corner of Kish Island. Mark squinted, protecting his eyes from the sun and gritty wind that blew across the dry ground. A white Range Rover was coming, at about eighty kilometers an hour, across the plain. The car pulled up behind Mark's dusty jeep, and Michael Kir stepped out.

"Hi, Michael," Mark said, walking over to greet Kir. "How did the meeting with the generals go this morning?"

"Fine, Mark. They're all in good spirits, perhaps a little tense, but that is to be expected." Kir looked at his watch. It was a quarter to one. "Sorry to be back so late, but it was a long meeting."

"I can imagine," Mark said. "I'm just glad you got back when you did. I leave for Cairo at 2:00 p.m. I've been busy with the technicians here, running the last minute checks. Everything is in order."

"Come on. I'd like to take a look at the site, one last time," Kir said.

They walked across the sandy ground, cluttered with tall scrub bushes and sharp rocks. The grayish-green, ugly bushes grew thicker as Mark and Kir walked along. They pushed their way through a tangled clump of bushes until they were standing on a large area of freshly packed ground, surrounded by a windscreen of bushes.

Beneath the ground was a group of powerful missile launchers—all loaded. The missiles had been on Kish Island for thirteen years. They had been secretly built for the Shah in 1971 by the Israelis, when they were on Kish Island building the desalinization plant. The Israelis, willing to support the Shah, who had consistently supplied them with oil, agreed to secretly build the missile launches in exchange for continued oil.

The Shah had always been fearful of a coup d'état by his own generals, and he wanted an armed fortress outside of mainland Iran, but within reach of it. The Shah had envisioned a scenario in which, in the case of a coup, he would escape from Tehran and, with his loyal officers, go to Kish. From this island, he would be able to strike back: the whole of Iran was in range of these secret underground missiles. These lethal missiles lay just below the surface of Kish Island, unbeknownst to the Shah's generals, or the rest of the world.

"Everything checked out thoroughly this morning," Mark said. "We'd better get going. My plane leaves for Cairo soon."

They walked toward the cars.

"I'll be back from Cairo with the businessmen at 11:45 p.m.," Mark said.

"Good. After I greet them they can retire for the night," Kir said.

"Ours will just be starting. I'm going to sleep for

465

a couple of hours on the flight to Cairo. Try to get some sleep this afternoon, Michael. You look beat," Mark said.

Kir nodded. "What's the schedule?" he asked.

"After the businessmen and I get back here on Kish, our pilot will refuel, and then turn right around and take off for Zurich immediately. His E.T.A. in Zurich is 7:00 tomorrow morning. He'll make the pickup, and turn around again and fly into Tehran."

Kir and Mark walked back to the cars in silence. Both of them were preoccupied with the events of the next twenty-four hours.

Everything was in readiness: the aircraft, the weaponry, the men, ready to embark on one of the most startling military operations of the twentieth century.

By tomorrow it would be completed.

Michael Kir slept fitfully. Disturbing, tangled dreams plagued him. He dreamt that he was a boy playing backgammon with his grandfather; then he dreamt that he saw Parvis Gazvini making love to Mitra, first in his grandfather's large wooden bed, and then in a tangled mess of mutilated and decomposing bodies floating on top of the salt lake near Qom.

Kir awoke, drenched with perspiration, his heart pounding. The sight of the familiar illuminated clock by his bedside was particularly comforting, as its red numerals flashed the time: 5:00 p.m. He had only slept for three hours and, although he was still groggy, he could feel the adrenalin flowing. All of the planning and preparing, for two years, for Project Norouz was coming to a close—sixteen hours to go.

Kir shaved and showered quickly, and dressed for dinner. Dinner was early, at six-thirty, to give Andreas time to prepare for the party of guests arriving from Cairo at midnight. Also, it would give Kir time for a leisurely dinner with the girls. He wanted the girls safely tucked away in the Crown Prince's villa well before midnight—before the businessmen arrived.

Mark looked out the window of the VIP lounge at Cairo International Airport. He watched as the black Cadillac limousine carrying Mr. David Blake, president of Martin Aircraft, sped across the tarmac, toward the Boeing 707 parked on a distant parking apron. The aircraft was in darkness, only the interior cabin lights were on. On board the aircraft were seven of the nine businessmen who would be returning with Mark to Kish.

Mark watched as the limousine pulled up in front of the 707. The president of Martin Aircraft was the second-to-last man to board.

Mark looked anxiously at his watch, it was nearly 9:00 p.m. He had anticipated taking off from Cairo at nine o'clock so that they could be back in Kish by just after midnight, but he was still waiting for Giovanni Agnellone's plane, which had been delayed by a strike at the Milan airport.

An attractive kohl-eyed hostess approached Mark. "Mr. Rowan, your party will be landing momentarily. Please, come with me," she said, as she escorted Mark down to a special gate that led to the tarmac.

It was a hot steamy night, and Mark unloosened his tie slightly as he watched the green-and-white Learjet 54/55 pull up. The high-pitched whine of the engines faded away as they shut off. The door to the small jet opened and a darkly tanned, silver-haired man hurried down the stairs.

"Mr. Agnellone," Mark said. "Good evening."

"Good evening, Mr. Rowan. I must apologize for the delay. I hope I haven't caused you any inconvenience."

"None whatsoever," Mark said. "This way, Mr. Agnellone." Mark led the way to the waiting limousine.

"Good evening, Lord Wilson . . . Mr. Lowell . . . Mr. Connelly . . ." Kir said, as he greeted the businessmen arriving at the court ministers' complex. Kir shook each man's hand heartily as the group of businessmen entered the high-ceilinged dining room of what had once been the villa of Amir Abbas Hoveyda, Prime Minister of Iran for sixteen years under the Shah, and executed by Khomeini's Revolutionary Council.

"Hello, Mr. Lowell. Nice to have you back on Kish Island. I trust you had a pleasant flight from Cairo?" Kir said.

"Yes, it was a very smooth flight," replied Winthrop Lowell.

Servants carrying silver trays of drinks, canapés, and sandwiches entered the dining room and began circulating among the guests.

Kir took Mark aside. "Did everything go all right?"

"Yes, fine, Michael. As you know, Angellone's plane was late leaving from Milan, but other than that, no problems. The Egyptian officials were very accommodating about our guests. They were whisked away without any customs or formalities."

"Mark, you'd better get up to the Communications Room. Inform the generals of the businessmen's arrival and wait for the call from Ali-Reza. I am expecting confirmation on the takeover of the air traffic control towers of Iran's airports. I'll be up to the Communications Room as soon as I can get away."

Kir milled around the dining room, chatting with the various guests. Jurgen Kripp came up to him.

"My last visit to Kish was most enjoyable. Tell me, Mr. Kir, where are your lovely girls?"

"I sent them shopping to Paris," Kir said. "They were getting a little bored on the island, and I thought some new clothes would cheer them up."

"How long will they be in Paris?" inquired Mr. Kripp.

"A few more days."

"Perhaps I shall stop in Paris on my way back to Germany."

"Fine," Kir replied. "I will tell them to expect you."

"That would be very nice indeed," Kripp said, taking a caviar canapé off a tray as he walked away.

"Gentlemen," Kir said loudly, addressing the cluster of nine businessmen. These nine men, five from the U.S., the others from England, Germany, Italy, and Japan, were the heads of the most important aerospace, munitions, and industrial concerns in the world—companies that would be returning to Iran after the takeover.

"May I have your attention for a moment, please," Kir said. "I will make this as brief as possible. I know you must all be tired, and to say that we have a busy day ahead of us tomorrow would most definitely be an understatement.

"The Norouz ceremony in Qom will be televised on National Islamic Radio and Television tomorrow morning. Via the Shiraz receiver, we can pick up the broadcast, so we will be able to see what the rest of Iran will view of the ceremonies. It will be quite a historic occasion."

A murmur ran through the room.

"Cars will pick you up at 8:30 a.m. to take you to the residence. Breakfast will be served in the screening room, where we will see the Norouz celebrations being broadcast. Later in the morning you will be flown to Abu Musa to sign the

469

contracts.

"For now, I suggest that you avail yourselves of the refreshments we have prepared for you, and then retire for a good night's sleep. The servants will show you to your rooms, and if there is anything you need, just ask them."

Kir took a glass of white wine from the tray of a waiter passing by. "Cheers!" he said to the guests. They all responded to Kir's toast, and he slipped quietly out of the room.

Michael Kir entered the Communications Room. It was 1:20 a.m.

"Hello, Mark," Kir said, taking off his jacket.

Mark turned away from the CCTV screens monitoring the court ministers' villas. A screen showed the empty living room of Hoveyda's villa. The servants were picking up the empty glasses. "So, our guests have gone to bed," Mark said.

"Yes, they have. Tomorrow at 8:30 a.m. they'll be picked up to watch the Qom Norouz ceremonies, in the downstairs screening room. Have you talked to Ali-Reza yet?"

"Yes, at 1:00 a.m. He was still waiting to hear from a couple of airports. He will contact us at 0200 Hours."

Kir nodded.

Mark picked up his notepad. He spoke quickly and succinctly as he briefed Kir on the latest reports in.

"Commander Kalvani is in Dubai supervising the rollout of the C-130's. The last C-130 will take off for the Makran Plateau at 5:00 a.m., but Kalvani will be back on Kish before the hovercraft land. His E.T.A. here is 5:15 a.m., and the hovercraft will be on the beach at 5:30 a.m." Mark walked over to the map with multicolored markers at Dubai, Al-Ain, Jubail, Kish, and Abu

470

Musa, representing the transport and attack aircraft awaiting final mobilization orders.

Kir took a seat near a bank of telephones and crackling radios. "Mark, will you man the radios? It's time to call Singer."

Turning his chair so that he could monitor the CCTV screens of the court ministers' complex, the control tower of the Kish Airport, and the Conference Room on Abu Musa, Kir picked up a scrambler phone and called New York.

"Good afternoon, Walter . . . things are going as scheduled here . . . Yes, very smooth . . . The businessmen arrived at midnight from Cairo . . . The 707 took off for Switzerland immediately upon refueling.

"Walter, how are things going from that end? . . . Good, the pilot's E.T.A. in Zurich is 7:00 a.m. What about security in Zurich? Don't worry about him flying into Iran's airspace. I just received word from Mr. Raissi. A three fighter escort will accompany the 707 once it's over the border into Iran."

Kir put down the receiver. "Walter has arranged everything. Our plane will make the pickup at 7:30 a.m. Now let me call Dubai."

Kir picked up a black phone, a direct line to the palace of the Sheikh of Dubai.

"Michael Kir here. Yes, Your Majesty, very well. Thank you very much, Your Majesty. Yes, I would like to speak to him." Kir paused momentarily. "Hello, sir, yes, everything is going as planned. I understand Commander Kalvani met with you late this afternoon. Transportation to Tehran has been arranged, is that correct? The 707 will be arriving from Switzerland at 1600 hours. Your E.T.A. in Tehran is 1530 hours, correct? Very good, sir. *Khodofez*, may God be with you." Kir hung up the telephone.

Looking out on the pitch-black runway from the control tower cab at Mehrabad Airport, Tehran, Ali-Reza listened to the voice at the other end of the telephone. It was Kermanshah Airport reporting in. The airport had been secured by the team of Zurkhaneh that Ali-Reza had sent in under the pretense of checking the radar equipment at the Kermanshah control tower. The leader of the Kermanshah mission reported that the control tower had been secured without incident.

Ali-Reza put down the receiver. Inside the dimly lit cab of the control tower three Zurkhaneh controllers, hand-picked by Ali-Reza, were hunched over their radar screens, as the phones in the tower continued to ring incessantly.

The Pasdaran guard, bewildered, watched all the activity in the small room. Everything had been normal when he, and the three controllers, had come on duty two hours ago. The guard took a Winston from the package Mr. Raissi had just given him. He lit a cigarette and stopped concerning himself with all the activity in the room. Now that Mr. Raissi, one of the heads of Civil Aviation, had arrived, things would soon be under control, he thought. The Pasdaran guard counted the cigarettes in the package. He wanted them to last his whole shift.

Ali-Reza glanced at the Pasdaran guard in the shadows, leaning against the back wall. The red ember glow from the guard's cigarette punctuated the shadows.

Ali-Reza walked toward the tinted-glass, inwardly slanting windows, and looked out. He watched as the searchlight, coming from the guardhouse tower, moved between the control tower and the chain-link fence that surrounded the highly restricted area of the airport. Ali-Reza knew that there were only two Pasdaran guards out there in the darkness—one in the ground tower, and one patrolling the chain-link fence. Ali-Reza knew that two of his Zurkhaneh were out there in the shadows, and that it was their duty to kill the two guards. Ali-Reza peered out into the black night, then glanced at his watch. It was 1:30 a.m.; his men should be making their moves.

The shrill ringing of a phone nearby broke Ali-Reza's concentration. After the third ring he picked up the phone and handed it to the nearest controller, already occupied on another line. Ali-Reza watched as the searchlight cut a path, back and forth, across the open ground between the control tower and the fence.

Suddenly, the light went out in the guard tower. That was the signal.

Ali-Reza turned and walked toward the shadowed Pasdaran, who was now walking toward the window to see what had happened to the searchlight. Ali-Reza's heartbeat quickened, and the muscles in his body tightened as he walked past the guard, then turned.

Ali-Reza attacked from behind. He grabbed the guard's dark oily hair, and violently yanked the head back. Like ripping paper, the knife held in Ali-Reza's right hand cut through the tautly stretched skin of the guard's throat. There was a small pop as the veins exploded, then the crunch of cartilage collapsing under the sharp knife's edge. As Ali-Reza pulled the knife in an upward motion toward the ear, the jugular vein exploded.

Ali-Reza held on to the head of hair. His senses were finely honed. He was acutely aware of the damp, stringy hair caught in his grip, he could smell the pungent odor of the guard's unwashed hair, he could see the needlelike stubble on his victim's chin and torn neck.

473

The guard's mouth was gaping open, desperately reaching for air. His body jerked spastically, violently. Like air out of a deflating balloon, the dying man's last breath, a blood-clotted wheeze, leaked out of the slash.

Ali-Reza, standing, crooked one telephone with his shoulder as he reached for a second ringing phone. A Zurkhaneh picked it up.

"Mr. Raissi, Qom control tower on the line," said the controller, as he held out the receiver to Ali-Reza.

"Mr. Raissi here. Go ahead, Qom tower."

Ali-Reza lit a cigarette as he listened to the report from the leader of the Zurkhaneh who had taken over the Qom airport. The Qom control tower takeover had been accomplished swiftly and silently. The Qom Zurkhaneh leader explained how he and his seven-man crew of technicians had been working on the so-called malfunctioning equipment in the control tower cab at Qom airport at 0100 hours when they made their move to seize the tower. The three controllers on duty were killed.

"They didn't even know what hit them," said the voice on the other end of the line.

Ali-Reza listened to the head of the Qom operation describe the stationing of guards at the entrance to the Qom control tower. Ali-Reza took a step—he could feel something sticky underneath his foot. He picked up the phone and moved away from the drying pool of blood, stepping over the body of the control towerl guard.

"Keep me posted," Ali-Reza said as he put down the receiver. With this final report in from Qom, all air traffic in Iran was now under Zurkhaneh control. It was 1:35 a.m.

Ali-Reza looked out the window of the control tower cab. A Zurkhaneh reached for one of the ringing phones. Ali-Reza reached for another.

# CHAPTER TWENTY-FIVE

The crescent moon shone high above the Persian Gulf, casting faint light on the choppy black water. A warm breeze carried humid air off the water onto the eastern shores of the Arabian Peninsula. Under the black night—in Al-Ain, Dubai, and Jubail—men were working as if it were the middle of the day, and not three o'clock in the morning.

At the military airfield on the outskirts of the oasis town of Al-Ain, in the United Arab Emirates, the airstrip was alive with activity. The twelve Hercules C-130's were lined up one by one. Forklifts loaded with crates of munitions drove up the rear doors, which opened outward and served as ramps into the bellies of the Hercules transport planes. On the runway, the first C-130 prepared for takeoff, its turboprops revving. Lumbering down the runway, it slowly lifted off and began heading north, toward Zahedan.

On a distant runway at Dubai's airport, out of view of the main terminal, the huge C-5A Galaxy heavy transport plane stood on the ground. Its upward-hinged nose was open, and into the gaping mouth of the cavernous aircraft rolled an M-113 personnel carrier, another lined up behind it. Side panels of the rear fuselage hinged outward, providing additional access to the interior of the gigantic military aircraft, in the process of being loaded with heavy equipment.

On the far side of the Dubai airport, the airfield was crowded with helicopters. CH-47, 214ST, and AH-1J helicopters prepared to take off for Zahedan and the Makran Plateau. As the helicopters ascended into the black sky, heading northward in formation, the noise of engines and the whirring rotor blades filled the air.

In a brighty lit hangar at Jubail, Saudi Arabia's port on the Persian Gulf, drab-green and mustard camouflage-painted SeaCobra helicopters received last minute checks by the flight line crew. Armament technicians checked the weapons systems. Beyond a glass partition at the end of the hangar, a group of former Imperial Iranian Navy officers and pilots were being briefed.

The six Wellington fifty-ton hovercraft cut through the stygian darkness of the Persian Gulf—only the narrow shafts of bright-white light coming from their spotlights marked their paths. The hovercraft had left Persian Gulf Fleet Headquarters, Kharg Island an hour earlier and were heading full speed toward their destination—Kish Island.

Inside Supreme Command Headquarters on Abu Musa, General Vanak paced about the situations room, puffing on a cigarette. Aides scurried back and forth from the radio room, carrying messages received from General Pakdal in Baluchistan, Commander Kalvani in Dubai, and Michael Kir on Kish. General Asman, a glass of tea in his hand, stood talking to Parvis Gazvini as an aide charted the movements of the hovercraft from Kharg Island toward Kish.

A report was brought to the aide standing in front of the map. He picked up a number of plastic markers from Al-Ain and moved them northward, toward Zahedan.

Hundreds of pointed tents dotted the flat fields around the Zahedan airport. Small fires could be seen outside some of the tents.

Standing outside his tent, breathing in the cool mountain air, Colonel Bahman scanned the still-dark sky. He could hear the noise of the approaching Hercules C-130 coming in from Al-Ain. A moment later, he spotted the flashing red lights on the wing-tips of the C-130—the first aircraft to arrive—as it began its descent into Zahedan airport.

Inside Bahman's tent, radio operators hunched over Collins radios, communicating with the nearby Zahedan control tower and with General Pakdal on the Makran Plateau. The tent was filled with the crackle of radio static and short, rapidly spoken phrases.

Colonel Bahman, coordinator of the major cities operation, walked to the next tent. Seated at a table were the leaders of the strike forces for the cities of Shiraz, Isfahan, Kermanshah, Bandar Pahlavi, Tabriz, and Mashad, as well as the commanders of the special border patrols for Iran's northwestern and northeastern frontiers.

"Gentlemen," Colonel Bahman said, addressing the commanders of the strike forces, "it is time to move out."

The officers stood up without speaking. They knew their assignments. They had been waiting five years for this moment and they were ready. Beneath their Baluchi rags were the crisp uniforms of the Immortals.

At 5:00 a.m., the airport on Kish Island was alive with movement. The door to the hangar was open,

477

casting a wide tongue of light onto the tarmac as the AH-1S heavily-armed helicopters were rolled out. Technicians, navy pilots, and crew moved in and out of the service equipment on the flight line.

Mark stood at the fringe of the activity, watching the movement, communicating by walkie-talkie with the Kish control tower, and with Michael Kir in the Communications Room at the residence.

Scanning the skies to the south, Mark saw a pinprick of light in the clear black sky. He followed the light as it approached the helipad. The noise of the helicopter grew louder.

Shading his eyes from the searchlight on the nose of the RH-53, Mark watched as the helicopter settled on the ground. Commander Kalvani climbed out of the helicopter and greeted Mark.

"Everything went smoothly in Dubai. The last C-130 has left for Zahedan, and the first one should have just landed," Commander Kalvani said.

"Commander, the E.T.A. of the hovercraft is 0530 Hours," Mark said.

"Yes, I received word from Admiral Mahmoud at Gulf Fleet Headquarters in Kharg. We'd better get down to the village immediately."

Mark and Kalvani, followed by an aide weighted down with radio equipment, hurried toward the waiting jeep.

On the southwest corner of Kish Island, Mark waited on the beach for the hovercraft. He could hear the sounds of the marine commandos in the Arab village behind him preparing for the arrival of their transports. Mark looked to the north: the sea was calm, but the horrendous noise coming out of the darkness drowned out the gentle lapping of the water. His eyes strained to see the dark hulks moving across the water toward the shore. Mark put his mouth to his walkie-talkie.

"Michael, the Wellingtons are here."

The spotlight of the lead Wellington hovercraft aimed for a brightly lit concrete ramp. Inside the hovercraft cockpit Mark could see a number of figures, but he quickly turned his face away from the blowing sand as the force generated by the giant propellers at the aft of the amphibious craft pushed it up the concrete ramp. Once landed, the downward-hinged door of the hovercraft opened out, forming a loading ramp. Units of battle-dressed marine commandos stood at attention on the beach.

Kalvani was on hand to greet the hovercraft commander. The two men moved to the side of the loading ramp as the marine commandos marched in silent precision into the mouth of the hover-craft.

Mark watched as the ramp to the lead hover-craft was closed. The hovercraft's flexible skirt puffed up and, as the noise of the turbine engines filled the air, the craft slipped down the ramp and into the black water. On board was Commander Kalvani.

The other hovercraft, one by one, pulled up, landed, troop-loaded, and pulled out. The hover-craft moved across the water, traveling in a north-westerly direction toward the head of the Persian Gulf. Their destination: Kharg Island.

A floodlit runway marked out the length of the Makran Plateau. The noise of CH-47's emanated from the darkness. The rotor-wash from the continuous landing of 214 transport choppers, HueyCobra gunships, 212's, and CH-47's on the plateau created a duststorm, diffusing the beams of light cast by the headlights of the forklifts. A steady stream of forklifts, loaded with crates of ammunition and supplies, traveled back and forth from the tunnels to the waiting helicopters.

General Pakdal spoke briefly with the leader of a force of counterinsurgency rangers, as the first CH-47's and AH-1J's took off, bound for Tehran. The force leader, an officer of the Immortals, saluted General Pakdal, then hurried toward the waiting CH-47, loaded with fifty combat-ready Immortals.

The CH-47 took off, followed by another, then another, heading out in a northwesterly direction. They would fly out of Baluchistan, across the Dasht-e-Kavir desert, then west to Tehran.

The first light of dawn was brightening the blue-black sky.

Colonel Bahman stood in the control tower of the Zahedan airport, speaking with Ali-Reza Raissi in Tehran.

"The C-5 for Tabriz just took off," reported Bahman. He watched as the big-bellied C-130 accompanying the C-5 lifted off the runway. Moving out of the holding bay was another C-130. A line of transport planes, fully troop-loaded, stretched across the airfield.

"Runway cleared for takeoff," the controller radioed to the aircraft waiting for the final clearance before departure for Kermanshah.

Colonel Bahman looked at his watch. It was 5:45 a.m. He left the control tower; he wanted to get down to the runway to supervise the final troop-loading of the C-130's designated for Bandar Pahlavi.

A slight wind was blowing in from the Gulf across the island of Abu Musa. The only sound was the Gulf waters against the beach.

The hangar on Abu Musa was buzzing as

General Pirayesh and General Mojat supervised the moving of the six F-4E's out of the brightly lit hangar onto the still-dark airstrip.

Inside Supreme Command Headquarters, the rest of the generals were busy following the deployment of troops from Zahedan and the Makran Plateau to Tehran and Qom.

The course of the Wellington hovercraft was being charted by an aide. He moved the markers in a north-northwesterly direction toward Kharg Island.

An aide brought in a message from the Radio Room. "General Pakdal is preparing to move out ASAP, as soon as possible."

Three hundred armed Immortals in combat uniforms—the Qom strike unit—stood at attention as their commander, General Pakdal, reviewed his troops. The early morning light above the Makran Plateau was a pale yellow-white, contrasting sharply with the dark-purple mountains surrounding the plateau. The noise of waiting helicopters filled the vast open space. Two soldiers stood by the open door of the RH-53 helicopter that would take General Pakdal to Qom.

As General Pakdal walked past the front row of troops, a soldier broke ranks, darted forward, and knelt before Pakdal. He grabbed the General's hand and kissed it, then kissed his boot. "General," the soldier said, overcome with emotion, "I have been waiting five long years for this day."

"We have all been waiting," General Pakdal said. He stepped back and surveyed his troops. Placing his right hand on his breast, his eyes flashing, General Pakdal gave the Immortals' pledge of allegiance.

*"Khoda, Shah, Mihan."* The strong words echoed

throughout the plateau.

The first day of the New Year brought beautiful weather to the city of Qom. The golden dome of the Shrine of Fatima, sister of the Shi'ite saint Imam Reza, glistened as the morning sun rose in the east. The turquoise-and-gold minarets and domes of the seventeenth-century Safavid mosques surrounding the shrine formed a strikingly beautiful tableau against the pink morning sky.

It was 7:30 a.m. National Islamic Radio and Television had been broadcasting from Qom for a half-hour. The television cameras focused in on the Madreseh-ye-Fayzeyeh Square, where the mullahs, all kneeling on individual prayer rugs, facing Mecca, convened for the first prayers of the day. They had not stopped chanting since dawn. As the minutes passed, the chanting increased in fervor. Through the open windows in the residential district of Qom the chanting, increasing in volume, could be heard.

On television screens throughout Iran was the flickering image of a sea of turbaned, black-robed praying mullahs anxiously awaiting the appearance of the Ayatollah Khalaghani. The television cameras focused in on the brilliantly tiled balcony on the Madreseh-ye-Fayzeyeh, from where Ayatollah Khalaghani would conduct the Norouz ceremony.

The six fighter pilots stood at attention, helmets in hand. Behind them, glistening in the early morning sun, was the squadron of Phantom F-4's. On the underwing mountings of each plane, on seven attachments under the wings and fuselage, were M117 bombs, and four Sparrow and four Sidewinder missiles—lethal complements of armaments.

The pilots saluted the generals. The commander of the squadron, General Haji Mojat, stepped forward, and spoke briefly to the five generals who would remain on Abu Musa. Mojat gave a sharp salute, and turned on his heels, leading his men across the tarmac to their waiting F-4 fighters.

General Mojat climbed into his F-4G Wild Weasel, put on his helmet, buckled in, and pulled the canopy down over the cockpit. Mojat gave the thumbs up sign as he started his fighter plane toward the runway.

As the morning sun traveled upward in the sky, General Vanak tugged on his peeked cap. He turned to General Asman. As the high-pitched whine of the F-4's filled the air, a broad smile spread across General Vanak's face.

The pointed nose of a F-4E lifted off the ground as the last of the slek, deadly Phantoms took off northward.

Screeching across the Persian Gulf, they raced over the parched deserts of Iran toward their target.


The noise of the whirring rotor blades was tremendous. Pilots and gunners from the elite unit moved out to their helicopters as the early morning sun cast a path of warm light on the runway at the Jubail airfield.

One by one, the SeaCobras and CH-47's lifted off, flying north toward the Abadan refinery. Other units remained on the ground, awaiting deployment orders to the oil fields of Khuzistan and the Straits of Hormuz.


The C-130 began its descent, having crossed over the snow-capped Alborz Mountains. The harsh, bare slopes of the mountain range gave way to lush, green rolling hills that met the Caspian shore. The C-130 flew west, following the shoreline of the milky, gray-blue waters of the Caspian Sea.

Inside the transport plane, the Immortals, sitting in rows of jump seats, checked their weapons and snapped up their helmets, awaiting final instructions from their commanding officer before touchdown at Bandar Pahlavi, only twenty-seven minutes away.

Michael Kir put his coffee cup down on his desk in the Communications Room.

"Mark," he said, "You'd better get downstairs. It's ten minutes to nine; the businessmen are in the screening room already. They'll wonder what happened to us." Kir watched the closed-circuit monitor that showed the nine businessmen standing around a breakfast buffet table at the back of the screening room, chatting with each other.

Mark stood up from his chair in front of the radios.

"I'm going now, Michael. I'll tell them you have some business to take care of."

"Fine," Kir said. "I'll be down shortly."

Mark shut the door behind him. Kir sat down in front of the bank of television screens. He focused his attention on the live coverage—being broadcast by National Islamic Radio and Television—of the Norouz ceremonies at Qom.

A procession of mullahs, beating their breasts and shouting, *"Allahu Akbar, Allahu Akbar"* in unison, were slowly winding their way down Fatima Boulevard, the main street leading into Madreseh-ye-Fayzeyeh Square. The scene changed to an overview of the square itself.

Kir watched as the mullahs in the Madreseh-ye-

Fayzeyeh Square prostrated themselves, their chanting increasing in intensity.

The NIRT television cameras focused on the empty balcony of the Madreseh. Suddenly, a black-turbaned figure, short and bearded, appeared on the balcony. Ayatollah Hassan-Ali Khalaghani, the head of the Third Islamic Republic of Iran, raised his hands to the multitude in the square below. The crowd of mullahs roared.

Kir turned his attention to the other television screen. The generals were standing around the television screen at Supreme Command Headquarters in Abu Musa. They, too, were intently watching the Norouz ceremonies at Madreseh-ye-Fayzeyeh in Qom.

It was zero-nine-zero-one. The Ayatollah Khalaghani raised his hands in the air, his eyes closed and his face turned heavenwards. He was surrounded on the balcony by a flock of mullahs, the ruling elite of the Third Islamic Republic of Iran.

"In this New Year of 1363, Islam will be even stronger, the nation of Islam will be stronger." The Ayatollah's voice increased in pitch. "The cancerous growths calling themselves Iranians and true Moslems who are against the rule of Islam, our Islam, the only true Islam, shall be punished." The Ayatollah's voice was reaching a frenzied pitch. "They shall be rooted out and destroyed, until, in this New Year, there will not be one left to corrupt this earth. We are victorious! *Allahu Akbar!*"

"*Allahu Akbar, Allahu Akbar!*" came the deafening cry from the courtyard of the Madreseh-ye-Fayzeyeh.

Over the jagged Kuh-i-Alia mountains just south of Qom, the needle-nosed squadron of Phantom

F-4's was fast approaching its target. Their high-pitched screams cut through the thin air.

Inside the cockpit of the lead Phantom, General Mojat glanced at the two silver fighters on his left wing, then at the two on the right. Behind him, in the slot position, was the sixth fighter.

General Mojat operated the TISEO, the target identification system. The vidicon TV camera's zoom lens moved in on positive visual identification of the ground target; Madreseh-ye-Fayzeyeh.

General Mojat's voice crackled across the radios of the five other Phantoms. "Target in sight."

The red digital readout flashed the time: 0905:45 . . . 46 . . . 47 . . .

At zero-nine-zero-six, Kir began counting down. His eyes never left the television screen.

"*Allahu Akbar*," shouted the Ayatollah Khalaghani.

At zero nine zero six and twenty seconds, Ayatollah Khalaghani stretched his arms out and up, indicating to the clergymen gathered in the square below him to rise from their kneeling positions. There was a rustling of black robes as the mullahs rose to their feet.

At exactly zero-nine-zero-seven and five seconds, the screen showing the televised Norouz celebrations from Qom went blank.

Within thirty seconds, a voice announced that there were technical difficulties with the transmission from Qom. A knotted length of film footage, the symbol NIRT that was always televised during programming difficulties, flashed on the screen. A few seconds later, a "Due to technical difficulties, broadcasting has been interrupted; please stay tuned" announcement appeared on the screen.

"Mission completed," came the terse message from General Haji Mojat to Supreme Command Headquarters in Abu Musa. "Am continuing to home base—Mehrabad."

The squadron of F-4's flew northward, toward Tehran.

Michael Kir focused his attention on the closed-circuit monitor that showed the Conference Room on Abu Musa. The generals were all standing in front of the blank television screen. An aide from the radio room walked into the situations room. The generals started shaking hands with each other. Their faces were portraits of frenetic joy.

At nine-zero-eight and thirty seconds, Michael Kir slid open the small rectangular door covering the electronic control panel beneath the television screens. Simultaneously, on the southeast sector of Kish Island, the earth slowly erupted. The double metal doors that had been camouflaged by earth and shrubs opened outward. The heads of two Chukar-R missiles emerged above the sandy soil.

"Missiles Surfaced," read the bright green letters on the control panel.

The missiles rotated into position. Their tapered gray heads now pointed in a south-southeasterly direction.

In the Communications Room, Michael Kir read the data racing across the control panel. "Target Checked."

"Kir pressed the black countdown button.

"10," the orange number flashed on the screen.

"9, 8," the numbers appeared and vanished with lightning speed.

"2, 1."

Michael Kir pushed the red firing button.

At 9:10 A.M., the television screen showing Abu Musa went dead. Every structure and every person on Abu Musa had been blown away.

# CHAPTER TWENTY-SIX

Ali-Reza looked at the clock on the wall in the cab of the air traffic control tower at Mehrabad. It was 9:25 a.m. Ali-Reza leaned over the radar screen. The blips on the radar screen moved closer and closer.

Ali-Reza adjusted his headset and spoke to the rapidly approaching F-4's. "IFF," he said.

The loud crackle of static made the reply unintelligible.

"Identify friend or foe," Ali-Reza repeated.

"Friend," came the reply. "Qom strike mission accomplished."

A few minutes later Ali-Reza and six armed Zurkhaneh stood on the runway at Mehrabad airport, watching the squadron of six F-4's land.

As the pilots climbed out of the cockpits, Ali-Reza walked over to the squadron commander, General Mojat, and congratulated him.

Moments later Ali-Reza and the Zurkhaneh escorted the fighter pilots toward a nearby hangar. At the entrance to the hangar, Ali-Reza ushered the pilots inside. He nodded to his Zurkhaneh, and walked away.

The sound of automatic-weapons fire echoed from inside the hangar.

At 10:30 a.m., Michael Kir entered the screening room. The blank television at the far end of the room was still on. The businessmen were sitting in comfortable armchairs drinking coffee and talking with each other. As Michael Kir made his way through the room, he was greeted with hearty congratulations from all the businessmen.

"Well, I guess we'll be leaving soon to go to Abu Musa and see the generals," John Watkins said.

Kir took a sip of his black coffee.

"I just spoke with the generals, and I'm afraid there's been a little change of plans. The contract signing will be done in Tehran, not on Abu Musa," Kir said.

"Why the change, Mike?" Burt Connelly asked.

"The generals were speaking with Pakdal, and it was decided that it is best to introduce the new military government immediately. They feel that it is necessary to project a strong image of authority to the people of Iran as soon as possible. The generals have already left for Tehran."

"I see," Burt said. "Well, when will we be signing the contracts with the generals? As soon as the situation stabilizes?"

"Actually, gentlemen," Kir said, looking straight at the group of men, "it will be this afternoon. The plane is waiting to take you to Tehran."

A silence momentarily fell over the room.

"This is preposterous, absolutely preposterous," Lord Wilson said, standing up. "Mr. Kir, you are mad if you think I am going to risk my neck going to Tehran to sign the contracts this very day." Lord Wilson, his face florid, jabbed his finger at Kir. "The generals can bloody well come here."

"I agree," said Jurgen Kripp. "I don't think this would be the right time for us to go to Tehran."

"That goes for me, too, Mike," Burt Connelly said. "Last revolution in Iran, I got out by the skin of my teeth. I don't want to risk it again."

"After what has just occurred, I'm sure the situation in Tehran is very unstable, to say the least," John Watkins said.

"I agree," said Giovanni Agnellone.

"Gentlemen, gentlemen," Kir said, raising his voice above the dissenting voices of the businessmen. "I can assure you that the situation in Tehran is completely safe. The whole country is securely in our hands. I just spoke with Commander Kalvani and General Pakdal before I joined you. Commander Kalvani experienced no opposition from the Iranian Navy. Admiral Mahmoud came over to our side; he and Commander Kalvani have secured the Persian Gulf area. General Pakdal's troops are in control of Qom, and his strike forces in the major Iranian cities of Tabriz, Mashad, Bandar Pahlavi, Kermanshah, Isfahan, Shiraz and, of course, Tehran, have secured the airports, radio and television stations—and have overpowered the Revolutionary Guard garrisons."

"Congratulations, Mr. Kir," said Jurgen Kripp, "but that is all beside the point. There has just been a chance of government in Iran. I do not think it would be a prudent move for us to go to Tehran at this time."

"Gentlemen, there has been a coup d'état, but the generals are in complete control of Iran. And they are very anxious to complete the contracts with you today.

"I think it would be wise of you to reconsider. The terms and conditions of the contracts that you have agreed upon with the generals are extremely advantageous to your corporations. Speaking more frankly, gentlemen, you have a lot at stake and I suggest—very strongly—that you reconsider," Kir said.

Kir paused a moment, letting his words sink in. "If you go to Tehran today, it would be a show of good faith to the generals. Security for your visit will be extremely tight. You are as important to the generals as the generals are to you."

Kir looked around the room for a reaction.

John Watkins spoke up. "All right, Mr. Kir. Let's just make this jaunt to Tehran short and sweet," he said grudgingly.

"You'll be out of Tehran by late afternoon," Kir said.

"Well, then you can count me in, too," Burt Connelly said. "Business is business."

"Since you've assured us that security will be provided, then all right, I'll attend," Lord Wilson acquiesced.

The other men voiced their concurrences.

"Fine. Shall we go, gentlemen?" Kir ushered the men out the door of the screening room. "The cars are waiting to take you to the airport."

Manuela stood in front of the steam-beaded bathroom mirror. Taking a damp bathtowel from the marble countertop she wiped the mirror clear. Manuela, her face flushed, her shiny black hair in wispy tendrils around her face, stared into the mirror. It was all over—or soon it would be, she thought; Michael should be here very soon to tell me that Parvis is dead. Manuela smiled. Soon it would all be over. She would be free.

Manuela selected a long jungle-print silk *pareo* and tied it just above her breasts. The rich browns and rusts of the gold-flecked material complimented her gleaming bronzed skin. Manuela reached for her hairbrush and slowly, methodically, brushed her hair. Holding her thick mane of hair in a knot at the nape of her neck, she reached for a long swatch of burnt-orange fabric, which she began to wind around her head, slowly building up the layers until she had created a turban. Manuela opened a brass box full of hair ornaments and selected a shiny object. She carefully positioned it in the folds of the material, securing the turban in place.

Manuela assessed herself in the mirror: the provocative silk *pareo*, the smokey line of kohl around her eyes, her gleaming sensual red lips. Dark tendrils of hair, peeking out from the richly-colored burnt-orange fabric, framed her face. She carefully adjusted the ornate silver decoration adorning the exotic turban. She wanted to look just right for Michael Kir.

Manuela walked into the living room of her villa. She glanced through the open door to her bedroom, past her still-unmade bed, to the swaying palm trees outside the patio, to the choppy, blue Gulf water. She prayed that all had gone according to schedule with Project Norouz thus far.

Manuela reached for a cigarette from the bar, then sat down in a beige leather chair. She waited for Michael to come in. She knew he would tell her everything, especially the thing she wanted to hear most.

Michael Kir hurried down the flower-lined pathway to Manuela's villa. His body was pumping adrenalin furiously, and he was filled by a sense of elation. He was flushed with the surge of power that had come from his victories. Kir mentally reviewed the hours to follow. He would not have much time at Manuela's villa, but he had promised her that he would personally bring the news of Parvis to her. He knew just how important it was to her.

Kir knocked, lightly but rapidly, on the door to the villa, and then opened the door.

Kir saw her. It was like that first time in Rio—she was so breathtakingly beautiful. Her eyes looked into his, begging for the answer.

Kir approached her. "He's dead, Manuela. Parvis is dead."

Slowly, she stood up. Manuela touched Kir's arm with her ice-cold hand.

"Thank God," she said. Moving closer to him, she embraced him. "Thank God, it's over, it's over," she murmured as she pressed her body against his. She could hear the pounding of Michael's heart, feel his rapid breath on her cheek.

"How did it happen? Tell me," she said.

"It happened exactly as I had said it would. Parvis' helicopter was the last to take off from Abu Musa; all the other generals had already left for Tehran," Kir recounted his well-rehearsed fabrication. Parvis truly was dead, but there was no way he could have let anyone, even Manuela, be privy to the secret double-cross.

"Parvis's flight plan was over the port of Chahbahar. Twenty minutes into the flight, our men, planted at the Chahbahar naval base, radioed that they had sighted Parvis's aircraft. They reported that his aircraft exploded above the hills behind the naval base at 9:50 this morning. They went to the crash site to investigate. There were no survivors.

"Parvis is dead, Manuela," said Kir, looking into Manuela's eyes. "Dead. You are free."

"My God," Manuela said, holding Kir tighter, pressing her cheek against his. Her lips traced a line along his cheekbone, down his cheek. She pressed her pelvis against his.

"Darling," she said, whispering in his ear, "I have some champagne in the bedroom. Let's celebrate." She felt his hesitancy and added, "Just for a few moments. Please."

Manuela moved her lips to his, her tongue explored his mouth, her lips ensnared him.

Michael Kir, aroused by his successes, was engulfed by Manuela's overwhelming passion. He reciprocated the intensity of her enflamed desire, enveloping her with his kisses. Half-intoxicated with excitement, he allowed Manuela to lead him to her bed.

Manuela undid the buttons of his cotton shirt with one hand as her other hand groped for the zipper of his khaki pants. Across the room, the champagne bottle lay untouched in the silver bucket.

Manuela pushed Michael back on the bed. She bent forward, and their lips met in a crushing embrace. As she writhed against him Kir pulled the *pareo* from her body. The rush of the cold silk as it slid away from her body and across his, the contact of Manuela's velvety skin against his, was electrifying.

Kir reached for her. With his hands at the nape of her neck he gently pulled her down to him.

Manuela kissed him hungrily. She could feel his hard penis pressed against her. She moved herself up against it—retreating, advancing—feeling his explosive energy. She could feel his hand moving to her hair, to her turban, to undo it, release it. She pulled back sharply, and mounted him.

Kir moaned with pleasure. Manuela continued to ride him; first inclining slightly toward him, then arching back. Her frenzy increased. With one swift pull, she unleased her luxurient hair from the turban. She slowed her movement atop Kir, rocking gently back and forth.

Kir's penis throbbed inside Manuela as he teetered on the brink of orgasm. He closed his eyes in ecstasy. He could feel her move toward him; he could feel her hair graze his cheek, envelope him. He savored the moment, inhaling the scent of her perfumed hair. The smell! His hot, coursing blood froze.

He opened his eyes and saw the metallic gleam. The razor-sharp blade flashed downward, and he felt a sharp but strangely painless shock as the knife bit into his chest.

Manuela jerked violently into the air, then collapsed across him. Kir grabbed for her, instinctively. A warm pulpy mass met his grip. He pulled his hand away, staring in horror at the crimson stream of blood flowing toward his elbow. He could feel the warm, sickeningly sticky blood dripping onto his body. He pushed Manuela off him, and she fell beside him. His hand reached for Manuela's neck, feeling for the carotid. There was no pulse.

Then he saw the steely-gray barrel of the Beretta pushing back the diaphanous white curtain of the glass terrace door. Kir could see a feminine form, a flash of blond hair. Victoria emerged, and stood at the threshold to the bedroom. Kir jumped up.

He moved to rush to Victoria, but his body was frozen. Images of the razor-edged blade flashed before him. He looked back at the bed—at Manuela, her beautiful body now grotesquely contorted by death. A smooth-edged creeping medallion of blood spread outward from beneath her body. The shiny knife on the carpet caught Kir's eye. He stooped to pick up the slender object. It was a scalpel—Manuela's scalpel. A chill shook Kir's crouching body. Kir turned the instrument over in his hand, examining the ornate handle. He imagined the methodical handiwork that had gone into disguising the scalpel's handle, to make it appear to be only a hair ornament.

For the first time he felt the pain. He touched his fingers to the raw edges of the fresh wound on his chest. He looked down, and saw the drying coagulated blood.

His gaze continued downward, across the cream

carpet. He saw the pink polished toenails, the golden tanned legs. His eyes moved upward, to Victoria's face. She picked a white bathtowel up off the floor.

"Here, Michael," Victoria said, handing him the towel. "Get up. We really must go. The businessmen are waiting for you at the airport."

Michael stood up and slowly wrapped the towel around his naked body.

Victoria went to the bed and covered Manuela's lifeless body with a sheet.

"Why?" Kir asked, his eyes taking in the scalpel, his wound, the corpse, and the gun still in Victoria's hand. "How did you know, Victoria?"

"Manuela was a mole, Michael. Parvis's spy. The night Parvis first visited Kish, she went to him as Manuela."

"But, Manuela," said Kir, bewildered.

"Parvis never recognized her, never knew she was Mitra Tabrizi. To him, she was only Manuela, a whore. I believe she went to Parvis that night to kill him, but when he offered her the chance to become his spy, she decided to play both of you off against each other. She couldn't take any chances. She feared that you might not keep your promise to kill Parvis—or that Parvis might not get the opportunity to kill you, as he intended to do after Norouz.

"Manuela understood enough about Project Norouz—and knew both you and Parvis well enough—to know that one of you would kill the other. She would kill the survivor. Manuela wanted to destroy the two men she felt had destroyed her. Only then would she be free."

Victoria looked back at the bed, at the human form outlined by the sheet. "Manuela was a tragic, tormented creature. Now there is no more hurting. Her pain is over," Victoria said.

Kir, his voice numb, asked, "How did you know all this Victoria?"

"It was my job to know. I did not work only for you, Michael. I work for Walter Singer—I was his eyes on the island. Nothing could go wrong with the plan."

Kir stood on the tarmac at the Kish Island airport. Mark and Victoria stood beside him. The last businessman boarded the Falcon 50 jet.

A light, warm breeze blew across the nearly deserted airstrip. No one spoke as a service truck pulled up by the cargo door. The black plastic body bag on the stretcher was lifted into the cargo hold of the aircraft.

"We'd better get going, Michael," Mark said softly.

Kir, jolted out of his daze, replied quickly. "Yes, Mark, of course. Let's get going."

"Goodbye, Victoria," Mark said as he walked toward the plane. He carried a large aluminum photographer's case in his hand.

Victoria turned to Kir. "Walter Singer has arranged for for a private plane to come this afternoon to take me to New York. We'll•refuel in Rome. If you want . . ."

"No," Kir replied. "A plane is flying in from Dubai this afternoon. It was supposed to pick up all three of you. Now it will carry only Gabriella." Kir thought of how it had all been planned—and now the painful reality. Manuela was dead, her anguished life over, her body being taken back to Tehran, to be buried in her homeland. It was all over.

Kir saw Mark standing in the doorway of the plane. Kir knew they were waiting for him. He looked at Victoria. The wind blew a swirl of fine sand across the tarmac. Victoria stood staring straight ahead. She raised her hand and brushed a strand of hair, a grain of sand, out of her eye.

She turned to Kir and said, "Goodbye, Michael. I know we will meet again."

# CHAPTER TWENTY-SEVEN

The early afternoon sun was high overhead as Ali-Reza waited on the tarmac at Tehran's Mehrabad Airport. He watched the wheels of the Falcon 50 touch down on the runway.

Heavily armed guards moved into position as the aircraft taxied up. The jet came to a halt in front of Ali-Reza and the guards. Michael Kir opened the door of the plane, and Ali-Reza walked forward to greet Kir.

Ali-Reza and Kir, followed by the businessmen and Mark, descended the stairs. A cordon of armed Zurkhaneh guarded the area between the plane and the waiting helicopter.

"Where are we going?" Burt Connelly shouted to Kir as the group headed toward the helicopter.

"The *Majlis*, the Senate."

The 214ST lifted off and headed into the city. Ali-Reza and Kir were sitting in the first row of seats of the seventeen-passenger helicopter.

"A nation-wide twenty-four-hour curfew was announced on television and radio at one o'clock," Ali-Reza said.

Kir looked at his watch. It was 2:15 p.m.

"The streets should be clear by now," Kir said.

"They are, for the most part, throughout the country. I spoke with General Pakdal shortly before your arrival. Qom is well-secured. Pakdal is already on his way to Tehran. So is Kalvani, from Abadan.

"The latest information is that Mashad is calm; the Zurkhaneh seized control there easily. Pakdal's special border patrol units have spread across the northeastern and northwestern borders. The latest report from Kermanshad is that there is still sporadic fighting at the Revolutionary Guard garrison in the northeastern sector of the city, but the commanding officer in Kermanshah says it is diminishing, and that the city should be relatively calm by nightfall."

Kir nodded. He looked down out of the helicopter window. Tehran looked deserted. The streets were devoid of people. There was no traffic except for a few armed personnel carriers traveling along Mossadeq Avenue. Tanks were stationed at the major intersections and *meydunehs*, squares. An occasional ambulance could be seen traveling along the wide tree-lined avenues. The shadow of the helicopter passed across the roof of the Intercontinental Hotel, in the center of Tehran, as the 214ST headed toward the heart of the city.

"The Zurkhaneh were largely responsible for securing this sector of Tehran," Ali-Reza explained. "We met with little resistance."

The helicopter flew over Meyduneh Ferdowsi. Armed personnel carriers and tanks blocked the arteries leading into the large square. "There were some incidents in this area," Ali-Reza said. "Lavizan Base sent down some reinforcements."

"Mr. Raissi," said the pilot. "Mehrabad control tower."

Ali-Reza picked up his headset and listened to the radio communication.

"Word just came in from the 707 pilot," Ali-Reza said to Kir. "He has just crossed over the northwest border. He is over Lake Rezaiyeh. He radioed in that he has spotted his escort of three F-4's. Our man is on board; E.T.A. at Mehrabad is 1600 Hours." Ali-Reza smiled at Kir.

The 214ST approached the Majlis. Hovering above the former Senate building were three Cobra gunships.

The 214ST landed right in front of the Majlis. A high wall, mounted by armed guards, surrounded the white, modern building. Chieftain tanks encircled the wall, and protected the gates. As soon as Mark, Kir, and the businessmen got out of the helicopter, it took off and headed back toward Mehrabad.

Kir led the way down the marble corridor of the Majlis to a Senate office, a small room with a number of straightback chairs, a desk at the front of the room, and a television in one corner.

"Gentlemen, in here, please." Kir said, ushering them in the door. "Take a seat, please."

The businessmen took their seats in the first row of the wooden chairs. Mark, still carrying the aluminum case, walked to the back of the room.

Kir stood behind the desk in the center of the room. He snapped open his briefcase and took out nine marked manila envelopes. Kir gave an envelope to each of the men before him.

"If you please, gentlemen, open the envelopes and review the contents," Kir told the group.

Within three minutes, foreheads began to furrow. After five minutes, there were definite looks of consternation on the businessmen's faces. After ten silent minutes, the businessmen began conferring with each other.

"Hey, John," Burt Connelly whispered to John Watkins, sitting to his right. "Is the Bening contract different than it was supposed to be?"

502

"Quite different. How about yours?"

"Mine, too." Burt looked around the room and saw similar hushed conversations taking place all up and down the room.

"Hey, Mike," Burt said loudly. "What the hell is going on here? There has been some kind of screw up."

"There sure as hell has been," said John Watkins, shaking his contract in the air.

Emboldened, others found their voices.

Mr. Ozawa of Mitsutanaki spoke out. "Mr. Kir, there has been some mistake. These are not the terms that my colleagues and I agreed on with the generals."

"Just what the fuck is going on here?" Burt said, standing up.

"That's what I would like to know," said Dick Smith, the president of Chessman.

"So would I," said Winthrop Lowell, the oil consortium representative.

"Gentlemen," Kir said, raising his voice above the din in the room. "A coup d'état occurred this morning. It has been successful and the new government will be installed within the hour. However, some other events have also occurred which I would like you all to be aware of. This film footage should make things clear." Kir pulled down a projection screen. He opened his briefcase and pulled out a cassette; it was the one Mark had given him that morning in the Falcon cockpit. Kir walked over to the video-cassette machine that had ben set up in the back of the room. Mark turned off the lights.

An aerial view of Abu Musa came into view.

"I trust you all recognize the island," Kir said.

The large warehouse, Supreme Command Headquarters, could be seen from the air. "This film was taken at 8:45 this morning," Kir said. He then turned the video-cassette player off.

"And this is Abu Musa at 9:30 this morning," Kir said, as he started the machine again.

The men in the room gasped as they continued to stare at the screen. The camera showed the smoking remains of what had been Abu Musa, slowly circling in closer to what had been Supreme Command Headquarters, now reduced to a pile of rubble. The warehouse and military installation had been totally obliterated. The images became smaller and more distant until Abu Musa was a mere speck of the Persian Gulf.

"Oh my God," exclaimed a voice in the first row. "What went wrong?"

The lights went on in the small Senate office. Kir walked to the front of the room.

"Nothing went wrong," Kir stated flatly. "Gentlemen, for the good of Iran, and for the good of the world, this had to happen. The generals are dead. The generals' plan was to topple the Islamic Republic, and establish a military dictatorship—pro-West, but still a military dictatorship. 'Fine,' you all said. 'Anything is better than letting Iran—and her oil—lie in ruins in the hands of the mullahs.' And, gentlemen, to a certain extent, you were right. You reasoned, 'Better in the hands of a military government than a fanatical Islamic one.'

"You knew that a hard-line military government by the generals would bring Iran back up to the level of oil production and prosperity it enjoyed during the 1970s. And you knew that with the oil revenues, the Generals would buy your fighter planes, helicopters, tanks, and weapons in quantities equal to or even exceeding the Shah's purchases. Frankly, gentlemen, I must congratulate you on your pragmatic attitudes."

Kir looked around the room. A stunned silence had fallen over the businessmen.

"But a military government would have been a dictatorship, a corrupt dictatorship, which quickly would have become more hated than either of the old regimes—the Shah's, or that of the Ayatollahs . The generals were power-hungry, self-seeking men; they were one of the main reasons Iran fell in 1979. They had not learned their lesson. Under the Generals, Iran would have exchanged the yoke of religious fanaticism for the yoke of militarism. Under the generals, Iran would soon fall again, perhaps into more dangerous hands—to the Russians. I'm sure you all agree, Iran is too important—strategically and economically—for us to allow that to happen.

"Yes, gentlemen, there has been a coup d'état, but one different than you anticipated. The nucleus of the new government is already formed. You will meet the new government shortly."

John Watkins stood up. "Why shouldn't we tear these rags up?" he said loudly, shaking his contract in the air. "We don't have anything to lose, because, Mr. Kir, if we withdrew our support now, what is going to keep your new government, whatever the hell it is, standing? We don't need you, Kir, but you sure as hell need us."

In a calm voice, Kir continued. "Let me assure you all that the new government wants your presence in Iran. We want your goods, your technology, and your expertise. The government is fully aware that it desperately needs the goods and services that your firms can supply to revitalize Iran's economy. But I am afraid that this government will not offer you the same golden contracts that the generals did: exclusive rights, ten-year automatically renewable contracts, cost-plus increases, nor the staggeringly high profit percentages, and whatever you want whenever you want.

"I suggest that you review the contracts we are offering you. The privileges and financial conditions set forth in the contracts you are holding are not as favorable to you as those in the contracts you had with the generals. But they are still excellent, and certainly more than competitive by today's market standards."

Lord Wilson stood up. "This contract, Mr. Kir, I consider pure bunk. Hilland Motors' contract was with the generals, and therefore I consider this contract null and void." The industrialist held his contract in his two hands and began to rip it in half.

"Don't do that," Kir said sharply. "If I were you, I would not do that," he warned.

Winthrop Lowell stood up and addressed Kir. "I supported this operation with certain returns expected. I don't have to tell you, Kir, that the oil consortium carries a lot of weight with the U.S. government. We will break you, Kir. Without the support of the U.S. government, you and your goddamn mystery government will be dead."

Before the other men in the room had a chance to dissent, Kir spoke again. "Perhaps you should not be so hasty in your decisions, gentlemen," said Kir, his voice icy.

Mark opened his aluminum case and out a couple of cassettes.

"There is one more thing I think that I should show you," Kir said.

The room went black.

A pair of cellulite-rippled hairy buttocks filled the screen. The camera zeroed in on a small half-flaccid penis, surrounded by the mossy-gray pubic hair of the great English Lord, moving slowly in and out of a golden-haired pussy. The scene changed to a shot of a pair of spread male thighs; a woman pushed her long chestnut hair out of the

506

way, a look of disdain on her beautiful face as she expertly tongued the hanging balls of the head of Mitsutanaki. The scene changed; a naked black-haired beauty was sucking the president of Chessman's cock while he ordered her to shove her fingers up his asshole; first one, then two, then three fingers disappeared. The film was in color, and the voluptuous darkly-tanned body of the girl contrasted with the pasty-skinned man she was servicing.

The cries of the chairman of Agnellone Industries grew louder as the beautiful blond's mouth encircled his short penis while she pulled at his nipples. The scene changed. Jurgen Kripp moaned as the black-corseted woman pulled the nylon stocking tied around his penis even tighter. The scene changed again, and the powerful and influential oil consortium representative recognized himself and another member of the consortium as two of the players in the cast of naked bodies writhing on the floor.

"Lights," Kir said.

Kir walked to the front of the room. "Not the prettiest movie I have ever seen," Kir said, his voice cold and hard. "We took some of the best clippings from hundreds of meters of videotape of your activities. Naturally, there are copies of this film in safekeeping elsewhere. I am sure that you gentlemen are as anxious as I am to keep these films our little secret."

There was a stunned silence in the room.

"I suggest that you look over the contracts again and reconsider," Kir said.

"Why . . . why . . . this is blackmail!" sputtered Lord Wilson.

"Yes," Kir replied.

Hesitantly, Burt Connelly opened his briefcase and pulled out his calculator. He began to study the contract again.

Pen in one hand, contract in the other, calculator propped on his knees, each of the businessmen began to figure out exactly how much he would be losing on the new contract, as opposed to the one with the generals. Within a few minutes, voices began to buzz.

It was still dark in New York City. East 75th Street was wet; the Department of Sanitation's street-cleaning truck had just traveled over it. Joseph Sullivan's black limousine pulled up in front of Walter Singer's townhouse.

The predawn telephone call from Walter Singer had puzzled Sullivan. Singer had asked him to come over immediately to discuss the latest developments in Iran. Sullivan wondered what news Walter Singer could have on events in Iran that he himself would not have received first.

Sullivan hurried up the stairs of the brownstone. Walter Singer greeted Sullivan in the entrance hall, and ushered him into the richly-paneled study.

Sullivan took a seat in a wing-back chair.

"Coffee, Senator?" Singer asked.

Sullivan declined. He was anxious to find out what Singer knew. "So, Walter, you've heard the reports about the coup in Iran?"

"Yes, I have," replied Singer, standing in front of the fireplace. "And the new government of Iran has asked me to deliver a message to you."

Joseph Sullivan was stunned speechless. What contacts does Singer have with the generals, Sullivan wondered anxiously. Sullivan could feel his heart start to pound.

"First, Senator, I think I should explain that there has been a slight change of plans concerning Project Norouz," Singer said.

Sullivan's mouth dropped. How did Walter Singer know the code name of this most classified . . . Sullivan's mind was reeling, as he tried to take in the implications of Singer's statement.

"The change is this," Singer continued. "Abu Musa was bombed. The generals were all killed."

"What?" Sullivan said, his face white. "What the hell happened?"

"At 9:10 a.m., Kish time, missiles were deployed from Kish Island. Their target was Abu Musa; Supreme Command Headquarters was destroyed."

"Singer, what the hell is going on here? Who is behind this?" Sullivan asked, his voice trembling, unable to comprehend what had happened. "Who's behind this?"

"The new government of Iran," Singer replied calmly.

"Who is that?" Sullivan asked, raising his voice.

"Michael Kir has informed me that, within the hour, a full cabinet will be announced from the Senate building in Tehran."

"Well, that is just too damn bad," Sullivan said, spitting out the words. "It is the generals or no deal, and you can tell that goddamn traitor Kir that."

"Perhaps you'll reconsider that statement, Joe," Singer said.

Singer took a cassette laying on the table and inserted it in a video machine. He walked over to the television across from Sullivan and turned it on; then the he pressed down the button on the video machine. He only let it run a minute; from the look on Joseph Sullivan's face, Singer knew that Sullivan had seen enough.

In a room at the Majlis, the businessmen were poring over their contracts, talking with one another.

"Hall Helicopter Industries would be losing about twelve percent under this new contract," Burt Connelly said.

"Really?" said Dick Smith. "Chessman would only be losing ten point five percent."

"That's exactly what we would be losing," said Jurgen Kripp.

"This contract isn't quite as bad as I thought it was at first," Lord Wilson said. With a flourish, he pulled a Dunhill fountain pen from his jacket pocket and signed the contract. Within twenty minutes, all of the businessmen had signed their contracts.

Two helicopters landed outside the Majlis. A crowd of Zurkhaneh guards surrounded the men climbing out of each helicopter. NIRT camera crews followed them into the Senate building.

In the small Senate office, Michael Kir picked up the signed contracts and put them in his briefcase. He looked at his watch.

"I'm sure, gentlemen, you are all interested in seeing the announcement of the new government," Kir said. He turned on the television at the front of the room. "This is being televised live, only a few hundred meters from you—from the Senate Chamber," Kir said.

The television cameras focused on the Iranian flag in the front of the Senate Chamber. A tall, distinguished-looking man, followed by six armed guards, entered the Senate Chamber. A tall man went up to the podium. The cameras focused in on the face of Shapour Bakhtiar.

"Today, Iran took the first step toward re-entering the twentieth century.

"There is now a new government. I, Shapour Bakhtiar, shall assume the position I held five years ago—that of Prime Minister of Iran.

"Finally, after years of oppressive rule, Iran will become a progressive democracy. Iran will rejoin the modern world. Iranian oil will flow again, and our country's economy will be revitalized. The fruits of our labors, the prosperity brought by our natural resources, will be used for the benefit of all.

"We will no longer be a weak and ineffectual nation, but a strong and proud one. Iran will assume its responsibilities in the world community. I pledge that Iran will preserve the integrity and stability of the Persian Gulf region; we will join the regional security pact with our friendly Gulf neighbors.

"My new government will be one which will serve but not dominate the people of Iran. Shortly, I would like to present the members of my new cabinet."

The new cabinet ministers stood by the door of the Senate Chamber, waiting to be presented on television to the people of Iran. The new ministers, nearly all Zurkhaneh, all well-qualified to head the various portfolios of the new government, had been chosen months before by Bakhtiar. Ali-Reza Raissi, Minister of Information; General Pakdal, Minister of Defense; and Commander Kalvani, Minister of the Interior, were among them.

In the small Senate office, Michael Kir, Mark Rowan, and the businessmen watched as Bakhtiar presented his government.

"At this time," Kir said, addressing the businessmen, "I would like to introduce the new U.S. Special Envoy to Iran."

Mark Rowan stepped forward.

"Our country is rich in history and tradition," Bakhtiar said. The cameras focused in closer on him.

"With the exception of the past four years, Iran has had a monarch continuously for more than two thousand five hundred years. The monarch is a symbol of our country's strength and unity. He represents our national heritage. Iran needs a monarch, and the new government requires one who will reign, but not rule. I present the new monarch of Iran."

Dressed in a white military uniform adorned with gold braid and ribbons, the son of the late Shah of Iran, Reza Pahlavi—ex-Crown Prince, now King—walked into the Senate Chamber and saluted the new Prime Minister of Iran.